Beautiful

as

Yesterday

Beautiful

as

Yesterday

A Novel

FAN WU

ATRIA BOOKS
New York London Toronto Sydney

ATRIA BOOKS

A Division of Simon & Schuster, Inc.
1230 Avenue of the Americas
New York, NY 10020

First Atria Books hardcover edition July 2009

ATRIA BOOKS and colophon are trademarks of Simon & Schuster, Inc.

For information about special discounts for bulk purchases, please contact Simon & Schuster Special Sales at 1-866-506-1949 or business@simonandschuster.com.

The Simon & Schuster Speakers Bureau can bring authors to your live event. For more information or to book an event contact the Simon & Schuster Speakers Bureau at 1-866-248-3049 or visit our website at www.simonspeakers.com.

Designed by Jill Putorti

Manufactured in the United States of America

10 9 8 7 6 5 4 3 2 1

Library of Congress Cataloging-in-Publication Data
Wu, Fan.
Beautiful as yesterday / Fan Wu.—1st Atria Books hardcover ed.
    p.cm.
I. Title.
PR9450.9.W76B43   2009
823'.92—dc22   2009002096

ISBN 978-1-4165-9889-3
ISBN 978-1-4391-0955-7 (ebook)

To the Eadys and John Joss for trust, wisdom, and friendship

Beautiful

as

Yesterday

IN THE YEAR

2000

ONE

November

IT'S A SUNNY DAY in California. The sky is a transparent blue. Occasionally a plane flies by, very high, tiny as a bird, dragging a straight white contrail. Somewhere in Mary Chang's Sunnyvale neighborhood, a lawn mower hums, disturbing the otherwise quiet Saturday morning. Mary, standing in her backyard, arms akimbo, inhales deeply to take in the aroma of freshly cut grass, one of her favorite smells. Thirty-seven years old, she looks good for her age, with a petite but firm body under a pair of well-washed jeans and a blue sweatshirt with rolled-up sleeves—her usual gardening out-fit—though fine wrinkles have begun to climb to her forehead and surround her eyes. She has large, beautiful eyes, almond-shaped, nar-rowed habitually when she is in thought, and if you saw her in this state of mind, you'd think she's quite a pensive person while in fact she might just be wondering what to cook for dinner.

A man sneezes loudly inside the house. That's her husband, Bob Chang, who is rushing to close the sliding window in his study. Medium-built, fair-skinned, with hair closely cut, wearing a pair of silver-rimmed glasses, he looks more like a doctor or a teacher than an engineer, which is what he is.

"Honey, could you shut the backyard door?" Bob shouts from inside.

"Didn't you take your medicine today?" Mary says as she starts for the French doors, and after taking off her outdoor shoes and arranging them neatly beside the straw doormat, she steps inside the house, shutting the door behind her. "You know Richard always mows the lawn on Saturday mornings." She washes her hands in the kitchen and gets a glass of water from the fridge dispenser, meeting Bob in the living room with a Claritin pill in his hand. Bob swallows the pill with the water and hands the glass back to her. "I have to go to the office to restore a corrupted database. I'll have lunch with my co-workers." His voice is apologetic. Since he joined a communications networking start-up with forty-plus employees one month ago, he's been working often on weekends.

"But you worked until midnight yesterday." Mary frowns and is about to complain. What about the afternoon walk in the community park he promised her earlier? But when she opens her mouth, the words that come out are "You need to look after your health. You don't want to get burned out so soon." What else can she say? She knows that working for a start-up is not just a job, it's a lifestyle, as people in Silicon Valley like to say. Also, it was she who suggested that Bob join a start-up. But it's not all her fault, she reasons. He was bored at Santa Clara University and wanted a challenge. It was his idea to go into the private sector. If she were to blame, it was because she suggested that he join a pre-IPO company—she had heard so many stories of people becoming millionaires overnight because of stock options.

"Pick up Alex on your way back then," she adds as Bob plants a casual kiss on her lips. Alex is their only son, six years old. To help him learn Mandarin, they have hired a Chinese teacher, a student at De Anza College, sharing with a friend who has two children under ten. The teacher comes to their house every Wednesday evening; every Saturday she goes to their friend's house in Mountain View, a few miles north. Earlier this morning, Mary dropped Alex at their friend's house.

After seeing Bob off in the driveway, Mary returns to the backyard. This autumn has been unseasonably warm, and her flowers are lush, basking in the unfiltered sunlight. Along the fence, to the east, a row of camellias blooms; they were planted more than thirty years earlier by the house's first owners, a family from Japan. The palm-size scarlet, pink, white, and yellow flowers attract bees, butterflies, and humming-birds. Too bright and gaudily colorful these camellias are for Mary's taste but she has never considered getting rid of them; after all, they are the house's real owners; besides, the plants form a nice hedge, offering privacy between her yard and the two-story pink house next door.

The star jasmines she grew in late summer in both side yards are thriving and in her mind's eye, she can see their soft white flowers quivering in the spring breeze like tiny hands waving. They're the type of plant she likes, leafy, small-flowered, a little subdued. Her favorites are clivias, however, and her fascination with them started six years ago, when she visited a flower show in San Francisco's Japantown, around the time she and Bob bought their first home, a tiny two-bedroom condo in downtown San Jose, two blocks from San Jose State University.

She squats and tends the clivias in the shady area along the back of the house, loosening the soil, removing the weeds and wilted leaves, then watering the plants thoroughly. It is not flowering season yet for clivias; in another few months their orange or white flowers will blossom, wedged between the leaves like slightly parted lips. She strokes the wide and glittering leaves as if talking intimately with them—to her, even the leaves are pleasant to look at, elegant and graceful, reflecting the plant's Latin name: *Clivia miniata,* which she had learned from a saleswoman at Spring Winds Garden, a local nursery where she bought all of her clivias. She likes even more the plant's Chinese name, *Junzi Lan,* referring to its resemblance to a gentleman with noble appearance and virtue. A perfect translation, thinks Mary now.

A while ago, she wrote a friend in China who had studied horticulture in college, seeking advice on growing clivias. Instead of offering advice, the friend told her that the plants, though precious in China in the mid-eighties, when Mary had come to the United States—easily costing a month's salary and commonly used to bribe officials who liked flowers—were no longer pricey. Even an average family could now afford to display them on their balconies. She suggested Mary grow rare orchids, saying that they were now in fashion and could also be a good investment. When Mary saw her friend's reply, she laughed: why was everyone in China so pragmatic these days?

"You've been away from China too long. You're out of date on what China is like," the friend also wrote. Though Mary visits China every year for a week to see her mother, widowed eight years earlier, she has always been called by her friends there "a half-foreigner" or "a Chinese-American." Thinking of her friends' mockery, Mary shakes her head with a smile: well, whatever they say. But she admits they're right that she wouldn't be able to live in China anymore—she simply cannot image herself in a condo in a concrete high-rise, without immediate access to a garden. Her and her husband's current Sunnyvale house, their second—with three bedrooms, two bathrooms, and a two-car garage, a yard of slightly over three thousand square feet—though standard in this neighborhood, would be a huge luxury in China.

Mary also cherishes their Sunnyvale house because they spent nearly a year having it renovated right after they moved in: the original dark green carpet in the hallways became maple floor; a double door replaced the single front door; recessed lights superseded the ugly fluorescent ceiling lights in the family room and living room; the master bathroom was enlarged and equipped with a Jacuzzi. She redesigned the kitchen herself, after having read stacks of *Better Homes & Gardens*, *This Old House*, and *Dwell* and borrowed ideas from friends' houses, turning a dull and claustrophobic space into a spacious, open area with a black marble countertop, wooden cabinet doors, a large bay window, a skylight, and stainless-steel appliances. Though she and Bob have lived in this house for barely three years, she's developed an attachment to it. Of course, now, since her mother might emigrate to the United States and live with them, it'd be nice to buy a house with an in-law unit so her own family can still have privacy. It's only three weeks until her mother's arrival: this time she's staying for six months, the maximum stay her visitor's visa allows, to see how she likes living here, living with them. Mary sinks into thought, fancying what kind of house she and Bob will get next. Then she remembers that she hasn't eaten her breakfast. It's almost ten now. Since Bob and Alex are not at home, she decides to fix herself a bowl of *pidanzhou*, "century egg" porridge, topped with green onion rings. Though Bob and Alex like Chinese food, they refuse to try this porridge. "Yuck!" Alex would cry out at the prospect. "Mommy is eating rotten eggs!"

No matter how exhausted or upset she is, whenever she enters the kitchen, Mary becomes joyful, like a thirsty person downing a glass of cold water. A skilled chef, she can cook various Chinese cuisines, her specialties being Sichuan, Shanghai, and Hunan. Her three best friends, Mingyi, Julia, and Yaya, who all go to the church she attends, nag her to cook for them when they crave certain dishes. Sometimes they bring ingredients to her house and make her cook them. She welcomes and even longs for these occasions: she likes to have her friends over, to chat, to gossip, to laugh, and since they are all from China, they converse in Mandarin, though each can also speak her hometown dialect. Some days, her friends come to help her in the garden, and afterward the four of them sit outside, at the teak table, chatting over tea and dessert Mary has prepared.

Mary met Mingyi at the Sunnyvale Chinese Christian Church

two years ago, and they have been friends ever since. Yaya and Julia didn't come to the church until last August. Mary sees them as a blessing from God. Since Alex started his Saturday Chinese class, the four of them have become accustomed to meeting at her house every Saturday for lunch. Bob has gotten used to their meetings and hangs out with his own friends that day, watching sports or playing golf (of course, these days, he might just as likely be working in his office). This week, however, Mary and her friends have had to cancel their rendezvous because Yaya is in China, Julia's daughter, Sophie, is sick, and Mingyi needs to volunteer at a shelter for homeless people in East Palo Alto, a well-known troublesome area separate from the exclusive Palo Alto itself. Mingyi works as a manager in the human resources department at Intel, and after work she often volunteers. She lives close to Highway 101 in Menlo Park, next to a gas station where police cars are often seen patrolling. Just a few days ago the gas station was robbed by two armed men. But whenever Mary asks her to move to a better area, Mingyi just smiles, saying that she has become used to her community and has made friends with her neighbors.

As Mary cuts a semitransparent, greenish century egg into tiny cubes and throws them into the boiling rice soup, she recalls those happy luncheons with her friends, and their lively conversations. It'd be nice if she and Bob could talk like that. This thought makes her regret, once more, that Bob speaks so little Mandarin. Not his fault, of course. After all, he is a fifth-generation Chinese, whose ancestors came to the United States from Fujian Province in the late nineteenth century to build the California Central Railroad over the Sierra Nevada. Maybe she should be glad that he understands at least some Mandarin and can manage a few common greetings, she tells herself. Also, he was very supportive when she suggested they hire a private Chinese tutor for Alex one year ago.

"What do you talk about with Mingyi, Yaya, and Julia?" Bob once asked.

"Everything," Mary said. "Husbands, kids, movies, books, cooking, gardening, shopping, work. Just . . . everything." As she replied, she remembered a Chinese saying: three women together is a show. Unlike men, who seem incapable of sharing things intimately, women talk with each other about almost everything.

Afterward, Bob called Mary and her friends "The Gang of Four," not knowing that this term, to Chinese, refers to a leftist political faction arrested in 1976, the year the Cultural Revolution ended, following the death of Mao Zedong. Mary once considered telling Bob about that period of China's history, which she had experienced, when what Mao started as an anti–liberal bourgeois campaign turned violent, causing millions of people their lives. But what was the point? A person like Bob, who grew up in a well-to-do neighborhood in Los Angeles, wouldn't be able to relate to it. And even she herself wanted to forget about that unpleasant time.

After finishing the porridge, Mary continues tending the clivias in the backyard, noticing now that the bark mulch she applied several weeks ago is thin around some plants, because of rain, wind, or animals like squirrels, cats, or raccoons. She saw raccoons in the yard the day before yesterday, an adult and two babies moving along the fence. Luckily they didn't do any damage to the lawn and plants, but neighbors later complained about missing pond fish and destroyed plants in their vegetable garden. Mary walks to the white plastic shed hidden behind a Kentia palm tree in the other side yard and takes out a half bag of bark mulch. She spreads the mulch evenly, remembering that the tree man she talked with a while back had told her that the palm tree needed to be felled because it had grown dangerously tall and thin for trimming. And the street-facing fence has been infested with woods ants and should be replaced, according to a contractor. The gutters also requires a thorough cleaning now that winter is approaching. She sighs: having an old house does require a lot of work. Bob promised her that he'd take care of these matters, but with his crazy work schedule . . . Mary's face darkens, and her large eyes narrow. A breeze brushes her face, and she breathes deeply, feeling the gentleness of a lovely late autumn day. "Things will get better. They always do," she says to herself as she dumps the empty mulch bag into the recycle bin.

She calls the tree guy and the contractor to schedule appointments. As for the gutters, it seems easy enough for her and Bob to clean them themselves. She'll have to talk with Bob tonight to decide on a time.

Mary met Bob the fourth year after she had come to the United States. She was a Ph.D. candidate in analytical chemistry at U.C. Berkeley, observing rows and rows of bottles and tubes in her lab most of her days and nights. After eight years studying chemistry, four for undergraduate and another four for graduate studies, she suddenly realized that she had neither the talent nor the passion to become like Madame Curie, her idol through college. But she was determined to complete the Ph.D. program, to be called "Doctor," so that her years of hard study would pay off.

Her adviser, an ambitious Russian with a heavy beard, bushy eyebrows, and coarse white hair, had his eye on the Nobel Prize. He was strict with her from the day she joined his team, and while he chatted and joked with his American students, asking them about their pastimes and even their romances, he grilled her and a few other Asian students only on their experiments and test results, as if Asian students knew nothing but how to work hard, a stereotype secretly shared by many professors in the department. After she failed in a few experiments, he warned her that should she not make significant progress she wouldn't be able to pass her thesis defense coming up in a year.

Mary began to toil through her days in the lab. Her stress and exhaustion did little to help the experiments. She knew better than anyone else that she couldn't afford to lose her scholarship, because she had already brought her younger sister to the United States. Ingrid was studying accounting at San Jose State University, an hour's drive from Berkeley. Mary had paid most of her sister's tuition with what she had saved from her scholarship and the little money she made from grading undergraduates' papers. It was quite a financial stretch, but she faced it without complaining.

The pressure weighed her down, though, and sometimes she wished she could talk with her parents in China about her depressing situation. But what could she say to them? In their letters they only asked if she ate well or slept well or had enough to wear, and what they wrote about was so trivial: a colleague in her mother's factory just had twins, her father's working unit was organizing a study of Deng Xiaoping's Collection, Old Wang's hen died of plague, there were a lot more mosquitoes this summer than last year. When she read their letters, Mary would sigh, knowing that she would never be able to tell her parents the truth about her life in America. She could have talked with her sister about her worries—after all, Ingrid was her only family in the United States—but she refrained from doing so, fearing that her sister would refuse to take her money if she knew her situation.

One day, Mary had a severe fever but had to complete a report on an experiment. When she finally got out of her lab, it was four a.m. and pouring outside. Without an umbrella or raincoat, and having eaten no dinner, she biked to her dormitory. The freezing December rain beat down, soaking her. It was dead quiet save for the raindrops splattering and her bike's skidding on the slippery street. The sky, huge and dark, resembled a grim face. A sensation of unbearable sadness and loneliness suddenly hit her as she realized that her hometown and her friends were thousands of miles away, and on this strange land under her bike wheels she was nothing but a rootless and pathetic foreigner. Her future, if she had one, was as foggy as the view in front of her. Every raindrop seemed ready to crush her, to propel her into an unknown darkness.

She burst into sobs, wailing like a three-year-old. Ahead was a church, which she had passed often but never thought of stopping at. That night, however, as if called by a mysterious voice, she parked her bike and walked up the stairs. She peeked through the gap between the door halves—she saw nothing but darkness, and she slid down onto the threshold, leaning back against the door. She stared at the slanting rain and listened to the drops splashing on the ground. She felt safe and peaceful, and soon fell asleep. She did not open her eyes until an early jogger woke her up. For the following three weeks, she was confined to her bed, stricken with pneumonia, and more than once she pondered death.

After she recuperated, the first thing she did was visit the church. A month later, she met Bob, a graduate student in computer science, at a Bible study there. They married a year later, and before long she left the graduate school with a master's degree and joined Advantage Biotech as a statistician.

To this day, she recalls clearly that early morning ten years ago, cycling to her dorm with a fever. It so haunted her that she had sworn she would never get sick again, or allow herself to be so vulnerable. However absurd her resolution might seem, her psychological strength prevailed, and she rarely fell ill afterward, not even so much as catching a cold, as if her spirit indeed affected her body. Once, she hiked in Yosemite with friends and they were caught in an hour-long, icy rain. Everyone except Mary went home with a terrible cold or fever. This trip won her a reputation as "an iron woman." Mingyi said that studying chemistry must have done something magic to her. Even now, Mary seldom needs to see a doctor apart from annual checkups.

At three p.m., Mary drives to her church for choir practice. With Christmas less than two months away, the choir has asked its members to rehearse every Saturday afternoon. If not for the church or other special occasions, she would wear jeans year round, a habit that she conveniently blames on the influence of the engineers in Silicon Valley, who have a reputation for dressing tastelessly. Though she is not an engineer herself, most of the people she works with are, and in her company even the executives sometimes wear jeans to work. It's not uncommon to see people at the office wearing sneakers and T-shirts printed with the company's logo on the chest and back. If she dressed up a bit, her engineer colleagues would tease her, asking if she had just returned from interviewing with another company. Today, however, because of the rehearsal, Mary has put on a knee-length, A-line print skirt, a white cashmere sweater, and a mother-of-pearl necklace that Bob bought her last Christmas. Before she left the house, she examined herself in the mirror and smiled with approval.

Her church, recently remodeled with an exquisitely carved maple door and off-white stucco exterior walls, sits on a spacious property surrounded by oak trees, a fifteen-minute drive from her house. The parking area has been enlarged and each parking space widened. Most of the church members are from mainland China, Taiwan, and Hong Kong, and there is also a small group of American-born Asians. Eight years ago, when Mary first visited this church, there were fewer than ten people from mainland China, but that number has increased to over one hundred. Even the newly appointed pastor, Pastor Zhang, is an immigrant from Zhejiang Province, a former Communist who later devoted himself to Christianity. Preaching in his deep and resonant voice, he is full of passion, gesturing often to stress his points. It amazes Mary that he can recite long Bible passages without error. Unlike her previous pastors, whose preaching focused on literal interpretations of the Bible, Pastor Zhang knows how to incorporate facts and stories into his sermons, preaching about topics that people can relate to, such as relationships with parents, spouses, and children; communication skills; balance of work and personal life; and health issues.

On entering the church, Mary spots Mingyi, who is arranging a basket of fresh flowers on the rostrum, not looking a bit tired from the six hours' volunteer work she has done.

"Hi, Mingyi," Mary calls out, appreciating her friend's impeccable appearance: a mauve silk jacket on top of a long black dress, smooth forehead, black and lustrous hair, and sensuous lips with a slight touch of natural-colored lipstick. Though her waist has thickened since Mary first met her, Mingyi still looks good, especially for her age, forty-eight.

They hug each other warmly and chat a little before the choir starts to rehearse. They'll be singing three songs: "O Holy Night," "Angels from the Realms of Glory," and "Joy to the World," Though none is professional, years of training have taught them to sing harmoniously, with the male and female voices—soprano, tenor, and bass—well-coordinated. Mingyi is the lead singer. Her voice has a wide range, and her face is serene. When the time comes for Mary to sing, she feels her voice rising from her chest like a clear spring. Her praise is transforming her, bringing peace and joy to her heart: she feels she is communing with God in her singing. At the last note, she regards the sculptures of Jesus on the cross against both side walls and the stained-glass windows, where the soft sunlight streams through, praying silently: My Father in Heaven, please bless and enlighten my body, my heart, and my soul. I admire you, praise you, and I will follow you forever.

When Mary returns home she sees that the message light on the phone is blinking. The first message is from Bob: he has to stay in the office for at least another hour to fix the broken database and might not come home for dinner. "I called your cell phone, but it was turned off. I guess you're at church. Could you pick up Alex?" Then there is a message from American Express, notifying her that they have suspended her credit card because of a suspected fraudulent charge in Africa. The last is from Alex's dentist, reminding her of his appointment next Tuesday morning.

She drives to Mountain View to pick Alex up and chats with her friend briefly. On their way home, Alex talks excitedly about the Chinese characters he's just learned how to write and says that writing them is like drawing a picture. "Teacher Huang praised me five times today. One, two, three, four, five. Five times." He counts his fingers, eyes gleaming.

"Wow, you have to tell Dad that when he's home," Mary says and smiles encouragingly, feeling the pride of being a mother.

She and Bob would have loved to have had more children, but since Alex they haven't been able to get pregnant. Believing that children are gifts from God, Mary consoles herself that God has already blessed her with Alex. When he was diagnosed with asthma at one year old, she had a hard time accepting it. Seeing him struggling to breathe, his small, lovely face twisted with pain, she was heartbroken, wishing it were she who had the disease instead of him. Despite her bitterness, she kept going to church and praying, and when, two years later, the doctor told her that Alex had improved significantly and his asthma was under control, she praised God for his healing. Though she was baptized years ago, it was not until that year that she began to experience a closeness with God.

As Mary pulls into her driveway and parks, Claudia Dawn, her manager at work, calls her cell phone. Mary lets the phone ring and then listens to the message: Claudia wants her to conduct a conference call with the European division about some market research data for the upcoming quarterly earnings report. "Please be sure to be in the office at seven o'clock Monday morning" is her last sentence, her voice distant yet aggressive as usual.

Claudia is a fresh MBA graduate from Stanford University who joined Mary's company three months ago. In her early forties, divorced with no kids, she treats her employees the way a general treats his soldiers: telling them what time they should arrive in the office, what time they can leave. She imposes a twelve-hour e-mail reply policy and demands that people check e-mails and phone messages after work. Once she called one of Mary's colleagues at eleven in the evening and asked her to present a report at nine o'clock the next morning. She is temperamental and capricious, sometimes all smiles, but a moment later, sullen and cold. When she is dissatisfied, she calls employees to her cubicle and loudly accuses them of deficiencies, knowing that the other employees are listening. Mary and her colleagues used to call Claudia a psychopath behind her back. Within one month of Claudia's being hired, three of Mary's colleagues quit, and though they had complained about Claudia to HR before they left, she remained and was even given more responsibility. Only recently, Mary and her colleagues realized that she is the chief operating officer's sister-in-law. This knowledge immediately turned some of Mary's colleagues into Claudia's most loyal followers, which first surprised, then disgusted Mary.

Maybe I should quit soon, Mary thinks, stepping into the house. It's not the first time she's told herself this, but she has yet to update her résumé. She has been with the company for nearly ten years, and its convenient location—less than ten miles from home—comprehensive medical coverage, and generous 401(k) package are attractive to her. Of course, she has seen people around her hopping jobs like restless bees buzzing to find a better, sweeter flower, but it never seemed to her that they were any happier despite the higher salaries; there was always something wrong with the new company. If she switched to a new company, she now reasons, she might have to commute much farther or her new boss might be just as terrible as Claudia. Perhaps she should wait to look for a new job until she cannot tolerate Claudia any longer.

Her younger sister, Ingrid, once called her "pragmatic," an adjective Mary dislikes. Easy for Ingrid to say that, Mary thinks bitterly. If she had a mortgage and a child, she wouldn't use that word about her older sister; she would know having these responsibilities changes things.

Ingrid had left a message on Mary's home phone last Wednesday—she had called during the day to avoid speaking with her directly. The message was in English, businesslike, not a single unnecessary word, saying that she would visit San Francisco at the end of November or early December. Though Ingrid came to the

United States four years after Mary, her English is much better than her older sister's.

Of course, Ingrid's English is better than mine, Mary thinks, frowning at the recollection of her phone message. She hangs out with bohemian Americans every day, and she may have even forgotten how to speak her mother tongue.

Mary hates it when Ingrid speaks English with her; she views it as a deliberate way to create distance between them, to deny their kinship. Isn't Ingrid still Chinese? Isn't Mary the only sister Ingrid has? If not for her, how could Ingrid have come to the United States?

As Mary cooks dinner, she thinks of Ingrid once again. It had been a year since Ingrid had called her and three years since they saw each other. Their last meeting took place at Mary's previous house, where they had a falling-out. That day, right before supper, Ingrid—without informing Mary beforehand—brought over a dark-skinned man, a DJ at a nightclub up in the Haight in San Francisco, a hippie area to Mary's knowledge: Ingrid introduced him as Steven. Bob was at Berkeley for an alumni reunion, so only Mary and Alex were at home.

At the first sight of Steven, who wore a tight, shiny black shirt and snake-shaped sterling-silver earrings, Mary disliked him. Ingrid's appearance was even more unpleasant: newly dyed blue and red short hair, baggy jeans with holes front and back, and shoes with transparent plastic heels. Though she had become used to Ingrid's habit of bringing friends to her house for dinner without prior notice, seeing her and Steven that day upset Mary. Besides, she noticed that they were intimate: Steven would stroke the back of Ingrid's head now and then, and Ingrid would whisper into his ear with her hand on his shoulder.

Steven was a strict vegan, who didn't eat eggs, fish, or meat, so Mary had to make two special vegetarian dishes for him. It was a silent dinner except for Alex's gibberish about his preschool and some polite yet unnatural exchanges between the adults. Apparently the two dishes didn't suit Steven's taste; after only a few bites, he put down his knife and fork, claiming that he was full. He didn't stay long after dinner, saying he had to go to his nephew's birthday party. Ingrid saw him out. Through the kitchen window, by the light from a lamppost, Mary saw them leaning against the trunk of his car, kissing. Before Steven hopped behind the wheel, he squeezed Ingrid's hips and pulled her pelvis tight against him.

As soon as Ingrid entered the door, Mary blew up.

"What do you think my house is? A Motel Six? You could at least tell me before you bring people over."

"It isn't the first time I've done it. Why didn't you say anything before?" Ingrid was irritated, then her expression changed to a sneer. "You didn't like Steven, did you?"

"Who is this Steven, anyway?"

"A friend."

"A friend? You kiss all your friends on the lips? You let all your friends pinch your hips?"

"Mary!"

"If you had any respect for me, your older sister, you should have told me about him before you began to date him."

"Well, now you know I'm seeing him."

"You'd better be a little more responsible."

"Am I irresponsible?"

"Just look at yourself in the mirror. I'm not picking on you for dressing like a punk, but dating a black guy is too much."

"He isn't black. He's Indian." Ingrid paused, raising her eyebrows. "Does it matter?"

"Of course it does. What do you think?"

"It doesn't matter to me."

"You can't date him. You can't date an Indian or a black."

"Don't you Christians always talk about equality? What's with this no-dating-an-Indian-or-a-black thing? Are you telling me you're a racist?"

"It has nothing to do with being a racist. You have a different background and culture from theirs. Look at Steven! What do you know about his family and upbringing? I'm thinking about your future, about your children."

"You didn't complain when I was seeing Peter last year. He's a Caucasian. He didn't share my background and culture, either."

"His father was a professor. He grew up in a good family."

"How do you know that Steven's father or mother isn't a professor? How do you know he didn't grow up in a good family?"

Mary was silent, knowing that this argument would turn ugly. Of course, it was stupid of her to assume Steven had a seedy family background. But how unpleasant his appearance was! And the way he'd pinched her sister's hips and pulled her toward him.

"I just knew," Mary insisted.

"Let me get this straight. You're okay with me dating a white guy but not a black or an Indian. Are Caucasians and Chinese more similar to one another than Chinese and blacks and Indians? Are children by Caucasians and Chinese prettier and smarter? Bob is Chinese, but how much does he know about China? How much Chinese can he speak, read, or write? How much of your background does he share? He's a banana, yellow on the outside and white on the inside. I can't see anything common between the two of you."

Mary was enraged. She pounded on the countertop. "I'm your older sister. How can you talk to me like this? You know how much I have gone through to bring you to the States? Your tuition, your apartment, your food and clothes, your car—which one of those things wasn't paid for by me?"

Ingrid kicked over a stool, and it bounced into the side of the dishwasher. "Mary, listen! I'll repay every penny of your money, with interest. From the day I arrived in the U.S. you have manipulated me as if I were your pawn. I've had enough. Enough!" She stormed out and slammed the door, leaving Mary stupefied, then weeping with her head buried in her crossed arms on the countertop. Minutes later,

Alex walked into the kitchen and said timidly, "Mom, don't cry. Mom is a good kid and Mom doesn't cry."

Mary clasped her son's head against her chest, holding back her tears. "Mom is fine. Mom isn't crying." She managed somehow to suppress her sobbing for his sake.

Three weeks later, she received a brief letter from Ingrid, with a three-thousand-dollar check enclosed, saying that she had found a job in New York. More checks followed in the next few months, in varying amounts. She tore the checks to pieces, but more kept arriving.

As Mary and Alex eat dinner, she still cannot put Ingrid out of her mind. She listens halfheartedly to Alex's chattering about his friend Jenson's hamsters, wondering if Ingrid is doing well in New York. At least, being an accountant, she concludes, Ingrid shouldn't have trouble finding a job. Maybe she even works on Wall Street, with a big-name firm like Morgan Stanley or Merrill Lynch, receiving a handsome year-end bonus and spending it on a shopping spree, who knows? Between them, Ingrid has always been the luckier one, hasn't she?

When they were little, Ingrid was cuter, cleverer, and more likable, and she would sing "Red Stars Are Twinkling" in a sweet voice when asked by the neighboring aunts, who would then reward her with candy or a picture book. But they ignored Mary, rarely praising her or giving her gifts. It might have been because she smiled little; even if she did smile, she did not have deep dimples, as Ingrid had. At age five, a few months before Ingrid was born, Mary's parents sent her to the countryside for two years to stay with a family they barely knew. She did not return to the city until Ingrid had learned to walk and talk. Probably thinking that Mary was too young to remember things, her parents never explained why they had sent her away, as if it had never happened.

Many days Mary and Ingrid were left home alone since their parents both had to work. Mary was Ingrid's babysitter. Behind their parents' backs, Mary pinched her little sister's cheeks, kicked her, and drew on her face with pens. Their age difference made it easy for her to bully Ingrid with tricks and punishments, though she was careful not to make her sister cry—somehow Ingrid's tears would soften Mary's heart and make her realize their kinship. Whenever Ingrid was about to cry, Mary mimicked the mythical characters such as Monkey King or Pigsy, or danced around like a manic wizard; then Ingrid's tears would freeze in her eyes and she would laugh and clap wildly at her older sister's performance.

Now Mary is thirty-seven and Ingrid thirty-one, yet they're like strangers to each other. Mary sighs at the thought but changes her sigh into a smile when she sees Alex's bright eyes gazing at her. "Mom, are you okay?"

"My little angel, want to help me clean the table?" she asks and winks at her son.

Bob is still not home; earlier he'd called again, saying that he wouldn't be able to leave the office until ten or later. "Both the founder and the CEO are here. That corrupted database contains a lot of advertising data, and it's crucial to fix it," he told Mary. His voice sounded stressed.

Alex sits at the piano for his daily forty-five-minute practice, with Mary next to him. Alex has been taking piano lessons for a year, but his progress is slower than that of the kids who started at the same time; his teacher blames his lack of interest and his inability to concentrate.

"You just skipped these two legatos." Mary knocks on one side of the black Yamaha upright piano. Alex is playing a piece by Bach. He purses his lips and mumbles a complaint then restarts the piece.

"Your little fingers are sticking up. Also, press the keys with your fingertips, not the flats of your fingers. Teacher Li said that if you cannot correct your posture, she won't teach you new songs." Mary has to interrupt Alex again a little later. Then, again. Finally, a fourth time.

"Mom, I don't want to learn how to play piano." Alex turns around to face her and speaks defiantly. "I don't like any other musical instruments, either. Why must I do this?"

"Music is very beautiful. People who know how to play an instrument are happier and more inspired than those who don't. When I was little, I dreamed of having a piano." She strokes Alex's head. "Teacher Li said you're very talented and all you have to do is concentrate on your playing. I'm sure you'll catch up with Amy and Jenson soon."

"But if playing the piano doesn't make me happy right now, how can it make me happier later? And I don't like Teacher Li. She's too strict. She always scolds her students. She even hits us. Last week, she slapped Leo's hand and said it was as clumsy as an elephant's foot."

"Teacher Li is strict because she wants her students to be good and play well. She used to teach at the Central Conservatory of Music in China and performed solos. A lot of kids want to learn how to play piano from her. You're lucky to be her student."

Alex sighs like an adult. "Jenson told me last week that he'd put his hamsters inside his piano and let them chew through all the strings. He hates playing piano."

"Jenson was just joking. I met his dad two days ago and he said Jenson played for an hour and a half every day and planned to take a test next year."

"Really?" Alex pouts.

Mary feels guilty about her lie, and as a way to make up with Alex she says, "Okay, you can take a break today. Want to watch the cartoon movie Dad bought yesterday?"

"Of course, yes!" Alex jumps off the piano bench and drags her by the hand to the family room.

After the movie starts, Mary walks to the master bedroom and turns on her work laptop—she has to compile some data for tomorrow's conference call with Europe. Barely five minutes into working, she returns to the family room, checking to see if there is inappropriate content in the movie. Bob always laughs at her concern and says she is oversensitive. But Alex is only six, and she must make sure he's not exposed to any violence or indecency. Even if it's a cartoon, it may contain content inappropriate for children.

Since the shooting at Columbine High School, she no longer buys toy guns for Alex. Every time she meets Julia and her other Chinese friends who have kids, she share their worries. They have endless worries: when their children were small, they complained about the loose curriculum at school, fearing that their children would learn very little compared with kids in the same age-group in China, whose curriculum was much stricter, whose school bags were filled with textbooks and homework, and who wrote compositions by age six or seven. In the United States, Mary's friends said, it was not uncommon that kids couldn't recognize all twenty-six letters of the alphabet by the time they needed to go to primary school. How absurd! they exclaimed, feeling ashamed for America's public-school education.

They lectured Mary on the importance of starting Alex's education early, telling her she had to develop his intelligence and talent; send him to after-school tutoring to learn math, chess, English, history, and geography; enroll him in a Chinese-language school and classes to learn music, dancing, swimming, or drawing. Some of them have sent their children to private schools, paying thirty thousand dollars a year just for tuition despite the fact that they live in a neighborhood with good public schools. Sometimes, Mary was afraid to talk with these parents, for they always gave her the feeling that she should have done more for her only child. It was a competitive group, no doubt. When these children reached their teens, their parents began to worry about whether they will do drugs or date too soon, whether their sons will make a girl pregnant or their daughters will get pregnant. Last month, Julia told Mary pensively that her son had not dated, nor had he brought any girl home.

"Isn't it great? George is focusing on school," Mary said.

"But what if he's a homosexual?" Julia said. "One day I found an opportunity to chat with him about homosexuals, but before I could finish he squinted his eyes and said, 'What's wrong with being homosexual? They have their opinions, their rights. They're cooler and more stylish than heterosexuals.' You tell me, shouldn't I worry? I didn't dare tell his father what he said. His father wouldn't let him step into the house if he turned out to be a homosexual. And his grandparents . . . oh, I can't imagine."

The next time Mary saw Julia, Julia talked about her son again, but this time she looked cheerful. She said that she had checked his computer when he was not at home and found pictures of female movie stars and singers. "At least he's interested in girls. He's normal," Julia said with relief.

Julia's concern seems ridiculous to Mary, but she can still empathize with her.

The cartoon movie looks fine, so Mary returns to her room. After working a little longer, she pushes away the documents on her desk, the numbers on the computer screen staring at her like malicious eyes. She decides to take a break by cleaning Bob's study, which will be her mother's room during her stay. She begins to tidy the desk, where files, software, and music CDs pile up. The floor around the desk is just as chaotic. Though Mary tries to clean his study every week, she doesn't want to mess up Bob's belongings, so all she can do, usually, is dust the desk and vacuum the floor. Today the messiness irritates her. She has asked Bob more than once to empty the room for her mother's stay, but he has done nothing yet. She takes an empty plastic container from the garage and dumps the cascade of files and CDs into it. If there was one more room in the house, that would be nice, she thinks.

Two nights ago, Bob told Mary that he had just been granted a significant number of new stock options.

"Do you know what these shares mean?" he asked, waving the letter excitedly.

"We may become millionaires overnight," she said.

"You don't look like you care. Isn't it your dream to buy a house in the best school district? Wasn't it you who urged me to join a pre-IPO start-up?"

She was slightly hurt: he sounded like he was doing all this for her, instead of for the family. But she feigned a smile, like she always did when facing a possible confrontation. "Of course I'm happy. After your company completes its initial public offering, we'll buy a big house in Palo Alto. Two-story, with a nice garden and an in-law unit. Alex can go to Gunn High School and attend Stanford University someday."

She didn't care so much about money, but if her mother emigrated to the United States, they would have to buy a house with an in-law unit to accommodate her. That was the plan they had agreed on before she started to prepare immigration documents, so Mary could take care of her mother while they still had their privacy. She felt fortunate that Bob had agreed to her plan despite some hesitancy; she knew that this kind of living arrangement was unusual among Americans, who, in her eyes, weren't sufficiently committed to caring for their elderly parents. But since their initial discussion, years ago, they hadn't talked about it seriously again; a few times she'd brought it up, but Bob had put her off. Now, with her mother visiting soon, they need to talk about it without delay. It takes time to save money and find the right house.

She shouldn't have asked him to join a start-up, Mary reflects gloomily as she continues putting files into the plastic container. They don't need a million-dollar house in Palo Alto, she tells herself. Somewhere in Cupertino or West San Jose, where the school districts are excellent yet houses are less expensive, would be more realistic. Of course, it still costs more to buy in these communities than in Sunnyvale. But at least there's a possibility they could afford a house there, if they can sell their current house at a good price. She suddenly becomes agitated. If Bob was more involved in running the house, she'd be less stressed. It's time for her to sit down and have a good talk with him.

She goes to the kitchen and drinks a glass of iced water. Feeling better, she returns to Bob's study to finish clearing up—when she starts something, she wants to get it done. Also, besides tending the garden and cooking, she likes to clean; it feels good to see the house tidy. She pushes the container into the hallway and begins to vacuum. There is a futon under the window. She opens it and lies down, bouncing to test its firmness. It's a Simmons and fairly firm. She figures she'll let her mother try this first; if she doesn't like it, Mary will buy a real bed. She takes a set of sheets and pillowcases from the dresser in her room and makes the bed, then empties the closet, finding a few of Bob's sweaters that are fairly new but that he no longer likes. She folds the sweaters, puts them in a half-filled plastic bag in the garage, and takes the bag to the sidewalk. Tomorrow morning, a Salvation Army truck will stop to collect donations. She looks into the distance for a while, in the direction from which Bob usually drives home. She has to ease up, she thinks, as the night deepens and the air gets chillier.

TWO

August

WANG FENGLAN FINALLY RECEIVED her passport: a crimson cover, twenty-eight pages, a poor photo. Few people in this small city have ever needed a passport, and as she took hers from the uniformed girl behind the glass window at the local police station, the girl said to her, "How lucky you are!"

Two days later, she bought the train ticket to Guangzhou to apply for a visa from the consulate of the United States there. When she checked in at a hotel near the embassy, as suggested by her older daughter, she heard a conversation between two people sitting on the antique-looking sofa in the lobby. They spoke loudly, as if wanting to be heard by everyone in the immediate vicinity.

"Sixteen people passed today."

"Passed what?"

"Aren't you here to apply for a visitor's visa to the U.S.? Most people in this hotel are here for this purpose."

"Yes, yes, I'm here for a visa too. My daughter lives in Chicago and is doing her postdoctoral studies at a university there. My wife and I haven't seen her for almost four years."

"I'm planning to visit my son in Boston. He practices law there. He and his wife just had their first baby. I hope I'll get a visa."

"Is sixteen people a lot?"

"Well, two more than yesterday, but three fewer than the day before. It depends on the visa officers' mood, I guess."

"When do you plan to go to the embassy?"

"This morning I arrived at seven, but there was already a long line. Before it was my turn, someone came out and told us to go home, saying that they already had enough applications for the day. What the hell!"

"Doesn't the embassy open at nine?"

"You won't stand a chance if you go there at nine. There's always a line."

"My heaven! The line must be longer than that one for food during the Three-Year Natural Disaster in the late fifties. Remember that? I thought that was long."

That evening, Fenglan went to bed early but couldn't fall asleep, thinking of the conversation about the long line, afraid that she would oversleep. Guangzhou is much more prosperous and busy than her hometown. It was one o'clock in the morning, yet cars and motorcycles were still whizzing by. The neon lights from the nearby skyscrapers penetrated the gap between the linen curtains in her room and danced on the walls. If she listened carefully, she could hear a woman's dreadful singing from a karaoke bar somewhere nearby.

After tossing on her bed for a while, she began to think about her late husband, wishing he was here with her; his mere presence would have calmed her down. She got up and turned on the TV, just in time for the rerun of the seven to seven thirty daily news by

Central Television: during that half hour, every channel broadcasts the same news. The first few items were about the Party leaders' trips and their meetings with several foreign leaders, who praised China's economic and social developments and asserted their support of the One-China policy on Taiwan. Then came the news of important Party conferences. The two formally attired anchors, one male and one female, read the lists of attendees, all high-ranking Party officials, whose names and positions were so familiar, having been mentioned day after day and year after year on the TV, that Fenglan remembered each of them. After news of the conferences, she watched the achievements of provinces or cities in manufacturing, agriculture, and trade. Nanyi, her city, was mentioned, to her surprise and happiness. The anchors and journalists commented that these achievements had come from following the latest instructions from the Party. Everything was rosy, positive, promising, not a negative word. And the two anchors' familiar faces were reassuring; they had been broadcasting the seven p.m. news since before Fenglan retired from her factory.

She was glad that she hadn't missed the news. At home, she watched it every day, despite its formulaic content.

A comedy starring a popular Hong Kong actor was now playing, a terrible movie, but she watched it till "The End" appeared on the screen. Then she opened her suitcase to check her visa-application documents, placed inside a used DHL envelope: passport, personal identity card, retirement certificate, invitation letter from her older daughter, and other required paperwork. What if she couldn't get a visa? she asked herself, gripped by anxiety. As she squatted to close her suitcase, her heart palpitated. She remained squatting until her heartbeat returned to normal, then walked slowly to the bed and lay down.

At six the next morning, she arrived at the embassy, finding a line of more than one hundred people. Some sat on the ground, dozing, their heads resting on their tucked knees, but most were talking. A woman in her fifties complained about the embassy's inefficiency, fluttering her arms wildly as if she were about to hit someone. An old couple said that it was the fourth time they had applied for visitors' visas to see their son in Ohio. "We don't even know why we got denied the first three times. What's the trick of getting a visa?" the wife asked. All sorts of advice was offered. One person remarked that it was crucial to be confident so the visa officer knew you were not desperate. Another said that a few family photos would certainly help, for they would make the officer sympathize with you for not having seen your children for such a long time. Who didn't have a family, after all?

"That's useless!" a man wearing a hat with the Great Wall printed on it declared authoritatively. "Those visa officers don't even look at your application. They deny you right away, saying that you intend to immigrate to the U.S. In their eyes, all Chinese who want to visit the U.S. plan to stay forever."

His words received a lot of eager nods of agreement.

"There's no shortcut," the man continued. "In my opinion, it's all about being persistent. You try again and again. Just don't give up. The wife of one of my neighbors went to study in New York two years ago, and her husband didn't get a visa to visit her until his sixth attempt."

"All in all, you just have to meet a nice officer," a red-faced woman sitting on a stool chimed in. "I heard that the officer wearing silver-framed glasses has issued a lot of visas. The meanest officer is a short, old black woman. Her face is as dark as ink. You can bet a person with that kind of face is never in a good mood. Keep your fingers crossed that you won't end up at her window."

Fenglan listened carefully, seeking tips. She worried that her immigration application would make the officer deny her the visa, but there was nothing she could do about that now. At this moment, someone from behind patted her shoulder. She turned and saw a girl in her mid-twenties in a Chinese-style white blouse with butterfly-shaped buttons and a suit skirt.

"Old Aunt, why are you going to the U.S.?"

"I'm visiting my two daughters," Fenglan said.

"How did they get there?" the girl asked, looking interested.

"They went to study."

"Wow, you must have a lot of money, sending them there to study."

"Where did *I* get that kind of money?" Fenglan laughed. "They didn't ask me for a penny."

"I wish I was as lucky as they are. I've been applying to study abroad for three years and have spent forty thousand yuan on classes and my applications. What a waste! Later, I just decided to get married. My husband is an overseas Chinese, twice my age but very kind and generous. Look!" The girl pointed to her skirt. "He bought this for me. Two thousand yuan. That's my two months' salary. Not bad, huh?"

"Do you get along well?" Fenglan asked with concern.

"It doesn't matter. I met him only once. He calls often, though. His wife passed away a long time ago, and they had no children. Having no children is a good thing; it will be easier to divide his assets when we get divorced. He doesn't look very healthy and maybe won't live for too long. Who knows?" The girl took out a pocket mirror and lipstick in a gold case, and began to apply a thick layer of shimmering color to her lips.

"Do your parents know about him?" Fenglan asked. She felt her heart tightening, thinking that girls nowadays could do just about anything.

"Of course they know. But they have neither money nor power and can't send me abroad. They're useless."

Fenglan turned away, not wanting to continue this conversation. Luckily, the girl began to chat with the person behind her.

Around eight forty-five, a crowd arrived, taking the positions of some people already in the line. Money exchanged hands, and the people who had received the money left: obviously, the newcomers had hired these people to stand in line for them so they wouldn't have to get up so early.

"When did the people at the front of the line arrive?" Fenglan asked the person before her.

"Them? They came after dinner last night."

At nine, the embassy doors opened, but after letting in about ninety people, an embassy representative walked out, telling the rest of the applicants to return the next day.

That evening, after eating a bowl of fish fillet noodle at a street stand, Fenglan returned to the embassy. More than thirty people were waiting already, including the man wearing the Great Wall hat and the old couple who had been rejected three times. At eleven p.m., she was so tired that she wished she could just sleep on the ground.

It began to drizzle. She wanted to take shelter under the awning of the building but worried about losing her place. She remained in line, using her imitation leather purse to cover her head. The man with the Great Wall hat suggested that everyone take a number according to his or her place in the line. "There are no policemen around, so I'm volunteering to keep the order," he said. He waved a stack of white paper. "After you get your number, you can leave. When the rain stops, you come back, to the same place you had before. Please, no quarrel, no fight."

Fenglan and those without umbrellas took numbers from the man after he verified their positions and walked to the dry area under the awning, but those with umbrellas stayed where they were. The line looked funny now, with gaps of varying lengths. More people showed up, and some of them refused to acknowledge the numbers held by the people under the awning. Bickering, cursing, and jostling ensued before peace was restored. Despite the rain, now heavier, the people under the awning returned to the line. A few vendors now appeared with cheap foldable umbrellas and colorful plastic stools, their relaxed expressions indicating that they had been doing business outside the embassy for quite a while.

After considerable hesitation, Fenglan bought an umbrella and a stool—they cost three times more than in a store. But being able to sit and stay dry made her feel less tired. Leaning the handle of the umbrella against her shoulder, she massaged her legs, which had gone numb from standing for so long.

Wind turned her umbrella inside out, and it took her a few tries to get it back into shape. As the night progressed, the temperature dropped. Wearing only a long-sleeved shirt and a pair of pants made of thin fabric, Fenglan had goose bumps all over, and her knees and ankles ached and swelled from rheumatism. She should have brought a jacket, she blamed herself. But how could she know that a coastal city had such weather? Since birth, she had been living inland, where summer nights were usually hot. She held her umbrella as low as possible to block the wind, stealing a look now and then at the old couple whose son lived in Ohio—they were four spots ahead. She noticed that some places on their backs, poorly covered by their umbrella, were wet, and though they held their arms around each other's waists to keep warm, they were both shivering, their heads bowed. The other people in line also seemed exhausted by lack of sleep and the bad weather. Most people had stopped talking, except a few who were cursing the embassy under their breath.

The wind and rain intensified. For a while, the line was so quiet that Fenglan could hear the squeaking of her plastic stool under her weight.

At close to three a.m., four policemen holding truncheons appeared, asking everyone in line to show their identity cards and declaring that only people with passports could stay. At this announcement, those hired to stand in line called or paged their clients hurriedly; for a while it was very noisy, like a market. The policemen left at four.

The rain didn't stop until daybreak. At nine, as a neatly dressed blond young man opened the door to let people in, a roar of complaint and cursing from those who had been waiting spread like a wave, as if it were the embassy's fault that they had had to stand in the rain through the night.

Three hours later, Fenglan was issued a visa. It was a miracle to her.

*   *   *

The first thing Fenglan does in the morning is fetch the milk bottle and newspapers. Newspapers are dropped in a locked box outside her apartment building and are quite safe, but the milk bottle, placed in the wooden box she has hung on the door, is often stolen. Twice last week she didn't get her milk; it is impossible to catch the thief: it could be anyone, a neighbor, a visitor, a maintenance worker, even the deliveryman himself. It happened before, and the milk company apologized and offered the victims one month's free supply of milk. Unlike in old times, when everyone knew one another, there are more and more strange faces in her complex now.

When the jail union assigned her husband their apartment, every family in this complex worked for the jail or its affiliated work units. In the beginning, though they could not own the apartment, they did not need to pay rent, and the only required fee was a symbolic main-tenance fee. In 1991, however, the residents were told that they had to buy their apartments with a one-time payment or pay rent every month. The prices of their apartments were based on the length of their tenure with their work unit; the longer the tenure, the cheaper the apartment would be. Fenglan's husband had worked in the jail since the mid-seventies, and the sum they had to pay was not extrava-gant, but it was still way beyond what they could afford. By then, both their daughters were living overseas, but how could they ask their daughters for money when they knew how difficult it was for them to survive abroad? On the other hand, they felt that not buy-ing their apartment would be a waste of his long tenure with the jail. They finally made the purchase after borrowing heavily from friends; it was not until their older daughter began to send money regularly that they managed to pay off the debt.

Two years ago, the smelly lake near Fenglan's complex was made into a park, with two man-made islands shaded by real and fake palm trees, a cluster of big and small temples, and a local folk art museum, which is now one of the city's main attractions. The muddy river meandering through her district has also taken on a new look. Five bridges have been built, each named after an ancient artist who once lived in the city. Along the embankments, high-rise condominium towers with ceiling-to-floor windows form an impressive view, advertised as Venice Garden and Monte Carlo Paradise; in the evening, the lights from those apartments reflect on the water and brighten the sky.

The new development has had an immediate impact on her complex. In the past year, more than ten original residents sold their apartments at prices they didn't dare dream of just a few years ago. The new homeowners come from different walks of life. Her next-door neighbors, for instance, are a couple selling dried fruit at the market. They speak a dialect she cannot recognize. They have installed a brass lion head with big mane and glaring eyes in the middle of their solid iron security door. They pass her in the stairway without returning her greeting. To this day, she doesn't know their names.

New construction replaces old houses rapidly; even houses built only two or three years ago have been torn down, making way for more grand buildings. Humongous cranes, concrete-mixing machines, trucks loaded with sand and lumber have become permanent parts of the cityscape, and the construction noises don't subside until long after dark. Fenglan has seen her old familiar alleys and small roads turn into wide boulevards with traffic lights, and the mom-and-pop shops and noodle stands she used to patronize are losing their battle to high-ceilinged and mirror-glassed real-estate offices, boutique stores, foreign-named fast-food chains and other fancy businesses. Crossing the street is now a nerve-racking task. Pedestrians must watch for cars, trucks, buses, motorcycles, scooters, bikes, three-wheeled rickshaws—drivers frequently violate the red lights. Each time she crosses a major intersection, she makes sure that she walks in the middle of the crowd to minimize her chance of being knocked down by an impatient driver.

Sometimes she loses her sense of direction on a busy street. Even the major streets, such as Marching Road, Liberation Street, and People's Boulevard, are becoming stranger by the day. More than once she has gotten off at the wrong bus stop, something she is embarrassed about, for she was born in this city and has lived here for over half a century.

She is aging quickly, she feels. To walk from the entrance of her building to her fourth-floor apartment, she has to stop twice to regain her breath. She gets dizzy just from lowering her head to pick vegetables or fruit in the supermarket. As she boils water, she has to wait right there, staring at the kettle, or she'll forget to turn off the gas stove—her forgetfulness has cost her a few pots and pans, including her favorite blue clay pot with a glass lid. Her eyesight is failing, and after the sun sets, everything looks blurry to her, though some days are better than others. The doctor at the Municipal Women's and Children's Hospital has told her that she has cataracts and suggested surgery, but she has been delaying, in part because she once read in *Seniors' Health* magazine that a woman went blind after an unsuccessful cataract surgery. Now she is about to visit the United States, another excuse to put the surgery on hold. Today's milk bottle is where it is supposed to be, but the milk looks thinner and is tasteless. She knows why: yesterday's evening paper reported that some dairy companies had been found to dilute their milk with water.

"These businesses will go bankrupt sooner or later," she says to herself while drinking the milk, which she has warmed on the stove. After a light breakfast, she sits in her wicker chair near the window in the living room and begins to read the newspaper. She reads from the first to the last page, without missing advertisements, lost and found listings, job recruitment ads, wedding and birth announcements.

Afterward she boils some *longjin* green tea and, holding a mug with both hands, walks to her bedroom to look at the calendar. She flips over three pages. A date in November is circled with a thick red marker.

The flight is nine that morning.

It was her older daughter's suggestion, after Fenglan's husband passed away, that she emigrate to the United States to live with her and her family. She didn't consider it at first but was later convinced by her daughter, who kept telling her how nice it would be for her to see her grandson growing up. She sent a stack of forms to Fenglan, some already completed in English. A lot of photos were required. For a while, Fenglan frequented the photo studio two blocks from her apartment, and the owner of the studio would say to her each time, "You're blessed, to be able to live off your daughter! You must have done a lot of good deeds in your previous life. I heard that in America you can find TVs and mattresses in the garbage dumps."

But she wonders what she will do in a country where she cannot even read the street signs.

She is fifty-eight this year, and according to the custom, a big celebration should be held for her fifty-ninth birthday, rather than for her sixtieth, to give her the blessing of longevity—9 is a good number, as it is pronounced the same way as the word for "forever." It would be nice to spend her fifty-ninth birthday with her daughters and her grandson, she thinks. At her age, she doesn't have ambitious dreams or goals for herself. She only hopes that her daughters will have stable jobs and good incomes, and that they will have happy marriages and clever children. She dreams of playing with her grandchildren, hearing them call her *wai po*. Someday, when she is too old or too ill to walk, she imagines, she'll lie quietly in her own bed, in her own apartment—not in a bleak-walled hospital room—waiting for the final moment, her daughters and their families at her bedside. Later, after she is gone, she fancies that they'll remember to visit her grave, burn paper money, light incense, and remove the weeds every Qingming Festival.

In her heart, however, she knows, with both of her daughters living abroad, she might die in a hospital or a senior citizens' home, and even if she died in her own apartment, she might die alone.

When her husband went into coma, she was with him. It was the second day after the new year in 1992, the year of the monkey, and they had just left a party held by his jail. It was raining and snowing that day, and the rockets from the fireworks the night before were scattered on the ground like dried-out blood. It was four p.m., yet the gloomy sky made it feel much later. Both wore bulky cotton jackets and pants, his the jail uniform. He walked into the apartment with his hands clasped behind his back, as when he was lecturing the prisoners. He commented that the room felt humid and stuffy, and smelled of mildew. She replied that it surely was because the weather had been so terrible, then added that when it turned warmer she would open all the windows to air the apartment out and take the blankets and clothes to the balcony to dry. He nodded silently, even solemnly, and settled in his favorite wicker chair, a reward he had received years ago for capturing a prisoner who had escaped from the jail. The wicker on the armrests had darkened with age, sweat, and dirt, and some loose bindings along the edge had been secured with light brown twine. He turned on the TV to watch the news, the volume high since he was a little deaf, while she went to the kitchen to prepare dinner. Half an hour later, she came back to the living room and saw him lying on the floor, facedown, a step away from his chair, his hands extending forward, his mouth open wide with saliva still wet in one corner, as if he had tried to howl for help before losing consciousness. The ambulance came and rushed him to the hospital, where he was in a coma for three days before the doctor announced his death.

Massive brain hemorrhage.

Both her daughters flew back home for their father's funeral.

"Ma, didn't you hear Ba falling from the chair?" they asked, their eyes filled with blame.

This is the question that Fenglan has asked herself repeatedly in the past eight years. Was it because the exhaust fan in the kitchen was too noisy? Because the TV was too loud? Or because she had been completely absorbed in her own thoughts?

Now her husband is gone and she lives alone. If she collapsed in the apartment as her husband did, there wouldn't be anyone to call an ambulance, and it is likely that her body wouldn't be discovered until days later. Perhaps it was because of her fear of dying alone that she agreed to emigrate to the United States, to live with her older daughter and her family.

At nine a.m., Grandma Li, her downstairs neighbor, visits and asks her to accompany her to You-Ming Temple, the one right behind the twelve-story department store on the other side of the river. Grandma Li says that she has been dreaming of a golden snake for a few nights now. "Snakes and dragons are from the same family. Gold, of course, means fortune. Maybe the Dragon God was telling me to buy a lottery ticket. It's my time to get rich," she says.

Although it is the smallest of the five temples in the city, You-Ming has the most visitors. Unlike the other four, destroyed during the Cultural Revolution and rebuilt, it survived the tumultuous times intact. Rumor had it that one day in 1967 a truckload of Red Guards arrived at the temple, planning to destroy it. As they were about to unleash their hammers, they heard a roar from underground. They stopped. So did the noise. They lifted their hammers again, and the same roar rose, louder and more resonating. It went on like this for a few rounds, and in the end the Red Guards decided the Earth God was warning them, so no one dared touch the statues for fear that a spell would be cast on them. But they had to do something to show the victory of their revolutionary spirits over superstitious demons, as Mao had advocated, so they took down a few inscribed plaques and left. This story has made You-Ming Temple famous, and it is always busy, with its plaques now inscribed with real gold, donated by rich businesspeople. The visitors and donors include not only Buddhists but also those who pray to the gods for all kinds of things: a date, a wedding, a baby boy, a promotion, a job change.

Fenglan is not a Buddhist, nor does she believe in reincarnation. If she could be reborn, she doesn't know what kind of life she would want. But she believes that dead people have souls and can talk with the living. Whenever she dreams of her late husband or parents or sister, she feels they're talking with her from a different world.

Each holiday, or whenever something significant is happening in her family, as when her two daughters went to college in Beijing or later went abroad to study, she goes to You-Ming Temple, where she lights a long red candle and a stick of incense and kneels in front of every god, asking for a blessing. As she performs each supplication, she first closes her palms in front of her chest to pray, then touches the floor with her head and both hands. She stays in that position for a while, praying again. The god she prays to the most is Ru Lai, the grandest statue in the temple. She is always in awe when she regards Ru Lai's colorful costume through the smoke from the incense and the flickering candlelight, marveling at His hugeness and authority; at this moment, she believes in His omnipotence and His ability to control fate. When she leaves the temple, she is filled with calmness and peace.

Today, with Grandma Li next to her, Fenglan kneels in front of Ru Lai, saying her prayers silently. "Please, Mighty God, take care of my husband, my parents, and my sister in heaven, and make them sleep and eat well, spare them any worry; please, Mighty God, send happiness, health, and harmony to my older daughter, Guo-Mei, and her family in the U.S.; please, Mighty God, find a responsible husband for my second daughter, Guo-Ying, and give them smart kids." On second thought, she repeats her prayers for her two daughters, this time using their English names, which they assumed as soon as they left China. After she finishes her prayers, she shakes her head, wondering why her daughters decided to take English names. Can Chinese gods remember those odd-sounding and meaningless foreign names?

After leaving the temple, Fenglan realizes that she has forgotten to pray for herself. But her old bones, as she refers to herself, won't get any younger or healthier because of a prayer. So she decides to let it be.

She has knelt in front of Ru Lai, Guan Si Ying, Guan Gong, Earth God, Fortune God, Dragon King, and other gods she cannot name, and she has followed some grannies she knows from her morning exercise in the park to Taoist temples to pray to Xu Xun, a Taoist transcendent. Like her, they pray to just about any god they can find. Their rationale: if those gods are revered in a temple, they must be powerful, and praying to them is better than not. Perhaps those gods are looking down from heaven to see if they are pious. Who knows?

She has lived long enough to know that nothing is guaranteed.

THREE

May

THE ALARM CLOCK GOES off like a fire siren. A quarter to six. Ingrid opens her eyes but stays in bed, covering her head with the blanket, extending a hand from under the blanket to shut off the clock. Two minutes later, she leaps out of bed and scuttles to the bathroom to wash quickly—no time for a shower. Then she returns to her bedroom, slips off her sleepwear—an oversize T-shirt—and changes into a black and white striped top and a pair of pale blue jeans. Before leaving, she glances in the mirror, frowning at the dark circles under her eyes from lack of sleep. Good morning, panda, she teases herself.

She jumps into a taxi. "Chinatown," she says, her voice crisp and urgent. The taxi stops outside a travel agency on Mott Street at her direction. She pays, with a good tip. Inside the office, she is handed a small triangular flag printed with the agency's logo and a bag of identical white caps with the same logo. An air-conditioned bus takes her to the Manhattan Broadway Budget Hotel in the Garment District, where a dozen Chinese tourists—men in suits and shiny leather shoes, women in print dresses and makeup, as if they were going to a wedding rather than on a sightseeing tour—are waiting at the entrance.

It's the tenth time this month that Ingrid has guided a tour group from China. May is a good time to visit New York, not too hot, not too cold.

"The bus is here! Let the leaders and female comrades get on first." A burly man with a conspicuous stomach waves his hand to the others, speaking Mandarin with incontrovertible authority. "Don't push. Keep in line. You don't want Americans to laugh at us, do you?" He then chuckles good-humoredly.

"There's a seat for everyone. Get on one by one. Watch your step." Ingrid stands beside the door, also speaking Mandarin, and gives a cap and a bottle of Arrowhead water to each person, smiling. Though she knows little about this group's background, her experience tells her that these people are government employees, who, typically, visit the United States in the name of attending a conference or investigating business opportunities, their expenses paid either by the government bureau they work for or an American company eager to win a contract from the government bureau, while their main purpose is sightseeing. Over the course of the week, the group will visit Florida, Washington, D.C., Las Vegas, and Los Angeles, accompanied by other tour guides.

The bus lurches off. Standing in the front, Ingrid welcomes her guests and announces the itinerary. As they approach each point of interest, she talks about its history and the facts appealing to first-time tourists. Times Square, the Empire State Building, Fifth Avenue, Wall Street, Union Square . . . she knows her speeches by heart.

Only a few people listen to her, something she has gotten used to: many Chinese tourists seem to know quite a bit about New York's landmarks, thanks to Hollywood movies and TV travel programs.

Also, they are more interested in poking their heads out the windows, taking pictures, and commenting on what they see. Ingrid does her best to talk over the chatter:

"That building is just okay. The Jin Mao Tower in Shanghai is much taller and looks much grander."

Ingrid: "The Empire State Building was the world's tallest building from 1931 to 1972. It has 102 stories . . ."

"You can bet that someday those billboards in Times Square will have some Chinese brands on them, like Tsingtao beer and Haier."

Ingrid: "Times Square is the junction of Broadway and Seventh Avenue, and it's famous for its giant billboards and bright lights in the evening . . ."

"Did you see that big pile of garbage by the road? I don't understand. Manhattan is so rich. Why doesn't the mayor hire more street sweepers?"

"Hey, hey, look at that white woman! There, at the bus station we just passed. Oh, my heaven! She's *huge*! Her arm is thicker than my waist." The person making the remark flashes her camera, taking a photo of the fat woman.

At midtown, after a brief stop at Rockefeller Center, the tour continues. An old man wants to go to the bathroom. Ingrid explains that it is hard to park, and even more difficult to find a public bathroom—unless they stop at Macy's or Saks Fifth Avenue. She asks him to wait until the driver can stop. The old man mumbles crossly, as if it were Ingrid's fault that he cannot go to the bathroom right away.

The bus finally arrives at Battery Park and Ingrid leads the group to the ferry to the Statue of Liberty. After showing them around a little, she tells everyone to explore by themselves and meet her in an hour. She sits on the curb facing the Manhattan skyline, and—thirsty from the heat and all the talking—drinks half a bottle of water in one gulp. Then she leans back on her elbows, looking at the sky. It's a beautiful day, the cloudless sky a piece of smooth silk.

She looks down at the peaceful bay, at the circling seagulls, feeling rejuvenated and relaxed. She breathes the salty air and stretches her back.

Before her, the twin towers thrust into the sky, modern and spartan. New York's monument, Ingrid thinks. The smell of fresh air and the sight of the open space always remind her of the wonderful things about New York: theaters, museums, shopping, dining, and its diverse population, and make her forget the misery of being stuck on a steamy subway train in the summer or the stress of worrying about next month's rent. In her eyes, this enormous place, with its charm and energy, even its congestion, pollution, and high crime rate, seems to promise endless freedom and hope, attractive not only to its residents but also to its visitors. She certainly thought so when she landed at JFK Airport: whatever the difficulties she encountered here, she felt, she could get over them sooner or later.

She closes her eyes, again pleased by her freedom and relaxation. And it occurs to her that she likes herself, her attractive looks and offbeat, free-spirited personality. She's five foot seven, tall for a Chinese female, with a small head, a long neck, wide and thin eyes, resembling a nimble feline. Both dignified and enthusiastic, she loves a wild party but is also perfectly content in solitude. Other things about her tend to be two-sided as well. She can enjoy a five-course banquet at an exclusive, candlelit French restaurant as much as she can appreciate a buttered poppy-seed bagel. She shops at Bloomingdale's and Saks Fifth Avenue but also at H&M or T. J. Maxx. She won't go to secondhand stores, though, for she feels that she wore enough hand-me-down clothes from her sister when she was growing up.

"A beautiful day, isn't it?" she hears a man's voice behind her.

She opens her eyes, turns, and finds a man in his late thirties sitting several steps to her left, in a white Che Guevara T-shirt and a pair of kahki shorts. Deeply tanned, he wears tawny aviator-style sunglasses, and his hair and eyebrows are bleach blond. He must be into surfing or diving, Ingrid thinks. He smiles at her charmingly, his perfectly aligned, porcelain-like teeth glittering. She notices the ring mark on his left ring finger, despite the fact that he has discreetly placed his right hand on top of his left.

She smiles back. "Yeah, it's beautiful." On normal days, she wouldn't mind a little harmless flirtation with a stranger, especially one as handsome as this guy, but now she wants to be alone to enjoy her free time, a rarity these days since she's taking on more jobs than she can handle comfortably. She feigns a yawn, then takes a big gulp from her water bottle. Just as she is wondering how to get rid of this intruder without appearing rude, two plump middle-aged women wearing flower-decorated straw hats and beaded sandals hurry over, waving affectionately at the man.

The man stands unwillingly, addressing the two women. "Didn't know you'd come back so soon." They must be his mother and aunt. He gives Ingrid a frustrated and helpless smile as their eyes meet.

After the man disappears with the two women, Ingrid thinks of the night she spent one month ago with Marvin Allen, a guest pianist with the New York Philharmonic, at the Ritz-Carlton. She leaned down to kiss his forehead, and he smiled up at her contentedly. His face was no longer young; there were wrinkles at the corners of his mouth, along the ridge of his nose, and around his eyes, like musical staffs. But whenever he sat at the piano, his hands on those black and white keys, he looked like a young man in love, his deep-set blue eyes full of wisdom and life. Half a year back, outside Carnegie Hall, those eyes had mesmerized her; she knew she had caught his attention too, with her sequined empire-style chocolate gown and her smiles. Marvin said he had separated from his wife and was waiting for the divorce papers, seemingly suggesting a future for him and Ingrid. Despite the fact that her instinct told her Marvin's affection would change as often as his music, she embraced the risk: she was in love, to her surprise.

It was, however, their last night together, though she didn't know it then. Two days later, she got a call from a woman through her travel agency. The woman, with her soothing voice, claimed to be Marvin's wife and said she wanted to meet Ingrid. The day before, Marvin had left for California for a performance. Ingrid accepted the invitation, and Marvin's wife, Victoria, received her in their rented apartment near Central Park. She cooked and served dinner in their spacious and brightly lit dining room. A crystal chandelier hung from the ceiling, above the cherrywood table that could sit ten people. Tall red candles stood on either end of the table, their silver bases meticulously polished. On the wall facing the door was a massive landscape oil painting, signed by the artist at the right bottom corner. As they dined on filet mignon, vegetables, and French wine, they chatted about light topics, Victoria adding anecdotes about how she and her husband met, how she had sacrificed her career for his, how they planned to spend three months in London to be with their college-age son next year. There was no bitterness or hostility in Victoria's face or voice; she treated Ingrid like an old friend. Two hours later, Ingrid left the apartment after being hugged good-bye by the hostess. As she roamed the park, burning with shame, she knew it was the end for her and Marvin. Since then, he hasn't called or written; neither has she. And she has sworn that she won't see anyone for a while.

Relationships should follow a natural course, shouldn't they? Ingrid reflects as she lowers her cap to block the sunlight. If they must end, it is for the best.

She had met other men before Marvin, like Ahraf Victor, an assistant professor at City College of New York, intelligent, garrulous, witty, holding two Ph.D.'s from Cairo University. He could talk for hours about art, history, politics, travel, or any other subject with unfailing exuberance. Also Frank Blanc, a French management consultant at McKinsey who loved beluga caviar and Huître plate oysters and told everyone that China was the best place to invest in in the twenty-first century. There had been several flings before Frank, but they hadn't amounted to anything.

She seems incapable of maintaining a relationship, and none of the men she has seen is right for her, as Ingrid has come to realize on this sunny afternoon, overlooking the bay. "Conceited popinjays," she suddenly recalls the expression from a story by Conrad. And she sees her vanity, which she used to deny. She had rarely questioned her taste in men, though admitting that she often ended up with men who were either too smug, or too egocentric, or both. And a high percentage of her dates were non-Americans, expatriates, which meant that they often had no control over the length of their stay in New York, or even in the United States. She blamed neither those men nor herself for the doomed relationships; she actually felt lucky to have remained single and independent.

She never saw herself as unserious or flirtatious, yet being in a committed relationship somehow daunted, even suffocated her. It didn't bother her not to have a stable partner, though sometimes, after a stressful day or a particular unpleasant incident, she longed for a passionate embrace or a shoulder to lean on. But there were always things to do and places to visit. She knew how to get around in the city, and, with her flexible work schedule, she had undertaken many spontaneous trips, hopping on a plane to another state, or another country. That was probably why her bank account was often overdrawn. She had friends—only a few close ones, but enough. She had troubles and frustrations, though you wouldn't know it by looking at her shimmering, youthful face and her confident stride.

Mary used to tell her that she was too emotional and too irrational. "Your love only flowers, but bears no fruit," she said.

"Why does one have to bear fruit? Is getting married and having children your only measurement of love?" Ingrid asked.

"If I had known you were so decadent, so debauched, I wouldn't have brought you to the United States," Mary had said more than once.

Decadent and debauched. That is how Ingrid is in her older sister's eyes.

With her mood dampened and perplexed at herself, Ingrid finishes her bottled water and wipes the sweat from her cheeks with the backs of her hand. The sun is scorching, but she's too lazy to move to a shadowy area; also, she has told the tour group to find her here. She closes her eyes.

If being decadent and debauched is the opposite of what Mary has achieved in her life, Ingrid thinks, she wouldn't mind. Mary is easily satisfied! To her, the meaning of life is in a detached single-family house in a suburb surrounded by well-trimmed trees and blooming flowers, a responsible husband, an obedient and clever kid, and a stable job at a Fortune 500 company. And her religious devotion.

Loud laughter interrupts Ingrid's ruminations. She opens her eyes and sees people from her tour group posing for photos not far from here. They are talking, laughing, jostling, blocking other tourists' views, utterly unaware of those tourists' glances. Though Ingrid sits quietly, alone, she has also received a few such unfriendly glances: she is wearing the same white cap.

"Huh, these Chinese!" an old Caucasian man in a Bermuda shirt mumbles indignantly when passing her, a remark not unfamiliar to Ingrid. She doesn't think this old man understands any Chinese; it's just that to him all Asians are Chinese. On other occasions, in other places, she has heard this comment made about a loud Korean or Vietnamese group.

She considers telling the people from her group to lower their voices and mind their behavior. But on second thought, she decides not to bother—her experience has told her that doing so would only arouse hostility toward herself. Even if they quieted down, their compliance wouldn't last; soon they would go back to their boisterous behavior. Ingrid knows that people in China are used to talking loudly in public; it's not uncommon for two people to chat comfortably about private matters on a jostling bus, over many strangers' shoulders. Moreover, her tour group members are government employees, who tend to be arrogant and intolerant of criticism.

She doesn't want to intervene also for another reason: this group is from the city where she was born and raised. It is the first time that she has guided a group from her hometown. Hearing their local dialect amuses her, though she admits that the dialect is harsh and unmusical—sounding as though the speakers are arguing, not conversing normally. When they talk about the odd and funny things that have happened in China, she listens attentively, smiling, nodding, or frowning depending on the content. When she went to college in Beijing, she stopped speaking her dialect. Even when she talked with her sister and her parents, she spoke Mandarin.

Of course, if she tries to speak her dialect now, she will likely remember it; she might even be able to guide the tour in it. But she has decided to speak Mandarin only—she doesn't want to be close to the tour group, to let them call her *ya tou*, the way they would local unmarried girls. She feels momentary guilt about distancing herself from these compatriots, recalling the old Chinese saying "When hometown fellows meet in a foreign place, they cry buckets." But apart from having once lived in their city, she is so different from them.

She observes them with curiosity, knowing that they are watching her the same way. In their eyes, she is an American-educated Chinese who has lived in the United States for ten years, on both coasts, who has a blue-bound American passport that lets her travel to Europe, Oceania, or Latin America without a visa, who perhaps eats hamburgers and steaks more often than rice, who speaks English as if born with it. She senses the young people's jealousy, especially that of the girls: her shoes, clothes, jewelry seem more stylish than their own. Perhaps because of this jealousy, they like to criticize America and Americans to her face: the littered garbage, fat or homeless people, run-down neighborhoods, high tax rates, unimpressive food . . . They seem to want to tell her: don't think you're superior because you live in the United States. The United States is no big deal! China will be the next superpower!

Yet their admiration for the United States is betrayed by their eagerness to learn about college application procedures, tuition, school rankings, and programs—they know that having a U.S. education will give their children a big edge in the job market.

How much has happened since she left China, Ingrid reflects. The Berlin Wall fell, the Soviet Union collapsed, Yugoslavia dissolved, China took over Hong Kong and Macau, and East Timor voted for independence from Indonesia. People now talk about globalization and the Internet era, instead of the "Cold War," which used to divide the world into the East and the West. And of course, the start of a new millennium was just celebrated. It amazes her to think about having lived through all these events. She wonders what students study in their history and political science classes in China these days. If a student asked his teacher why Communist countries have collapsed if they held the most advanced social notions, how would the teacher reply? Do students still have to recite the Four Cardinal Principles— keeping to the socialist road and upholding the people's democratic dictatorship, leadership by the Communist Party, and Marxism-Leninism and Mao thought—as she did? Her generation grew up with the propaganda of the Four Modernizations, which predicted that China would realize the modernization in four key areas by 2000. That had been the goal for every Chinese since the mid-1960s. She remembers in her first class at primary school, a few months before Mao died, the teacher taught her and her classmates to write "Long Live Chairman Mao" and "Four Modernizations." But, on this sunny May day in 2000, Ingrid wonders how many Chinese still remember the Four Modernizations.

At this moment, Ingrid hears a young man from her tour group say to a colleague, "Americans are immature."

He continues, "Americans spend money like there's no tomorrow. They can't survive without a credit card. The more they buy, the more they owe the bank. When they can't afford to pay, they go bankrupt. They're like little kids without discipline. On the other hand, Chinese live on a budget, know how to save, and are much more careful with their finances."

She smiles—he's right. It is not only the Chinese; Asians in general seem to know how to increase their assets, though she cannot say the same about herself. In the United States, she reflects, among all the ethnic groups, don't Asians have the highest average household income and the highest saving rate?

After the Statue of Liberty, she drops the tour group at their hotel. Another guide will take them to dinner and show them the city's nightlife.

The next morning, Ingrid doesn't get up until noon—one hour later than usual: she's a night owl. Her room is chaotic, as if it's been visited by a thief: books and clothes are lying around on the hardwood floor and on the red, modern-looking Nelson marshmallow sofa with crepe upholstery; two unmatched shoes sleep under her desk. Against the walls are several bookcases, in different sizes, and most of the books they hold are classics. All the walls are filled with lithographs and oil paintings acquired from her international trips.

Thinking of her apartment in Astoria always cheers Ingrid: she has a roof over her head in this city that countless billionaires and millionaires call home. Her apartment is on Steinway Street, a two-story unit with stained glass windows, boasting a 120-year history. Reportedly the writer who received the National Book Award three years ago lived here when he was an office clerk. Not long ago, the landlord, a Korean, had the exterior walls and main entrance door painted bright green and the few big cracks on the cement stairs fixed. But nothing has been done to the old window frames, which have turned a dirty brown, chipped paint hanging in many places like tears running down cheeks. From the outside, the whole building looks like a garishly dressed and made-up showgirl.

Inside, a square entryway is covered by a patch of wine-colored carpet. To the right, against the wall, is a Victorian-style buffet table with a dark, laminated-plywood surface, an apparent acquisition from a treasure-hunting trip to a flea market. On the table are old magazines—*Time, The New Yorker*—or expensive-looking ads from Saks Fifth Avenue or Tiffany. The main provider of these ads is a model, nicknamed Tooth, who lives on the first floor and sings three nights a week at a Brooklyn bar. *The New Yorker* is from Ingrid and her roommate, Angelina Pérez—they share the subscription. Angelina has been playing small off-Broadway roles for five years, but she has never abandoned the hope of becoming the lead in a major Broadway production. The hallways and stairs are narrow. Rather than using the wine-colored carpet in the entryway, the landlord has covered them with secondhand Persian rugs, whose intricate patterns of black and red flowers easily hide tracked-in dirt and mud.

"Ingrid!" It's Angelina. She must be in the kitchen—Ingrid hears her open the fridge. Their apartment has thin walls.

"What's up?" Ingrid opens her door.

Angelina leans against Ingrid's doorframe, a bottle of Corona Extra in her hand. She has thick, wavy black hair and enormous brown eyes. Her nose is thin and straight, as if carved, a gift from her grandmother. Her full lips look as if they were about to burst from her skin. Her healthy dark brown complexion, inherited from her father, and her firm legs give her confident sex appeal. Typically she wears as little as she can without risking arrest, often meaning that half her chest is exposed beyond her tight top or dress. As she walks in high heels, her breasts rise and fall like two wild animals breathing. Whether you know her or not, man or woman, the moment you see her you notice her deep cleavage. She has less desirable features—

stubborn, light gray freckles, slightly crooked front teeth—but these defects are minor compared with her overall charm. Today she wears a knee-length, strapless black dress that clings to her hips like another layer of skin.

Ingrid whistles. "You look fantastic! What's special?"

"I lost the role in *The Wild Party* to Teresa Lurie. That fucking bitch!" Her voice sounds dulcet even when she is cursing. "Carl just told me. He sounded plenty sorry for me, offering all kinds of explanations. You know, all the poppycock." Angelina is fond of picking up words from her performances.

"Hmm, I thought you had it."

"I thought so too. But she's probably slept with Carl. You know that fox." She giggles, her breasts shaking. She takes a swig from the bottle. "If he were a bit taller and his legs a little thicker, I might have slept with him. Then I'd have the role. But no, thanks. I can't imagine screwing him. Anyway, I thought I'd boost my morale a bit by putting on something . . . comfortable. How about a little party next week? Maybe not an orgy like that in the show. No guns, no fights. The usual crowd."

"Swell! I need that. I've been working like a dog."

"Written much lately?"

"I wish. Haven't had the time."

"Heard anything from that New Voice something short story contest?"

"It's probably bogus, you know. A bunch of poor writers putting together some event to make money. Twenty-five bucks per submission. If they got one hundred fools like me, that's twenty-five hundred bucks."

"I never believe these contests anyway. Don't let Molly talk you into that kind of shit next time."

"Molly just loves these contests. I don't blame her. It's like buying lottery tickets—there is always hope."

"That's right, hope. We all need that." Angelina holds the bottle up, moving the thumb and index finger of her other hand up and down it suggestively. "I need to get drunk . . . and laid."

"Good luck!" Ingrid says.

"You betcha, honey." A ripple of laughter. "I'll leave you alone. I'd better make some calls."

Ingrid had found the apartment through a newspaper classified ad: low rent, easy-going and artsy roommate, it had said. The day she moved in, she caught Angelina making love to a man on the sofa in the living room, both naked. They were so passionately engaged, like two hungry lion cubs, that they didn't hear Ingrid open the door. At the sight of Ingrid, Angelina got off the man slowly, calmly, covering her breasts with her right arm and her crotch with her left hand, smiling charmingly as if she had been expecting her. The man snatched Angelina's lace bra from the floor and threw it on his erection—the whole thing looked like a funny-shaped mushroom.

"Oh, darling, you timed it perfectly!" Angelina said to Ingrid, as the latter tripped over her luggage trying to back out the door. After Angelina and her lover got dressed, they introduced themselves properly. Angelina gave Ingrid a hug and a kiss on both cheeks, while the man offered a handshake. "Tolstoy, nice to meet you." As if knowing that Ingrid would ask his name again, he repeated, "Tolstoy, that's my name. I'm a TV producer." There was a shrewd smile on his face, and he gave her a wink.

Later, at various times of day, Ingrid encountered more of Angelina's lovers just as she had met Tolstoy. Some of the men were embarrassed, others weren't. One suggested, half-jokingly, a threesome, which received a long and hearty laugh from Angelina and a cold shrug from Ingrid. Angelina once confessed to Ingrid that the danger of being caught having sex stimulated extra pleasure. "Danger and excitement are brothers," she said. "Adrenaline, you know."

Though Ingrid was a little put off initially by Angelina and had considered moving, she has since learned to appreciate her as someone who is genuine and enthusiastic about life. Her generous hugs and kisses warm Ingrid's heart. She feels comfortable being with Angelina and her friends, knowing that they accept her for who she is.

"Hope, my sweet New York hope," she hears Angelina singing theatrically from her room. Then her voice turns into an indolent "mi amorsito"—her phone call has gone through.

Ingrid smiles. She'd better call her mother today. It's been a while.

FOUR

November

ANOTHER WEEK GOES BY, and it's Saturday again. At noon, Mingyi and Yaya arrive at Mary's house. Julia shows up a short while later, explaining that she just squabbled with her husband.

Today's menu is steamed dumplings. Mary has prepared three kinds of stuffing, shrimp with *baichai*, ground beef with chives, and mixed vegetables. Julia has brought the handmade wrappings from home. They sit at the dinner table, making dumplings.

Since stepping into the house, Yaya has been talking, first about an eccentric ex-colleague who sold everything he owned on eBay and bought a boat, planning to sail alone through the Caribbean, then about a piece of lingerie she recently purchased at Victoria's Secret at Valley Fair Mall. Short and slightly chubby, Yaya has an animated face that never seems to show tiredness. The youngest of the four, she just turned thirty-five, and the birthday gift she got from Mary, Mingyi, and Julia was a limited-edition pink Hello Kitty watch. She is fanatic about Hello Kitty, a baffling hobby in Mary's opinion since Yaya is a senior graphic designer at a major architectural firm in San Francisco. Though she is married, her husband spends most of his time in Beijing, where he founded an investment management company half a year ago, after he quit Microsoft, with two ex-classmates from the Wharton business school. While listening to Yaya talk, Mary admires her friend's energy and enthusiasm: how fast she talks! Like a quick summer shower. And the way she bursts into laughter is reminiscent of thunder in a blue sky.

"Pink again?" Mary winks at Julia. "Looks like our pinky girl cannot wait for her man to return."

"I didn't buy it for Daming. It's for my own enjoyment. It's a beautiful piece. Silk, well-designed, with a nice pattern," Yaya responds, then adds, "Daming likes white laced lingerie anyway."

"Mary, is the heater on? It's hot!" Mingyi waves her hand exaggeratedly. Mary laughs: it's always nice to see Mingyi lighten up. Mingyi is the only single among them. Secretly Mary views her as her closest friend and wishes she could be like her. Though they are both quiet and good listeners, Mingyi acts like a big sister to her friends, and her quietness, seems to be part of her upbringing, consistent and in character, unlike Mary's own, which one might associate with a bashful yet sociable person who can become lively if the occasion is right.

"What a beautiful jasmine flower! So fresh, so fragrant." Julia begins to sing a Chinese song popular in the eighties.

"What did you suggest?" Yaya guffaws. "At least I didn't read *O* magazine or *Marie Claire* to get the tips about firming breasts and toning hips and thighs."

"Hey, hey, hey, I didn't say anything. I was just singing," Julia replies, scooping some stuffing from a bowl into a wrapping with a pair of chopsticks. "When I brought over the articles, who was the one so eager to borrow them to make copies?"

"Neither do I use egg white and fresh cucumber slices to clean my face every week," Yaya continues, smiling brilliantly. "Or eat black sesame seeds and weird herbs to make my hair black."

Julia holds up the chopsticks, threatening Yaya. "Just wait until you're forty."

"What are you fighting about? I'm the oldest here, and I haven't said a word about aging," Mingyi says. "Want to hear? I have plenty to tell."

"You're the last person who can say anything about aging. You simply don't age!" Yaya exclaims. "Your face is smoother than mine. That's so unfair. Just look at mine. It's like the surface of the moon. And I got another zit yesterday." She turns toward Mingyi and closes her eyes. "Here, did you see? Right on my eyelid."

"Who asked you to eat so much spicy food?" Julia says, dipping her fingers into the flour spread thin on the plate to keep the dumplings from sticking and marking two white lines on Yaya's forehead. Yaya pops open her eyes, jumps up, and takes revenge by splashing a few drops of water from her drinking glass onto Julia's face. Laughter fills the house.

Mary stands and places two plates of dumplings on a bed of lettuce inside a multilevel bamboo steamer, then walks to the stove to steam it. As she brings a pot of water to boil, she is surprised as always at how much she enjoys chats with these friends and how intimately they share. Though they meet at the church every Sunday, it's the Saturday rendezvous that she anticipates the most, in which they rarely talk about God, the Bible, or other religious topics but indulge in gossiping and sharing their thoughts on varied matters. Not all their thoughts are in line with Christian values, she is aware; sometimes they get so carried away by their conversations that they simply forget they are Christians. But that doesn't bother Mary; on the contrary, she feels that she and her friends are like girls from a college sorority who have sworn honesty and loyalty to one another, who share secrets and speak their minds candidly. That kind of trust, makes her feel young and lively. How lucky she is to have these friends!

As they wait for the dumplings to cook, Julia talks about her work. A real estate agent specializing in the South Bay area around Sunnyvale, Santa Clara, and San Jose, Julia has helped both Yaya and Mary buy their houses. She has a girlish voice, slight but high-pitched, giving the impression that she is much younger—in fact, she's forty-two and has two kids, George fourteen, Sophie eleven. She is as talkative as Yaya, sometimes losing all sense of time, but her subjects tend to be practical, related to investments, housework, shopping bargains, children's education, and so on. Whenever Mary has questions in those areas, she turns to Julia for help.

"I was busy all day yesterday, showing houses to five different clients. The first was a Taiwanese couple with four children. The wife doesn't have a job and the husband is just a normal engineer. They wanted to buy a house in Saratoga with five percent down. I suggested more affordable areas, like Milpitas, San Jose, or Santa Clara, so they wouldn't have to worry about interest rate hikes. But the wife was angry with my suggestion, as if I were looking down on them. Then there were three Vietnamese families buying a house together. They told me that they would buy one first and live together, then buy another with the equity from the first house, then buy third in the same way. In the end, each family would have a house. Smart, isn't it? Another client was a flipper, looking for houses to sell within three months at a profit. I'm telling you, people here are crazy."

"This kind of double-digit annual growth can't last forever," Mary says and looks concerned. "Don't you think the housing market will crash soon?"

"No, I don't." Julia shakes her head firmly. "Where can you find a better place on the earth than California? It has great weather, beautiful mountains and oceans, and countless scenic attractions. Not to mention Silicon Valley's huge job market. Also, homeowners here account for less than twenty percent of the population, and if prices drop only a little, many renters will rush into the market and that will raise prices in no time. Though your school district can't be com-

pared with those in Cupertino and Palo Alto, it's good enough to attract buyers with children. You have nothing to worry about."

"Cupertino is a no-no," Yaya says. "A friend of mine showed me
her daughter's class photo. Except for two white boys, the students
were all Asians, most Chinese and Indians. Sisters, wake up, give kids
some fun and childhood. Life is not all about the Ivy League."

Julia ignores Yaya and continues, "Mary, your house sits in the
south and faces north and gets a lot of sunlight. That's good feng
shui."

"Oh, my goodness, not feng shui again!" Yaya laughs. "All the
crap about not buying a house with stairs aligned directly with the entrance door, or not with a 4 in the number, or not with a severely slop-
ing roof. I don't believe any of this for a minute. It's all superstition
among Chinese. In my opinion, wherever there are a lot of immigrants, the housing market will hold firm. The first thing immigrants
do when they arrive in a new country is try to buy property, either for
themselves or for investment. They can't sleep tight unless they have
a piece of paper under their pillows proving that they own a property
somewhere. Chinese, Indians, Vietnamese, Mexicans, they're all like
that. I bet you a million dollars that if Chairman Mao were still alive
and had emigrated to the U.S., the first thing he'd do would be to buy
a house. He had a peasant's blood, you know."

"Who says feng shui is nonsense?" Julia disputes. "Americans
also ask about feng shui when buying a house."

"Don't be silly. You know they don't believe it. It's all because
of the Chinese—those Americans are afraid that Chinese won't buy
their houses when they want to sell them." Yaya snorts. "Everyone
knows that Chinese like to bid on houses, especially Taiwanese and
Hongkongese who have a lot of cash."

"When you were buying your house, didn't you tell me that you
didn't want a house at the end of a T intersection? Admit it! Feng shui
is an old art, a science. It's about health and energy. Mingyi and Mary,
isn't that true?" Julia says, looking for support.

"I'm not a judge, okay? I don't want to get between you two. You never agree on anything," Mary declares and walks over to the stove, turns off the heat. "Hey, gals, the dumplings are ready!"

Mingyi helps Mary take out the steamer. "Wow, that looks good!," she says. "I'm starving. Yaya and Julia, just forget about feng shui. Let's eat!"

Julia's cell phone rings. She talks briefly, speaking English. After she is done, she says, "It's George. He said he's going to have dinner with some classmates. Last night he went to San Francisco to see a movie with a friend. Boys his age see parents as enemies and only want to avoid them. He can't drive yet. Just wait until he has a car. I probably won't see him for days. Sophie is just as much of a worry. Her class learned about sexuality last week, and the teacher demonstrated how to use a condom. Part of the homework for her father and me was to explain about sex. Well, you know, what can people from our generation say about sex? The day Wang Wei and I got married, both of us were still virgins. He knew no more than I did about what to do in bed. Wang Wei asked me to do the teaching. He said he did it with George, and now it was my turn with Sophie. So I had to do it. I stammered into an introduction, but you know what Sophie did? She patted my shoulder with sympathy, handed me a glass of water, and said, 'Mom, don't panic. I know all that stuff already. It's no big deal.' I'm not kidding, I almost wanted to cry. Maybe I shouldn't have brought them up in the U.S."

"Hallelujah, welcome to America!" Yaya exclaims and applauds.

"You think China is any better?" Mary asks as she adds soy sauce and vinegar to her friends' dipping plates. "Nowadays, kids in big cities there know quite a bit too. One of my college friends told me the other day that she had found a bag of cocaine in her sixteen-year-old son's schoolbag."

"Julia, why do you worry so much?" Yaya says through a mouthful of food. "When your kids were small, you barely had time to sleep. Now that they're older, you should just relax and enjoy yourself."

"I wish. I'm not as modern as you. You don't even want to have children!" Julia says. "Apart from the kids, there are millions of other things to worry about at home. Let me tell you about the fight I just had with Wang Wei. He said I had sent too much money to my family in China, a few hundred here, a few thousand there. He said it was unfair because he sent far less to his parents. I said that his parents work for the government in Shanghai, while my parents are retired primary-school teachers. He's the only child in his family, yet I'm the oldest with three brothers and sisters, two of them without jobs. If I didn't send money home, what would they eat and wear? He said, 'Doesn't the government subsidize them?' I said, 'Look at you! Didn't you come from China? You know those subsidies are barely enough to buy a *jin* of lean meat.' Wang Wei is so calculating, a typical Shanghainese. You'd think he'd be more generous since he has a Ph.D. and works for a big company like HP. Quite the opposite. Whenever he has time, he'll make this or that chart to calculate the value of his investments. If I want to buy something, even just a piece of clothing, I have to get his permission or he'll be grumpy. Have you ever seen a man like him? Maybe I should divorce him."

It's not the first time that Julia has complained about her husband. Knowing that she and Wang Wei actually get along well despite their disagreements over domestic matters, Mary and Mingyi only smile, offering no comment.

"Aha, speaking of divorce. A friend of mine just divorced her husband," Yaya says. "She's from Guangdong, and her husband is British. That guy didn't eat chicken with bones and skin, and used many measuring cups when he was cooking. He ate slowly, chewed his food without the slightest sound, and moved his knife and fork like they were trained soldiers. He wouldn't even use chopsticks! You'd think he was a robot if you saw him eating. When he got home, the first thing he did was listen to Mozart. My friend was very different. She loved Cantonese-style chicken—with bones, blood, skin, and all that. She loved chicken feet, porridge, preserved eggs, and beef-tendon soup noodles. It's hard not to slurp when eating porridge and soup noodles. Don't you agree? She also liked to invite friends over for potlucks instead of listening to Mozart. They were together for a few years but just couldn't continue the marriage. The guy even got depressed and had to see a psychiatrist."

"Westerners love to see psychiatrists," Julia remarks. "In China, who does that? So many people here are treated for depression. If I told my mother I was depressed, she'd surely say, 'Drink some ginseng soup and go to bed early and you'll be okay.' "

"Ha-ha, my mother would say the same thing." Mary laughs. "Isn't it a bit like the Jewish cure for everything? Chicken soup, right?"

"Mary, what's the secret of your marriage? Bob is never angry or gloomy. Whatever you say, he listens. And you never quarrel," Yaya says.

"Well, English is his first language, but it's my second. I guess you can only quarrel in your mother tongue. If he speaks slang or idioms, I just don't understand him. To me, speaking English is like taking a bath with my clothes on. It's always awkward. I also don't know how to swear or curse in English. If I translated Chinese cursing into English literally, it simply wouldn't work. If I said, 'You're the son of a turtle!' he'd think I was wishing he would live as long as a turtle; if I said, 'I'll give you some color to see!' he'd ask, 'Which color?' "

All her friends burst out laughing: they know those Chinese curses.

"That's so true!" Julia says. "When Wang Wei and I get into an argument, sometimes he speaks Shanghainese, of which I don't understand a word. So in the end I can do nothing but laugh. Then we reconcile."

Yaya has just returned from visiting her husband in China. "You know what I bought in China this time?" she asks, mysteriously.

"Another *qipao* or some other Chinese dresses? Or more knockoff Louis Vuittons or Gucci?" Julia mocks her. "You have enough of those to start a department store."

"Helloooo, I haven't bought any knockoffs since I began going to church. Mary can be my witness." Yaya pauses, moving her eyes from friend to friend. "I don't think you can guess. I should just tell you. I bought my great-great-grandfather's snuff bottle! Don't ask me how much I spent on it. If I told you, you'd think I'd lost my mind. Here is how it happened. Daming was busy and didn't have time to hang out with me, so I wandered around by myself. One day, I went to Pan Jia Yuan antiques market. I spotted this snuff bottle in a store and knew instantly that I had seen it somewhere before. A few hours later I finally remembered that my grandfather once showed me a picture of it. He said *his* grandfather had given it to him before he died, but during World War Two a Japanese soldier took it from his house. He also told me that my great-great-grandfather had carved his nickname on the bottom of the bottle. I walked back to the store and asked the owner to show it to me. Indeed, my great-great-grandfather's nickname, Little Monkey, was on the bottom of the bottle! Too bad that my grandfather has passed away. Just imagine how surprised and happy he would have been to see it again! Now I've got an idea. I'm going to do some treasure hunting to find the antiques that the Red Guards took from my parents during the Cultural Revolution. I have some of their pictures."

"You're dreaming. Where can you find them? They were either destroyed after being confiscated or now belong to some ex-Red Guards," Mary says.

"I bet some of them will show up in an antiques market somewhere, just like this snuff bottle," Yaya says.

"Yaya, why not spend the energy thinking about what you are going to do with Daming? How long do you want to be separated like this?" Mingyi says.

"I don't want to live in Beijing. It's too crowded. Too much pollution as well. Also, I like my job here," Yaya says.

"Aren't you afraid that he might run away with another woman?" Mary teases her.

"We grew up as neighbors, and I know him inside and out. Even if a girl talked to him, he wouldn't know how to answer."

"People change, don't they?" Julia says. "If you want to do business in China, you have to invite your clients for dinner. After dinner, you go to a nightclub or a karaoke place. There are so many pretty young girls there. What's the saying you told me last week? 'Men turn bad when they have money, and women can't have money unless they turn bad.' Honestly, I don't even let Wang Wei go to China alone. Girls are no longer innocent, as we used to be." She frowns. "I watched a Chinese talk show the other day and the subject was 'Should extramarital affairs be condemned?' What kind of discussion is that? Isn't the answer obvious?"

"I trust Daming. And if something bad ever happens to me, God will take care of me, right?" Yaya points her right forefinger upward. "When I was in China, a friend of mine said that what is important in a relationship is not staying together forever but momentary possession. I know God wouldn't approve, but I kinda like the idea. Isn't it a little boring to look at the same face every day, every year, every decade? If there's no more love between a couple, they'd better get divorced rather than maintain the marriage. Christians divorce too. Reading the Bible, praying, and listening to sermons don't always help. Lucky us, we're not in China, or we'd have to ask permission from our work units to get a divorce. I read somewhere that two thirds of marriages in China are 'dead.' Scary, isn't it? I think all of them should just get divorced. Julia, forget your worries. If Wang Wei left you, you'd be a free woman and could look for your new love. At least you could fantasize about a handsome single man without feeling guilty. God doesn't like divorce, but the Bible doesn't say it's a sin to fantasize about someone if you're not in a marriage. Andy Lau? Hmm, maybe not. I want to save him for myself in case I become single again. How about George Clooney?"

Julia takes away Yaya's plate, where there are still a few dumplings, and hides it behind her. "No more food for you. You're getting drunk from eating dumplings. You'd better pray hard tonight or God won't forgive you for what you've said."

Mingyi slaps the back of Yaya's head playfully. "Don't talk trash! Are you trying to destroy others' marriages?"

"I'm just kidding, okay?" Yaya laughs heartily.

"It looks like Daming should be worrying about you." Mary says, affecting seriousness. "Before he left, he asked me to keep an eye on you. Well, maybe I should call him and ask him to fly back to the U.S. tomorrow."

As soon as her friends leave, Mary goes to the master bedroom and lies on the bed, thinking about Yaya's comment that she and Bob never fight. It's not true, though she didn't want to admit that to her friends. Unlike Yaya and Julia, she rarely speaks about her family troubles, or complains about Bob, even to close friends, even to Mingyi. There's no perfect couple, no perfect family in the world, that's her belief, and you just have to work out the problems. Perfection belongs to God, not to human beings. Still, it bothers her to think that she and Bob had a fight the night before, or an argument to make it sound better. It was innocent enough to begin with, but then it took a wrong turn.

Bob had returned home at eleven. He said that the company had ordered sushi for everyone who had to stay late. Mary took his laptop bag and helped him slip off his jacket, something she always did when he got home.

"When will this project end?" she asked, hanging the jacket in the hallway closet.

"Who knows? Our founder has been sleeping in his office for weeks. Shirat is still at work, and it looks like he'll have to spend the night in the office again. I don't think he has the energy to drive two hours to get home at this hour." Shirat, Bob's manager, lived in Sacramento.

"Doesn't he have three small children? Even if his wife doesn't work, it must be hard for her to take care of them by herself."

"He doesn't have a choice. He's waiting for a green card, and if he loses his job he might have to move back to India. Also, he's been counting on the IPO to make him rich, so he can buy a house closer to work."

More and more foreigners at Mary's company were H1B visa holders applying for a green card through their employer, so she understood Shirat's situation. If these people lost their jobs, they would lose their visas as well and would have to leave the United States. To secure a visa, they were willing to work long hours or accept lower-than-market salaries. Recently, at her church, Mary had met a Taiwanese girl who worked for a Korean company in Santa Clara. The company had sponsored her H1B but paid her only thirty thousand dollars a year, one half to one third of what they would have to pay an American or someone with a green card who could leave for another job at any time, despite the fact that she had a master's degree in computer science and worked more than twelve hours a day.

Bob walked into their bedroom and lay down on the bed, stretching his arms and legs comfortably. She followed and sat on the edge of the bed.

"Teacher Chang, I'm exhausted. It looks like we have to cancel our Chinese class today," he said, smiling. On Monday, Mary had started to teach him some Mandarin every evening, in preparation for her mother's arrival. "Fire drills," Bob had called their classes.

"Oh, we can skip it."

"Even if I studied hard, you know, I would never be able to understand you and your friends' high-speed chatter in Mandarin. It's as incomprehensible as ducks quacking or birds chirping." Bob mimicked their talk, making a fast nonsense sound.

Mary laughed. His sense of humor, that was what she had always liked about Bob. When they were dating and even in the first few years of their marriage, he had often made her laugh by telling her jokes and teasing her.

"So, the project is going well?" Mary said, guessing the reason for Bob's good mood. He'd been stressed the whole week.

"Today, yes. We made good progress. Tomorrow, a big question mark. That's what it's like working at a start-up."

"Why not quit and join a more established company?" she suggested. "So you don't have to work so much."

"I wish I could, but what about all the stock they've promised? And the economy is slowing down; many companies are actually laying off people. It isn't that easy to switch jobs. Not like before."

"You haven't been to church for a while. Why not go this Sunday? You might feel less stressed afterward." Bob's church, an English-speaking one, unlike Mary's, where the pastor gave sermons mainly in Mandarin, was in Palo Alto.

"I don't have time."

How could lack of time be the real reason? Mary questioned silently. Born of devout Christian parents, Bob had been baptized young and was very active in church affairs at Berkeley and at Santa Clara University. It was after he started his job at the communications networking company that he'd begun to go to church less. She had imagined many reasons for his alienation from religion, including his disgust and bafflement by the recent news of a priest reportedly raping an altar boy in Waltham, Massachusetts. But Bob had denied all her speculations and wouldn't discuss the matter further.

"But it's important to go to church," she finally managed to say.

Bob was silent, then he asked, "What do you go there for?"

She was taken aback by the question. "Of course, for spiritual enlightenment, so we can connect with God and with people."

"Not out of habit and for comfort?"

She hesitated. "That too."

"Or because it makes us look like good people?"

Another pause. "No."

"Or out of the fear of going to hell when death comes?"

This time, she didn't answer.

There was a disturbing lull. Then Bob said, "I need some time to think about it."

She leaned back against the headboard, her heart sinking: so it was true, Bob was turning away from God. In her heart, she felt that she should try harder to find out why he had stopped going to church. It had been a while since she'd inquired. It was too bad that they went to separate churches; though she had been to his church a few times, she had little idea what it was like. On the other hand, she could see where his question came from; she'd had it herself. Sometimes, as soon as she walked out of church, she felt that her life resumed being as ordinary as always. There was a disconnect between her daily life and her church life. However, despite this, it was comforting to know that God was watching over her and taking care of her, and to know that she had a chance to be saved and go to paradise after she died.

Should she keep pressing Bob? she wondered. Obviously, there was something he was hiding from her. But no, it was unlike her to be pushy. Maybe she should just put the matter behind her, assume that as soon as his workload lessened, he would start to go to church again. Also, she didn't want to trouble herself with the issue right now: she had a busy day herself. She wished she could speak Chinese to Bob; it was such an effort to speak English when she was tired. She is careful with her English at work, trying to make it as good as possible, so her professionalism wouldn't be jeopardized by embarrassing grammatical errors in her speech, but at home, she doesn't have to try so hard. If she is in good spirits, she speaks just fine; if not, such as now, her English fails her and she lapses into Chinese English.

"My mother is arrive two weeks from now, you know. It'd be nice if we could go to the airport together," she changed the topic. She realized the mistake in her sentence but ignored it.

"I'll try. But it's not for sure that I can take time off."

Her face darkened. "It's the first time she visit us. I'm not asking your whole day, just a few hours."

"I said I'll try."

"And maybe we should talk about our plan of buying a house with an in-law unit. It doesn't have to be big or in an expensive area."

Bob linked his hands behind his head, staring at the ceiling. "I just don't think it's a good idea for her to live with us. I mean in the future, permanently."

"But we agreed on that, don't we?" Mary straightened up. "We said that for our next house we'll buy a place with an in-law unit. Separate entrance for her and our privacy, separate kitchen too."

"I know, I know. But how can we afford a house like that? If it's decent, you're talking about $750,000, if not more. In this economy, it's not guaranteed that my company can swing its IPO. And some companies that have tried that haven't been doing well at all. A few Wall Street analysts have predicted a recession."

"We should be able to make a good profit from selling this house," she muttered after a pause. "It'll be at least another four or five years before my mother can immigrate to the U.S. anyway. We has time save more money."

"Well, I just don't think it's a good idea that she live with us. But, of course, she can visit whenever she feels like it. Isn't that better?"

That was why Bob had been unwilling to talk about this issue, she thought. "She getting old. It's difficult for her to travel so long a distance. And she not in great health. I can't let her live alone in China, don't I?" Her mind throbbed momentarily as a headache came over her. She was almost angry that she had to speak English.

"Mary." Bob put a hand on her arm, looking up at her. "I understand where you came from, but I've been thinking about it too. Your mother can't speak English, can't drive, doesn't have friends. She'll need us to be around all the time. On weekends, on holidays, we won't be able to go anywhere unless we bring her with us. Even if she has a private kitchen, most likely she'll have dinner with us every day. You know it's true. Have you thought about all this?"

She avoided Bob's eyes. "Do I has a choice? I don't think Ingrid can take care of her. She in New York, single. She have no house. I'd be happy if she could support herself."

"Of course you have a choice. Just look around. How many of

our friends live with their parents or in-laws?" Bob's voice was slightly impatient. "How many would have their parents or in-laws over for six months? Half a year is a long time, don't you think? I understand that it means a lot to you to have your mother here, but it's just too inconvenient for us. I have to use the computer in our bedroom. Just look at the mess in that corner! Books, CDs, power cables—"

"But it because we don't have an in-law unit yet. If we did, you'd have your own study and my mother live in her own unit."

"Don't fool yourself. Even if we had a house like that, your mother would be over at our place most of the time."

Mary wanted to say he was being selfish, but she knew what he said was true: he was the one who was making the compromise, the sacrifice. After all, his mother lived comfortably in a four-bedroom home in Florida. Yet she felt that Bob should have supported her decision to have her mother live with them, knowing that she, as the older child, was expected to take care of her according to Chinese custom.

Bob continued, "Also, our family life would be affected. For this six months, it'll be hard for us to make love. I'd always feel there was a stranger living in the house, watching us."

"A stranger?" Mary shook off Bob's hand. "How can you say that? My mother a stranger? It is her first time visit us and you didn't even help with clean the guest room."

Bob didn't answer, which made her regret instantly her harsh tone—it was uncharacteristic for her to speak this way. And he was right, it would be hard for them to make love with her mother in the next room. But the truth was that even now they hadn't made love much—she hadn't felt the desire and she doubted he had; many nights he fell asleep as soon as he got into bed. He was just using their lost opportunities for lovemaking to argue that her mother shouldn't live with them. Though when they first got married they'd had a passionate sex life, it had faded soon, especially after Alex was born. Now, it had become like this: if he didn't initiate, she wouldn't ask.

For a while Mary listened to the wall clock ticking; it seemed to urge her to end the argument before she and Bob started quarreling more seriously.

Bob finally spoke: "We could rent an apartment somewhere for her. Or send her to a complex for seniors."

She shook her head firmly. "No, definite not. It don't sound right."

"But we're in the U.S. It's common that parents and children live separately. Even in China, how often do you see three or four generations under the same roof in the city? Just the other day I read an article saying that young couples there prefer to live on their own."

"Ziyang's parents live with her and her husband for five years, and her husband never complain." Ziyang was someone at Mary's church, whom Bob knew too.

"He's Chinese. I am not!"

She was startled by this reply and gazed at Bob's face for a few seconds as if it suddenly looked different.

He seemed to regret what he'd said. He closed his eyes and sighed.

The unflattering ceiling light exposed the exhaustion on Bob's pallid face, where the muscles hung a little loose on his cheeks and chin. Though he was only thirty-nine, his hairline was receding. Mary looked away from her husband to her own image in the closet mirror. In faded green pajamas, with her shapeless, permed hair, her flat chest, her bent neck, she looked plain and unattractive.

Plain and unattractive, as Mary lies on the bed in the master bedroom, mentally reviewing what happened last Friday between her and Bob, these two words pop up again and bother her like sand in the eye. She gets up and walks to the closet mirror, where she sees a young-looking and slim yet well-proportioned woman wearing a pair of tight jeans and a black V-neck sweater. Well, maybe a little plain, but definitely not unattractive, she says to herself. She turns to look at her profile: she doesn't have a big chest or buttocks, but she's curvy; not by a black woman's standard but certainly by an Asian woman's. Didn't Julia once say that she wished she had Mary's figure?

A sudden urge to prove something overtakes Mary. She fumbles in the closet and finds a blue silk *qipao* which she'd had tailor-made when she visited China three years ago. She wore it only once, at her company's year-end party at the Hyatt in San Francisco, and it had won her a lot of admiration from her colleagues. She takes off her jeans and sweater and puts on the *qipao*. Sleeveless, high-collared, with white plum flowers embroidered along the bottom, it reaches her ankles and opens to the middle of her thighs on both sides. She studies herself from different angles with a sense of wonder. Then, with abrupt determination, she removes the *qipao*, then her bra and pantie. When was the last time she looked at herself naked? She doesn't remember. Her skin is creamy and smooth, though there are several light stretch marks on her lower abdomen and upper thighs, thanks to childbearing. Her breasts, though not very big, are cone-shaped, fulsome, with dark brown nipples. Under her abdomen, her pubic hair seems a bit too long, too dense; it could use some trimming. She blushes, embarrassed by the thought. Do women actually do that, trim their pubic hair? she asks herself. Even the outspoken Yaya and Julia have never mentioned this. At this moment, she hears footsteps from outside. Startled, she quickly puts her jeans and sweater back on, thinking it might be Bob, who had gone to Dave and Buster's in Milpitas for a friend's birthday lunch. But it is only someone running along the sidewalk outside.

Now, with the urge to assure herself that she's still attractive gone, she sits on the bed, her thoughts going back to what Bob said on Friday night. Why was she surprised by his answer? she asks herself. Didn't she always know that her husband was American-born and American-raised? Then she thinks that she should take him to China someday, so he won't feel that it is completely alien. Once or twice, he had wanted to go along with her, but somehow it had never happened—he wasn't insistent, perhaps because he feared meeting her parents, and she wasn't enthusiastic, thinking of the poverty and backwardness in her hometown. They had honeymooned in Hawaii, then for vacation, other than visiting his parents in Florida every year, they took a cruise to Mexico and stayed one week in Paris. Since Alex was born, they haven't traveled outside the United States.

It wouldn't make any difference even if Bob had visited China. Mary shakes her head, realizing that there's something wrong with her marriage. Just admit it, she thinks. She and Bob communicate and make love less and less. Yes, they rarely argue, they sleep in the same room, in the same bed, they grocery shop together occasionally, Bob still calls her "honey" now and then, and in their friends' eyes, they are a good couple. But an unspeakable tension is there, hanging in every corner of the house like the sky on a rainy day: overcast, gray, heavy.

Maybe it's just her own imagination. Everything is fine between them, she counters. She should focus on the good times they have had together, like their annual vacation to see his parents. She, Bob, and Alex walked on the white powder sand at Siesta Beach, sunset tinting the sky with soft pink and lilac; they tasted pies made from freshly squeezed key limes; they took a private yacht trip through the swamp infested with alligators. They had a lot of laughs, didn't they? And she thought herself lucky to have Bob and Alex in her life, didn't she? But those good times . . . how come they seem so far away? A rush of sorrow attacks her.

Her eyes move to two silver-framed photos on the wall facing the bed. In the left one, she is wearing a beaded ivory-colored lace wedding gown, her hair in a classic braided upswept style accented by a jeweled hair clip, a bouquet tied with a lavender ribbon in her hands. Sporting a tuxedo, Bob is standing behind her, embracing her waist with both hands, kissing her behind her ear. In the other picture, they are wearing traditional Chinese costumes: for her, a scarlet, high-necked *qipao* with golden silk piping and frog buttons; for him, a long silk *magua* printed with a pattern containing four Chinese characters:

fu, lu, shou, and *xi*—fortune, wealth, longevity, and happiness. She is leaning against one end of a mahogany table, bending slightly to pour tea for him, while he is sitting at the other end, holding out his teacup, looking at her, smiling. They had this picture taken at a studio in Chinatown on their way back from City Hall, where they had just been issued their marriage certificate.

Maybe her mother's pending arrival has exposed the hidden, unspoken crisis in their marriage, Mary speculates. Maintaining a lukewarm marriage isn't that difficult, especially when you have kids. You go to work, you come home, you cook, you clean the house and tend the garden, you take care of the kids; little time is left for the couple themselves, and sex becomes an obligation, a burden, a nuisance. She suddenly remembers the idiom "seven-year itch." How funny is it that the Chinese have the same expression! Is it true that most divorces happen after a couple has been married for seven years? She and Bob have passed that threshold; they have been married for almost ten years. Should she worry about their marriage? She throws another glance at the two wedding pictures on the wall.

Her cell phone rings: not the familiar ring tone of Bob or any of her close friends. She walks to the living room to pick up the phone, thinking it might be Alex's Chinese teacher.

"Hi, Guo-Mei, long time no talk." The man speaks Mandarin. Then he asks Mary to guess who he is; after she makes some futile guesses, he laughs.

"It's Han Dong!"

"Han Dong!" She almost drops the phone, her heart racing. "Where are you calling from?"

"Berkeley. I'm here for a three-month business course. I now work for the international loan department at the Bank of China. I got your phone number from one of our college friends. I surprised you, didn't I?"

"You surely did," she says. She still cannot believe she's speaking with Han Dong. Fourteen years have vanished since they've seen each other. Is it a dream? But that voice is undoubtedly his: confident, magnetic, vibrating, as she remembers it.

"Did you bring your wife and kid?" she asks.

"We divorced last year, and the boy is with his mother right now. She remarried not long ago, and her husband is a European. They live in a mansion in Guangzhou. How are your husband and kids?"

"My husband and I have been married for almost ten years. We only have one child, and his name is Alex. He's six. He looks like his father."

"Can he speak Mandarin?"

"A little bit, but he's taking classes. His father doesn't speak Mandarin, though. He was born in the U.S."

"How're your parents?"

"Actually, my father passed away eight years ago. My mother still lives in Nanyi, and she's visiting the U.S. soon."

"Sorry to hear about your father. He was quite a character. I still remember him in his jail warden's uniform. I used to be very afraid of him, honestly. Remember our signal when I needed to visit you at home?"

She remembers: if her father was home, she'd hang her red scarf on the clothesline on the balcony, which Han Dong could see from downstairs so he wouldn't come up.

They talk a little more and, before saying good-bye, agree to meet in Berkeley on a Saturday in December.

Han Dong's phone call deprives Mary of any chance for peace of mind.

They had been classmates since middle school, even shared a desk for a few years. At the end of their first year in high school, he lent her Sartre's *Being and Nothingness,* and though it took her many tries to get through the book, she fell in love with philosophy and decided to study it in college. One year later, when the time came for students to be separated into classes according to their intentions to study either arts and humanities or science and technology at college, her father told her that she had to go to the science and technology class.

"Philosophy?" he growled. "There's no future for idealists in China or for people with abstract ideas. If you think differently from the people high above, you'll be in deep trouble. I've known many people tortured and exiled because of what they said or wrote. I saw with my own eyes a philosopher jump from his fourth-story apartment, his brains spilling everywhere." Her father's Adam's apple rolled violently as he spoke, like that of a fighting rooster.

"But the Cultural Revolution has ended," she replied.

"It only ended four years ago. How do you know there won't be another one?"

They were having dinner when their fight broke out. Her mother looked anxiously at her father, then at her, and put a roasted duck leg in her bowl. That night her father stormed into her room and ripped up the philosophy books Han Dong had lent her.

Her teachers tried to persuade her too. "Studying philosophy won't get you anywhere!" they said. "Since the Industrial Revolution, you don't hear people mention philosophers' names. China is on its way to the Four Modernizations, and the most important projects are in agriculture, industry, science and technology, and national defense. Who has the leisure to discuss philosophy? Don't you know the saying 'You'll succeed wherever you go if you've learned math, physics, and chemistry'? You're the best student in the class. Look at your classmates who have good marks! They've all chosen science or technology. Most of the leaders in the central government in Beijing studied science or technology. If you choose philosophy, you won't find a job after graduation. You don't want to sell tea eggs on the street, do you?"

So she gave in and chose science. When it was time to pick a college major, she took her teachers' advice and studied chemistry—a discipline, her teachers said, more becoming to girls than math and physics, which were too theoretical and abstract.

Han Dong, however, chose to study philosophy and attended the same college in Beijing that Mary did. They soon began to date, and he promised her that they would get married upon graduation.

But he was not the type for commitment. He was a poet—artsy, passionate, easily distracted by his emotions. Tall and slender, he had elegantly chiseled facial features. His hair, not too long, not too short, was parted to the left, with a few wayward tufts over his forehead, like his restless heart. When he was lost in thought, he looked cold and arrogant and was thus called Truculent Shelley, a nickname that had made him famous on campus. He was the center of attention wherever he went, and his readings always attracted a lot of girls. The more poems he wrote, the more pretty girls surrounded him, and at the beginning of their fourth college year he confessed to Mary that he had been secretly seeing a girl from the English Department. Mary was caught completely off guard by his cheating. She began to apply for overseas study: she swore she would leave China and never see him again.

Soon after she arrived in the United States, she assumed the English name Mary, a derivation from the last character of her Chinese name, Guo-Mei.

Mary paces the living room, reminded of the old intimacy she and Han Dong shared and the time when she was still living with her parents in their gray apartment. Her father had worked at the same jail since the 1970s, but by the time he died, in 1992, he hadn't been promoted even once. Some of his friends suggested that he bribe the jail management, but their suggestions were invariably rejected.

"I damn them all to hell!" he roared. "My grandpa and my father lost their lives for the revolution, for Mao, but nowadays our leaders are barely old enough to grow beards. If it hadn't been for their connections, how could they have taken such prominent positions? I'd rather die than beg these milk-drinking brats for a raise. I can't afford to lose face."

His colleagues, even those who started their jobs much later, had received titles and been assigned apartments in a new ten-story building with an elevator and a garden. But Mary's father and his family remained in the ramshackle, five-story apartment building, whose stairways were narrow, uneven, and always dark because there were no windows and no ceiling lights. The two buildings stood not so far from each other, one red, the other gray; seen from the side, the new building was twice as wide as the old one. Mary and her sister used to call the new building "sausage," and their own "dough stick."

Mary had her own room, but it was tiny, barely big enough for a single bed, a bookshelf, and a two-drawer desk. There was no space for a chair, and Mary had to sit on the edge of the bed to do her homework. The ceiling was low, with a fluorescent light often covered by cobwebs. The bookshelf contained all her textbooks and reference books starting from primary school, along with a complete collection of the Chinese Communism Party's history, which she had won in a school contest and had never read. A framed family photo, yellowed with age and sunlight, hung on the wall facing the closet, taken a week after the Gang of Four was arrested, at a shop called Serving the People. In the picture she wore a red cotton jacket that was too big for her, with her hair combed into two braids on her chest. Her father stood behind her, his hands rigid at his sides. Her mother was the only one sitting, with Mary's sister, Ingrid, leaning against her. Except for her sister, everyone looked serious, even anxious, as if they were afraid that the decade-long nightmare had not ended.

She knew her family's history more or less, though her knowledge came not from her parents but from a distant relative. Her parents rarely talked about their pasts, not even her grandparents' pasts. All they told Mary was that her paternal grandparents were born of a poor peasant family and had participated in Mao's revolution, while her maternal grandfather was an intellectual and her maternal grandmother's family were businesspeople. They also said that both her maternal grandparents died of illness in the 1950s. If she asked questions, they would say that they knew no more. As for their own pasts, they simply said, "There's nothing interesting for you to know." It was not until Mary went to high school that she learned from that distant relative that her father was a member of a Rebellious Faction when the Cultural Revolution began and had beaten wronged rightists and antirevolutionists and destroyed their homes. She also learned that her mother had married her father, eleven years her senior, not out of love but to protect herself from being persecuted because of her family background—her father was condemned.

How Mary despised her parents after she had learned all this! Though that relative also said that her father didn't stay with the Rebellious Faction for long and was later condemned himself, his history was there, shameful, unerasable. If she had respected her father for not bribing his managers for a promotion, she now felt that his pride might have resulted more from his guilt regarding his past than from his righteousness. Moreover, if he had asked for a promotion, his dossier would have been reviewed. What if the stigma was recorded there? Whenever she thought about it, Mary shivered with disgust and sadness.

She had never liked her father. He always returned home from work with a gloomy face, as if his family owed him a debt. After dinner he would go out for a long walk, still wearing his uniform. A few times, she followed him to see where he went and realized that he liked to visit a bad neighborhood, where drunkards peed in dark alleys and hooligans stopped female factory workers going to their night shifts. He wandered about, clearing his throat loudly every few minutes as if to announce his presence. Though he was quiet and self-effacing as a jailer, now he strode vigorously, hands behind his back, head high, like a high-ranking official on an inspection tour, his uniform making him look important. At the sight of him, the drunkards who were peeing would run away with their pants still unzipped. Hooligans saluted him and even bowed with reverence and flattery. "Uncle Policeman, good evening," they said. Street vendors selling fake medicines and certificates were afraid of him, mistaking him for a genuine security policeman. If they saw him, they shoveled their merchandise into plastic bags and ran away, not daring to slow down until the distance between them and her father was at least two blocks. These vendors were mostly unemployed city residents or farmers from nearby villages, and they shared a fear of policemen, regardless of function or rank: traffic policemen, wardens, or soldiers. They nicknamed them Big Caps, referring to their caps' wide visors.

The unhappier Mary's father was at work, the longer he walked after dinner. Some nights, he did not return home until after midnight. It seemed to Mary that these long walks were outlets for her father to get over his frustration and disappointment with being a total failure in his career.

While Mary despised her father, she felt pity and sympathy for her mother. If her mother hadn't gone through one political movement after another, with her family background she could have received a decent education and married someone she liked. And even if her looks faded with age, she would have maintained her elegance and good taste, instead of having turned into what she was now: unkempt, frugal, boorish, and narrow-minded.

Many of Mary's memories of her mother were of going grocery shopping with her when she was in her teens. Her mother didn't have enough strength to carry the groceries home, so Mary had to help. The market they usually went to was a farmers' market, where rotten vegetables, animal excrement, and buzzing flies were everywhere. Her mother would typically buy vegetables at the stands outside the market, because those peasants charged a little less than their competitors inside, who had to pay a management fee.

"How can you ask so much for such shabby *baichai*?" her mother would say, her hands rummaging inside the vendor's bamboo basket. After tedious bargaining, usually ending in a savings of one or two cents per *jin*, the deal was made. Mary's mother took her time picking the best vegetables, peeling off the less fresh-looking outer leaves and swinging each *baichai* back and forth several times to get rid of the water before having them weighed. "Nowadays, you can't find a single businessman who's honest," she would lecture Mary. "They all soak their vegetables before selling them, to add extra weight." When the vendor weighed her purchase on his scale, Mary's mother never failed to examine the number carefully to make sure it was correct.

As the garlic vendor counted the coins her mother had given him, her mother would quickly take an extra head and throw it into her basket. By the time the vendor realized what had happened and cursed in his country dialect, her mother had arrived at the meat section.

"So expensive! Do you think I own a bank?" Holding a pork rib, her mother exclaimed with a genuine surprise on her face, as if it were years ago that she had last bought ribs. She lingered for at least ten minutes, examining every rib on the counter, and at last picked two. Before handing them to the meat vendor, she asked him to give her a piece of finger-length lean meat for free. Not wanting to lose her business, the vendor always agreed.

This was how Mary remembered her mother, a crude woman who always wore a deep blue factory uniform stained with oil and grease. Before reaching forty, she already had white hair and was overweight. She had been a factory worker most of her life: at the beginning, in a steel factory, then in a papermaking factory, and finally, in the seventies, in a car-parts factory, where she was an assembly-line worker. Not until a few years before her retirement was she moved to the office.

Mary once saw an old picture of her mother, wearing a dark jacket like everyone else in the Mao era, both sides of her short hair combed tidily behind her ears, her right hand holding Mao's Little Red Book against her chest. Her eyes glittered with joy and hope, her eyelashes were thick and curly, and her bangs touched her forehead gracefully. There was no resemblance between the person in the picture and the obese woman who haggled shamelessly with the vendors at the farmers' market.

In Mary's teenage years, she often felt deep disappointment and shame. Why wasn't she born to parents who were intellectuals? While other families discussed books, movies, or world politics and economics at home, her family talked only about daily trivialities.

Her father was intimidating with his sullen face. Her mother liked to stay in the kitchen, where she could stand or sit undisturbed for hours. More than once, Mary caught her sitting on a paint-chipped stool in the middle of the kitchen, mouth agape, staring blankly into into midair like a retarded beggar often seen in their part of town. But as soon as she sensed her daughter's presence, she leapt to her feet with unexpected agility and her face assumed a broad smile.

Mary rarely invited friends to her home. Yes, the decoration in the apartment was tasteless, with secondhand-looking furniture and appliances, and the vulgar wall posters her mother had cut out from an out-of-date calendar. But a lot of her friends' parents' apartments were like this as well. In fact, what she feared was that her friends would catch her mother in a trance in the kitchen and think that she had some kind of mental disease.

She did not go home for the new year during her first winter break in college, telling her parents that she would be visiting a roommate's family in the countryside in Sichuan Province. The truth was that she stayed in her dorm room on New Year's Eve, alone, listening to the countdown on the radio, imagining fireworks bursting all over the night sky. She knew that at that very moment her parents and her sister were watching the Spring Festival Evening Show, in which singers, dancers, acrobats, and comedians tried their best to entertain the audience. Everyone was celebrating except her, who lay on her cold bed. For the first time in her life she felt desperately lonely; an unspeakable sadness seemed to have filled her, a sadness that, unlike that from a relationship breakup or job failure, had taken root in her heart, to breathe with her, to be part of her life, something she could not escape.

She did not cry at her father's funeral, and because of that, Ingrid called her "stone-hearted." Ingrid said those words in their mother's presence, but in English, so that their mother wouldn't understand.

Mary did not defend herself. What could she say? Ingrid would never know what was in her mind. When the Cultural Revolution broke out, Ingrid had not been born; when it ended, she had just started primary school. She had never lived in a remote village with strangers who called her "illegitimate." She had never experienced hunger. The six-year difference in their age was like a gap between generations.

Mary hears a car turning in to the driveway and then Alex's cheerful talking. "Dad, let's go to the aquarium in Monterey tomorrow. Jenson said there's a baby white shark there." She opens the front door for Bob and Alex, putting on a gentle smile, telling herself that it's time to leave the past behind, to embrace her life in the United States.

FIVE

September

THERE'S A KNOCK AT the door. Fenglan opens it, thinking it's the milk deliveryman.

"A letter from the United States!" Old Yu, the security guard for her complex, holds a white envelope high, his eyebrows shiny with sweat. "The mailman is new and he couldn't find your mailbox, so I told him I'd give it to you."

"Old Yu, sorry to trouble you. You have to climb so many steps to deliver the letter! Next time you can just yell from downstairs and I will fetch the letter myself." She takes the letter. It is from her second daughter.

"No trouble at all. This stamp . . . hmm, you know my grandson collects stamps."

"I'll give it to you later, just as I always do, of course."

"Huh, my grandson is waiting in the security room right now. You know, kids nowadays are stubborn and spoiled."

She goes to the kitchen, uses scissors to cut off the stamp, and hands it to Old Yu.

"I'm sorry to rush you, but my grandson . . . Next time you need to have your shoes repaired, just give them to me. I won't charge you." Old Yu has a small shoe-repair machine in the security room, a way to earn his cigarette money. "Also, the other day you said you didn't want to disconnect the phone while you're away; I can help you pay the phone bills."

"That's so kind of you. I'll leave some money for you before I go."

After Old Yu leaves, she closes the door and opens the envelope. In the letter her daughter asks her to bring some old family photos with her in November. "If they don't have negatives, have them reprinted. Make sure to find a good photo store so the photos won't get damaged." Also enclosed is a check for five hundred dollars. "Buy yourself a new television or a massage chair," she says.

What does her daughter need all these old family photos for? Fenglan wonders, remembering that her daughter asked her for her and her husband's wedding photo several months ago.

It has been a long time since Fenglan looked at those family photos.

There's another knock at the door. This time, it's two Workers' Union representatives from the state-run factory she worked for before retiring. Their visit is expected: they called last week and said they would stop by to drop off some gift from the factory for the upcoming Mid-autumn Festival. Newspapers sometimes would report on this kind of gift delivery, calling it "sending warmth to retirees' homes."

The gift this year is a box of moon cakes made by a local bakery and a one-liter bottle of Dragon and Phoenix peanut oil—every retiree from the factory gets the same gift. Fenglan invites them to sit on the sofa and pours tea for them. She also takes out a plate of South Fortune honey oranges and some roasted sunflower seeds.

As the visitors sip tea, they ask her if she is healthy, if she sleeps and eats well, if there are any inconveniences in her life, and if she has any feedback for the factory leaders and the Party committee. Every year, the same questions are asked.

She says everything is fine. She thanks them, thanks the factory leaders for their concern and generosity, thanks the Party committee for thinking of retirees. Every year, her answers are the same.

"After you go to America, no working units and no Party committee will care if you're well, no one will send you moon cakes and peanut oil," they tease her. Everyone in her factory knows that she's going to visit her daughters—she had to get a retirement verification letter from the Personnel Department for her passport application.

"That's very true. People don't have time to care for others in capitalistic societies," she echoes hurriedly.

The two women stay for another few minutes, sipping more tea and sharing an orange, then leave for the next retiree's apartment.

After they've gone, Fenglan feels tired, so she lies down on the sofa. But she dares not fall asleep or she won't be able to sleep in the evening. Lately, she has had many fragmented dreams, and though she forgets most of them as soon as she awakens, she recaptures those about her husband. Like the dream she had two days ago, in which she saw him walking out of his coffin, telling her that he was craving steamed codfish. The next day, she steamed a two-*jin* codfish and presented it along with some fresh fruit in front of his black-framed picture on the top of the dresser.

Her husband did not like to have his photo taken, and this picture is from their fifth marriage anniversary. The part below the top jacket button was cut off because there was a Chairman Mao badge next to it. She has planned to use her own half of the photo as her portrait on her gravestone, so she and her husband will be united again—space has been saved in her husband's grave for her and there is also space for her picture on the gravestone. When it's time for her to be buried, all that will need to be done is to add one more ash urn, one more picture, and one more name to the gravestone.

The phone begins to ring. She has to get up from the sofa to answer it. The call is from an ex-colleague, asking her to buy a digital camera for him in the United States—he has heard that it's cheaper to buy electronic products there. Then another call comes: this time it is a classmate at the paper-cutting class at the senior center asking her to bring back some English picture books for her granddaughter. In the past few days, Fenglan has received many calls with different requests; as long as she feels she can manage, she does not say no. She knows that any rejection would provoke gossip, saying that she is arrogant because her daughters live overseas. Moreover, these friends, ex-colleagues, and neighbors have helped her here and there, doing favors like carrying a big bag of rice for her, fixing the clogged sink and toilet, or sending her TV to a repair shop. When her husband was alive he did all this, but now he is gone. Unless it's absolutely necessary, she does not call a handyman to her apartment; she doesn't want a stranger to know that she lives by herself. Who knows if people are trustworthy?

Then her older daughter calls.

"Ma, travel light. Don't bring any gifts for us," her daughter says.

"Most of my luggage is clothes. It's not heavy," Fenglan says.

"The quality of the clothes here is much better. I've already bought some for you."

"Don't waste your money. I have a lot of clothes already. It's much cheaper to buy in China."

"It's not expensive here, either. I just don't want you to exhaust yourself. It's your first air trip."

"I should be fine. I just went to see a doctor. She said I am very healthy," Fenglan lies.

"That's good."

"How's Dongdong? How tall is he now?" she asks about her grandson, referring to him by his Chinese name.

"Alex's one point two meters tall now. Very naughty. He can't wait for your visit. You'll love him."

Fenglan suddenly remembers that her daughter forgot a sweater the last time she visited, but before she mentions it, Guo-Mei says that she has to go to bed. Then she says good-bye and hangs up.

Her older daughter's calls are usually brief, and her voice sounds tired, which makes it difficult for Fenglan to ask questions.

Nor does her daughter write long letters. Though most of her letters look bulky, they contain mainly photos. At first, these were group photos of her and her classmates and professors at U.C. Berkeley, then of her and her husband, and now, since their son, Dongdong, was born, most of the pictures are of him. Dongdong turned six two months ago, yet Fenglan has never met him. Her older daughter says he has asthma and is very sensitive to air pollution—that's why she cannot bring him to China, where the air quality is poor.

In the next few weeks, Fenglan begins to buy gifts for her two daughters, her son-in-law, and her grandson. She asks neighbors and friends with grandchildren and salespeople at toy stores what six-year-old boys like. Some say animal picture books, some say toy guns and fire trucks, others say clothes printed with pictures of Mickey Mouse. The more thoughtful ones say, "Your grandson lives in the United States, the richest country in the world. He must have a lot of toys and clothes already. Buy him snacks and sweets." In the end, she is confused by all the ideas and decides to buy a bit of everything. One of her suitcases is packed with gifts for Dongdong. The other suitcase contains her clothes and shoes for different seasons, a big Chinese chopping knife, said to be unavailable in America, and various Chinese cooking ingredients, like dry pepper flakes, fermented black beans, star anise, and fennel seeds.

The gift for her son-in-law gives her a headache. She doesn't know if she should see him as a Chinese or as an American. He speaks little Chinese, yet he has a Chinese face and even a Chinese name: Bohan. She thinks it's a very elegant name, quite traditional, even poetic; according to her daughter, it was given to him by his grandfather. After telling her this, however, her daughter quickly added, "Call him Bob. It's his official name. No one calls him Bohan now that his grandpa has died." Bob? Fenglan shakes her head. It sounds like a firecracker bursting. Bohan sounds much better, with a lot of Chinese culture in it. But what does her son-in-law's name have to do with her? Whatever he prefers, she will have to call him. So his name is Bob and he is neither a Chinese nor an American, she decides at last. After thinking long and hard, and having gone to many stores, Fenglan eventually buys him a cashmere scarf at the oldest department store downtown. The salesgirl is friendly and helpful, spending half an hour suggesting colors and styles. The final purchase is dark gray, made of the best wool from Xinjiang Province.

It is much easier to choose gifts for her daughters. Fenglan wants to buy jade pieces of their astrological signs: Guo-Mei is a rabbit and Guo-Ying a rooster. She consulted Granny Li before making her final decision, and Granny Li said that a rabbit is responsible, amiable, and stable, and a deep green jade pendant will be a good match; a rooster, sensitive, adventurous, and passionate, should wear a light green bracelet. Fenglan doesn't know anything about jade, so she takes Granny Li's advice, thinking that, even if she bought the wrong styles, jade would be the right choice: it is known for being auspicious, and it looks nice on girls. These two jade pieces cost her quite a lot, but she is happy: she feels she now has something to leave to her daughters, who might even pass them on to their children. Also, since her daughters have been sending her money regularly, buying nice gifts for them, she reasons, is a good way to return some money to them.

Whenever her daughters send her money, she tells them not to. "You've worked hard to earn your money. You should save it for the future in case you need it," she says. To sound more convincing, she adds, "My retirement salary is not much, but it's enough to live on. I also get a pension from your father's jail regularly." But her daughters continue sending her money anyway, asking her to buy better-quality food, to replace the fridge and washer, to hire a maid instead of cooking and doing housework herself, to buy American or European-brand medicines rather than less trustworthy Chinese ones. "You should enjoy yourself after being poor for most of your life," they say to her.

Her Wanbao fridge and Water Lily washing machine, both purchased ten years ago, are still in use. The Wanbao is a little noisy but keeps her food cold, and the Water Lily, though it does not spin well and often leaves the clothes too damp, does a decent cleaning job— she just needs to hang the clothes on the clothesline on the balcony a little longer. In one of her bedroom corners is a Butterfly sewing machine that her husband bought her as a New Year's gift thirty years ago; she used to love it, taught herself how to sew, and later made most of her daughters' clothes and shoe pads with it. But she doesn't use it anymore; it is a souvenir from the past.

People from her generation tend to keep everything. If a product still works, they don't replace it until it breaks. The advertisements in newspapers and on TV are, of course, attractive, but older people don't open their wallets easily, as young people do. The popular notion that "the old has to give way to the new and the better" doesn't take root in their minds.

As much as Fenglan doesn't want her daughters' money, feeling herself a burden to them, she needs it, and feels fortunate to have it. She deposits most of it in CDs, with half-year, one-year, and five-year terms. Her husband's grave is in the countryside, and she has to send his family temple and his relatives there one thousand yuan every year—not long before her husband died, he asked her to do so. Her health is deteriorating: she suffers from shoulder and back pain, diabetes, high blood pressure, heart disease . . . the list on her health record keeps getting longer. I'm like an old piece of furniture that can collapse anytime, she sometimes says to herself. Every visit to the hospital and the pharmacy costs money, and though her factory reimburses a certain percentage, she has to pay a good chunk of it out of her own pocket. If her factory delays the reimbursement, which often happens, she has to take money out of her savings account. Last year, half her retirement income and her husband's pension went to medical bills. If not for the money her daughters had sent, she would have had to stop some of her medications.

She knows she's lucky compared with many of the people with whom she goes to morning exercises. Not being able to afford to see a doctor, they either leave their diseases untreated or buy cheap medicine from an unlicensed doctor or even a street vendor. The media often report that hospitals throw out patients because they can't afford to pay. The fear of getting sick has compelled many old people to exercise diligently. All kinds of *qi gong*, which are said to be able to cure diseases, are popular. Fenglan practiced *xiang gong* herself when it first became popular, but she never managed to exude fragrance from inside her as some loyal followers claimed they could.

Fenglan also saves for her daughters. She fancies that they might move back to China someday, with their husbands and children. How fast China is developing! Whenever she sees a new high-rise, a new supermarket, a new park, she marvels, thinking that it's a world for young people, like her daughters and their children. She has heard and read many stories of the government promising privileges and high salaries to lure overseas talent back. Some of the promises include free housing, free transportation, and no-interest business loans. But even with those, she imagines, if her daughters did come back, they would need money, and her savings could subsidize them. Whenever she thinks of her daughters moving back, she smiles. They can live in Beijing, Shanghai, Guangzhou, wherever they choose, but at least they would be able to visit her on every holiday, and sharing the same time zone, they could call her more often.

Old Tian, a neighbor, often says to her with admiration, "How nice it is to have daughters! They're considerate and sensitive, like inner cotton vests to keep you warm. Unlike sons—they only think of

their own families, and you're lucky if they don't ask you for money."
He envies her, but she actually envies him too. Every weekend, Old
Tian's two-bedroom apartment is filled with his sons and their wives
and children, and even if they bicker and fight constantly, there are at
least sounds and activities in his apartment. She has only the TV and
radio to keep her company, the emptiness of the room saddening her.
In the afternoons, when the sunlight fades, her heart dims. Sitting in
front of the TV, she glances at the telephone often, hoping that one of
her daughters will call; it is nice to hear their voices. Often, as if her
younger daughter has sensed her mother's thoughts from across the
world, she calls, and they usually talk for a while.

Yet her older daughter rarely calls.

It puzzles Fenglan that her second daughter calls often but hasn't
been back to China since she attended her father's funeral, while her
older daughter visits her every year but rarely calls.

Her older daughter must look down on her and her father, she
surmises. She was a factory worker for twenty years, and her husband a low-level warden for fifteen years. Her older daughter was
especially cold to her father, which used to upset Fenglan because she
knew how much he cared for her.

"People who use their brains manage people who use their muscles." She remembers her husband telling her this ancient saying,
which he had heard first as a small kid from a teacher in his village.
Later, after he went to school, he learned that it was from Confucius.
Even during the time Mao was promoting the slogan "The poorer,
the more glorious," her husband's only thought was to give their
daughters a good education. Some of his friends laughed at him. "A
dragon's son is a dragon, a phoenix's daughter is a phoenix, but a rat's
son only knows how to dig holes. You aren't an intellectual yourself,
isn't it ridiculous to dream of sending your children to college?" He
ignored their sarcasm and carried out his plan all the same. He used
to be a chain smoker, a pack a day, but after their daughters started
school, he quit smoking and used his cigarette money to buy them

textbooks. If they stayed up late preparing for an important examination, he did not go to bed until the lights in their rooms were off, killing time in his room by reading the newspaper over tea. The last few months before their older daughter took the entrance exam for college, he packed up the TV and the radio and put them in the closet, so there would be no distraction. He took two shifts at work to earn extra money to buy fish and meat for her. All these things he did joyfully, as if every little sacrifice he made would reward him generously in the future.

Though he inquired with their daughters' teachers often about their grades, he rarely asked their daughters directly because he was ashamed of his ignorance. He had never studied chemistry or physics, knew nothing about algebra and English, and his knowledge in history and geography was minimal. Once, their younger daughter, then in middle school, asked him about the major lakes and deserts in China, but he had no answer. The next day, he bought a topographical map and a geography book, hiding both purchases from his daughter, afraid of being laughed at. He studied them industriously, but when he was ready to answer his younger daughter's question about the lakes and deserts, she cut him short, saying she already knew the answer.

Despite his concern about their daughters' studies, he was careful not to put pressure on them—he had read that some children rebelled, left home, or became mentally disturbed because their parents were too strict with them. A colleague's son, a classmate of their older daughter's, was an example. When Yizhong was in the last year of high school, his father checked his homework daily and would reward good marks with money and punish him for less satisfactory marks with more homework. For a while, his father was pleased with his method, telling all his friends that his son had leapt into the top five in his class. But on the first day of the college entrance exam, Yizhong had an anxiety attack and couldn't finish his test. He retook the exam three years in a row but did poorly each time. He finally gave up and became a clerk in a supermarket. Whenever Yizhong's father talked with Fenglan's husband about his son, he would burst into tears.

The day their older daughter received the admission letter from Beijing Normal University, her father cabled every relative he could think of, and though he was usually quiet and self-effacing at work, he distributed ten-*jin* candies and numerous packs of cigarettes among his colleagues. Even the prisoners in his ward got some. In his jail, he was the only one to have a child go to college, not to mention that she was going to study in Beijing, the capital. What could have brought more honor to him and his ancestors?

But their older daughter alienated herself from them further after she went to college, spending little time at home during breaks, and even when she was home, mostly locking herself in her room, reading. To please her, her father bought her a set of newly translated works of Roman and Greek philosophers, which cost him a month's salary, only to find out a few months later that they had been eaten by termites under her bed. Once, Fenglan and her husband peeked at the books that their older daughter was reading: the authors were all foreigners, and the translated titles contained terms like *democracy, freedom, human rights,* and *right to vote.* They were scared by their discovery: they knew that these words and phrases were typically used by political radicals or dissidents. Both their work units had organized studies of the anti-westernization documents issued by the central government in the past few months.

To their relief, their older daughter did not get involved in a political movement and went to the United States after graduation, not breaking the news to her parents until she got the visa. Four years later, she helped her sister go abroad.

Then, in another two years, Fenglan lost her husband.

At three p.m., it occurs to Fenglan that she needs to get some cash from the bank—she has to buy decent clothes for her trip, mainly for the autumn and winter. Her visa allows her to stay in America till May, but she plans to return home earlier, though she's not sure how much earlier. She considers going to the department store where she brought the scarf for Bob, but a quick calculation changes her mind. For that kind of money, she reasons, she could ask Young Song, the seamstress who lives on the first floor of her apartment building, to make her more than ten jackets.

Young Song used to work at the same car-parts factory as Fenglan did, as a production line worker, but she was forced out when the factory went through a staff reduction.

Compared with Young Song, Fenglan feels herself in a much better position. After all, she retired before state-run companies all over the country had begun to lay off their workers. Also, she retired as an office employee, with guaranteed benefits.

She knocks at Young Song's door and is greeted warmly— Young Song hasn't had any business for a week. After choosing a few styles from Young Song's fashion books for seniors and being told how much fabric is needed, Fenglan says good-bye. If she stayed a little longer, she knows, Young Song would complain about her life. "When I was about to go to school, I was told 'Knowledge is useless.' Then I became a Red Guard, then was sent by the Party to a remote village to be re-educated. When I finally returned to the city, it took me a long time to get a job. Then, you see, I was laid off for lack of education and now have no money to send my son to college." She cries as soon as she starts her story.

Fenglan sympathizes, but what can she do to help other than giving Young Song business now and then?

After purchasing the fabric and delivering it to Young Song, Fenglan cooks some vegetables at home and eats them for dinner. Since last week, she hasn't been feeling well and has been eating only vegetables. She has lost over ten *jin*, which she thinks is good—she is overweight. Also she believes the old saying "Nothing is more precious for an elderly person than being thin."

She needs to get a haircut the day before her trip, she reminds herself, so she will look good to her son-in-law and grandson. She used to have her hair cut at a salon in a small street just outside her building, but Old Wei sold his business and moved back to his hometown a month ago. A young couple now owns the place. Within two weeks they renovated the salon, making it look more like a disco than a barbershop. The huge double-glass doors are framed with colored lights that twinkle in the evenings; the walls are pink, with entertainment celebrities' photos hung at odd angles. Everything looks new: the shiny, full-size mirrors; the black leather chairs; the color TV mounted in a corner playing the latest Korean romance movies. No one working in the salon has black hair. The men look like women with their tight pants and long hair, while the women look like men with short hair pointing upward like the quills of a hedgehog. A few days ago, passing the salon, Fenglan saw a man walking out, his arm tattooed with a half-naked woman. Since Old Wei moved, she has not patronized the salon. She heard that a haircut there now costs thirty yuan, six times of what Old Wei used to charge, and it is said that the barbers there don't know how to cut old people's hair. She will have to walk a few blocks to the barbershop recommended by Granny Li. It's owned by a man in his fifties, and he charges the same price as Old Wei used to.

Fenglan looks out the window, wanting to see if the moon is full—it's the fifteenth according to the lunar calendar—but it's blocked by a half-built high-rise. She turns on the TV: an advertisement for a Japanese whitening cream is on. The model's face is as white as paper, and her curvy eyelashes are fake. Fenglan tunes to another channel: MTV from Taiwan. Four feminine-looking boys are running and jumping on the stage like they're going mad. She turns off the TV, thinking of her younger daughter's letter. She walks to her bedroom and opens the closet, where half the hanging space is still occupied by her husband's uniforms. Stacked on the right are three identical black-lacquered wooden chests, the top two containing her daughters' old clothes and the bedding they used during their college years.

It takes her a while to move these two chests. Her heart flutters, and she can hear her heartbeats. She walks to the kitchen to get a glass of water and returns to the bedroom to take a heart pill. After she feels better, she opens the bottom chest. It is only half filled, mostly with the gifts she and her husband received when they got married in 1962: a square mirror with text in red paint: "I wish you will be together for a hundred years," a handmade embroidery of a fat baby boy and girl, a plastic-covered Chinese dictionary. Inside the chest there are also a few dozen Chairman Mao badges, in varied sizes and styles, which she and her husband wore in the sixties and seventies.

In addition to the wedding gifts and the Chairman Mao badges, there is a long, narrow tin box, tarnished and considerably dented.

She hesitates before opening the box.

SIX

September

ON A SUNNY FRIDAY, Ingrid leaves her apartment for the New York Public Library, bringing her Apple notebook with her. Besides guiding tours, Ingrid does freelance translation and interpretation, Chinese to English or vice versa. She has received several highly paid jobs through an agency this month, including interpreting and proofreading for international conferences in New York, Boston, and Miami. Though she doesn't have a degree in translation and interpretation, she has built, mainly through word of mouth, a solid client list with premium commissions. But unless she needs money urgently, she prefers projects with flexible schedules, like translating a book or a long article. Now and then, something interesting turns up, concerning history, arts, or social issues, but most of these projects are boring, typically product descriptions, travel brochures, survey questionnaires, or research papers. The brochure she's been working on since Monday is for a Chinese pharmaceutical company and contains numerous medical terms. That's why she is going to the library: to look up the terms in a special dictionary.

Terminology is one thing, writing itself is entirely another. Recently, Ingrid translated a product description for a Chinese electronics company which said that its products had been highly rated by the provincial and central governments—an advertising cliché used in the seventies and eighties in China. It also said that the company owed its success to the Communist Party's encouragement and support. Yet another cliché. Should she tell them that Americans couldn't understand these expressions? One would never hear Bill Gates say that Microsoft couldn't have achieved what it has without the Republican or Democratic Party's encouragement and support.

But why bother? She charges by the word. Also, she does this kind of translation only to pay her bills; it has nothing to do with her ambition or passion. Sometimes, she thinks this way. But other times, she remembers why she took up translation and interpretation three years ago: she feared losing her fluency in Chinese. In fact, she has forgotten how to write some common Chinese characters, and without a computer's help, she wouldn't even be able to compose a letter without making embarrassing mistakes. It was out of the same fear that she became a tour guide for visitors from China—in addition, this occupation allows her to observe and listen to those visitors, a good way to be informed about what's happening in her birth country.

As for her ambition, her most recent thought is to go to graduate school and study art history. Before that, she had considered a law degree and a master's in library science. She has an inquisitive mind and is willing to try things out. But going back to school doesn't thrill her because she has gotten used to a flexible schedule; that's why she has been procrastinating on her decision.

Ingrid plans to move to San Francisco in a few months to be closer to her mother, during her visit. She has been taking more jobs than she would like. Moving always costs more than one expects, and renting in San Francisco is hardly cheaper than in New York. No, she won't stay there long, she has decided; she will return to New York as soon as her mother goes back to China.

Not having seen her mother for eight years, Ingrid wants to make up for it this time. Though she calls every week, hearing her mother's voice is different from seeing her in person. Ingrid has not told her mother that she freelances and guides tours for a living; her mother has always thought that she works for the government—the ideal job, in her opinion, because it is safe. To her mother, being a contract translator or a tour guide is not a real job.

How could it have been eight years since she was last in China, attending her father's funeral? Ingrid wonders. How fast time has passed! She also imagines what it will be like to see her sister, Mary, again. Yes, she was a bit too harsh three years ago with her comment concerning her brother-in-law, whom she actually liked and whom she enjoyed talking to a lot more than she did to her sister. But Mary had started the whole thing, hadn't she? With her bullshit about not dating blacks or Indians.

Ingrid gets off the subway at Fifth Avenue. She stops by Saks Fifth Avenue and, though she thought she'd only take a quick browse at Max Mara's new arrivals, she ends up purchasing a top and a skirt. Great, I've broken my promise not to buy more clothes this month, she says to herself while paying.

Before she goes into the library, she decides to stroll around Bryant Park, one of her favorite places in midtown Manhattan. When the weather is nice, she sometimes brings her translation work here and sits in one of the portable chairs the park provides. She's watched many free movies in the park and has learned how to ice skate and play pétanque here.

The lawns are crowded. Unlike on weekdays, when businesspeople with laptops can be seen here and there, some holding serious-looking meetings, today's mass of humanity is mostly here to enjoy the view and the sun. The grass is very green, unusual in a public park, suggesting a recent renovation or special care. Ingrid finds an empty chair near the end of the lawn. In her immediate vicinity, a few girls in bikinis are sunbathing on colorful towels, facedown, arms at their sides, the thin straps on their backs untied. A young couple has fallen sleep, the woman's face against the man's chest. Three old men with walking sticks sit on the park's portable chairs, chatting gaily about a recent cruise to Alaska. Ingrid looks farther. Several kids are chasing one another on the walkway with water pistols in their hands, their wet faces glistening.

She assures herself that she is happy in New York, and though she hasn't found her career yet, at least she doesn't hate what she is doing. Being adrift is not that bad, considering its freedom. If Mary hadn't forced her to study accounting at San Jose State University, she might never have lived in New York, might never have chosen to be self-employed. The idea of thanking Mary for what she's enjoying right now amuses her. Ironic, really, she thinks.

Perhaps she shouldn't have listened to her older sister's insistence that she study accounting, but did she have a choice? She was only twenty, a college junior, and she was desperate to leave China. When Mary sent Ingrid the financial aid documents, she sent along the application form from San Jose State University's accounting program. As a history student, Ingrid had no interest in accounting, but she completed the application and mailed it. She was lucky to get a student visa, and later, under Mary's pressure, she finished the bachelor's program. Not a day went by while she was studying accounting that she didn't hate Mary's manipulation. But she had to listen to her long lecturing, for her sister was paying most of her tuition and expenses.

As an outlet for her frustration, Ingrid began to wear bohemian clothes and dye her hair in bright colors, she drank and smoked; all this, she knew, her churchgoing sister disapproved of, and when she saw Mary's sad face, she felt a taste of victory. She never followed

Mary's advice—get a scholarship, take extra classes, prepare for the CPA exam; quite the opposite, she skipped classes often and did only the minimum on homework assignments.

After trying smoking and drinking, she used marijuana. It was not difficult to get it at weekend dorm parties saturated with beer, dim lights, and throbbing hip-hop music. The first time she smoked from a pipe handed to her by a classmate, she only felt dizzy and a little nauseated, like having jet lag. She tried a second time. She still felt okay at first, but as she stood to get a beer, the music suddenly sounded very close, like a band playing right next to her. A light seemed to sparkle inside her brain. She sat down, staring content-edly at a table fountain and a lit candle, and in her reverie, she saw herself sitting next to a tall waterfall, her body light as foam. She felt lazy, she wanted to fly—she imagined herself flying. Barely a week had passed before she bought LSD from a "pharmacist," a senior student. She took some while reading George Orwell's *1984* on the sofa in her dorm room.

The effect kicked in half an hour later: before her eyes, the sofa fabric separated into individual threads, slowly and audibly, then the threads inched toward her and climbed onto her arms, her legs, and her stomach like snakes. Paralyzed by fear, she couldn't make a sound; her breathing was heavy but hollow. To add to her fright, the book in her hand started to melt, the words falling off the pages one by one, turning into sharp knives as they hit her thighs. After this nightmarish experience, she never touched drugs again.

Ingrid blamed her cowardice (as she thought of it then) on hav-ing grown up in China, where she had never seen drugs, let alone used them. She and her teenage friends, compared with their Ameri-can peers, were like sheets of blank paper, ignorant of sex and drugs. When they watched a movie, if there was a kissing scene, even if it showed just a light touch on the lips, they would blush and their hearts would race. She was thought adventurous and bold by her friends in China, but she did not kiss a boy until high school. As for sex, it didn't happen until she was twenty, already in the United States. From China to the United States was, to her, a big leap, as if a homebound country girl was entering a dazzling city for the first time.

She'd had so many firsts here: using a clothes dryer; watching a baseball game; drinking vodka; taking a tub bath; eating a hamburger, cheese, and pizza; using a microwave oven and a vacuum cleaner; owning a credit card; wearing lace underwear; having her ears pierced; and letting a boy kiss her in public. Of course, she remembers vividly the bewilderment in her first American boyfriend's face when she told him that she was a virgin.

And the first time she read porn. A classmate had told her that the college library carried *Playboy;* it was not displayed on the open shelves, but all she needed to do was ask. She was tempted, having heard about the magazine in China, where it was considered incontrovertible proof of a corrupt and doomed capitalist society. How obscene could it be? She finally asked, when the librarian was alone behind the counter, presenting her query cleverly, as instructed by her classmate, for Jimmy Carter's interview in 1976, in which he famously admitted that he had looked on many women with lust. She was researching a class paper about left-wing political interviews, she claimed. She got a copy of the interview, as well as the latest issue with missing centerfolds, and read them in the dimly lit archive room. Though the first few nude or seminude photos, including the bikinied Barbi Twins on the cover, were shocking and arousing, she quickly came to feel jaded. This was tasteless and demeaning, she concluded. And it was simply beyond her comprehension that the same issue, with its shameless focus on enormous breasts (were they real? she wondered) and buttocks featured an interview with the governor of Virginia. It was like saying that porn and politics were in fact one big family, that porn revealed too much, while politics hid too much.

Despite her low opinion of the magazine, Ingrid was stimulated, much to her surprise, and in the following days, she was obsessed with sex, making love to her boyfriend incessantly, being unusually restless and aggressive. Was it because of the lingering impact of the porn, or the exotic and forbidden act of reading porn itself? She didn't know. As she lay on the bed after a satisfying orgasm toward the end of her sex marathon, barely able to move, it struck her that what she had been doing was an attempt to sever her ties with her past, with her innocence, ignorance, and naïveté, everything in her that wasn't American.

America was a huge whirlpool, taking her down gradually; she knew she would never be swallowed completely, yet she couldn't seem to escape, either.

It was not until she came to New York, until she met Angelina, that Ingrid began to like herself, feeling more at home in Angelina's Latin culture than in her own, which seemed to her too pragmatic, formal, and restrained. Also, by hanging out with Angelina and other non-Chinese friends, she felt free from the burden that had weighed her down. Occasionally, it occurred to her that she was like a hermit crab in a tight shell looking for a well-fitting one to protect herself better and let her self grow faster. It was an unpleasant thought, but it didn't bother her the way it used to, for she had begun to consider herself a global citizen who travels, experiences, and enjoys various cultures, and calls everywhere home.

But in the depths of her mind, Ingrid knew her concept of a global citizen was just an illusion.

Ingrid senses that she is being watched. She looks to the right and meets the gaze of a pair of brown eyes a yard away: the Asian girl looking at her is wearing a red, hooded windbreaker and has a black sack under her chair; she is drawing something in a notebook with a pencil. Seeing that Ingrid has noticed her, the girl puts her notebook down on her lap and beams nervously. This girl was sketching her, Ingrid speculates. She'd like to see the drawing.

As if guessing what is in Ingrid's mind, that girl stands and walks to her, the notebook under her arm. She has short hair and tanned skin, appears to be in her early twenties. "I'm sorry. I sketch you without permission. I hope you not mind."

"Oh, really? I didn't know I could be a model," Ingrid says, sizing up the girl. Now she can see four holes on both her earlobes—only the two in the middle bearing tiny silver rings. She also detects the girl's Chinese accent.

The girl hands Ingrid her notebook. "I'm not done yet," she explains. "I haven't drew your shoes."

Ingrid takes the notebook and looks at it. It's her, beyond a doubt: her hair, eyes, mouth, black top, and long, pleated skirt. She has never had a portrait of herself drawn, and it surprises her how much the drawing resembles her; she likes it. She raises her eyes from the notebook to the girl's face. "It's very good."

"I hope so." The girl seems skeptical of Ingrid's praise. "You must been thinking of something serious. Your eyes . . . I don't know, they were intriguing. In-tri-guing, did I pronounce it right? Anyway, could be better. If you want it, it's yours. But let me finish your shoes. You have time?"

"Sure." The girl looks so eager that Ingrid feels she has to say yes.

The girl runs back to her chair and moves it to a spot facing Ingrid, a step away. Ingrid gives the notebook to the girl and watches her as she draws. After the girl draws her shoes, she does more work on her eyes. Then she holds the portrait up in front of her and tilts her head sideways, studying it. "Well, could be better. I don't know what's wrong with me today," she says to herself, obviously disappointed. She signs the sketch, tears it out of her notebook carefully, and hands it to Ingrid.

"You're Chinese?" Ingrid says, now in Mandarin. The girl's signature is in Chinese.

Excited, the girl replies in Mandarin, "Are you Chinese too? I wasn't sure. You don't have an accent. I'm Bing'er, living in Toronto.

I've been there for two months. I emigrated there from Hubei Province. It's so nice speaking Mandarin."

"Only two months? Your English is good."

"Thanks. I studied English a lot before I went to Canada." She looks proud. "I listened to the Voice of America radio program every day for more than two years. You know that program, right?"

Ingrid nods, remembering how unclear the program was because the transmissions were interfered with by the Chinese government. She had to carry her radio to her dorm's rooftop and listen to it there; even so, there was constant static in the background and she had to walk around with the radio and adjust its antenna often to hear better.

"I didn't dare listen to it in my dorm. You know, I lived in a government-assigned dorm," Bing'er continues. "Luckily, there was a school playground nearby. Oh, what's your name?"

Ingrid tells Bing'er her name and what she does for a living. Then she asks, "Toronto? Why there?"

"It's a long story. Anyway, I went there as a chef. I was told by my friends that it was easy to emigrate to Canada as a chef. But, of course, I wasn't a good chef. I took some classes and got a certificate. But that kind of certificate is easy to get. You might even be able to buy it from a street vendor for several hundred yuan. God knows how my case was approved. I think I was just lucky. Or Canada must be desperate to increase its population. You know, there's so much land there, with so few people. Have you been to Canada?"

Ingrid says that she has visited Canada at least six times.

"Six times? So you've been to a lot of places in Canada then. I love those little towns and have done a lot of sketches of them. Do you travel much? Where have you been?"

Ingrid mentions some of the places she has visited. Bing'er leans forward, eyes wide with admiration, feet tapping lightly as if she wanted to fly to those places at this very moment.

"Even Egypt and Ghana? That's so cool. I need to pay off my debt first, then I can start to travel. You know, I borrowed a lot of money for my emigration application and the plane ticket," Bing'er says. She moves her chair closer to Ingrid, as if saying "Now, you're my pal."

"What did you do in China? Why did you move to Canada?" Impressed by Bing'er's portrait of her and also liking the way she talks and acts—she looks candid and natural—Ingrid finds herself drawn to the girl, whose eyes are restless, glancing with curiosity at the people passing.

Bing'er tells Ingrid about her boring typist job at a government bureau after she failed to go to college; quitting to sell clothes with her best friend, Tingting; her longing to travel abroad; waiting on tables to make a living in Toronto. All this Ingrid takes in with immense interest and unwittingly compares her own experience with Bing'er's. Though there is something in common between them, she sees more differences, the unfamiliar characteristics associated with the new generation in urban China, the generation born after the Cultural Revolution, who have little recollection of the poverty and dogmas of the seventies and eighties. A generation free from the burden of that history.

"Tingting also wanted to emigrate to Canada, but her parents didn't allow her," Bing'er says. "Her grandma even threatened her with suicide. She's the only child in the family, poor thing. Whenever she writes me, she asks a lot of questions. Are white people nice, funny, or are they difficult to make friends with? Do white women shave their legs every day? Do white women wear sexy lingerie under normal clothes to work? Do white people often visit strip clubs? God knows where she has gotten all these ideas about white people."

Ingrid laughs: she has been asked similar questions by the people in her tour groups. "Aren't you the old child?" she then asks, thinking of the one-child-per-family policy implemented in China in the past twenty years.

"Lucky me, I have an older brother. He was born prematurely and was often ill when he was little, so my parents bribed the people in charge of the Planned Reproduction Work Unit and had the second child. They almost lost their hospital jobs for that. Both my parents are doctors."

"But you're the young one. They probably worry about you more."

"My parents don't like me much," Bing'er says quickly, seemingly happy with the fact. "My brother is very good-looking. He's tall and slim, has a fair complexion, a cute nose, thick eyelashes, and nicely curved lips, a perfect showcase of my parents' best genes. I think he looks like a girl, but that's just my opinion. But I have inherited the worst of my parents' appearances, with my father's dark skin and small eyes, and my mother's flat nose and thick lips." She opens her arms, as if to invite Ingrid to have a better look at her ordinary face. "Also, he went to college and is an engineer at a state-run railroad company. A lucrative job, you bet. I didn't go to college, and for a while I roamed the streets, befriending 'bad kids'—that's what they were called—and learned how to smoke and play mah-jongg. My parents had told me many times that they wished they didn't have a child like me."

"They were just saying that," Ingrid says, feeling the need to console Bing'er.

"It doesn't matter. I'm actually glad they don't like me, I'm free to do what I want. I can support myself, that's not a problem." Bing'er shrugs. "When I was in China, I didn't get along well with my brother and his wife, either; they were both living with my parents because they were saving to buy their own house. That woman has a small face, small eyes, small nose, small mouth, and small hands and feet— I am sure she has a small heart too, and a small mind. That makes a matched set. My brother had always been cold to me—of course, he too thought he was much better than I was. With his wife bad-mouthing me constantly, he had little to say to me. The day I moved to the government's dorm, my sister-in-law persuaded my parents to remove the wall between my room and her and my brother's bedroom, saying that she was planning to get pregnant and needed more space. So if I went home, I had to sleep on the living room sofa. Oh, I've got to tell you about my ear piercing. I got my ears pierced when I was in middle school. That evening my mother didn't allow me to eat dinner and my father told me to sleep on the floor. My family was fascist."

Ingrid thinks of her own father, who was also very strict with her, and she was rebellious just like Bing'er. Though she's a decade older than Bing'er, she feels close to her.

"Don't you miss your family at all?" Ingrid asks.

"Hmm, no, at least not right now. Maybe later. Maybe never. Now, I only want to travel all over the world." Bing'er strokes her chin with one hand and squints at Ingrid. "Do you write?"

"Write what?"

"I mean, are you a writer?"

"What made you think so?"

"I don't know. You just look like someone who writes. Literature stuff."

"Maybe. I haven't written much."

"So, you are a writer!"

Ingrid shakes her head. "I don't know about that. I've not been published yet. You know, in New York, there are lots of wannabe writers. All the big publishers are here. Greenwich Village, Chelsea, and SoHo are also here. Well, not many writers can afford to live there anymore, but they're still nice places. And Columbia University is here too. It has a respected writing program."

"I like New York, but it's too expensive. Even deli food is not cheap. I'm glad all these nice parks are at least free."

At last Bing'er talks about her new brush-and-ink paintings. "How do you like the idea of painting Chinese characters? You know, you translate them into English, while I draw them. I'm not talking about calligraphy; it's more about telling a story. If you look at the Chinese character for crying, it looks like someone is crying, and the character for laughing looks like someone is laughing. The English words don't have that effect. Also, just look at how much is embodied in Chinese characters! The characters for rape, wizard, envy, prostitute, and shrewd all have 'female' as part of them. Doesn't that mean that women's social and familial status was low in the old days? If they're translated into English, they lose that kind of intrinsic culture. I've started to draw certain photographic characters: *mu* becomes different trees; *shui,* creeks or waterfalls; *ma,* galloping horses." She pauses and bends to extract a thin stack of paper from her bag. "Look! Here are some ideas in sketches. Back in Canada, I have a few brush-and-ink paintings at home. They're just experiments. I don't know exactly how I'm going to draw Chinese characters right now. Later, I may have more ideas."

Ingrid studies the highly abstracted images. "Brilliant. Very creative. You should go to art school. You have talent."

"I've got to save money first." Bing'er smiles. "Unless I can get a scholarship, which is unlikely. I've never had any formal training in drawing. Not even summer school. My parents thought drawing was a waste of time. And I want to travel for a while." She pauses, giving Ingrid a trusting glance. "I do have some money. I made it with Tingting doing business in China, but I'm putting it aside for traveling. I like waiting on tables. I can leave when I please. There are so many Chinese restaurants in Toronto. I can always find jobs."

Bing'er checks her watch. "Jeez, I didn't realize it was so late already. I'd better get going. Today is my last day here. I came to New York with a friend two days ago. She'll pick me up at a bus stop on Forty-second Street."

They exchange e-mail addresses, and Ingrid invites Bing'er to stay with her next time she is in New York.

Ingrid doesn't go inside the library until the sun is behind the clouds and the air has cooled slightly: somehow, Bing'er's drawings of Chinese characters linger in her mind. It has been a long while since she thought about the beauty of those ideographic characters.

When Ingrid arrives home, it is almost dinnertime. Today is the day that Angelina is having a party. Though none of the guests is here yet—all are habitually unpunctual—the music of "Margarita", is playing cheerfully on the stereo, with its accordion and saxophone duet. On the living room table Ingrid finds two trays of mixed finger foods: chicken drumsticks, triangle samosas, spring rolls, cheese, olives, pâté, and some tortilla chips. Angelina is making the salsa for the chips; she always makes it herself, saying that nothing from the store can beat her grandmother's recipe.

Ingrid sees a big Mexican flag nailed on the wall above the sofa: it looks brand new.

"Did you just get another flag?" she asks as she walks into the kitchen, leaning against the counter watching Angelina prepare the salsa. Angelina has changed into a red Mexican dress embroidered heavily across the chest and along the hem, which she bought at the Cinco de Mayo Festival in California last year, and her hair is combed into two thick braids, with a pink carnation on either side.

"Sí. Isn't it pretty?"

Angelina is a patriot. In addition to a Mexican map taking up two thirds of a wall in her room, she has a few Mexican national flags. One is placed in the bonsai pot Ingrid gave her as a birthday gift—Angelina claims to love plants. The bonsai's leaves long ago turned yellow and its roots have dried out. The plant's lifelessness brings out the flag's vivid colors, as if the flag had killed the bonsai.

Though Angelina doesn't like reading (she claims that she's too busy "reading" men), she has an impressive collection of literature by Spanish-speaking writers, some first editions, hunted down from secondhand bookstores all over the United States and Mexico. More than five hundred books fill her three tall bookshelves, mainly in Spanish, some in English, some in other languages she can neither speak nor read. Gabriel García Márquez, Jorge Luis Borges, Octavio Paz, Pablo Neruda, Gabriela Mistral, Camilo José Cela . . . both well- or little-known authors. Ingrid credits Angelina for her increasing interest in Latin American writers.

On last year's Mexican Independence Day, Angelina hung a big Mexican flag outside her window. The commotion it created on the street exceeded her expectations—she couldn't have been more excited if she had been given a leading role in a Broadway show. As soon as it got dark, chaos ensued: small stones and paper balls were thrown at the flag, accompanied by expletives that American TV and radio would beep out. The indignant people included passersby in the mood for a prank; the most loyal American citizens, who couldn't tolerate the sight of a flag that didn't contain thirteen stripes and fifty stars; anarchists, who hated all national flags; and drunkards constantly looking for opportunities to spit and throw stones. An Irish bar sits two blocks down the street, so there is no shortage of drunkards in the neighborhood; some have developed a habit of peeing in the few half-dead boxwood bushes outside Ingrid's building. When Ingrid comes home in the evening, she can sometimes hear them mumbling or humming while doing their business in the bushes.

Seeing Angelina's Mexican flag, these drunkards felt the need to express their political views.

"Italian bastards, get the hell outta here!"

"Ya go back to Africa! All of ya!"

"Kiss my ass, Canada!"

Ingrid was leaning against the window, wanting to peek at the people who didn't recognize the Mexican national flag, when she heard a yell: "Down with Japan!"

Their Korean landlord, Kim Choi, knocked on their door, asking Angelina to take down the flag. Having lived in the United States for more than two decades, Kim has transformed herself into a perfect hybrid, blending Korean industriousness, American practicality, and immigrant frugality, along with a deep fear of trouble. She is in her late forties and lives in the smallest apartment, on the first floor. Her face is big and round; her eyes, nose, and mouth squeeze together, making her face look like a spacious room with furniture crowded into the middle. She seldom smiles, though her comic face makes it impossible for her to look serious.

Now Angelina tells Ingrid, "I got something for you too." Seeding an avocado, Angelina motions with her chin toward the fridge. Ingrid sees a magnet of a Chinese national flag on its door. "Where did you get it?" she asks.

"From that Chinese grocery store on Thirty-eighth Street. When I passed the store, I saw this magnet. What's the meaning of the pattern?"

Ingrid tells her: red stands for revolution, the big star circled by the four smaller ones signifies the gathering of the people under the leadership of the Communist Party. Each of the four smaller stars has a corner pointing at the big star, symbolizing unanimous assistance and support for the Party. She learned all this in primary school. As she talks, she remembers the first time she observed the national flag-raising ceremony at Tiananmen Square at dawn, in 1988, her first college year. Along with thousands of tourists, she watched the flag be raised by uniformed soldiers. As the national anthem was played, many people cried. Ingrid was one of them. Her tears glistened on her cheeks and glued her eyelashes together, and through her tears she saw the flag billowing like burning fire against the sky. At that moment, she was filled with the pride of being Chinese, of being born and raised in a country with a long history and tradition of civilization.

"Hmm, good design." Angelina nods. "I have no interest in politics or party membership. I love no political parties. It's not like my love for Mexico, rooted in me even before I was born. That's about the land and the culture. Oh, did you read the news today? Something about the Chinese national flag. The newspaper is on the sofa."

Ingrid opens *The New York Times* and finds the article Angelina referred to: a company specializing in Chinese immigrants' affairs hung a Chinese national flag on the top of their building in Queens on the day of their opening. Within minutes a crowd of protesters had gathered, led by a Korean War veteran, demanding that the flag be taken down. The police intervened, and the company was ordered to remove the flag.

"What are these people afraid of? It's just a flag," Angelina comments, chopping a tomato into small cubes. "Isn't America supposed to be a free-speech country? I've never seen another country as fearful of Communism as the U.S. Fifty years ago, they were afraid. Now, they're still afraid. Actually, is China a Communist country nowadays? I'm not sure about that. All the news about the economic boom and the new rich. And big American corporations setting up offices there. Well, if Chinese people shop at Wal-Mart, eat at McDonald's, drink Coca-Cola, use IBM computers, and drive Toyota or Honda cars, they aren't Communists to me."

"I don't think people in China care much about politics these days. The economy is the key now," Ingrid says. That's the impression she has gotten from the media and the tourists from China. But isn't it too arbitrary for her, someone who hasn't lived in China for a decade, to make such a statement?

"I think you're right. Oh, I read the other day that Starbucks opened an outlet inside Beijing's Forbidden City. China has to be very capitalistic to let this happen. It's not even good coffee! Ingrid, if I were you, I'd go back to China and open a teahouse in the Forbidden City. It goes well with the temples."

"We'd have to ask Donald Trump to be our investor."

"You bet he'd jump onto the deal. Who doesn't want to invest in China nowadays?" Angelina laughs, then says, "I saw Kim's lover today."

"Are you serious? I've never seen any guys visiting her." Ingrid is glad that Angelina changed the topic.

"I knocked on her door this morning and was going to tell her about our party. A black woman with a thin neck and long legs opened the door. She was in Kim's pajamas, and she said Kim went to buy breakfast. Pretty cool, huh?"

Angelina often says that you can meet any kind of person and see anything in New York. She once talked about a homicide that took place not far from their apartment. She told the story as if it were from a novel, and with the same easy, calm tone, another time she described to Ingrid how she saw a middle-aged man in a white shirt and pink underwear jump from the roof of a spectacular house: his brains spilled all over the brick pavement and her shoes and dress—he had landed right in front of her.

New York is the city that suits her best, Angelina sometimes remarks, leaving Ingrid to wonder which city tops her own list. Ingrid has lived in New York more than three years: not too long a time, and not too short, in her opinion. She always remembers how lonely and miserable she was in her dimly lit, scarcely furnished studio in Chinatown during her first Christmas in New York. She'd had a fight with her sister, broken up with Steven, given away all her belongings, and left California on a Greyhound bus. She had little money because she had just written a big check to her sister to pay off part of the debt she owed. She'd worked as a waitress and door-to-door salesgirl. Some days, after working twelve to thirteen hours, she arrived home exhausted, and the moment she threw herself onto the bed, her body seemed to be collapsing into a pile of loose bones and flesh, and trivial things like brushing her teeth and taking a shower were difficult tasks. If someone had pushed her off the top of the Empire State Building, she imagined, she would have fallen asleep before hitting the ground: that was how tired she was. She had never before liked sleeping so much, and nothing was better than lying spread-eagled in bed in her tiny room, which she nicknamed Womb, where the windows and mirrors would fog up when she took a shower. Though she didn't do menial jobs for long, she has made herself remember those days not with shame but with pride: all this she sees now as part of what she had to go through to become independent, physically, financially, and psychologically: thinking of the times when she depended on her sister's money fills her with self-loathing.

Their guests—six of them—arrive finally. Except for Molly Holiday, Ingrid's friend, the rest are either Angelina's colleagues from the theater or people she has met at a bar or in a club. They are mostly little-known actors, artists, or aspiring writers. The apartment is now noisy, vibrating with music, chatter, and the clinking of glasses. Angelina carries drinks between the kitchen and the living room, stepping gracefully around the legs of the guests sitting on the floor.

Ingrid sits next to Zonta, listening to her talk about a religious dance she has just designed. Zonta, a petite American Indian, is a frequent visitor. She is a dancer and goes on tour with different troupes. She has played trivial roles in *Cats, Miss Saigon,* and a few other Broadway shows. But what interests her is to dance her own dance and create her own show. She once performed at Ingrid and Angelina's apartment. Her long black hair was her most powerful and expressive weapon, generating endless metaphors: a sword, a horse whip, a tree, a river, lightning.

"I'm going to cut my hair at the end of the performance as a sacrifice to God," she announces to Ingrid and Molly.

"Where are you going to perform?" Molly asks. Molly is a short, energetic, red-haired woman, a New York native. She has been writing poetry and fiction since high school; now forty, she has received more than three hundred rejection letters. She has saved them and filed them in different folders: domestic literary magazines, international literary magazines, agents, small presses, trade publishers. Most of her rejection letters are typed form letters, unsigned, but some are handwritten notes from editors with encouraging comments. These rejections represent only a small proportion of the submissions and proposals she had sent out. She has speculated to Ingrid often about what happened to all the other hundreds of stamped, self-addressed envelopes she included. Did the recipients steam off and reuse the stamps?

"Well, I don't need an audience. I dance for myself," Zonta says matter-of-factly, her dark-skinned face slightly arrogant. When she isn't on tour, she teaches yoga at a YMCA gym. No matter whether she's dancing or practicing yoga, she is completely engaged in the process, and her mind and body seem to be filled with pleasure and purity. Ingrid likes Zonta and likes to see her dance; she is impressed every time by her fluid movements, expressive eyes, and creative choreography. If she were a few inches taller, Ingrid believes, Zonta would have gotten more important roles in the shows she has appeared in. On the other hand, Ingrid is aware how competitive the entertainment business is. Isn't Angelina good? Still, she has to wait patiently for her turn.

"That's nice. I wish I could say the same thing. I'd certainly love to be published. Even just a poem in a small magazine," Molly says, sipping the margarita she is holding. "So I could convince my children that their mother isn't locking herself in her study for nothing." She turns to Ingrid. "Any good news with your writing?"

"My writing? I got another rejection letter, if that interests you. From *Tin House*. For a manuscript I submitted half a year ago. The letter was handwritten by the editor, so I guess it wasn't all that bad. He didn't say much, just that he thought it was a good read but one of the characters was a little weak."

"There's always something wrong for each individual reader, isn't there?" Martin Freeman, a thin-faced, curly-haired black young man, Zonta's boyfriend, chimes in. He's a primary school teacher, writing screenplays in his spare time. "You could rewrite *forever* without pleasing them. Have you thought about applying for a writing program? Getting an MFA in writing might help. At least you can teach after graduation. A good way to make a living. I'm applying for a writing program at George Mason University."

"No, no, Ingrid, you aren't going to do that." Molly shakes her head. "This MFA, that MFA, can you nowadays find a university that doesn't offer some sort of writing degree? I bet most of the students write without any individuality, trying to become the next Faulkner, Hemingway, or Steinbeck. Yes, they write well, their stories are perfectly structured, their language is superb, but so what? There's no life in them! They haven't lived. They have nothing to say. You don't call that art, do you? Let me ask you: Did Victor Hugo have an MFA? Did Dostoevsky have an MFA? How about Mark Twain or Dickens? The best way to learn how to write is through reading and living."

Divorced twice, mother of three children, ages thirteen, seven, and four, Molly has been a sports journalist, bartender, dental assistant, gardener, and truck driver, and has worked in many other professions that don't require a master's degree in anthropology and biology, which she has already earned from Princeton University. Now, she runs a flower shop. For her, these are just day jobs. In her heart she is a writer, and the rest of the time is just waiting to write. Ingrid met her when she had one of her wisdom teeth extracted. While waiting for the dentist, who was late because of traffic, they chatted, about traveling, anthropology, Whitman's *Leaves of Grass*, and Sun Tzu's *Art of War*, and afterward they met for lunch or coffee regularly.

Martin and Molly start to argue about the worthiness of getting an MFA, each with convincing examples. Zonta joins in, supporting Martin, as she always does in an argument. Ingrid sides with Molly, doing it more for fun—having started to write creatively only one year ago, she doesn't have a strong opinion about writing programs. Two other guests join in, and the debate soon turns into a passionate discussion of the creative process of writing, music, dancing, and art making.

Whenever there's a gathering in their apartment, Ingrid can expect a fun conversation. Though she isn't an artist herself and has never thought she'd be one, she is becoming more enthusiastic about art and writing day by day; sometimes she considers writing seriously.

Angelina is in the kitchen, making more salsa. She shouts out her ideas. "Art is about letting go of yourself. Reaching deep into your subconscious to find your voice. The deeper, the better. The louder you holler, the more exciting it is. You cannot be afraid, cannot hold back. Babe, it's just like having wild sex."

"Well said." Zonta stands and belly-dances, her arms swimming in the air like snakes. She holds out her hands, so Ingrid gets up and dances with her. Someone whistles, another person applauds.

Martin and Molly are still debating heatedly. Irritated by a comment Molly just made, Martin exclaims, "Molly, those artists you mentioned are geniuses! They aren't like us. They were born with exceptional talents!"

"Geniuses start from humble beginnings," says the man leaning against a sofa leg. It's Diego Lopez, who's been drinking silently. He always looks sad and vulnerable, especially when he's a little drunk. Ever since he made the announcement two years ago, that he was writing a historical novel about the Alamo, he hasn't been talkative. None of his friends knows about the book's progress. If they ask him, all he offers is that he's "working on it." He doesn't have a job and depends on his parents' and friends' financial support. Last winter his landlord evicted him for being delinquent with his rent, and he has since been living in the kitchen of a friend's restaurant.

"Let's toast our Diego, the upcoming genius." Angelina, walking out from the kitchen, holds up her wineglass.

Everyone clinks glasses and says "Cheers!"

After a few sips of her margarita, Angelina begins to sing in Spanish, which she always does at parties. When she sings, her voice becomes deep, a little raspy, perfect for sad songs. Diego and two other Spanish speakers soon join Angelina, their eyes closed and heads shaking gently. Ingrid knows some Spanish and understands that they are singing about a heartbroken girl wishing the man who has abandoned her a happy marriage with his new lover. She'll survive, the girl says in the song, for she has the beautiful mountains and forests and her dear family to be with her. Ingrid loves Mexican songs, is often moved by the passion in them, whether they are sad or cheerful. She likes the sad songs better, and whenever she hears them, she feels that Mexico has gone through many tragedies and much suffering and the songs themselves are a tribute to the country's history. She cannot say why, but these songs remind her of China, of the passing of time.

Angelina asks Ingrid to sing a Chinese song. Ingrid is shy when it comes to singing: she doesn't think she has a good voice, but today, influenced by the margaritas, she sings "In That Place Far Away," a folk song everyone knows in China. She starts an octave too high but manages to go through the high-pitched sections by humming. She hasn't sung this song for a long time, and it surprises her that she remembers most of the lyrics. Angelina and her friends hum along. "So beautiful!" they say, though they don't understand a word.

Ingrid has to fly to Boston to interpret at a conference early the next morning, so after singing, she excuses herself and retreats to her room. She takes a bath, then sits at her desk to sort her mail.

In addition to the credit-card bills and junk mail, there are two letters.

She picks up the thinner one. The handwriting on the envelope is her own—it is the self-addressed, stamped envelope she put into a manila envelope with a short story and sent to a literary magazine several months ago. She opens the letter. A tiny piece of yellow paper drops to the desk. A typed rejection letter from "The Editors" thanking her for her submission but regretting not being able to use it because it "does not meet our present editorial needs."

It must be the eighth or ninth rejection letter she has received since she began to write, encouraged by Molly. At first, she wrote merely to prove to Molly that writing fiction wasn't as difficult as Molly had claimed; she wasn't serious—she was considering getting a law degree at that time. But Ingrid soon discovered that she liked writing fiction, which allowed her to retreat to her mind after a busy day. To her, the process is like solving a puzzle with endless layers, twists, and turns. She remembers the story she sent to this magazine: a country-born girl goes to the city to work in a factory, but unable to resist materialistic temptations, she ends up becoming a prostitute. It was Ingrid's first attempt to write about China and Chinese people, based on an interview she conducted during a brief internship when she was studying in Beijing.

Before, she had tried to write about Americans' lives, about the middle-class families or blue-collar workers who populate John Cheever's or Raymond Carver's stories. She thought she could write about them well because she had lived in the United States for a number of years and seen people from different walks of life. But somehow she couldn't seem to grasp the face and voice of that Mr. Smith or Ms. White; on the other hand, Old Aunt Zhang or Grandpa Wang loomed in as if from nowhere, demanding to be written about. But Ingrid didn't think she knew those Chinese people well enough, either, to write good stories about them.

She sometimes wonders whether, if she had lived in the United States since she was little instead of coming here as an adult, she would still have so much attachment to China. It seems to her writers always identify more closely with the cultures where they were born and raised. Jewish writers write the best about Jews, and Asian-American writers tend to focus on Asian Americans' lives, while black writers such as Toni Morrison and James Baldwin are masters in depicting the black experience. A famous writer whose name she has forgotten once said that literature is the extension of a keen nostalgia about one's ancestors. Maybe it is true.

Or is her problem the language? Which language to choose, Chinese or English? She remembers a story from *Autumn Flows*, written by Zhuangzi, the most renowned Chinese Taoist philosopher. In the story, a person from the Yan Country admires how the people in the Zhao Country walk, so he travels there to imitate their walking. By the time he needs to return to his own country, he has forgotten how to walk like a Yan person; meanwhile, he cannot walk like a Zhao person, either. So he ends up crawling back to Yan. In the back of her mind, Ingrid fears she no longer has a first language: she has lost intimacy with Chinese, yet she's still learning English despite the fact that she speaks with only a slight accent and has begun to build her name in the business translation world. When she writes in English, especially creatively, she sees her limits; the words seem to be floating on the surface of the water, instead of being part of the water.

She glances at the folder on her desk where she has collected her rejection slips, which amount to nothing compared with what Molly has received. Ingrid resolves to stop writing for a while, until she knows what she wants to write about.

The second letter is from her mother, enclosing a wedding photo of herself and Ingrid's father. Since Ingrid began to write, she has become interested in old photos and visits antiques stores to look for them. To her, each photo contains a story about the past.

The wedding photo, with serrated edges, is black and white. Her father is wearing a Mao-style jacket, the neck button tightly fastened, and looks serious, his lips locked tight. Her mother is not smiling, either, but she seems relaxed, her head leaning toward her husband's shoulder. Ingrid remembers that her mother once told her that her life was easier after she met her father.

Ingrid always feels that she owes her father. Whenever she thinks of him, she thinks of 1989.

Then a sophomore at People's University in Beijing, like many other college students, she was involved in the demonstrations in Tiananmen Square led by students, intellectuals, and labor activists.

They marched, they sat in, they undertook hunger strikes, condemning corruption and demanding a democratic government.

The night of June 3, Ingrid left her tent in the square with her boyfriend to fetch pamphlets from her dorm. When she arrived, she saw her father squatting outside her room. He was scrawny, his eyes red, as if infected, his lips dry and flaky. At the sight of her, he leapt up, his legs quivering. He gripped her arm and said that he had been looking for her all around Tiananmen Square. "Go home with me," he demanded. "No," she replied, shaking off his grip, and after getting the pamphlets, she told him to go home right away.

Her father knelt, holding her right leg with both hands, saying she and her friends were putting themselves on the road to death. "Do you have guns? Do you have tanks? Do you have an army?" he asked. "You're just a bunch of unarmed students. You think you can stop the guns with your chests? You're too young, too naïve. It's not worthwhile to kill yourself this way. Listen to me this time. Just go home with me." He leaned his head against her leg, sobbing. It was the first time that Ingrid had seen her father cry.

Other students were in the hallway. Some threw paper balls at her father, saying that China was so conservative and backward because there were so many cowards like him. She felt ashamed of her father's presence. She tried to loosen his grasp on her leg, but though he looked weak and sick, his grip was strong. In her fury and frustration, she kicked him and slapped his back, yelling, "Leave me alone!" He wouldn't budge, his fingers seemingly sinking into her flesh. Eventually, helped by her boyfriend and a few other students, she broke free, and they locked her father in her dorm room. As she darted down the stairs with her boyfriend, she heard a heavy pounding on the door, followed by a long howl.

She would never forget that howl. It sounded like a wolf mourning its dead cub.

It was after midnight, but the streets were seething with people as if it were a carnival—it had been like this since April. There were uniformed, fully armed soldiers on some roads, stopping people from passing through. They took a taxi, a free ride when the driver learned they were students. They got out when the taxi was stopped by armed soldiers. They walked toward Tiananmen Square. Then they heard gunshots, not one or two but many, tearing the night as if right in their ears. They soon saw people falling to the ground covered in blood. For a few seconds, Ingrid thought that she had imagined all this, or that they had accidentally stepped onto a movie set and she was just seeing special effects. But her instinct told her to run, as fast and as far as she could: in fact, her boyfriend was already running, dragging her behind him. People kept falling around them, and then her boyfriend fell, blood spurting from his head, spilling onto the roadside flower bed. She pulled him, by the arm, hearing a man alongside shouting at her. "He's dead! Run for your own life!" She didn't listen and kept pulling the body. It was not until she collapsed against a tree that she realized the gunshots had stopped.

In the following days, she sometimes dreamed of herself running from guns she couldn't see. When she woke up, suddenly, and sat up in bed, panting and weeping, she touched her chest to see if there was blood there. And she thought of her boyfriend, whose death she had witnessed near Tiananmen Square; and of her father, howling his rage and fear behind that locked door.

Her father had come to her dorm to save her life, yet she hated him. Though what happened on the early morning of June 4, 1989, had proved him right, she still hated him for a long time afterward, because he had shown himself to be a coward in front of her friends and didn't manage to stop her and her boyfriend after all. For a long time, her temper was volatile and her grief made her irrational and unreasonable.

This was not the first time that she had hated her father. Her first year in high school, Ingrid fell in love with a boy in her class. Though they only wrote love letters to each other and held hands when no one was around, when her father found out, he went to the boy's parents, asking them to promise that their son would never speak with his daughter again. Not long after, the boy moved to a different city. Then, during her last year in high school, her father insisted that she study science, as her sister had. If she hadn't run away for a few days, staying with friends and making no contact with the family, he wouldn't have given in.

One year after the Tiananmen protest—referred to by the authorities as the Political Turmoil Between Spring and Summer of 1989—was put down, her sister helped her move to the United States. Because the U.S. embassy officials sympathized with students, it was easy to get a visa. Ingrid didn't know at the time that she would never see her father again.

The singing in the living room has faded into intermittent humming—Angelina and her guests must be a little drunk. Ingrid imagines them lying on the carpet or leaning against the sofa, sleepy and relaxed, half-empty glasses in their hands. It's a little chilly now, so they probably have covered themselves with blankets, bath towels, the tablecloth, or one of Angelina's coats. Sometimes, at earlier parties, they would fall asleep on the floor, and after they woke, with hangovers, they would drink more, till there would not be a drop of alcohol left in the apartment. It will be the same this time, Ingrid is sure.

She hears Angelina's tremulous laugh. Whenever she and Diego are kissing, Angelina laughs like this. They kiss like brother and sister, rather than lovers, kisses more for consolation than for passion.

The night has turned the window into a mirror, and Ingrid gazes at her reflection. She thinks of Bing'er and recalls her fascination with Chinese characters. She also thinks of some places in Chinese books she used to like: Lao She's old Beijing, Zhang Ailing's war-stricken Shanghai, and Xiao Hong's snow-clad northeastern provinces. She feels something awakening inside her.

SEVEN

November

AN AIRPORT IS A city's heart. Whenever Mary is in an airport, she can feel its restless pulse. When she was in her twenties, she loved traveling, always asking for a window seat so she could look out through the double glass at the thick clouds and passing oceans, the mountains and fields, feeling the slight shaking of the wings. Now, though the airport's energy still excites her, she would rather stay home, tidying the house or tending the garden.

United Airlines Flight 858 will be one hour late—the matter-of-fact female voice is announcing both in Mandarin and in English. Mary sits in the waiting area reading the Chinese *Sing Tao Daily* that she has brought from home. Its front page offers detailed bi-ographies of George W. Bush's newly appointed cabinet members. Mary scans their names and quickly flips to the next page, then the next, until she reaches the Home and Garden section. Realizing that her eyes are merely browsing without comprehending the content, she puts the newspaper down to look at the screen suspended from the ceiling in front of her. Now and then people pushing carts loaded with luggage show up, but of course, they are from other flights.

It's raining outside, the overcast sky dark gray. The weather worries Mary, and she prays silently for her mother's safe arrival. Bob had wanted to take a few hours off from work to be at the airport with her, but at the last minute, he had to meet a client. Newly promoted to senior manager, overseeing an eight-person team, he is on call twenty-four/seven.

Lately, Bob has become addicted to computer games. To wind down from work, he claims. Some days, once Alex has gone to bed, Bob sits at his desk playing racing or war games. Mary doesn't mind the racing games much, but she hates the war games, where Bob plays the hero, using all kinds of weapons to kill his enemies. "I bet the two kids who did the Columbine High School shooting grew up playing these kinds of games a lot," Mary once said. "But it's not real." Bob shrugged, smiling. But he did promise that he wouldn't allow Alex to play his games. Eventually Mary gave up, after Yaya and Julia had told her that their husbands also liked playing computer games. "It's a man's thing. It's like shopping to women, I guess," Yaya said.

And Bob now watches more sports on TV. He's always been a sports fan, particularly baseball, football, and hockey. When he started to see Mary, he tried to cultivate her interest in baseball. He explained the rules to her patiently: how to pitch, how to hit, each player's position, scoring . . . He took her to Candlestick Park to see the Giants play the Dodgers, always in the best seats. All his effort, however, did not convert Mary to a baseball fan; quite the opposite, she concluded that baseball games were boring and the players weren't even fit. Bob's tutoring in football didn't go well, either. Mary thought the game cruel, with players knocking one another down constantly. But she hid her boredom and sour views of these sports, continuing to accompany Bob to stadiums and arenas, where she was more entertained by the crazy costumes and makeup and cheering in the bleachers than by the game itself. Bob did not give up hope until Mary fell asleep during a game between the Yankees and the Red Sox in New York, where they had flown specifically to watch it.

Maybe Yaya was right, playing computer games and watching sports are what men do in their spare time; it's not like they use these things to avoid their wives. As long as Bob prays before each meal and they still sleep on the same bed, she shouldn't worry too much, Mary thinks with little comfort.

The plane arrives finally. Not knowing how long customs will take, Mary continues looking at the screen, rising periodically to stretch. It is not until an hour and a half later that the first passenger from Flight 858 comes out the exit, welcomed by a big family. She finally sees her mother on the screen, dragging behind her two suitcases, one of which—apparently with a broken wheel—zigzags dangerously. Mary recognizes the broken suitcase as the one her father bought her for her first year of college in Beijing, remembering that she hated it because it was too brightly colored and had no style. Dangling on her mother's right shoulder is the black purse Mary gave her at least six or seven years ago, during one of her visits to China. To the purse strap is tied a stuffed plastic bag, which bumps into her mother's waist with each step she takes. The bag must be heavy, for her mother walks with her right shoulder much lower than her left. Her jacket is two sizes too big, making her appear fatter and shorter than she is. Mary finds herself slightly irritated by her mother's shabby looks—didn't she tell her to buy good-quality suitcases and clothes?—but immediately she feels guilty for thinking ill of her own mother, who has come thousands of miles to see her.

Mary darts to the banister by the exit.

Her mother appears at the exit, but instead of continuing to walk, she drops one suitcase on the floor and begins to massage her upper chest over the area of her heart with her free hand, as if she were feeling pain there. Then she picks up the suitcase and looks around eagerly.

Mary raises her hand and waves, but after seeing her mother still looking vacantly into the waiting crowd, seemingly overwhelmed by the noise and chaos, she runs over.

"Ma!" she shouts, startling her mother.

"Guo-Mei, you're here!" Her mother calls out Mary's Chinese name, her face suddenly radiant. "Why didn't I see you? I was just thinking that you got stuck in traffic. You must have waited a long time."

Compared with the last time Mary saw her, her mother has more wrinkles on her forehead and more white hair. The veins on the backs of her hands show prominently.

Without thinking, Mary gives her mother a bear hug, as many people around them are doing with family, relatives, or friends who have just arrived. Her mother, taken aback by this American greeting, remains motionless in her embrace, arms stiff at her sides. After a brief moment, she hesitantly places her hands on Mary's shoulders. Mary realizes that she is being very Western with her hug; she knows that Chinese, even within a family, usually shake hands or pat each other's shoulders in greeting. In fact, in all her previous visits to China, she has never hugged her mother, not even when saying good-bye—it is just not the custom there. But somehow, being in the United States has made her forget that custom, at least momentarily. She loosens her arms awkwardly, her face flushed with embarrassment, and quickly grasps the handles of her mother's luggage.

On the way to the parking lot, her mother keeps asking questions: How's Bob? How's Dongdong? How's Mary's work? How's Guo-Ying? A few times she tries to take the broken suitcase from

Mary, saying that she knows the way to drag it easily. Mary insists that she can handle it. When they get to the car, Mary opens the door, helps her mother in, and fastens the seat belt for her. Her mother peruses the car as though she has never ridden in one before. "Is this your car? So big! The seat is so soft."

After they reach the 101 freeway, heading south, her mother looks out the window attentively, saying repeatedly, "I see, America is like this," while in fact, apart from the sound-reflecting walls on both sides of the freeway, advertising billboards, fast-food chains' garish signs, and some commercial or residential buildings, she can see little. But Mary refrains from commenting on her mother's remarks—fourteen years ago, when she sat in an airport shuttle on her way to Berkeley, she made the same remarks.

Forty minutes later, they arrive home. As Mary unloads the luggage from the trunk, her mother stands in the driveway, surveying the front yard and the house. "You don't see this kind of mansion in Nanyi," she says, shaking her head in apparent disbelief. "How do you keep the grass so green?" Following Mary, her mother steps into the house and immediately takes off her shoes. Mary shows her Bob's study, which will be her bedroom during her stay, and suggests she wash herself in the hallway bathroom, then take a nap. Her mother says that she isn't tired at all, and it is not until she takes a look at the whole house and the backyard that she sits down to drink the water Mary has poured for her. Then she tells Mary she is hungry and wants porridge.

"You and Bob must have to work very hard to pay for this house," her mother says, with both pride and worry in her eyes, while eating the fish fillet porridge Mary just made. "I cannot help you at all. Not just that, but now, I'm a burden to you."

Mary is touched, but other than assuring her mother that she isn't a burden, she doesn't know what to say.

"When will Dongdong be back?" her mother asks eagerly. She asked the same question twice at the airport and later on the drive home, and Mary told her that she needed to go into the office for a while in the afternoon to get some work done, then she'd pick him up at his kindergarten on her way back. But rather than pointing this out, Mary repeats her answer.

Despite her denial, her mother is indeed exhausted from the twelve-hour flight, and after washing herself in the bathroom and changing into the flannel pajamas Mary has prepared for her, she lies down on the futon and soon falls asleep, snoring slightly. Mary closes the door for her mother and stands against the doorframe briefly, knowing that from now on her life won't be the same.

At four, Mary is home with Alex. Before they enter, she reminds Alex how to say Granny in Mandarin. "*Wai po*, remember? W-A-I-P-O. The fourth and then second tone." Alex frowns. "*Wai po, wai po, wai po.* Is it enough now?" At this moment, the door opens, and her mother stands there with a broom. "I was sweeping the backyard. There were some fallen leaves," her mother says to Mary, though her eyes fix on her grandson. She has changed to a blue cardigan with shiny gold buttons and a pair of fat-legged black pants with creases down the front, and her hair has been combed carefully, with pins on both sides above the ears.

"Call *wai po*," Mary urges Alex, speaking Mandarin.

Alex steps back and hides behind Mary.

"Dongdong." Her mother squats. "It's *wai po*. You're so tall. I dreamed of you often in China."

"Call *wai po*!" Mary orders.

Silence, then "No. I don't understand her."

Mary turns to grab Alex's arm, speaking English. "Be polite!"

"*Wai po!*" Alex yells at the top of his lungs, then runs into the house through the gap between his grandma and the doorframe, into his room, and slams the door shut.

Her mother stands slowly, managing a smile. "Dongdong is taller than I thought. I hope the clothes I bought for him fit."

"They'll fit, I'm sure." Mary wants to console her mother. "You know, Dongdong . . ."

"He's so tall already," her mother murmurs. "Let me finish sweeping the yard."

Mary sees Bob's white Volvo turning in to the street: Bob had called her earlier to make sure he wouldn't get home before she did. "Ma, Bob is here."

Her mother looks over her shoulder. Their eyes meet: Mary sees doubt and anxiety in her mother's face. Her mother drops the broom and walks to the door, stretching her cardigan left and right. "It's not too big, is it?" she asks.

Mary says it looks good on her, then adds, "Ma, no worries. I'll be the translator between you and Bob." While she's saying this, it occurs to her that she's playing the role of a diplomat.

To her relief and gratitude, Bob behaves naturally and warmly. *"Ning hao. Huan ying. Hen gao xing jian dao ning,"* he says and holds out his hand to his mother-in-law. Then he switches to English, inquiring about her trip and her health. Mary translates for both sides, adding her own words here and there to spice up the conversation. Her mother keeps smiling as if impressed by her son-in-law's friendliness and liking him. Bob smiles constantly too, as if genuinely welcoming his mother-in-law to live with them for six months. As they're chatting in the family room, Alex slips out of his room and sits next to Bob, staring at his grandma.

That night, they have dinner at a Shanghainese restaurant in Mountain View. At the rectangular table, Bob and Alex sit on one side, Mary and her mother on the other side. To avoid silence and keep everyone engaged, Mary jumps from subject to subject, switching between Mandarin and English, speaking a lot, laughing a lot, not realizing until the end of the dinner that she has done most of the talking. When they get home, Mary goes straight to the master bathroom and only now runs her hands across her face and releases a long sigh.

*   *   *

The next day, Mary takes the day off from work to show her mother around. They stroll in Mary's neighborhood. She points out the local streets, various architectural styles—ranch, Eichler, Victorian—different trees and flowers. Then they walk to El Camino Real, a thoroughfare thronged with shops and restaurants. When they pass Safeway, her mother says that she wants to go inside to see how Americans shop, a request that doesn't surprise Mary because a few of her friends visiting from China had asked the same thing. If Mary had never lived in China, she would have laughed at this request. Don't people from everywhere shop for groceries the same way? But she knows exactly what it's like to be Chinese and visiting the United States for the first time, especially for a Chinese person like her mother, who has lived in a small inland city since birth and never traveled.

Mary clearly remembers the first time she entered a grocery store in the United States, the day after she arrived in Berkeley in 1986. For three hours, she indulged herself in the smells and colors of merchandise that was completely new to her, studying the brands and ingredients and nutrition lists. Fruit jam, cereal, pasta, wine, yogurt, butter . . . especially cheese, piles of various shapes and textures and smells, often with odd names, a lot of French or Italian that she couldn't even pronounce. Why on earth do people need all these different cheeses? she wondered. She wrote down the words she wasn't familiar with, but soon she gave up and pushed a cart around like everyone else. Walking from one aisle to another, she couldn't help but recall the farmers' market in her hometown, where rotten vegetables and animal intestines littered the ground, the farmers with callused hands and bitter faces stood in front of their stalls waiting for customers.

She thought of her mother too. If her mother was here, would she pick a bundle of vegetables and swing it left and right to dispose of the water inside? Would she fumble in a pile of neatly arranged Fuji or Gala apples to look for the most perfect ones? Or maybe she wouldn't dare touch the produce and would end up buying nothing. All of the produce here—after converting its price into Chinese currency at the one-to-eight exchange rate between the dollar and the yuan—was so expensive that her mother's monthly salary could purchase only ten pounds of broccoli. Even Mary herself, with a full scholarship from Berkeley, held her breath at the sight of the price tags, which she swiftly converted into Chinese currency in her head, a habit that she retained for years.

However, she had to buy something: since she couldn't afford to eat out, she had to cook. At last she found what she could afford: a big bag of potatoes at half of its original price and a package of beef sealed with clear plastic wrap, on sale because it was close to its expiration date. They were good bargains; she rarely had a chance to eat beef in China because it was so expensive there. Also, beef stew with potatoes was considered a delicacy for Chinese. When she was little, people always said that the best thing in a utopian communist society was that you could eat beef stew with potatoes at every meal. Then she had often dreamed of this dish, imagining its taste and smell. Now, to her amusement, she would eat it for days, if not weeks.

The memory provokes a comfortable sigh from Mary: many years have passed, and how different she is today.

Her mother stops here and there to peruse certain products, like Italian prosciutto or premade pizza dough, with curiosity and caution, carefully picking something up and putting it back with both hands as if it were fragile; afterward her mother shakes her head, seemingly having decided that it wasn't something she could cook. Mary and her mother keep walking. A few times, Mary unwittingly looks to see if anyone is watching them: they've been walking around the store for half an hour with an empty cart.

It is not until her mother stands in front of big bags of potatoes that her eyes shine with excitement. She reaches out and lifts a bag. "Is this one on sale? Two dollars for such a big bag! In RMB . . ." She calculates with her fingers. "It's only eighteen yuan, not bad for so many potatoes. What do you think?"

"Ma," Mary whispers, "just get whatever you want. It's not much money for me. This place is just like a farmers' market in China."

"It's not easy to live abroad, and if you can save, why not? I like eating potatoes anyway." Before Mary can stop her, her mother quickly tears open a bag and takes out a potato, feeling it like an expert. "Look! It's heavy and its skin is smooth. There are no sprouts, either. A very good one."

"Ma, you're not supposed to open the bag." Mary looks around again. "Put the potato back. Let's just take this bag."

Fifteen minutes later, they walk out the door with the bag of potatoes and a package of beef.

Her mother is delighted. "I haven't cooked beef stew with potatoes for years. You see, now that you and your sister are both living abroad, I just need to cook for myself, and there's no point spending time fixing a fancy dish like this." There is an awkward lull, then she adds, "You know, it was your father's favorite dish."

It is windy outside, the ground wet from yesterday's rain. As they walk home, Mary carries the bag of potatoes, her mother next to her holding the package of beef—she has insisted on helping.

Mary hasn't walked to buy groceries for a long time: you drive wherever you go, that's life in the suburbs; she's used to it. Especially in this kind of windy weather, Mary thinks, only people without a car would walk more than half an hour to bring home groceries, as she had done when she was a student at Berkeley, before she had a bike. By the time she arrived home, her hands were burning from the plastic bags' handles.

Ahead of them two Asian women in colorful sweaters—Vietnamese or Thai, Mary surmises—are trudging along, arms locked tightly, grocery bags in their other hands. The younger woman is pregnant, presumably the daughter of the older woman. Three boys are with them, the oldest about ten, and they keep poking one another in the armpits or ribs and giggle all the way. Twice the younger woman stops, dropping the bags in her hand, and fixes the older woman's silk shawl, which has been ruffled by the wind. While she does it, she speaks gently into her mother's ear.

Mary finds herself watching these two strange women with admiration, even jealousy. Their intimacy looks so natural that she imagines the daughter must have been doted on by her mother when she was growing up. Walking next to her own mother, Mary seems to have returned to China, to the time when they went grocery shopping together, but instead of the resentment and disdain she felt toward her mother back then, she now has only a sense of responsibility and pity.

Why can't she be as close to her mother as that pregnant woman is to hers? Why can't she hold her mother's arm as she does? Mary wonders. Was it merely to satisfy her conscience that she had decided to bring her mother to the United States to live with her? Is she doing all this to show her church friends that she is a good Christian who takes care of her elderly mother? Or is it her cultural duty, her heritage?

She wishes there were such a thing as a memory eraser that could help her forget the unpleasant past, make her love her mother sincerely, but it is not as simple as that. She has too many memories that keep her from giving her arm to her mother to hold on this windy day. She remembers an American bishop in the nineteenth century said: "Duty makes us do things well, but love makes us do them beautifully." So all she has done so far—visiting her mother once a year, sending her money regularly, inviting her to the United States to live with her—is just fulfilling her duty as a daughter, with little love involved.

But if she didn't love her mother before, how can she love her now? Mary now defends herself. You don't expect a plant will still grow when its leaves and roots have already died from lack of water and sunlight.

Mary longs to become a good Christian, to be loyal to God, to follow the gospel, to enjoy the peace her belief can bring her. But as time passes, she senses increasingly her failure as a wife, a daughter, and a sister. Her lack of intimacy with Bob, with her mother, and with Ingrid bothers her, yet she cannot imagine what to do to change the situation. No matter how hard she tries, the result seems miles away from her hopes and expectations.

She recalls her baptism ceremony in Half Moon Bay. She had expressed to her pastor her desire to be baptized in the ocean. Having grown up in an inland province and not seeing the ocean until she was in the States, she had always had a fascination with the ocean, its mystery, hugeness, and depth. That day, she wore a white blouse and an ankle-length white skirt; besides the pastor, Bob and a few other church brothers and sisters were her witnesses. Standing in the shallows, facing the sweep of blueness and the gliding seagulls, she felt elation and peace. She'd have a new life, she said to herself as the pastor plunged her head into the cold and salty water. That day and many days after she lived in a state of idyllic happiness, until family and work and other mundane routines consumed her.

In one of her confessions to Pastor Zhang, she mentioned her resentment toward her parents, and he told her that she should let God lead the way, then everything would be like a stream running down into a river and the river into the ocean. He also said that forgiveness was the biggest virtue one could possess. It was after one such confession that she had decided to apply for her mother's permanent residence in the United States, to take good care of her in her old age.

In the days following her decision, Mary was filled with the hope of reconciling with her mother. She kept telling herself that her resentment toward her mother would vanish once they lived together. Now, walking beside her mother without feeling intimacy toward her, Mary realizes that if her motive for inviting her mother to live with her was selfish to begin with, she won't be able to reach the harmony she desires in their relationship.

Her mother rubs her nose, reddened by the wind, and coughs slightly. Mary turns to look at her, noticing that her mother is also watching the mother and daughter ahead of them, so attentively that she has slowed her pace.

Halfway home, her mother trips over a fallen tree branch. Instinctively, Mary reaches to grab her arm. After her mother regains her balance, Mary lets go of her hand, but her mother thrusts her arm underneath Mary's and holds it. Mary allows her, feeling the warmth of her mother's arm inside hers. She also tightens her grip, though she feels awkward walking with her mother like this. Her mother begins to stride like a young person, as if her daughter's arm has given her extra strength.

They walk home with their arms linked.

Alex is playing with a Lego fire truck in the hallway outside the guest room. He pushes the truck forward on the hardwood floor, mimicking its piercing siren.

"Why don't you go to your room to play for a little while? You don't want to wake up *wai po*, do you?" Mary says to him and gathers the truck and its scattered pieces into a box.

"My room has a carpet and the truck doesn't run on it." Alex purses his lips, following his mother to his room. "Why did *wai po* go to bed so early? It's not even eight. I was waiting for her to continue the story of San Mao's Adventure! Yesterday she stopped at the place when San Mao became homeless and had to sell newspapers on the street to make a living."

"*Wai po* still has jet lag. She needs more rest."

"Mom, maybe *wai po* doesn't like Chinese food. Let's order pizza tomorrow. I bet she'd like the kind of pizza with pineapples and chicken on top. She said she has bad teeth and likes soft food. She can eat the pineapples and chicken and give the dough to Dad. Dad likes pizza dough. He always eats mine. I think *wai po* will like Coke too. It goes well with pizza."

"Look who's talking, my pizza lover! Just tell me if you want to eat pizza and drink Coke yourself."

Alex sticks out his tongue and makes a face at his mother.

It surprises Mary to see how fast Alex has made friends with his grandmother. The first three days Alex refused to call her *"wai po"* other than the single time he was forced, and he ran to hide in his room when his grandma tried to talk with him. On the fourth day, he began to tell her in Mandarin what he had learned in school that day. On the fifth day he played with her in the garden, asking her to push the swing for him. He even taught her some English words.

"*Lu* in English is *green*. You repeat after me, *g-reen* . . . , " Mary heard her son say to his grandma. His grandma pronounced *green* cautiously, sounding like a pigeon cooing, which made Alex laugh wildly. He then asked his grandmother to say *yellow* and *purple* after him. She tried. He laughed again.

Whatever Alex asked his grandma to do, she obeyed eagerly. Mary has never seen her mother so happy, almost like a child. To please her grandson, she had tried all kinds of tricks, like using her handkerchief to make a rat or a rabbit, mimicking the sounds animals make, or paper cutting, which she had learned from her seniors' college back home after she retired. If she didn't have a weak neck and back, she would have let Alex ride her like a horse. When she started to tell Alex the story of San Mao's Adventure, Mary thought Alex wouldn't be interested. How could a child born in the United States relate to a homeless child's journey in old Shanghai in the thirties? But Alex got hooked completely and nagged his grandma every evening for more. When he heard that San Mao was beaten and had no place to sleep in the winter, tears streamed down his cheeks.

Grandma and grandson had developed a creative way to communicate. If Alex didn't know how to say something in Mandarin, he wrote down the English words, then looked them up in an English-Chinese dictionary and showed the Chinese translation to his grandma. His grandma did the same thing, using a Chinese-English dictionary. If Alex was too impatient to use the dictionary, he gestured and drew to express himself, which his grandma also did. Because he had to speak the language with his grandmother, Alex's Mandarin had improved quickly. He sometimes even spoke it with Mary, which he had seldom done before. As for his grandma, she had managed to remember a few English words, such as *this, that, good,* and *bad,* words she sometimes used.

Mary is both happy and sad seeing Alex play with his grandma. Before her mother arrived, she worried that her son would treat her like a stranger, ignoring her. Now her worry has proved groundless. Maybe she has been too strict with Alex, rarely playing with him so intimately, while Bob has been busy at work all these months, having little time for Alex. Work has taken a toll on Bob, Mary has to admit. He has become more preoccupied and easily irritated. Once, working at home under a deadline, he shouted when Alex kept pestering him to put together a jigsaw puzzle. He regretted it profoundly afterward, swearing to Mary that he would spend more time with their son, but it was a promise that he hasn't been able to keep because of all the deadlines at work, with the IPO date approaching.

Now Alex has his grandma, who doesn't force him to play the piano and doesn't tell him that she is too busy to play with him.

As far as Mary can remember, her mother never played with her when she was a child, and she always looked tired and worried. When Mary was Alex's age, she played alone with sand and mud every day in the countryside, far from her parents.

Alex's room is crowded with toys, some from his grandma, others from Bob, who has bought a lot for him in the past few months, as if to make up for the time that he couldn't be with him. "When will

Dad be home?" Alex asks, hugging a panda his grandma gave him to his cheek. He puts the panda beside his pillow every night when he goes to bed.

"Dad will be back soon. Now it's time to brush your teeth and change into your pajamas." Mary sits on the floor to sort out his toys. "I'll read you a story when you're done."

Alex falls asleep before Mary finishes the story.

EIGHT

December

RAIN STARTS IN SAN Francisco. The weather forecast has predicted a steep temperature drop in the next few days because of a cold front from the Gulf of Alaska. Last night there was even a thunderstorm, a rare phenomenon in this part of California.

Before Ingrid left New York, she had contacted a few motels and apartments offering short-term housing in San Francisco. After comparing prices and locations, she had picked a bed-and-breakfast on Russian Hill. The price is higher than she'd like to pay even after a discount she was able to negotiate, but she has always wanted to live in this neighborhood, home to a lot of Victorian mansions, and with a spectacular view of North Beach, Telegraph Hill, Alcatraz, and the Bay Bridge. It's fun to watch cars lining up every day, waiting to drive down the block on Lombard Street, famous for its extreme corners, between Hyde and Leavenworth, which has earned it the name "the crookedest street in the world." She has planned to stay here for only one week—it'll be her well-deserved vacation—then she'll move to a cheaper place and stay there until her mother goes back to China. As for her shared apartment with Angelina in New York, her landlord has allowed her to sublease it to an art student from Italy during her absence.

Standing on the top of Coit Tower, Ingrid can see colorful Victorian row houses in many neighborhoods and steep streets meandering between skyscrapers and low-level apartment buildings, as Telegraph Hill blends with the downtown area. Somehow she always imagined that San Francisco was bigger and more populated, but in fact, it's a city with fewer than eight hundred thousand residents, one fifth the population of her home town in China.

Having returned to the Bay Area from New York, Ingrid realizes how much she loves San Francisco. It's energetic and dynamic, not quite as busy as New York but with its own special character. Wherever she looks there are always more vistas, more greenery, more flowers, and more people walking at an unhurried pace. Every morning, even when it rains, she jogs in Golden Gate Park or visits a museum, the San Francisco Museum of Modern Art, the De Young Museum, the Palace of the Legion of Honor, with Rodin's *Thinker* in the courtyard, or one of the many galleries on the streets around Union Square. She once biked along the Great Highway, watching surfers ride the Pacific waves, seeing the hang gliders floating on the air currents on the escarpments to the south.

Of course, she could have lived with Mary—her sister asked her in their last phone conversation. It would have helped her save money. But Ingrid likes her freedom: she can eat or sleep whenever she wants and lie on the sofa reading a book over tea or coffee for hours without being disturbed. More important, she likes to live in the city, close to activities and attractions—what could she do in the suburbs anyway?

She needs a few days to herself before she sees Mary. Just imagine how many questions her older sister will have for her! It will be like an interrogation.

On a Sunday afternoon, Ingrid saunters in the Mission District. She has been invited to an ex-classmate's housewarming party at six p.m. Violet Wilson lives on Valencia Street, not far from where Ingrid is. So Ingrid decides to walk there. She hasn't seen any of her classmates from San Jose State University for more than three years, and it will be nice to catch up with them, especially Violet, who had let Ingrid copy her homework and driven her around when Ingrid didn't have a car. In Ingrid's memory, Violet was loud, talkative, rowdy, a partygoer, a cheerleader, but she was also warm and helpful. Violet had taught Ingrid how to put on makeup, how to smoke, how to dance. It was also Violet who took her to underground bars in San Francisco and Oakland, advised her on sex, and told her about the *Playboys* in the school library.

Two days ago, Ingrid went with an agent to look at a studio apartment on Eighteenth Street in this neighborhood. It was on the second floor, a little over four hundred square feet, with a cherrywood floor and cabinets. It looked dark even with the lights on. As Ingrid walked into the bathroom, she spotted mildew and soap scum around the tub. The whole place had been cleaned only casually.

"It's near the Muni bus lines, the BART station, and the 101 freeway," said the agent matter-of-factly. He was a young man with a crew cut and a feminine voice, and played with the skeleton-patterned silver ring on his right index finger. "In this city, transportation convenience is very important." He was treating her as if she were a stranger to San Francisco, which she was forced to admit was somewhat true: clearly she had missed the tech boom.

San Francisco's high rents surprised Ingrid. Three years ago, apartments were much cheaper. She wondered where the artists who used to swarm the Mission District lived now. "Eighteen hundred a month for this?" she asked. "I thought renting had come down after the dot-com bubble burst. There aren't so many millionaires around anymore."

"Well, it's lower than the market price, believe it or not. You're renting month by month, you know." His deadpan expression seemed to say, "If you don't take it right now, someone else will."

It was the fifth apartment Ingrid had looked that day. When she walked out the door, she decided that if she couldn't find a better one under $1,800 the next day, she would have to take this studio. What a downgrade from the Russian Hill neighborhood to this ghetto-looking studio! But she must start living on a budget—since she left New York, she hasn't worked. Also, a week earlier, she leased a '98 Volkswagen. She didn't need a car in the city, but visiting her sister and mother in Sunnyvale every weekend could be troublesome without a car: public transportation in the South Bay suburban area is underdeveloped.

Ingrid likes the Mission District, its large Latino population and the overall vivacious and laid-back atmosphere. Of course, the neighborhood is also packed with restaurants serving the cuisines of Mexico, El Salvador, and Guatemala. Just now, she passes two Mexican delis with banners above their doors advertising their family-recipe meals and various burritos and tacos. She can live on burritos and tacos alone.

It's only four p.m. The rain has dwindled to a mist. The morning fog has burned off, and the sky is clear. Maybe in another hour or so the sun will come out. The weather here can change so quickly at this time of year, and a crisp, warm morning can be followed by a chilly and overcast afternoon. Rather than use her umbrella, Ingrid puts up the hood of her black Burberry trench coat, which she bought in London last year. Roaming in the mist with a map in her pocket, passing blank-faced pedestrians and half-filled buses, she feels the leisure of being aimless. Half an hour later, she stands in front of the murals painted on the walls, fences, and garage doors in Balmy Alley, said to have been inspired by the work of Diego Rivera.

All the murals have vivid colors, and many are political. One shows a colored, bespectacled man against a red background, where block letters declaim: "No one should comply with an immoral law." Another mural, two yards long, has surreal, beautiful plants, flowers, and birds on one side and metallic monsters on the other, a protest against oil companies drilling in the Amazon area. One mural, titled *A Past That Still Lives,* catches her eye. A mother sits in a truck bed, her sleeping baby on her thighs, and looks skyward defiantly. Behind the truck the artist has depicted a winding road, huts, and people going about their daily chores peacefully. Across the road, in the other half of the painting, the mother's face is full of dread: she is surrounded by fire and soldiers with guns, apparently an image from her memory.

Ingrid stands in front of this painting for a long time. Later, as she walks onto a busy street, she thinks that most people's lives are mediocre, filled with small incidents and trivial emotional twists. That's what real life is about, anyway. It's with this thought that she heads toward Valencia Street.

"Ingrid!" Violet gives her a big hug at the door. It's not the same Violet that Ingrid remembers: the woman in front of her has gained at least sixty pounds, and her plump body looks like a sausage wrapped inside her tight print dress. Her black mascara is too thick, gluing her eyelashes together and making her look old and tired. "I was so happy when you called. Welcome back!"

Ingrid hands her a bottle of wine and gives her chubby cheek a peck. "Congratulations on the house. It's nice to be back. It's much warmer here."

"You bet. Didn't you watch the news? There is a blizzard in

New York. I watched TV last night—it showed people clearing piled-up snow outside their houses and scraping ice off their windshields. Everyone is wrapped up like a pregnant bear. Thousands of travelers are delayed at the airports due to flight cancellations. Well, you don't need me to tell you that. You lived there. I don't understand why a place with such a terrible climate can be so expensive." Ingrid has noticed that whenever people in San Francisco discover she has lived in New York, they try to talk down the Big Apple. It seems these two cities are competing to see which is the better place to live.

As Ingrid follows Violet into the house, she says, "I actually don't mind snow. I like to have a white Christmas." She feels like arguing for New York.

Violet continues, ignoring Ingrid's remark. "It's not just the East Coast. The news said that Europe is also freezing. And there's hurricane somewhere in Asia. And of course, there are always wars going on in Africa or the Middle East. Australia is having a drought right now. Do you know that people there aren't allowed to wash their cars at home? How absurd! Even if it didn't have the drought, it is just too far from everywhere. Who wants to live there?" A native San Franciscan, Violet has made it clear that no other place on the planet is better than her hometown. Though Ingrid used to be attracted to Violet's bubbling personality, considering her outgoing and bold, she now thinks her shallow and annoying. And God, she's gained weight!

The room is packed, with both adults and small children. Sharing a long, cumbersome sofa, several women are talking about their children, while the children crawl on the carpet or play with toys. They wave at Ingrid and say their names, but Ingrid cannot remember any of them. One woman with permed hair winks at Ingrid and says loudly, "No children?" a question that makes the other women laugh heartily, as though it were a joke. Their husbands, presumably, are listening to Violet's husband, a former engineer who has become a junior financial consultant, talk about investing for retirement and children's educations. Her husband makes a small chart on a page he tears from a notebook he has been carrying, to show his attentive audience major index funds' growth rates compared with that of the benchmark Dow. "Do you have a 401(k)?" Violet's husband suddenly stops drawing his chart and asks Ingrid. She shakes her head. "You don't? You really should." Violet's husband nods seriously while eyeing his audience, as if saying, "Believe me, you don't want to be like her."

"Maybe soon," Ingrid says politely.

Violet's husband extracts his business card from his pants pocket. "Call me when you're ready. I'd love to help."

Other than Violet, three of Ingrid's old classmates are at the party. She wasn't friends with any of them at school and hasn't seen them since graduation. Ted owns an accounting practice, and Alison works at the financial software company where Violet works. Violet leaves to greet the newcomers—all with children—so Ingrid tries to hang out with Ted and Alison, who were talking about new accounting rules when she showed up. Ted and Alison hug Ingrid with feigned enthusiasm—"Oh, my God, Ingrid! Long time no talk. How wonderful to see you! You look gorgeous," Alison says. Since Violet mentioned that Ingrid has lived in New York for the past three years, Ted and Alison ask about her life there. But after learning that she didn't work on Wall Street and isn't even in the financial industry, their enthusiasm gives way to disappointment, then boredom: clearly, Ingrid is not someone they can add to their professional networks. Ingrid realizes that she has little to say to them. To keep the conversation going, they begin to talk about their professors and classmates. At this moment, another classmate, Joseph, shows up.

"Remember Jerry Pike?" he asks, excited.

"Sure. He was quiet, I think. Didn't he try to kill himself because his parents were getting divorced?" Alison screws up her eyebrows.

"What's with him? Did he attempt another suicide? Did he finally succeed?"

"I remember him," Ted says. "Man, he wasn't in a good shape. He had a crush on you, didn't he?" He elbows Alison. "Didn't you go out with him for a while?"

"He wasn't my type," Alison answers and coughs out a dry laugh. "He couldn't get a job here after graduation. I don't know where he went."

Ingrid contributes her impression of Jerry: a guy who liked to read science fiction. She wants to say a little more: after all, they were classmates for four years. But she cannot think of anything to add. In those four years, she now regrets, she spent most of her time and energy confronting her sister like a belligerent child. Except for Violet and a few others, she rarely hung out with fellow students. She was a shadow in her classes, on the campus.

"He is doing extremely well now," Joseph says. "I just heard from Diana Gilbert that he retired. I mean retire retire."

"Really? How so?" both Ted and Alison ask.

"The lucky bastard joined Amazon in 1996, before the company went public and got stock options. Then, right before the company's stock tumbled, he sold all his shares. He must have made millions. Diana said he was planning to buy a private jet and invest in a baseball team."

"Jeez!" Alison says.

"Maybe you should divorce your husband and marry him instead," Ted teases Alison.

"My goodness! Did you seriously mean that Jerry Pike? The guy with bow legs?" Alison still looks shocked.

The discussion turns to organizing a class reunion and inviting Jerry to the Bay Area. Alison's voice is affectionate, as if she had always liked Jerry. Bored, Ingrid excuses herself and goes to the kitchen to get a drink. While sipping wine, Ingrid watches the exuberant mothers in the living room still talking about baby food, diapers, toys, breast feeding, schooling. The more experienced mothers share their wisdom with the newer ones. Ingrid doesn't dislike children, but she is none too fond of parents who cannot stop talking about their offspring. She decides that it was a mistake to come to this party, which is all about parenthood and professional networking. Honestly, though she likes San Francisco, she doesn't have friends here. The good thing is that she'll stay only a few months, like an expatriate, then go back to New York. This trip will be a proper good-bye to part of her life, to San Francisco—when she left this city she was in a rush.

Ingrid remembers that Angelina once claimed she was no one's woman and no one's mother, which brings a smile of approval to Ingrid's face. Maybe she's like Angelina, she thinks. At this moment, Violet walks into the kitchen. "Want to take a look at Emily?"

Before Violet reaches the crib in the baby's room stuffed with Disney soft toys, Emily makes a whimpering sound. Violet bends to scoop up the ten-month-old baby, "Isn't she the prettiest girl in the world?" Ingrid looks at the baby, her wrinkled forehead, swollen eyelids, beady eyes, and disproportionately big nose.

"Oh, my God, she's so adorable," Ingrid remarks, despite her negative opinion.

Violet covers the baby with loud, affectionate kisses, then looks at Ingrid. "Want to hold her?" Her voice suddenly trembles as if she were giving her child away to an enemy.

Ingrid doesn't want to but doesn't have the heart to say no. She locks her arms over her chest to make the cradling position.

"No, no, no. Not like that. Hold Emily in your left arm first, letting her head settle in the crook of your arm, then use your right arm for extra support." Violet sounds as though she were reciting from a *Parents* magazine article.

Ingrid follows the instructions, regretting again that she has come to the party. The baby is now against her chest: warm, smelling like butter.

"You look so natural!" Violet exclaims, in a way that makes Ingrid feel she has said this many times to a childless woman who has been coaxed or forced to hold her daughter.

Before Ingrid can say "Don't kid me," the baby wakes up and begins to scream. Ingrid hastily hands her back to Violet, but she's a little too late—the baby has already soiled her blue silk Miu Miu blouse with her milky saliva.

"I'm sorry," Violet says, though she doesn't look sorry. She wipes Emily's mouth with a small towel hanging on the crib's frame. "You know, babies are like this. They don't care if you're Princess Diana or Bill Clinton. They do whatever they want. There's Kleenex there.

"Oh, she just pooped," Violet says with a smile after checking the baby. "She poops a lot! Why don't you help me change the diaper?" She yanks off the baby's pants and asks Ingrid to fetch a new diaper from a big box of Pampers. "Thank God there's Costco. Until you have a baby, you don't know how many diapers they use a day!" After changing the baby's diaper, Violet puts her back in the crib, making her stand, and holds her puffy arms. "Emily, you can walk, can't you? Why don't you show Ingrid that you can walk?" She talks to the baby with that unnatural whining voice parents generally use. The baby doesn't walk but leans backward, her eyes bulging, looking angry. "Okay, okay, my princess doesn't want to walk today. How about stamping your feet? You did that yesterday. You were like Shirley Temple." Violet stamps her own feet to set an example, her eyes fixed eagerly on Emily. The baby makes a squeaking sound, a little bit like a rat, then whimpers.

"Little Emily is sleepy, aren't you?" Ingrid says to the poor baby, who is like a puppet in her mother's grip. As soon as she says it, she hates her voice—affected by Violet, she has used baby talk as well.

Violet lies the baby down in the crib and turns to Ingrid. "There are too many people here today. Usually, she smiles and moves a lot.

You should see her when she smiles. Oh, did you see her teeth? She has two! Bottom fronts." For the next half hour, Violet forces Ingrid to sit on the floor and browse through Emily's five oversize albums, explaining each photograph and entry with awe and wonder. A few times, Ingrid looks at Violet's beaming face, wondering at how motherhood has transformed such a rowdy girl into an enthusiastic baby lover.

Ingrid plans to say good-bye with the excuse that she has an appointment with her hairstylist, but Alice Yao, another former classmate, arrives with her three-year-old daughter. Her daughter soon begins to play with the other children in the living room. Violet leaves Ingrid to videotape the children. A housewife, Alice isn't interested in the financial discussions that Ted, Joseph, and Alison are having, so she stays with Ingrid.

Alice tells Ingrid that she was divorced last year. Her former husband is a real-estate investor who has made a small fortune in Florida and Las Vegas, where he predicted rising markets caused by baby boomers' retirements. Her husband recently moved to Palm Springs.

"With his lover." Alice's voice is bitter. "I think he's a guy, but I don't know for sure." Alice then tells Ingrid that she's going to live for a few months in Shanghai, where her parents own two restaurants.

"Both my daughter and I are learning Mandarin," Alice says. "My parents have moved most of their assets to Shanghai and have even bought a house there, planning to live there permanently after they retire. They were born in Shanghai. In 1949, when the Community Party seized power, my grandparents took them to Taiwan. Later, my parents moved to the States. They spoke English at home and didn't teach me Mandarin. It was a pity. I wish I'd learned some from you at college."

"I heard that a lot of Taiwanese live in Shanghai nowadays," Ingrid says.

"Indeed. I don't know how many, but it's a lot. Where my parents bought their house, more than one third of the residents are Taiwanese. I visited Shanghai for the first time two years ago, and I couldn't believe my eyes. It was so modern! Skyscrapers, designer boutiques, bars and clubs, upscale shopping malls, you name it. Both my brother and sister moved to China recently, one to Shanghai, the other to Beijing. My sister is at a language school, and my brother works for a local computer company." She pauses. "Ingrid, why don't you go back to China? With your double background, you could surely find a highly paid job."

"I've yet to figure out what to do there." Ingrid manages a smile.

After Ingrid leaves Violet's apartment, she is still thinking about Alice Yao.

Back at San Jose State University, Alice had been hostile to Ingrid. Initially, Ingrid had felt a natural connection with Alice because there were few Asian faces in the class, and she'd wanted to make friends with her. But Alice had turned a cold shoulder to her. If they were assigned to the same study group, Alice would ask to join a different group; at dorm parties, if Ingrid was hanging out with a group of people, Alice would say hi to everyone except Ingrid. Behind Ingrid's back, she called her FOB—Fresh off the Boat.

Then, Ingrid hadn't lived in the United States for long, and her English was limited. Often she had to use gestures to express herself. When she wasn't sure how to say a word, she tapped her right forefinger on her left palm, as though looking for something there, and she blushed. She rarely made steady eye contact with her conversation partner, instead glancing sideways or looking at the ground. Later she adopted the American way of looking at the other person while conversing, a disrespectful and threatening gesture in Chinese culture. Wherever she went, she brought a pocket Webster's dictionary in case she had to look up new words. She was reluctant to speak English, especially with a native English speaker, but gradually she began to speak more, to ask questions in class, and to attend school activities. Though she still made frequent mistakes, she no longer panicked but managed to finish her sentences calmly.

The language was hard enough, but learning about American culture was harder. To improve her cultural knowledge, she took classes in the arts and humanities departments; one of the classes was about media's influence on the popular culture. The professor mentioned dozens of celebrities in entertainment and sports. Ingrid recognized only three, all with names starting with *M*: Michael Jackson, Michael Jordan, and Madonna—well-known in China. But she had no clue about the rest. After asking an American student, she realized that Tiger Woods is a golf star who is one quarter Chinese, one quarter Thai, one quarter African American, one eighth Native American, and one eighth Dutch, while Oprah Winfrey is an Emmy Award-winning black talk show host who is also a book critic, an actress, and a magazine publisher.

Ingrid was self-conscious about her looks compared with the other girls in her class, who wore makeup, funky jewelry, low-cut, tight tops, and miniskirts that almost showed their buttocks. She didn't know how to drive, had a low tolerance for alcohol. She had brought most of her clothes, shoes, and other belongings from China. Whenever she passed Ingrid, Alice would shrug and snort, as if to say, "We belong to different worlds, you know." With her yellow skin, flat nose, and small, slanting eyes, Alice wore tight tops barely covering her navel and dyed her hair different shades of blond. Her cobalt blue eye shadow and shiny red lipstick made her resemble the Stars and Stripes.

One day, in gym class, Ingrid noticed that Alice was sneering at her Reebok running shoes. Ingrid had bought them at the airport store in Guangzhou to replace the made-in-Shanghai shoes she was wearing. She had always wanted a pair of Reeboks, but they were beyond her means. Now, with the money her sister had sent to her from the United States, she felt that it was time for her to own something from America—she couldn't even wait until she arrived at San Francisco. The Reeboks cost her six hundred yuan, three months of her mother's salary at the time, but she liked them and thought them comfortable and trendy. Why did Alice stare at her shoes? she wondered. After returning to her dorm, she compared her shoes with her roommate's Reeboks. To her embarrassment, she saw that the brand name on her shoes was spelled "Reabok," though the logo was the same. And only later did she discover, whether Alice knew it or not, that Reebok was a British company, not from the United States.

After a few quarters, Ingrid made some friends, Caucasians, blacks, and Hispanics, but she had few Asian friends and had rarely spoken with Alice. By then she had changed her name from Guo-Ying to Ingrid. She had gotten tired of having to repeat her Chinese name when introducing herself, and she had also felt awkward trying to explain what *Guo* and *Ying* mean in Chinese. "Your name means 'the country is splendid'?" the other person would always ask, with a cynical frown. Assuming a new name wasn't as difficult as she had thought, and she quickly got used to being called by her English name. Even her sister, who had adopted an English name herself, began to call her Ingrid.

It puzzled Ingrid that Alice and a few other Asian Americans in her class were so unfriendly to her. She concluded that they thought themselves superior to her, a fresh immigrant who had no money and spoke poor English. In other words, they were Americans while she was still a Chinese. But they seemed to be fairly friendly to non-Asian immigrant students, for example, those from Europe or Latin America. So she further surmised that they viewed her, someone with the same color eyes, skin, and hair as theirs, as a threat to their American identity; she was an unpleasant reminder of their unglamorous past or, more accurately, their parents or their ancestors' unglamorous pasts, more often than not associated with poverty and ignorance.

Another thing that puzzled Ingrid was that Alice and her American-born Asian friends usually hung out together instead of mingling with other ethnic groups. If any of the girls in the group dated a Caucasian, she would arouse gossip among her friends, being secretly accused of "selling out." But this kind of gossip sometimes contained jealousy, as if this girl were with someone from a higher class. The reaction was the same when an American-born Asian boy was seeing a Caucasian girl. However, dating a black or a Hispanic was disapproved of. Once, Ingrid overheard an American-born Vietnamese girl say to Alice, "My mother said that she wouldn't care who I'm with as long as I am not with a black or a Hispanic."

So where was she in Alice's and her friends' racial and social hierarchy? It amused Ingrid to speculate. Certainly below Caucasians and American-born Asians, and probably below American-born blacks and Hispanics as well, since she didn't even speak good English or possess an American passport.

But today, in Violet's house, Alice was friendly and kind, without any of the old arrogance. Maybe divorcing and being a single mother had changed her, or maybe it was because Ingrid speaks English almost as well as she does, or because her whole family is benefiting from the economic boom in China. Or maybe it was simply because when Alice acted unkindly to her she had been merely an immature teenager.

All this, of course, thinks Ingrid, matters little to her now; she doesn't care how others see her, and she isn't asking for acceptance. She turns onto Mission Street, passing a man holding a big sign that reads, "Culture contains the seed of resistance that blossoms into the flowers of liberation." She smiles, pondering the depth of what she recognized as Amilcar Lopes Cabral's words.

Three days later, Ingrid moves to the studio on Eighteenth Street. She has little kitchenware, but that's fine with her. She doesn't like cooking. It's convenient to eat out, sparing the hassle of doing dishes.

She shops at grocery stores now and then, but only to buy fruit, juice, premixed salads, canned food, snacks, bread, and cheese. Occasionally she eats canned beans and boiled eggs for supper when those are the only foods in her kitchen. If she remembers, she makes sure that she has cheese in her fridge: when she first arrived in the United States, she couldn't stand the smell of cheese; now, she's addicted to it.

Though she doesn't want to invite her mother and Mary to her apartment, Ingrid knows she must. In her mind, she can hear Mary asking her skeptically when she and their mother can take a look at her apartment as soon as they meet. Of course, Mary won't believe she actually has a place to stay in the city until she sees it with her own eyes. Ingrid can also see her sister cook a lot of food for her and put it in containers or Ziploc bags, and ask her to take them home.

To prepare for their visit and, more important, to convince them that she has a good income, Ingrid has decided to furnish the studio with decent furniture, instead of cheap IKEA stuff; when she leaves, she'll just sell it. She couldn't have been luckier: the day she moved in, she spotted a liquidation sale notice on her building's message board, advertising designer furniture including Aeron chairs, Noguchi tables, Tolomeo lamps, and Eames desks, the kind of furniture she likes but has often found too expensive. It was a small e-commerce company that had just announced bankruptcy. As Ingrid looked at the pieces of furniture, being sold at less than half their original prices, some of the employees were packing their belongings with grim faces. One young girl was shouting into her cell phone in a conference room clustered with computers and documents. "I know, I know, don't act like a smart-ass! I don't need you to tell me this right now. It wasn't like this a year ago. I really thought I'd become a millionaire. We came so close!"

The studio doesn't look bad at all after being cleaned and furnished. Now, Ingrid wants to ship the furniture to New York when she leaves.

She also bought a few nice flowerpots and has planted a Fire Dragon Japanese maple and New Zealand grass on the tiny balcony.

It's time for a family reunion, she says to herself, stretching comfortably as she stands on the balcony, looking up at the sky, which has just turned sunny. Of course, she's been missing her mother, but strangely, she has to admit that she's been looking forward to seeing Mary too.

NINE

December

TELEGRAPH AVENUE HAD BEEN Mary's favorite street in Berkeley when she was a student there. It swarmed with restaurants, bookstores, boutiques, bakeries and coffee shops, street vendors selling handmade crafts, jewelry, secondhand clothes, sunglasses, and cheap art. She used to like rambling from Bancroft Way to Dwight Way, checking out the various stores, enjoying the flowers and creeping vines, or just watching the eccentrically dressed people—there were many of them—and being amused by them. Basking in the street's dynamics and diversity, she could easily look past the garbage at the corners and the graffiti on the walls and doors, imagining that she was in a fairy tale. Now, when she thinks of Berkeley, she thinks of Telegraph Avenue, its noise and bustle, rather than the campus and classrooms, which remind her of her unpleasant time as a graduate student in chemistry.

She hasn't been back to Berkeley much since she moved to the South Bay to work, but whenever she is in town she feels a surge of excitement and knows that she must visit Telegraph Avenue, order a cup of steaming espresso at a coffee shop, and sit under a low-hanging tree for a while, listening to a musician play jazz or rock music nearby. Despite her liking the street, where time seems to go by faster, she prefers to live in her South Bay suburb. One is like a midnight party going wild, the other a serene spring morning in an exquisite garden; yes, periodically she longs for a party, but most of the time she would rather smell her freshly cut lawn and feel the breeze.

Before she came to the United States, Telegraph Avenue was what Mary had imagined the country would be like; now, after all these years, she still thinks it is for her one of the most representative images of the country.

For their meeting, Han Dong has booked a table at Le Bateau Ivre, a French restaurant on Telegraph Avenue. Since they talked on the phone, Mary hasn't forgotten him for a day. Though she informed Bob a week ago that she would be meeting an old classmate for lunch in Berkeley this Saturday and had canceled her usual Saturday get-together with Mingyi, Yaya, and Julia, she was occasionally desperate to find an excuse to call off her meeting with Han Dong. Even this morning, when she woke up at three a.m. she considered calling his hotel, leaving a message saying that Alex was sick and she had to take him to see a doctor; in fact, she wished that Alex would get sick, a light cold, a sore throat, for instance, nothing big, so she wouldn't have to lie—she is never comfortable lying. But in the morning Alex was naughtier than ever, running the length of the house, then the backyard, nagging his grandma to play Ping-Pong with him on the dining room table.

To kill time, Mary cleaned the kitchen though there was nothing to clean and swept the backyard patio though only the day before she had washed it with the hose. At ten a.m., as if being put under a spell, she rushed to the hallway bathroom to get ready. She was anxious when she came out of the bathroom, afraid that she had put on too much makeup. But when she said good-bye to her mother and Alex, neither commented on her face. Bob was on a conference call with a co-worker in India in their bedroom. As she walked in, he only glanced at her and, with one hand covering the phone, said that she must have slept well because she looked refreshed. Then he returned to his call.

Mary parks her car at Sather Gate Garage, where she usually parks when she visits this neighborhood. She remains in her seat for a while, praying to God not to let her lose her conscience and good sense, asking for His forgiveness for skipping choir practice. Almost reluctantly, she takes a bottle of Hugo Boss's Deep Red from her black leather Prada handbag, both purchased at Saks Fifth Avenue a week ago, inspired by a recent issue of *Vogue*. She sprays the perfume around her neck, behind her ears, and on her wrists a few times, then checks herself in the rearview mirror. Her hair, dyed recently at a salon called Fantasia, recommended by a co-worker, shines with a copper gleam in the soft sunlight. Before she walked into the salon that day, the color she had decided on was a more aggressive dark red, but as soon as she sat in the chair, she changed her mind. Her face looks pale and her lips a little dull, so she outlines her lips with a strawberry shade, fills them in with a plum color, and dabs a light bronzer on her cheeks. As she is doing all this, she is careful and focused, yet without enthusiasm, as if she were being forced into it.

Standing outside the restaurant, Mary wonders if she should go in. Several teenage boys carrying skating boards dash in her direction; to avoid being smacked, she steps forward, presenting herself right at the entrance. Without consciously willing it, she opens the door and enters. She spots him right away, sitting at a window table, a glass of red wine and a basket of bread in front of him. He is looking out the window at a long-haired white girl in a pink, low-cut top, a denim miniskirt, and a pair of knee-high cowboy boots. She saw the girl earlier, when she was standing on the street, but didn't pay attention to her. Now she does. The girl is leaning against a lamppost, smoking, an imitation mink coat hanging over her left arm. It's chilly, but she doesn't seem to care, sucking on her cigarette greedily. She is perhaps in her early twenties. She isn't pretty, is wearing too much makeup, but she has an ample bosom, curvy hips, and long legs. Now and then, she smiles at the passing men who look at her.

Mary feels a pang of envy. Young, tall, sexy, audacious, free— all the words that can be used to describe this girl have nothing to do with her, Mary Chang. But how ridiculous is her envy? She soon laughs at herself. That girl might well be a prostitute, while she, Mary Chang, is a highly educated statistician who works for a Fortune 500 company. Why compare herself with a slut? If it wasn't for Han Dong looking at the girl, she wouldn't have bothered to glance at her. At the same time, she snorts disdainfully: well, Han Dong is the same person he was before, easily attracted to women.

It is not until she calls out his name that he looks away hurriedly from the window as if waking from a daydream.

"Hi, Mei," he addresses Mary as he did when they were lovers. "You've not changed the slightest bit, still young and pretty." He seems sincere with his praise. He stands, circles to the other side of the table to pull out the chair for her, and as she sits, he pushes it in slightly to make sure that she will be comfortable. Then he returns to his own chair. Though he always behaved like an old-fashioned British gentleman when they were dating, she is still impressed by his natural, smooth movements. His well-practiced Western manners, she imagines, must have won him many women's hearts all these years. Even Bob, her husband, born and raised in the United States, had begun to ignore all this etiquette soon after they got married, and nowadays he doesn't even remember to open the car door for her.

"I wish you were right," Mary says. "But I must say, you look successful." She shakes his hand across the table, and when she withdraws her hand, his thumb strokes the back of it slightly. She blushes, but he looks normal, as if it were an accident.

The waiter arrives, and Mary orders a glass of house white wine.

Han Dong looks different from the way she remembered him. His face, once thin and angular, is now smooth, even a little chubby. He has no wrinkles, either around his eyes or on his forehead, and his hair has been styled carefully; those locks that once dangled over his forehead like a bird's wings, which once enchanted her, are gone. His facial features are still delicate, with a sensitive mouth and thoughtful eyes, though those eyes seem as if they belong to a seasoned businessman rather than a restless poet, the man he used to be. He has applied cologne, which she imagines to be Acqua di Gio by Armani—she once smelled a sample of it at Macy's when she was Christmas shopping for Bob. She liked the smell but didn't buy the cologne because Bob didn't use any. She recalls how Han Dong used to talk about Giorgio Armani with passion, calling him a poet who wrote his poems with fabrics, when no one else among their friends had heard of him, when he himself couldn't even afford to buy a pair of made-in-Shanghai leather shoes. That was in the early eighties, when people would be happy if they could eat meat every meal or wear unpatched clothes.

"Successful or not, it's hard to say, but after all these years I certainly have seen what I should see and have heard what I should hear." There is panache in Han Dong's demeanor. "I know how to survive, that much is true. No more bookishness in me now, for one good thing. Confucius, Taoism, Nietzsche, Aristotle, Spinoza, Thoreau—they all belong to history, my history. I'm not ashamed. You know, it's just that you can't live on the stuff called philosophy. Among my college classmates, after graduation, only one entered graduate school and eventually got a Ph.D. in philosophy. The rest of us went to work at banks, in the government, or for private companies. And you know what? Last year, that classmate of mine who got his Ph.D. in philosophy quit his college teaching job and is now running a model-training studio. You've got to be either a genius or a fool to study philosophy. Your father was wise to make you study science. Good that you listened to him."

"So I guess you don't write poems anymore," she says.

"Poems?" He shakes his head and chuckles. "No. I haven't written a line for years. Poetry is for little boys and girls. Who's got time to write or read poetry, after all? Everyone is busy making money, and even so-called serious writers must include some sex in their books or no one will buy them."

"But you were very good."

"Nah, I wasn't good. I don't care about poetry anymore, so it doesn't matter, really. Let's talk about you instead. How's your life in this free country? You must have had a few houses. Driving a BMW or a Mercedes-Benz? Are you a big boss at work? How much do you make?"

His questions offend her, but she knows that Chinese people always ask these competitive questions when they meet their friends; there is no such thing as privacy. "Oh, I'm doing just okay, not too rich, not too poor," she offers diplomatically.

He smiles shrewdly. "Sorry, I forgot that you're now an A-me-ri-can. Okay, I won't ask you about your financial condition, or your religious or political views; so, relax." He picks up a slice of bread and butters it, then takes a small bite.

Mary finds herself watching his slender and agile fingers: they used to slide through her hair, seeming to be speaking to her. She quickly moves her eyes away from them and asks, "How's your work?"

"Working for a state bank is the same as working at a normal state-run company. It's like eating chicken wings: it's a waste to throw them away, yet if you eat them there is little meat. But really, I can't complain. I'm a director in the loan department and have quite a bit of power. Almost every day I receive dinner invitations. People buy me gifts all the time. If I don't make a mistake, I shouldn't have any problem becoming a branch director in two years. I don't want to go higher than that. Visibility means risk. If you get high enough, you can't avoid politics, which is all about building connections with government officials. Those officials are always fighting for power or something else. If I weren't connected with the right people, my career . . ." He lifts his hand and makes a gesture of cutting his throat.

The man she once loved has turned into a bureaucrat, she thinks. Meanwhile she feels relieved, convinced that nothing will happen between them today: He is now a stranger to her, and all her trepidations were unnecessary. She straightens her back and sips her wine, looking briefly out the window, then puts down her glass and takes a piece of bread.

The waiter returns. Both order Caesar salads and, for the main course, he asks for grilled chicken breast and she vegetarian penne pasta.

Han Dong taps the table lightly with his fingers, as if trying to find something to say. Mary cannot help but glance again at those fingers.

"China today is different from what you were familiar with," he finally says.

"Well, I try to keep myself up-to-date by reading newspapers or watching TV, and I go back once a year to visit my mother. Also, some of my friends go to China often, and they share with me what they've seen."

Han Dong laughs. "Mei, that's just not enough. I live in China and still I sometimes have no idea what's happening. Haven't you heard the song 'It's not that I don't understand but the world is just changing too fast'? That's how I feel. You must follow your instincts. If there is a big opportunity somewhere, you must catch it and take advantage of it; if you can't find any, you don't just sit and wait; you take a detour and find your way around. Who knows, maybe you'll get lucky. Believe me, there is always a way around. Being honest and conscientious doesn't get you anywhere."

"But you don't want to break the law and go to jail," Mary blurts out.

"Law? Jail?" Han Dong shakes his head as if finding her comments ridiculous. "I believe in shortcuts and believe that you have to find ways to take care of yourself. These days, the word I hate the most is *serious*. Our generation lost big in believing the Party's ideology education. When we were little, the Party said it was most honorable to be factory workers and peasants, but the current reality is that many state-run companies have gone bankrupt and a lot of workers have been forced out of employment. As for peasants, they live at the bottom of the society and are looked down upon. Nowadays, there's even a cursing phrase 'So peasant!' The Party also said that soldiers were the most lovable people, and I used to dream of being enlisted, but now only people who cannot get into college join the army, and after demobilization they would be happy if they end up being a company's security guard or a rich person's bodyguard. Then it was said that knowledge is power, but take a look at wealthy businesspeople in Guangdong and other coastal cities. How many of them have even finished high school? Now their money has made them famous and respectable while intellectuals struggle to make ends meet. And also look at some of the business gurus in Hong Kong, who started their fortunes from gambling and the porn business. They're the biggest philanthropists and the government's best friends. Wonderful, isn't it? This world is changing faster than you can ever imagine, and if you can't ride the tide, you'll live in misery. The only thing real is money. Power is about money too. Look at those billionaires in mainland China. How many can you name who don't have kinship with a top-level official in Beijing? If you're a prostitute, people won't laugh at you, but if you're poor, people will. That's the reality."

She stares at his cynical face and feels sympathy: he must have stomached a lot of complaints that he cannot voice to any of his friends in China.

Crossing his arms over his chest, Han Dong shakes his head in distress. "The innocent dreams we took to heart when we were young are just naïve. Do you remember that I once said I'd use my poetry to change Chinese people's spiritual world? What a dreamer I was! You also said that you'd devote yourself to science just like Madame Curie. We used to think we were the happiest people in the world."

She is touched. "We were poor then, but we were happy."

"Now we're no longer poor, but we have forgotten what happiness is." A trace of sadness and bewilderment rises on his face, but it soon disappears. He uncrosses his arms and sips his wine, then holds it in front of his eyes, watching the red liquid with interest. "I must say, you have very good wine here in California. It wouldn't be a bad idea to buy a few cases and ship them to China."

It is that fleeting moment of bewilderment and sadness that evokes Mary's compassion toward him, making her recall their connected pasts. She asks softly, "What did you do after I left China?"

"Oh, that's a long story. Very long indeed. I almost didn't get my bachelor's degree because I had skipped too many classes, spending a lot of time writing poetry. Then I realized that I had to have a job to pay my bills. My girlfriend at the time helped me get a government job in Beijing, where her parents worked. Nothing fancy, just a clerical job, writing reports for our leaders, filing documents. I was still ambitious, dreaming of becoming a famous poet. I had actually been published by quite a few magazines, but then life played a trick on me."

He stops, meeting her eyes. "How do you like your wine?"

"Mine? Oh, it's pretty good." Afraid that Han Dong will ask to taste her wine, like lovers do, Mary lifts her glass to her lips.

Han Dong regards her with interest.

"What kind of trick?" Mary presses.

A feeble smile flashes on his face, but he continues. "Have you heard of the Anti-Spiritual Pollution campaign? Well, I was busted for a few poems I wrote. They were just love poems, mimicking Byron, but I guess there was a little political stuff in there as well. I don't even remember what it was. Anyway, a colleague of mine was so eager to please the leaders that he turned my poems in as evidence of my bourgeois decadence. That was then; now, who cares about a few subtle lines about sex and politics?

"But still I lost my job and soon broke up with my girlfriend— she just couldn't stop nagging me to write a penitence letter to the government. I went to help a friend run a hot-pot restaurant. We were making good money and thinking about opening two more branches in Beijing. Then the student movement for democracy started. My friend was always an advocate of democracy and free speech, so he turned our restaurant into a temporary hotel for students from outside Beijing and helped print and distribute pamphlets."

"Guo-Ying, my sister, was in Beijing at that time," Mary adds, an attempt to show that she wasn't entirely ignorant of the situation.

Han Dong acknowledges this information with an indolent nod. "Of course, I was fully involved as well, feeling like a newborn person. I began to write poems again and even made a few speeches in Tiananmen Square. I should have known better, but I was blinded by my passion. After the central government declared that the movement was an antirevolutionary riot and put it down, our restaurant was forced to close and my friend was sentenced to two years in jail."

"How about yourself?"

"I was lucky and was only detained at the police station for a few days. I was interrogated and threatened but was let go without being charged. Later, I tried my hand at different jobs before an old friend got me something at Bank of China. And I've stayed." Han Dong doesn't appear sentimental talking about his past; on the contrary, he looks relaxed, stretching his arms and suppressing a yawn, as if what he has just said was quite boring and unworthy.

"How about that friend who was put in jail?"

"He stayed in jail only for a year. Then a French journalist friend of his got him some kind of visa for political dissidents and helped him get to France. He didn't do anything related to politics in France, though. He did some odd jobs for a while, then opened a Chinese restaurant. He's certainly doing well and has all kinds of titles: this CEO, that board director. He even has a French wife, whose father owns some serious jewelry business. Just a few months ago, he came to Beijing for a trade show. He's been trying to persuade me to get into real-estate investment in China with him. Who knows, I might do it."

Han Dong extracts a package of Marlboros from his shirt pocket and shakes out a cigarette.

"Smoking is prohibited in restaurants here," Mary whispers.

He frowns, puts back the cigarette, and throws the package onto the table. "You Americans are all about rules. I don't think I could ever get used to living here." He runs the tip of his tongue around his lips and says casually, "You're lucky. You weren't in Beijing at that time."

She wants to tell him that she, in her Berkeley dorm room, watched on TV as tanks rolled onto Chang'an Avenue and how a slim man sporting a white shirt tried to stop a column of advancing tanks by standing in front of them, and how a squad of uniformed soldiers pointed their machine guns at protesters. She also wants to say that she heard a speech on the radio by a student leader who had escaped to the United States, who in a tearful and weary voice said that the tanks had knocked down the tents in Tiananmen Square where students were sleeping. In those days, Mary watched and read every piece of news about the Tiananmen Square massacre and the events that followed. The news sources varied, so did their reports. What was true, what was not, no one seemed to know for sure; even the surviving participants provided different versions of the story. And her calls to her sister were met with hesitancy or even silence. She ate and slept poorly and had nightmares of her sister lying on the ground, bullet-riddled and hollow-eyed.

"Han Dong, you know, in 1989 . . ." She stops, noticing the indifferent expression on his face. She swallows what she wanted to say and states instead, "I mean, if I'd stayed in China, I don't know what would have become of me."

"Let me guess. Hmm, a scientist at China's Academy of Sciences? Or a professor at Beijing University?" He sounds sarcastic.

"I meant if I would have gotten involved in the political movement, if I would have gotten myself into trouble. I used to like reading books about politics."

"You'd have been totally okay. You were only interested in theories and concepts, not in action. You read the books I lent you like you were reading classic novels, purely for the pleasure of reading. Actually, studying philosophy might suit you. You could lock yourself up in your room for a month while I'd go absolutely mad if I couldn't get out of my room for one day."

The waiter serves their salads, apologizing for the delay. "There is a birthday party over there." He points at a far corner. "They ordered tons of stuff." He is young, perhaps a student, has blond, curly hair and a nervous voice, and he blinks often. Mary asks for a glass of iced water in Mandarin—after speaking it for a while, she has a hard time switching back to English. Immediately realizing her mistake, she repeats her request in English. The waiter smiles mischievously and says in Mandarin with a Beijing accent, *"Hao le, yi bei bing shui,"* then switches to English. "I'll be back in a minute."

When the waiter returns with the glass of iced water, Mary asks him where he learned Mandarin. He says that he taught English for a year in Beijing, where he met his fiancée, a Beijing native. After the waiter leaves, Han Dong remarks, "You can't believe how many foreigners live in Beijing nowadays. You see them everywhere.

Before, they came for sightseeing or a temp job, but now they've moved their families over, the parents working locally and the kids going to an international school. Somehow it reminds me of the gold rush in California, except that this time everyone is coming to China. I've seen little white kids speaking perfect Mandarin. That's just amazing."

He leans across the table, staring into her face. "Mei, I have to say that you're even prettier than before; you've got that kind of classic look. I've seen many pretty women, and some of them were even beautiful, but they bored me to death. Like my ex-wife. She'd be all smiles if I just bought her a gold necklace. When we got divorced, she wanted the house, the car, all the furniture and kitchen appliances, even the Omega watch I was wearing. When we were at college, I must have been blind to have let you go. After all these years, I still recall the time we went for a walk after dinner, talking about poetry, about philosophy, about our dreams." He grabs Mary's hand.

Flustered, she pulls her hand out of his grip and places both her hands in her lap, her face turning scarlet and her hands trembling. After she composes herself, she says, "What's the point in talking about the past? We're both parents now."

"America hasn't changed you, nor has time." He leans back in his chair, takes a green leaf with his fork from his plate, and lifts the fork to his mouth. But his eyes, full of desire and affection, eyes that she has dreamed of more than once, fix on Mary's face. She looks toward the door, at two old women who are entering, but all she can think about is the captivated look in his deep-set eyes. She knows that she has never forgotten him, her first and only love before she married Bob. If not for him, she wouldn't have left China and her life would have been entirely different.

For a moment, she allows herself to be carried away by her reflection. She's frightened, confused, yet excited, like a caged bird suddenly facing an open door.

Han Dong, sensing Mary's dilemma, leans forward again, extending his hand, palm up, in front of her, staring into her face. In her daze, Mary places her right hand on his without looking at him, allowing him to lift it to his lips. She shivers when his soft lips touch her skin.

She finally meets Han Dong's eyes. She says to herself that she should just get up and leave the restaurant, but all she does is withdraw her hand mechanically after he has kissed it a few more times.

Both know what these few seconds mean. Han Dong whispers her name affectionately.

She lowers her head like a coy girl, her mind blank. At this moment, God, Bob, and Alex are nothing but empty words that have no influence on her. As she meets Han Dong's eyes again, she loathes herself for her inability to resist temptation, but she cannot seem to muster the strength to leave the table; in fact, she smiles at him.

From that moment on, everything seems like stage acting to Mary. They continue chatting over their meals and drinks. He asks about Alex and how she met Bob, and she asks about their old acquaintances and how he met his ex-wife. Several times, when he says something slightly funny, she laughs too loudly, flirtatiously. She is behaving, she knows, like the kind of woman she usually despises.

They mention the whopping trade deficit between China and the United States, and the pressure the United States has imposed on China to reform its currency policy. They laugh at the scandal between Bill Clinton and his plump, blowsy intern.

Throughout their conversation, Mary feels that she and Han Dong are like two politicians who have reached a dirty deal yet have to cover up their scheme with normal conversation in front of their voters, their public.

After Han Dong pays the bill, he invites her to his hotel for coffee. He's staying at the Claremont, a magnificent resort hotel; she's been there for a conference. She agrees without hesitation, as if believing this is an innocent offer. On her way out, she reaches into her purse and shuts off her cell phone.

They hail a taxi, and Mary insists on sitting in the front, next to the driver. As the car jerks into traffic and gathers speed, she stares out the window at the passing pedestrians, who look perfectly happy, saying to herself every few minutes that she should stop the car right here, right this second. Every inch from the restaurant is a step closer to a swamp, she reminds herself. But with time moving on and Telegraph Avenue disappearing behind them, she remains in her seat, trying to assure herself that she will just have coffee with Han Dong in his hotel lobby, then say good-bye after a handshake; she pictures the expression she will wear as she extends her hand to him: gracious and polite, even with a halfhearted invitation to pay a weekend visit to her and her husband's house.

They get out of the taxi and walk across the hotel's marble entryway, through the revolving door, into the lobby, and toward the elevators. A bellboy coming down with an empty luggage rack exits the elevator and holds one side of the automatic door for them. As soon as the door closes, Han Dong puts his arm around Mary's waist. Her heart misses a beat, but she allows him, her hands placed rigidly on her purse in front of her, her eyes gazing at the center of the closed stainless-steel doors as if wanting to force them open with the sheer power of her staring. The moment the doors open, he slides his arm to her hip; again, she doesn't stop him.

No sooner do they enter the room than Han Dong turns her and pins her against the door, hands on her hips, kissing her fervently on her mouth and neck. She drops her handbag, twists her head away from him, and kicks, trying to escape his kisses. Push him away, she commands herself, but then suddenly she gives up, turns back to him, and opens her mouth to take in his tongue. The moment their tongues touch, Mary throws her arms around his neck. Yes, she wants him! she exclaims in her heart. Hasn't she always been fantasizing about this moment? Hasn't she been yearning for a little craziness and boldness in her drama-free and mundane life? She sucks on her old lover's tongue greedily. She reasons further: they grew up together, were lovers—each other's first lover—for three years; they never made love—premarital sex was unthinkable in those years. Just once, maybe it is not too terrible a mistake. After she came to the United States, many nights, filled with shame and guilt, she imagined them having sex on the bed, in the woods, or on a beach; she even regretted that she hadn't made love to him while she still could. These dreams bothered her, making her doubt her sanity. Maybe her wild dreams, she thought then, were merely a way for her to escape from her onerous lab experiments and unsympathetic adviser.

Han Dong has never been out of her mind, she admits painfully, as she attacks him with hungry kisses on his face and neck. She plants her hands on his hips and pulls him toward her, feeling his erection against her body, which is swelling with heat and sexual stimulation. A vine clinging to a tree with its tendrils, that's how she sees herself. Is she taking revenge on him for abandoning her? she asks herself. Is she a victim of her buried desire?

On the other hand, through her panting and the pounding of blood in her ears, she hears clearly a cold voice inside her, "You don't love him, nor does he love you."

She closes her eyes, letting go of herself, a self that is now a stranger to her.

Han Dong leads her to the bed and lowers her onto it. Astride her, he takes off her sweater and throws it onto a davenport against the window. "Oh, my baby," she hears him say, his voice oddly twangy and pretentious, reminding her of bad acting in a cheap romance movie. She opens her eyes, expecting to see him looking at her face with flaming eyes, but instead he is gazing at her lacy, semitransparent, black bra, smiling mysteriously.

Why is he smiling? Mary wonders. Is it because he thinks her breasts are too small? Is it because he is so excited at seeing his first lover's half-naked body after all these years that he wants to take things slowly? Is it because he is contemplating some kind of fetish, such as role-playing stuff? Or is it because he thinks her hypocritical—if she didn't plan to sleep with him, why did she wear such a bra?

She feels goose bumps all over, and her conscience suddenly wakes up and hits her hard. She sees Bob and Alex and hears their voices. They're as real as the bed she's lying on.

"Don't . . . ," she manages to utter.

But Han Dong's hands are already at her belt. Soon he'll see her black panties, just as transparent as her bra, and her trimmed pubic hair. Terrified, she sits up and shoves him off her with all her strength. He rolls across the bed and falls onto the floor with a thud.

She buckles her belt with quivering hands and gets off the bed to pick up her sweater. She puts it on with her back facing him, then grabs her handbag. As she opens the door, she turns to look back: he still sits where he fell, looking at her contemptuously, his face red with fury, his mouth twisted as if saying something.

Bitch, he must be calling her, Mary thinks.

"Sorry, I'm terribly sorry," she hears herself say.

Before hailing a taxi to the garage where she parked her car, she fixes her makeup in the hotel's public ladies' room. She can't remember afterward how she got home; it is a wonder that she wasn't stopped for speeding.

"Mom is back!" Alex sees her first through the kitchen window and shouts merrily.

The door opens, and Alex jumps up and hugs her hard. Her mother and Bob stand at the door.

"Is your cell phone battery dead? I was so worried. I called you a gazillion times." Though his tone is unhappy, Bob looks relieved.

"You forgot to take a shawl with you today. Look at you, your lips have turned purple. Come in, don't catch a cold," her mother says at the same time Bob is speaking.

Ingrid appears from the living room, thinner than Mary remembers, smiling uneasily. "Hi, Mary, I arrived an hour ago," she says in Mandarin. She approaches her sister and, after a brief pause, holds out her arms to hug her.

IN THE YEAR

2001

TEN

January

THEY'VE ALL LEFT—HER older daughter and Bob to work, and her grandson, Dongdong, to kindergarten. Except for the periodic sounds from the fridge and birds chirping in the backyard, it is very quiet. Fenglan can hear her footsteps as she walks on the hardwood floor in her cork-soled sandals and, if she tries, even the clock ticking in her daughter's bedroom. The quietness disturbs her: something is missing, she feels. If she were in her own apartment in China right now, she would surely hear Old Aunt Huang scolding her unemployed daughter-in-law, saying that she never helps with housework, or the sounds of hammering, sawing, and drilling from a neighbor remodeling. Of course, there also would be street vendors' chanting, and buses' and cars' honking. She used to complain about these noises because they interrupted her sleep, or made it hard to hear the TV or radio, but now she misses them—they kept her mind occupied, made the days go by; they reminded her that she was still alive.

Now, she can sense clearly each minute, each second, as if time were invisible animals sneaking about with unhurried steps. It is just so quiet! Seen through the living room window, the street remains still, like a scenic poster: the light gray asphalt road, the trees, the lawns, the flowers. Cars or people rarely invade this stillness.

Where are the retired people? she wonders. Don't they stroll in the neighborhood or gather to play chess or cards on their front porches as older people like to do in China? What a waste of such nice porches, occupied only by flowerpots and reclining chairs! On the other side of the street, two houses to the left, a thick-trunked orange tree laden with fruit resembles a burning torch in the sunlight. But she has never seen the tree's owners pick the oranges: they just let them fall all over the lawn and, every Thursday evening, gather them, place them inside a plastic bag, and dump the bag into their garbage bin—garbage collecting day is Friday. She once mentioned this tree to her older daughter. "Those oranges must be very sweet and juicy. If sold at a store, they must cost good money. If this tree was in China—" Her daughter cut her short. "Ma, we aren't in China."

Her daughter's other neighbors puzzle Fenglan as well. Immediately to the right is a middle-aged white couple without children. A row of overgrown oleanders separates their front lawn from her daughter's. This couple go to work at eight a.m. and come back home around six p.m. every weekday, both driving massive SUVs with big tires, one black, the other red. They don't seem to worry about their gas bills. They have another car they keep in the garage and drive only on weekends. It's a monstrous yellow convertible, like a sailboat, with images of black flames on both sides, making a loud noise like a tractor when its engine starts. Her daughter has told her that this car is an antique and worth a lot of money, but Fenglan thinks it's ugly.

This couple rarely come out of the house unless they are in their cars. In the evenings, they watch TV. Whenever she passes their house, Fenglan glances at their windows; sometimes, if the blinds are not completely closed, she can see a huge TV screen flickering in their living room.

After dinner, she usually takes a stroll, from her daughter's house to the pink house with an impressive succulent garden three blocks away, across a wide street to the community park, around the loop in the park, then circling back via a small road flanked with trees and turning onto the street where her daughter's house sits. It is a pleasant route with even sidewalks, well-maintained lawns, and little through traffic. It surprises her that so few people here take a walk after dinner, something people do a lot in China, both the old and the young, believing that an after-dinner walk helps with digestion and is good for health and longevity. Occasionally during her stroll, she has come across several Indians and Chinese, but it doesn't happen often. Neither her daughter nor her son-in-law has the habit of walking after dinner—her daughter accompanied her the first few days, then stopped. If Fenglan mentions the old saying "If you take a walk after a meal, you'll live to be ninety-nine years old," her daughter tells her that she takes vitamins and calcium pills every day. Bob does the same thing, taking those pills as if they were fruit or vegetables. Her daughter even bought her a big bottle of multiple vitamins for seniors and other supplements, such as fish oil and lecithin. Sometimes Fenglan thinks that her daughter is more like an American than a Chinese.

On the far end of the street lives a white man who must be in his eighties. He's tall and bald, humpbacked, neatly dressed. He has a blue Cadillac, which he still drives a few times a week. As he cruises by her daughter's house, if he sees Fenglan in the front lawn, he slows down, lowers the window, leans out, and waves at her. She waves back and watches his car disappear around the corner, thinking that he is brave to drive on his own. Though she has never seen him out in the evenings, she has spotted him walking with a stick in his front yard a few times.

Once, early in the morning, on her way to the community park to exercise, she saw him sitting on his vine-covered porch, watching hummingbirds drink from a hanging bottle under the awning. He wore a checkered flannel jacket, and his legs were wrapped loosely by a wool blanket that reached the ground. "Hello," he said, waving. Fenglan said "Hello" back hastily—it was one of the few English words she understood. The man pointed at the hummingbirds, their wings flapping rapidly. He said a long word slowly, syllable by syllable, with a smile. Also smiling, she nodded and repeated after him— she was sure that her pronunciation was wrong—knowing that he was referring to the birds.

They watched the birds silently for a while, then the man stood and invited her to sit in another chair on the porch so she could see the birds better. She couldn't understand what he had said, yet knew that was what he had meant from his gestures. She felt awkward, accepting a stranger's invitation, but the man looked friendly and sincere. Also, somehow, she felt obliged to talk to this old man, who didn't seem to have visitors. So she walked to the porch and sat. "Mike." He extended his hand. That must be his name, she figured. She took his hand and said her own name. It took quite a bit of practice before he could say her name correctly; even then his into- nation was far off. They couldn't converse further, so they watched the birds quietly, seeing them poke their long beaks into the bottle's flower-shaped yellow openings and, after drinking, jerk their heads up alertly, then chatter as if communicating. One bird, probably a male, had brilliant iridescent feathers at its throat, reflecting the morning light.

Fenglan felt uncomfortable sitting next to a stranger, a foreigner, a person with skin of a different hue and eyes of a different color from hers. She pictured the questions she would ask him if they could talk—if they spoke the same language, she imagined, they would have much in common. A person his age must have experienced a lot. She assumed that his wife had passed away and his children and grandchildren must be living far away or in a foreign country so that they couldn't visit him often—or maybe he had no children. And what about his birthplace, the jobs he had held, his friends, his hobbies, his favorite dishes? It suddenly occurred to her that, despite the fact that he was a Caucasian and didn't speak her language, he was a human being just like her. Or maybe there was a natural bond among the elderly, who have seen and experienced the world, have gone through ups and downs.

The birds flew away after chasing each other for a while. She stood to say good-bye—another English word she had mastered. The man stood as well, nodding appreciatively, and said something, and she walked away across the paved path.

Later she asked her older daughter about this man and was told that he was a retired veteran and had served in South Korea and Vietnam. But other than this, her daughter didn't know anything about him.

Fenglan walks to the kitchen to see if there are any dirty dishes in the sink. Of course, there aren't—her older daughter always cleans the kitchen after each meal. The marble countertop shines, the plates and bowls are arranged by size and color behind the opaque glass cabinet doors. Her second daughter is unlike her older daughter when it comes to keeping things organized and tidy. Guo-Ying leaves a mess wherever she visits. She doesn't even make the bed in the morning. She eats breakfast before brushing her teeth and takes a shower in the morning, rather than in the evening as the Chinese do.

Thinking of Guo-Ying, Fenglan shakes her head. In her thirties, she still acts like a girl, sleeping with a pillow over her chest, talking in her sleep, just as she had done when she was little. A girl her age in China would have a child at least three or four years old, but she is still single and doesn't even have a boyfriend. Fenglan also worries about her job—Guo-Ying told her that she had quit her government job in New York and was now working for a small company in San Francisco.

"Government jobs are stable and provide good benefits. Why did you quit?" she asked.

Guo-Ying shrugged. "But small companies offer more opportunity for career development."

Career or not, Fenglan doesn't care; she just wants her daughters to be safe and well.

She takes the dirty dishes from the dishwasher and washes them with detergent herself. She dries them with a clean towel until she cannot see any water stains, then puts them in the cabinet according to her older daughter's arrangement. If she was in her own apartment, she wouldn't have been so careful with the dishes, but she is a guest here. After cleaning, she goes to the backyard and sits on the bench, watching two gray squirrels frolic on the trees and the power lines. After she is tired of watching them, she walks around the garden looking for weeds. She finds some and pulls them out. Just as she is debating whether she should take a walk or read the *Sing Tao Daily* that her older daughter has subscribed to for her, she hears a faint meowing behind her back. She turns and sees a green-eyed yellow tabby on the top of the fence between two camellias, her ears erect.

Her daughter has told her about this cat and said that she belonged to the house's first owner. When that family moved back to Japan, they gave her to a friend two blocks down the street. But the cat likes to visit the old house, then occupied by a family from Ireland, and would sometimes sleep in the backyard. The Irish family was allergic to cats but put food and water outside for her. A few years later, the Japanese family's friend moved as well, so the tabby became a stray. When Guo-Mei and Bob bought the house, the Irish family offered to send the cat to the Santa Clara Humane Society. But Guo-Mei and Bob wanted to adopt her and even gave her a name, Niuniu, meaning "little girl" in Chinese. They put food and water in the yard as well, trying to befriend her. Whenever they saw her, they would call out Niuniu, and after a while, on hearing their call, the cat would roll on the ground and purr and, if she wasn't in the yard already, would dart in from where she was hiding. However, she didn't let them pat her and would run away if they got too close.

This is the first time Fenglan has seen the cat. "Niuniu," she calls.

The cat swishes her tail, staring at her.

Noticing that no food is left in the tin bowl near the back door, Fenglan takes the bowl and walks to the garage. She finds the cat food and fills the bowl. After putting the bowl back where it was, she returns to her bench and sits, watching the cat.

Niuniu jumps down from the fence and walks to the food; as she eats, she looks up often to check on Fenglan, her hind legs poised as if ready to escape.

After Niuniu has finished eating and drinking, she rambles along the fence, seemingly inspecting her territory, then lies next to a flowerpot a few steps from Fenglan. She meows, rolls, and stretches. Suddenly a sparrow shoots out from behind a camellia, flying low over the lawn. The cat runs after the bird and jumps a few times, her body twisting in the air. On her last jump, she lands clumsily, and as if angry at herself for failing to catch the bird, she begins to chase her tail madly, running in circles.

Fenglan laughs. The cat stops chasing her tail and lies down on her side—this time, only a step away from Fenglan. She looks relaxed, licking herself all over and washing her face with her front paws. Fenglan closes her eyes, pretending that she has fallen asleep, her right arm dangling over one armrest. A few minutes later she feels something cold touch her fingertips—it's Niuniu's nose. Then the cat rubs her head against the back of her hand, her fur soft and warm. Fenglan opens one eye, but Niuniu jumps away immediately, across the lawn, onto the fence, and disappears.

Fenglan waits for a while and even stands on the bench, looking over the fence at the neighbors' backyard, where Niuniu disappeared. But the tabby is nowhere to be seen.

At lunchtime, Fenglan doesn't feel hungry. She turns on the TV and finds a children's program, then walks to the kitchen to warm up some leftovers in the microwave, which her grandson has taught her how to use. Since she arrived, her daughter has stuffed the fridge with meat and her mother's favorite vegetables and fruit, but Fenglan doesn't feel like cooking just for herself and always eats leftovers.

After lunch, she takes a nap on the sofa in the family room, where outside the window, a star jasmine hangs gracefully over the trellis. She dreams of her husband, who seems to have gained weight and whose facial wrinkles are less prominent than she remembers. In her dream, he walks with his hands locked behind his back and wears his warden's uniform. She calls his name, and he nods and smiles at her, as if saying, "I'm doing well. Don't worry."

After Fenglan wakes, her eyes meet the cross ornament on the wall facing her sofa, the white porcelain pieces trimmed with small purple flowers. There are half a dozen cross ornaments in the house. One used to hang on the wall in her room, made of peach wood and carved with the elegant-looking text "I love my lord" in Chinese on it. But she felt uncomfortable with it and put it in a drawer. Her older daughter must have noticed the missing cross, but she hasn't said a word about it to her mother.

Fenglan doesn't understand her daughter's religious belief. Who is Jesus? Who is God? Who is Lord? Why does a Chinese pray to a white god? These questions race through her mind whenever she sees the crosses in the house and when she hears Bob and her daughter pray before each meal. Bob usually leads the prayer. Eyes closed, head bowed, he thanks God for different things, then asks the loving father in Heaven to bless his family and his mother-in-law, while Guo-Mei and Dongdong hold the same posture, listening. At the end, they all say "Amen." As they pray, Fenglan feels awkward, not knowing what to do, only wishing that the prayer will end so that they can start to eat. A few times, she left the table and waited in her room until Dongdong called out in Mandarin, "*Wai po*, we're done!" The seriousness on her grandson's face when he listens to his father's prayer always amazes her. What does a six-year-old know about God? She decides that her daughter has taught him to believe in God just as China's Communist Party teaches kids to love the Party. How strange that she and her Communist husband would have a daughter who is a Christian! If her husband were still alive, he would undoubtedly give her daughter a long lecture on atheism and tell her not to be swindled by a capitalist religion. He was such an atheist that he would get angry with Fenglan for going to the temple. He used to say that she had been contaminated by feudal superstition.

Whenever Fenglan dreams of her husband, she lights a stick of incense and prays to Ru Lai, asking Him to look after her husband on his return to Heaven. Right before he died, his eyesight worsened severely. But he refused to wear glasses, with various excuses, for example, that prisoners wouldn't respect a bespectacled warden. After she pointed out that quite a few of his colleagues wore glasses, he insisted that glasses hurt his nose. The real reason, she guessed, was that he didn't want to admit he was aging. She gave up in the end, knowing how stubborn he was. She wished that he would stop going out alone for a walk after dinner, a habit he had kept for years. Those days, many buildings were under construction, and even people with good eyesight would trip over exposed pipes, pumps, or littered garbage. But he didn't want her to come along, saying that she walked too slowly and only wanted to go to the park.

She worried about him and would sometimes watch him from their balcony, seeing him cross a trench or a bump. In front of her or his colleagues and acquaintances, he always walked with his back straight, his steps firm, but when no one was around, he stooped and walked much more slowly, sometimes using a tree branch for aid when crossing potholed areas. He saw himself as so strong and capable that he refused to slow down at work and retained the habit of taking cold showers, even in winter.

When they first got married, he was like that too. In 1967, he was accused of sympathizing with rightists and taken away by the Red Guards. A week later he was released, after having been beaten repeatedly with belts and sticks. That evening, she saw him through the window, bent over, limping, scuffing, but as soon as he entered the door, he pretended to be fine and, to prove it, did a few push-ups. He took a small parcel from his jacket pocket and handed it to their older daughter, who had been crying because she was hungry: it contained a few biscuits. As Fenglan cleaned and dressed his wounds, he kept saying that he didn't feel pain, though a layer of cold sweat had formed on his forehead. On that evening she began to fall in love with him.

She has brought from China a picture of Ru Lai, which she purchased at You-Ming Temple right before her trip. She displays it on the windowsill, kneels in front of it, and bows deeply a few times.

It is still an hour before she has to pick up Dongdong from his kindergarten, something she looks forward to from the moment he steps into his father's or mother's car every morning. Mostly Bob or Guo-Mei picks him up, but when they are busy and cannot get off work early, or get stuck in traffic, Fenglan does. She likes walking, and it is only half an hour's walk from home to the kindergarten. Also, Dongdong likes walking with her, so he can catch bugs or pick flowers on their way back.

There is more to look forward to: Guo-Ying will drive down this evening and stay for a few days. Though it is not a long drive from San Francisco to Sunnyvale, Fenglan hopes that her younger daughter will move to Sunnyvale, so that she and her sister can see each other more often, which, she surmises, might help Guo-Ying settle down and start a family.

But Fenglan also dreads Guo-Ying's visit, knowing that she will inquire again about the old family photos, which Fenglan had brought from China upon her request. Last weekend, Guo-Ying went through each photo and asked many questions. Guo-Mei didn't show particular interest, though, only browsing through them before handing them back to her younger sister, then walking into the garden to fertilize her plants, as if she didn't want to have anything to do with the past.

"*Wai po*, I wanted to see Great-grandma and Great-grandpa's pictures," said Dongdong, jumping onto Fenglan's lap as she was explaining a photo to Guo-Ying.

She told him that she didn't have a picture of them.

"You must have at least one." He raised his head and stared at her innocently.

"It's been too long and I can't find them anymore," she said, recalling clearly how she threw their photos into the fire when the Red Guards' footsteps and shouting could be heard downstairs.

"I want to see them!" Dongdong insisted. He didn't stop nagging her until his mother told him that she was going to read him a story.

"Ma, how and when did my grandparents die?" Guo-Ying asked after Dongdong left.

"Didn't I tell you before that they died of sickness in the fifties?"

"Both of them?"

She looked away from her daughter's skeptical eyes. "It was difficult to get medicine at that time. There weren't many good doctors, either."

"How about Aunt, then?"

"She died of food poisoning during the Three-Year Natural Disaster." Fenglan replied hesitatingly, not sure if this was the same answer she had given before. "Right after the Great Leap

Forward campaign. You know, millions of people died in that famine. The weather was bad. There were droughts and floods all across China."

"Ma, the weather was just a small factor. The famine was largely due to the government's wrong policies. You knew that. If they hadn't built people's communes, hadn't forced peasants to leave their lands to produce iron and steel, hadn't promoted close cropping and deep plowing, hadn't killed all the sparrows, there wouldn't have been such widespread famine."

Fenglan looked at her daughter, a little taken aback by her bold statement. She remained silent.

Her daughter softened her tone. "What kind of food did Aunt eat—the food that poisoned her?"

"She ate poisonous mushrooms."

"Hmm . . ." Her daughter sighed. "Did you live together at that time?"

"We did."

"Did you eat the mushrooms too?"

"I did. They were mixed, some poisonous and some not. She saved the big ones for me and ate the smaller ones herself, the ones that were poisonous." It hurt Fenglan to say this, remembering her sister's sweating face, loud panting, and grip on her arm. She didn't want to go on, but she couldn't help saying more. "We had picked the mushrooms in the woods, near a village, and had started a fire to bake our harvest right there. She wanted me to eat the big ones, so she told me that she liked the taste of the smaller ones better. I was silly enough to believe her. Later, I managed to find the doctor from the village for help. He was young, barely twenty. He wasn't a real doctor, and all he had done before was treat pigs and dogs. But he was the only help I could find. He gave your aunt the wrong medicine. I shouldn't have trusted him. How stupid I was!" She realized that this was the first time she had revealed this information to her daughter.

Her daughter sighed again, then held up a photo of her aunt. "She was very pretty."

"She was. You have her eyes and mouth," Fenglan said and stood. "I'm very tired and want to go to bed now."

Guo-Ying looked into her eyes with concern and said that she would ask her more next time.

Now, alone in the quiet house, as Fenglan thinks of those faded old photos, the door to her memory opens slowly.

Her father used to be a superintendent at an all-female college. He liked to talk about politics with his colleagues and students. Deeply skeptical of the Nationalist Party's ability to run the country, he longed for a revolution and often wrote articles criticizing the government. He had many visitors, and they sometimes would talk over tea from dawn to dusk, their faces red with excitement. Apart from politics, her father enjoyed practicing calligraphy and began to teach his daughters to write when they could barely hold a brush. Her mother was born of a family that had become rich through selling fabrics. When her family's business was at its peak, they owned more than half the fabric stores in their city. Tutored at home by an erudite, old-fashioned teacher, she became a good painter and poet. Though she was never interested in politics, she was her husband's best listener and supporter. After the Japanese occupied the city, her family's business began to go downhill, and it was devastated further by the Civil War until it went bankrupt in early 1949, the year the Communist Party forced its rival, the Nationalist Party, to retreat to Taiwan.

Throughout the wars, the family moved often but never separated. In Fenglan's memory, she and her sister were always happy. Many days, they played games on their patio, their mother sitting on a stool next to them, sewing clothes or making shoe pads, her fingers adroit and her posture graceful. Their father, though often writing or reading in his study, would sometimes poke his head out of the window, brush in hand, and watch them play. One of their favorite games was invented by their father. When they played it, they slapped each other's hands and sang rhythmically.

"You slap my hand once, I slap your hand once, now let's tell the story about a kid playing with mud.

"You slap my hand twice, I slap your hand twice, now let's tell the story about two eagles looking for wizards.

"You slap my hand thrice, I slap your hand thrice, now we have a story of three monkeys crossing the mountains.

After they chanted all the way to "You slap my hand ten times," and indeed slapped each other's hands ten times, they would start the game over again, sometimes making up their own words. The song didn't make sense, but they loved the rhythm and never got tired of singing it. While playing the game, they glanced now and then at their parents.

When the Communists entered their city in April 1949, Fenglan, then seven years old, and her sister followed their parents to the widest street, greeting the Liberation Army with thousands of people, who waved small red flags and chanted "Welcome! Welcome!" A squad of young men and women who looked like students were dancing *yang ge,* a dance they must have learned from the people in the north, swinging their bodies exaggeratedly to the *suo na* music of "The Sky in the Liberated District." On that day, her father wore his best blue silk *changpao,* and his shaved face was smooth and youthful. He hoisted Fenglan onto his shoulders and held her hands to clap. They had pushed their way to the front of the crowd, where they could see clearly the uniformed soldiers marching with rifles against their shoulders. Fenglan had never seen her father so happy, so she clapped as loudly as she could, feeling like dancing on her father's shoulders.

When her hands hurt from clapping, she played with her father's glasses. She took them from his nose and put them on herself. She tilted her head upward so the glasses wouldn't slide down. Everything looked blurred and distorted through the thick lenses. The beautiful orange sun seemed to have exploded into a deep ocean that could drown her. She held the glasses in place with one hand and looked at the procession: the soldiers became slanting shadows. Dizzy and startled, she took the glasses off and wiped her eyes: now the sun was orange again, and the soldiers were striding with straight backs. She turned to look at her mother, who stood with her father, holding her sister beside her. She wore a pink *qipao,* her hair combed back into a bun, her powdered face illuminated with what seemed like a golden halo. How pretty she was! Fenglan thought. Her sister was applauding, jumping up and down, her long plaits, decorated with two red butterfly bows, bouncing on her chest, her red leather shoes shiny with polish.

Fenglan wanted to put her father's glasses on again, to see what her sister's bows and shoes would look like from behind those magic lenses. But her father took them away, saying that he couldn't see anything without them. At this moment, an official with a pistol at his belt walked over and shook her father's hand, then her mother's. They must have known one another. They chatted briefly, wishing one another a bright future in the brand-new society. Before that official returned to the procession, he pinched Fenglan's cheek lightly. "Little girl, you're very lucky indeed. Now, the Japanese devils are gone, Jiang Jieshi and his Nationalists have escaped to Taiwan. The Chinese people are their own masters. You'll go to school and go to college someday, becoming a scholar like your father. Aren't you the luckiest child in the world?"

As he pinched her cheek, she was still thinking about the orange sun that looked like a huge, deep ocean through her father's glasses, that seemed to be able to swallow her.

Was it an omen? Later, after so many things had happened, after both of her parents had died, she asked herself this question.

Not long after the Liberation, a series of political movements started. Within two years her father lost his teaching position, accused of using college money to buy books for himself, an accusation he denied. Though there was no evidence, her father was interrogated for months and forced to pay reparation to his college. He was also physically tortured. Angry and humiliated, he fell ill and died one year later. Lacking money to buy a coffin, her mother had to wrap her husband in a straw mat and bury him in it. He was wearing the blue silk *changpao* he had worn four years earlier to welcome the Liberation Army. Before long, her mother, who ate and slept little, calling her husband's name all the time, died from grief. That year, Fenglan was eleven and her sister thirteen. Then, when she was eighteen, her sister died. In 1962, she met a man from an Anti-rightist Working Team; the man liked her. Though she had no feeling for him—he was much older and had little education—she married him.

Her husband had been born of a poor peasant family, a background favored by the Party. He named their two daughters Guo-Mei and Guo-Ying, meaning "China is beautiful" and "China is outstanding," respectively. It had never occurred to them that the two names, if read in reverse—*meiguo* and *yingguo,* meant "America" and "Britain," and if the last characters of their names, *Mei* and *Ying,* were read with the last character of Fenglan's husband's name, *Qiang,* it became a statement: "America and Britain are strong." It was not until two years after the Cultural Revolution ended that one of her husband's friends pointed out this coincidence, which shocked Fenglan and her husband. If this naming thing had been used against them during the Cultural Revolution, they would have been condemned as counterrevolutionaries and thrown into jail. But now, there was no need to change their daughters' names. Of course, they didn't know that as soon as their daughters left China they would assume English names that meant nothing in Chinese.

Sometimes, Fenglan thinks that, with her bourgeois and capitalist family background, she wouldn't have survived all the political tumult had she not married her husband. She has never told all this to her daughters. If they asked how she met their father, she would say that a common friend introduced them, and if they asked how their maternal grandparents died, she would say that they died of diseases.

She doesn't want to tell them the truth. Not a single word.

To her, the history is a scar that never heals, the best medicine is to forget. What can she do about it anyway? she sometimes reasons with herself. She cannot rewrite the history, cannot bring the buried people back to life or retrieve her lost youth and opportunities. While a country or a people can leave the past behind and restart, as a marathon runner who lags in the beginning of a race because of an ankle sprain can catch up after relaxing his muscles and may even win, there is no recovery for a broken family or a lost life. However trivial a person's or a family's suffering may seem compared with a country's, it is substantial to that person, to that family. All lost lives are lost forever, and the survivors have to live with grief for the rest of their lives.

Of course, Fenglan cannot forget the past as she wishes. It was harder when she was younger. As she was cooking, or breast-feeding her babies, or boxing car parts on the production line, the images of her parents being buried and her sister's pain-stricken face would creep into her mind. But she didn't let herself be carried away. She would shake her head, as if this physical movement could wipe out all the memories that were about to explode in her brain. She was eager to distract herself, which was not difficult because her bored colleagues on the production line always had something to talk about: this person's child peed on the bed the night before, that person forgot to put a bag of tofu into the fridge and it went bad, yet another person discovered that the soup noodles sold by a vendor at a particular market had a few extra pieces of meat in them compared with those sold by other vendors. Fenglan listened and commented on each incident. If they laughed, she laughed with them; if they were angry about something, she told them that they had good reason to be angry. Time went by fast with all the talking. The easiest way to keep from thinking about the past, she realized, was to surround herself with sounds and voices.

At home, when she was alone, she turned on the radio or TV, setting the volume high, letting the sound fill her brain like boiling water filling a thermos. As soon as the water reached the mouth of the thermos, she pushed down the wood cork. At first, the water would bubble and sizzle, shoving the cork upward, but soon all the action would die down and the water would settle quietly. So it was in her mind. Fill, then still.

Later, in the mid-eighties, when a leader in her factory found out that she had beautiful handwriting—a gift from her parents—she was assigned to work in the Propaganda Department, transcribing the leaders' speeches and announcements, a job she liked because it required her to focus. That too filled her mind and obliterated the memories that were always waiting for her.

She is not the kind of person who likes to think about philosophical questions. If asked whether she has any complains about her life, she would say no. Didn't millions of Chinese live their lives just as she did in the past few decades? She has painful memories, so have they.

In fact, she feels that life has treated her fairly: her parents were kind and loving; she had a happy childhood, however brief; she didn't die of hunger or illness in the Mao era; her husband loved her and took good care of her; her daughters both got good educations and have done well in their lives. The old saying goes, "The key of happiness lies in being content." So she believes.

She has her secret, but she is determined to take it with her to the grave.

After dinner on a Tuesday, Fenglan and her older daughter sit in the family room watching Chinese news on TV while Bob and Dongdong are assembling a Lego plane in Dongdong's room.

"Let's turn off the TV. I watch it every day," Fenglan suggests. It is rare that her daughter has a free evening, so she wants to chat. These days, her daughter talks little; she is forgetful, less patient, and when she cooks, she often mistakes vinegar for soy sauce, salt for sugar. Once, making soup, she poured half a can of salt into it, and if Fenglan hadn't stopped her, she would have emptied the entire can. Often they have to eat out or order take-out because the food her daughter has prepared is not edible.

Even Dongdong has sensed her mother's absentmindedness and has been taking advantage of it. Every night, as she supervises his piano practice, she nods idly, saying "Good" to every song, even when he is obviously playing nonsense. Enjoying fooling his mother, Dongdong can barely contain his laughter: he has to bite his lips hard and twist his small body on the bench to keep from giggling.

Once, Fenglan overheard a conversation between her daughter and Bob. To Bob's inquiry about her recent absentmindedness, her daughter replied that she was just stressed out at work.

Her daughter now turns off the TV with the remote control. She yawns and lies half reclined against a sofa arm, two pillows stacked behind her back. She rubs her eyes, runs her hands over her face, and yawns again. Sitting in a single chair next to the sofa, Fenglan observes her daughter.

"Guo-Mei, have you been very busy at work?" she asks.

"Not too bad." Her daughter repositions her head on the sofa arm so it's easier to talk with her mother.

"Do you want me to fix you some ginseng soup? It isn't easy to work in a capitalist country, and you must take care of yourself. You aren't an eighteen-year-old anymore." She pauses. "I must have been a burden to you."

"Ma, what are you talking about? You're my mother. Don't speculate too much, everything is fine."

"Don't lie to me. I can tell that something is wrong." She lowers her voice, glancing toward Dongdong's room, though she knows that Bob cannot understand their conversation. "Did you have a fight with Bob?"

"No. We get along well."

"Bob doesn't seem to talk much."

"He has a tough job. When he gets home, he's tired."

"I can see that. Can he work less? It's not worthwhile putting his whole life into a job."

"He won't listen to me. I mean, it's not up to him. All his colleagues also work very hard. Things will be better after his company completes its IPO."

"What is that?"

Her daughter smiles. "You won't understand even if I told you."

"You two need to talk more. If he's not happy with me, you should just tell me. It must be hard for him to have me around in his house all the time. He can't even talk with me."

"What do you mean 'his house'? It's also my house. I own fifty percent of it. Ma, you think too much. Bob is fine with you staying with us. He and I have talked about it before. He can't speak Mandarin or he'd have told you that himself."

Fenglan doesn't believe this but decides not to confront her daughter. "Are you having trouble with your church? Or is there anything wrong with your sister or Dongdong? Do you have a problem paying your mortgage?"

"Ma, I've told you that everything is fine." Her daughter's voice is slightly higher now. "There's nothing to worry about. If you really want to know, it's just that I have a tough project at work. That's it. It's actually a good project and will help me with my career." She sits up, faces Fenglan, and smiles at her. "Ma, I'm glad you're here, taking care of Dongdong. It's a big help to me."

But Fenglan knows that her daughter said this just to console her.

"What will you do with your apartment in China after you move here?" Her daughter diverts the conversation.

"Let's just keep it. If I don't like living here, I'll still have a place to stay in China."

"I don't think it's a good idea for you to live alone. What if you get sick or have an accident? You have no one to look after you."

"I'm quite healthy. Doctor Du in the Women's and Children's Hospital said that I could live to at least ninety. It's normal for people my age to get ill now and then. No one can go against nature. But we won't die so easily. Haven't I been doing okay all these years since your father passed away? Of course, I wished I could see you and Guo-Ying more often. I used to think that you might move back to China. Now I realize that you like living here better." Considering that her daughter might think she was complaining about living alone, she adds, "I understand that you and Guo-Ying have your own careers. If you choose to live here, it's fine. I'm just happy that you are doing well."

"Ma, I still think you should live with me. The air quality here is better, crossing the street is safer. Also, don't you want to see Dongdong growing up? He'll be very sad if you leave."

"Of course I want to see him growing up, but . . ." She stops, feeling the dilemma. She has wanted to tell her daughter that she'd like to return to China in another few weeks so she wouldn't be a burden to her and Bob. The more she thinks about it, the more she is convinced that her daughter must have been fighting with Bob about her—that's why Guo-Mei has been beside herself lately. Bob is polite to her, but they cannot talk with each other. The first few days after she arrived, he would smile and say in Mandarin "good morning," "good afternoon," or "good evening." But now he avoided her. If she was in the living room, he stayed away; if she was in the kitchen, he asked Dongdong to get him a beer or a glass of water. A few times he was about to step out of his bedroom, but as soon as he saw Fenglan in the hallway, he withdrew into the room. And if he couldn't avoid her, he gave her an awkward and quick smile. She had sensed his discomfort and had tried to avoid him as well. Sometimes, she went for a walk so she wouldn't be in the way.

She understands Bob: it must be difficult for him to live with an old woman from China who doesn't speak English. Her being his mother-in-law must make things even more complicated. If her daughter were pregnant or had a newborn, Fenglan would feel more comfortable living with her and Bob because she could at least offer help. But Dongdong is old enough to play by himself, and with his schedule filled with school and all kinds of extra classes, he has little time to be with her. Extra, unnecessary: that's how she sees herself in her daughter's family.

Also, her life here is limited, as she has begun to see more clearly day by day: she cannot drive, cannot speak English, cannot read road signs, cannot take a bus, cannot go shopping, doesn't have friends, and doesn't dare walk far in case she gets lost. She regrets that she has agreed to emigrate. Now, her daughter has spent so much money on her. How can she just tell her that she's changed her mind? What's more, her daughter has tried hard to keep her entertained. On weekends, she takes her to beaches, parks, shopping malls, and other points of interest; she has subscribed to two Chinese newspapers and rents Chinese movies and TV shows all the time; she introduces her to her church friends and their parents and has hosted a few potlucks. Fenglan likes Guo-Mei's church friends, especially Mingyi, Yaya, and Julia. The three of them visit her often, bringing small gifts, this time a tin of tea, next time a pair of warm socks. Sometimes, Mingyi stays for hours to chat with her. Just a few days ago, her daughter said that she would take some days off and accompany Fenglan to Disneyland, Las Vegas, and the Grand Canyon. Whenever Fenglan thinks of what her daughter has done for her, she feels that she must stay a little longer before announcing that she wants to go back to China.

Apparently having interpreted Fenglan's silence as assent, her daughter says, "Ma, you'll get used to living here soon. You've met some of my church friends' parents, right? Didn't they say that they liked living here?"

They are all couples and have been here for years, Fenglan thinks. But she doesn't want to disappoint her daughter, so she says, "I'll try."

"It's a little cold. I'll start a fire," her daughter says.

"Isn't the heater on? Why waste money to burn logs?" She has seen firewood at Safeway—more than ten dollars, one fifth of her monthly salary from her factory, for only five or six logs. Ridiculously expensive.

But her daughter seems not to have heard her. She walks to the garage and returns with an armful of logs. As she starts the fire she says, "It is awfully cold tonight, don't you think? The weather is unpredictable these days. One day it's warm enough to wear shirtsleeves; the next day you have to wear a sweater."

The logs are dry. Soon the fire burns vigorously, its flames licking the chimney walls. "Now it's warm," her daughter says to herself, sitting on the floor next to the fireplace, her legs drawn up, her chin on her knees. She stares at the fire intently.

"I've never told you this, but your father and I met at an evening dance," Fenglan tells her daughter. "It was held outside, in an empty field, lit by bonfires. Most of the people there were young, and we did a group dance popular at the time."

"Did Baba know how to dance?" There is doubt in Guo-Mei's tone.

"He was a good dancer. Girls liked to dance with him because he knew how to lead."

Her daughter is silent, then asks suddenly, "Ma, did you ever love Baba?"

Fenglan is startled, thinking that her daughter is becoming an American now, asking her own mother such a question.

"Who talked about love in our generation? Your baba and I were together for almost thirty years."

"Did you love Baba when you married him?"

"We weren't intellectuals. As long as we had a place to live and something to eat, we were happy. In those days, people just didn't date like you do now. A lot of times, your work unit arranged your marriage for you."

"If you had the freedom, would you have chosen Baba?" Her daughter is strangely stubborn, looking into her face.

"Guo-Mei, what kind of question is this?" Fenglan pretends to be angry, avoiding eye contact.

Her daughter shakes her head slightly, as if to say, "I knew you wouldn't tell me the truth." Then she looks back at the fire. "Do you remember that our house caught fire once?"

"Of course I remember. You were barely seven at the time. If our neighbor hadn't found out and saved you and your sister . . . What a nightmare! Thinking of it gives me goose bumps."

"We lost a nice cabinet and a stool Guo-Ying liked."

"The cabinet was one of the only two pieces of furniture your baba and I bought when we got married. Your baba knew a carpenter and got a good price from him. The other was our bed, the one I still sleep in today."

"I set the fire." Her daughter's voice is low yet calm.

"Oh . . . hmm . . . Is it true?" She leans forward.

"Every day you and Baba left home early and came home late. When neither of you was home, I had to take care of Guo-Ying—feeding her, dressing her, playing with her, cleaning her. Once, in winter, Baba was gone for a few months. You said he went on a business trip. Of course you were lying to me. I thought that he didn't want us anymore. One day during Baba's absence, as soon as you left the house, Guo-Ying began to cry and wouldn't stop. Then she wet her pants. I took off her pants but couldn't find dry ones, so I used my face towel to wrap her. The scratchy towel must have been very uncomfortable. She cried louder. I was sleepy, hungry, and cold. There wasn't enough food in the house—and I had to feed Guo-Ying first."

Her daughter shoots her a quick smile as if this will somehow lessen the tragic effect of her words. Fenglan forces herself to hold her daughter's eyes: they are hers, her husband used to say. Her daughter looks away and continues.

"Somehow I remembered Hans Christian Andersen's story of a girl selling matches, which I had heard from someone. The little girl has to sell matches on a snowy and windy evening, wearing neither a hat nor shoes. She doesn't have much luck, and when she is freezing she lights a match to warm herself. In the match's faint flame, she feels that she is sitting next to a burning stove. But as the wind blows out the flame, the stove disappears. She lights a match again—this time, she sees delicious food and even a roasted goose. But again they disappear when the match goes out. By the light of the third match, she sees her grandma, whom she loves. Afraid of losing her, the little girl lights all her remaining matches. Then she dies, with a smile on her face.

"I went to the kitchen and got a box of matches, thinking that I might see something nice if I struck a match. As soon as I struck a match, Guo-Ying stopped crying and stared at the flame. I did another one; this time, she applauded and smiled. I suddenly thought that if I wasn't alive, I wouldn't have to babysit Guo-Ying and I wouldn't feel sleepy, cold, or hungry. How nice that would be! But if I died, what about Guo-Ying? She'd only cry louder. So I decided that we had to die together. I lit a bundle of dry straw in the kitchen, then sat with Guo-Ying in the outer room, where we could see the fire. You should have seen how happy she was. She was dancing, laughing, almost choking herself with giggles. I was happy too, forgetting my hunger and cold, and laughed with her. I saw the fire coming toward me, and I felt warm. I don't know when I lost consciousness, but when I woke up, I was sleeping on the neighbor's bed, with Guo-Ying next to me."

Fenglan is frozen in her chair; she has trouble breathing. She turns her head away from her daughter's gaze so she can recover.

"Ma, don't feel sad. It's all in the past. Aren't Guo-Ying and I doing well?" Her daughter stirs the fire with a wrought-iron poker to make the logs burn better.

Fenglan speaks after a long silence, her voice dry. "Your baba was condemned at that time. I had to work to make money and had to try to save your baba. We wanted to be with you and Guo-Ying, but we couldn't." What a weak explanation, she thinks. Really, she was a terrible mother, leaving her small children at home like that. But where could she find people willing to look after two children with a condemned father and a mother with a capitalist background?

"You don't have to explain. I understand your and Baba's situations. Few families could lead a normal life at that time. I hadn't wanted to tell you about the fire; somehow, it just came up. It's odd, but all these years I've always felt that I have to take care of Guo-Ying. I almost killed her, you know." Her daughter moves to the sofa opposite her mother. "Ma, there's one thing that I've always wanted to ask you."

"What is it?"

"Am I your blood daughter or not?"

"Why do you ask? Of course you are."

"I'm a mother myself now. I can take the truth."

"But you're your baba's and my blood daughter."

"I don't believe you. If I were your blood daughter, why did you send me to a village to live with strangers when you were pregnant with Guo-Ying? Everyone in that village said I was illegitimate, and no kids wanted to play with me. I just want to know the truth."

Fenglan sees bitterness and anger in her daughter's eyes. Maybe she'll have to tell her the truth, she thinks—it's impossible to keep silent or lie in front of those eyes. She had thought that she could take the secret with her to her grave. But now the time has come.

"You're our blood daughter, but Guo-Ying has a different father."

Guo-Mei's eyes narrow with disbelief.

"I never betrayed your father, if that's what you are thinking." As Fenglan launches into her speech, she plays every detail in her mind. If time is a jigsaw puzzle, she is putting it together piece by piece.

"One day, a group of Red Guards came to our house and told your father that it had been a crime to marry me, someone with an undesirable family background. They said that if he would divorce me, he would still be Mao's good soldier. He said no, he'd never divorce me. The Red Guards took him away, and that night he didn't come home."

"I remember that night," her daughter says. "But just a little. You sat on a stool, looking out the window for hours."

"You were only five years old. I thought you'd be too young to remember anything at all. The next day I looked for your father everywhere and was later told that he was in the hands of someone called Old Hu. It took me a while to find Old Hu. In his office, he told me that your father had damaged his house with some Red Guards one year earlier. Now the days were different, and he, previously a condemned rightist, had become a powerful leader. He wanted revenge. What a horrible smile he had on his face when he said that! I begged him to release your father. At last he said he would do it if I agreed to one thing." She pauses and takes a deep breath. When she meets her daughter's widened eyes, she turns away to look at the floor.

"I had no other option. I thought then that I'd kill myself after your father returned safely—at least he could look after you. Your father came back a few days later. By then I was so full of shame and guilt that I was determined to die. Among the people I knew, quite a few had committed suicide, so I wasn't so scared of this idea. Your father guessed what had happened and told me that if I died, he'd kill himself as well. I knew he said this to keep me alive. I listened to him eventually, but I became hysterical and often had nightmares and delusions. Once, I almost choked you to death while dreaming.

Another time, as I bathed you, I was so haunted by my memory that I imagined you being the vicious Old Hu. I pressed your head into the water, and it was not until your father heard you screaming and came to rescue you that I realized what I was doing.

"After all these accidents, your father suggested we send you away for a while, saying that at least you would be safe. We couldn't find anyone in the city willing to look after you. A friend mentioned distant relatives of his in a village who might let you stay with them temporarily, in exchange for food and money. So we sent you there. Then I found out I was pregnant by Old Hu. I wanted to get an abortion, but the doctor said I was too weak and the procedure might kill me. With so many doctors exiled to the countryside and the hospitals being chaotic, I might not even be able to find someone to perform the abortion. Your father begged me to keep the baby. I agreed, but behind his back I ate the herbs said to cause an abortion, and in the winter I went to the creek and stood in the icy water till I nearly lost consciousness. When all this didn't work, I began to think that I should give the birth to the baby: she hadn't done anything wrong and didn't deserve to die."

Fenglan hears her daughter's sobbing but decides to continue the story: Guo-Mei is a mother herself now, and she should know the truth, to know that her parents weren't as heartless as she thought.

"So Guo-Ying came into the world. I wasn't planning to raise her myself—whenever I saw her, I was reminded of my humiliation and guilt. I thought I'd leave her outside a decent-looking house and maybe that family would adopt her. But whenever I put her down outside some stranger's house, she smiled at me, as if I were playing a game with her. Then I didn't have the heart to abandon her. I took her out in a basket many times, but each time I brought her back home."

Though Fenglan's voice had faltered slightly at first, as she continues to speak, it becomes composed and smooth, and her face tranquil, as if she were telling a story from an ancient book. Only she knows that this calmness and distance have protected her, keeping her sane and alive. As for her tears, they dried a long time ago. What is left in her eyes is peace. Now she suddenly feels tired and cold, sensing the illusion that she was standing on a barren field, alone, surrounded by chilly wind: only the soft cream-colored carpet and the fire still burning in the fireplace, though no longer blazing, assure her that she is in her daughter's snug and cozy house.

Head bowed, her daughter covers her face slowly with the palms of her hands. She sits like this for a while, then walks over to Fenglan. She sits next to her, snuggles up, then embraces her with both hands, pressing a cheek against hers. Fenglan strokes her daughter's head and teary face.

In Dongdong's room, Bob and Dongdong burst into laughter. Dongdong shouts in Mandarin, "*Wai po,* Mama, come here! Look at the monster that Dad has put together for me! Come quick!"

ELEVEN

January

ON A THURSDAY AFTERNOON, Ingrid drives to Sunnyvale. Today is her thirty-second birthday. Mary has called several times, asking her to arrive early.

Her mother is in the kitchen making cold dishes: tofu and preserved eggs, spicy seaweed, roasted peanuts with small dry fish, and sweet-and-sour cucumber slices. Alex insists on helping his grandma fetch different ingredients. Not being able to reach the cabinet, he has to get a stool from his room. But when he comes back, his impatient grandma has already gotten them herself. He forces her to put everything back where it was, then stands on the stool and takes down the bottles one by one.

"Dongdong, you only know how to give me trouble," his grandma says, pretending to be angry, though she is smiling.

"The food will taste better if I help you prepare it," Alex disputes, speaking Mandarin, then turns to Ingrid, who is steadying the stool for him. "Aunt, isn't it true?"

"Of course, it's true. You have a magic hand. Everything you've touched becomes better," she says, passing the bottles to her mother. As Alex gets down, he puts his arms around Ingrid's neck. She holds him to her chest and whirls him around, making sure his flying feet won't hit anything. "Hold tight! We're flying." Alex presses his cheek to her neck. "Aunt and I are flying to Shanghai to see San Mao!"

"San Mao?" Ingrid asks.

"Mother has been telling him San Mao's story," Mary explains. She breaks a few eggs into a bowl and stirs them clockwise with chopsticks.

"How interesting! That was my favorite story when I was little." Ingrid puts Alex down. "Mary, I think you read me the story."

"I surely did. You bugged me every day to tell you more."

"And you made up a lot of stuff. I remember you once spent the whole evening describing a duck dish San Mao and another homeless kid cooked. The same duck was broiled, fried, roasted, baked, and smoked at least ten times."

"I must have been hungry." Mary laughs.

"You liked San Mao too?" Alex tugs Ingrid's shirt. "Aunt, let's go to Shanghai to see San Mao this Christmas. I have a lot of gifts for him. Do you think he wants to learn how to play the piano? I can teach him, and I won't hit him if he doesn't do well."

Ingrid squats to hold Alex's hands. "Yeah, let's go to Shanghai someday to visit him. Now you speak Mandarin so well, you can talk with him in it."

Alex leans forward and whispers in English, eyeing his grandma, "Aunt, you won't leave Mom and me again, right?"

She looks at his twinkling eyes. How fast Alex has grown in the past three years! When she left California for New York, he had just learned how to dress himself and started to speak in sentences. She nods hard. He smiles and gives her a high five.

She turns to look at Mary and their mother, who are chatting intimately at the sink, and feels a new appreciation for both of them.

"Oh, Ingrid," Mary suddenly says. "You have a letter. It's been here for a while. I forgot to give it to you. It's on the living room coffee table. From someone called Bing'er. Is she Chinese?"

"Yeah. I met her in New York." Ingrid goes to the living room to fetch the letter. "This girl dreams of traveling the world. Now, she's planning to drive across the U.S. alone. Amazing, isn't it? Also, she's a very good painter."

"I didn't know you had Chinese friends." Mary's voice is low.

"Mary, I heard that." Ingrid returns to the kitchen with the letter. "There are a lot of things you don't know about me."

Mary smiles, not wanting to contradict her in front of their mother, and continues with her chores.

Ingrid opens the letter. Bing'er says she just purchased a 1988 Jeep Cherokee for eight hundred Canadian dollars. She lists the U.S. cities and towns she wants to visit. She has also enclosed a sketch she drew on a trip to Niagara Falls: a pointed-roofed farmhouse against the setting sun. The "grand journey" will begin in mid-March, she wrote.

Since their encounter in Bryant Park, Ingrid and Bing'er have kept in touch through e-mail and letters. The week before Ingrid left New York for San Francisco, Bing'er showed up at her apartment. She stayed with her for four days, rising early to tour the city; in the late afternoons she drew portraits for five dollars each in different parts of the city—that was how she planned to fund her road trip when she ran out of money. Once, she was almost arrested for not having a license to perform on the street.

Thinking of Bing'er cheers Ingrid up. That girl has the spirit of a free bird! Ingrid liked to hear her talk about how she had traveled to Guangdong Province to purchase the latest fashions at evening markets teeming with vendors, and the people she had met in the government and while doing business. ("Do you believe that some factories in Guangdong limit how many times workers can go to bathroom during work hours? If they exceeded the limit, they have to pay a fine." "I once went to a small merchandise market that sold Chairman Mao souvenirs. All kinds of them. Pictures, badges, calendars, posters, mugs, vases, coins, sculptures. Just about everything. It was said that Chairman Mao could bless your safety and keep away disasters and ghosts, and if his picture was hung inside a car, you'd never have an accident. Who would dare to bump into Chairman Mao's car?" Bing'er had so much to tell, and Ingrid listened and asked questions as if she had never set foot in China. Though this girl is her junior by a decade, Ingrid somehow feels that through her she has reconnected with China.

Ingrid notices that there is a basket of fresh flowers in the kitchen's bay window.

"Mary, where did you get the flowers?" She walks over to take a better look. "The arrangement looks odd. So many on this side, so few on the other. And this leaf . . . hmm . . . Is this some kind of modern style?"

Mary raises her head from the cutting board and jerks her chin at their mother, chuckling. "Believe it or not, Ma did it!"

"Wow, Ma, when did you start to be interested in arranging flowers?" Ingrid asks.

"Your sister forced me to take a class offered by one of her church friends." Her mother looks embarrassed. "I told her I couldn't learn this kind of fancy stuff. It's Japanese, isn't it? I can't even hold my hands steady."

"But you can do beautiful paper cutting," Mary disagrees. "That requires a lot more work."

"Your grandma taught me that when I was little. You should see what she could do. She didn't even need to draw a pattern on the paper first. It was all in her mind. She just used a pair of scissors to cut here and there, and when she opened the folded paper, it was a nice image. On holidays, the neighbors always asked her to cut something for them to paste on the windows."

"I didn't know Grandma was an artist," Ingrid says.

"She was just interested in many things," her mother says, placing two plates of cold dishes on the dining table. Then she calls Alex to set the table with her.

"What other things did Grandma like to do?" Ingrid asks.

"She could paint, sew, play music, make dolls, crochet, and she was good with flowers."

"She sounds like a talented heroine in one of the classic novels," Ingrid remarks.

"If she could have lived to see you and your sister growing up . . ." Her mother's voice trails off. Then she switches the topic. "I think I should drop the flower-arranging class. The other day, the teacher asked me if I could differentiate red from orange and blue from green. I don't think she's happy with me."

"Ma, don't think too much," Mary says. "Mrs. Liu is very nice and patient. She'll never be unhappy with you. Oh, also, another church friend, Mrs. Zhou, a retired doctor, asked me if you'd be interested in taking an advanced *tai ji* class with her at a private studio. The teacher speaks Mandarin. She can pick you up and give you a ride home."

"I know you want me to have something to do here. But if I go back to China now, you won't have to trouble yourself so much to send me to this class and that class."

"Ma!" Mary looks at her mother. "Didn't you say yesterday that we wouldn't talk about it until next month?"

"*Wai po*, you can't go back to China. I won't let you." Alex grips his grandma's arm. "Promise you're not leaving or I won't let go of your arm."

"I won't leave you, I promise," his grandma says. "Now, let's take these plates to the table."

"No. I want to play on the swings now. Let's go out in the yard and play."

"Ma," Ingrid says. "Why don't you take a rest? I'll set the table."

After her mother and Alex leave, Ingrid asks Mary, "Is Bob still so busy?"

Mary nods. "Worse than before. His company recently laid off fifteen people, a few from his team. He has to do two people's work now. Last week his boss told him that he needed to visit clients every other week. His traveling schedule is grueling. The day before yesterday he was in Phoenix, yesterday in Atlanta, today in Boston. I hope he can get enough sleep. The economy is quite bad right now. An Internet stock Julia bought last year at $150 a share has dropped to below $5. It once reached $250 a share. She didn't sell at that time, thinking it'd go higher. Isn't it crazy? In fact, my company will have a staff meeting next week. The rumor is that our CEO will announce layoffs. At least a twenty percent reduction."

"Are you worried?"

"Worrying doesn't help. I pray every day, though," Mary says, without looking up from the cutting board, where her knife is making rhythmic chopping sounds. In no time, a few stems of green onions turn into a small pile of pulp. She pushes the pulp with her knife to a corner of the board, then picks up a Chinese squash from a plate on the counter. She cuts it into thin slices so that they stack together evenly, then slices them into thin strips—while her right hand does the chopping, her left hand moves the slices. Her hands coordinate harmoniously, as if they were dancing. After placing the strips in a bowl Ingrid has handed her, Mary starts to work on the fish, a silver cod. She scrapes the scales off and guts it. After washing it, she makes several diagonal slices along both sides of the fish so that the sauce can seep into the meat. She looks absorbed, a faint smile at the corners of her mouth, as if she were preparing a work of art.

Ingrid has wanted to tease Mary, asking her when she stopped buying live fish—Mary used to say that the trick to a good fish dish was to start with a live fish. But seeing how immersed her sister is in her cooking, Ingrid refrains from asking; she even feels the need to remain silent. When she is alone with Mary, silence doesn't make her uncomfortable, and she knows that it doesn't bother Mary, either. Because of their age difference, as they grew up, silence between them was more usual than chitchat. When Ingrid started primary school, Mary was already in middle school; when Ingrid entered middle school, Mary was preparing for the college entrance test. By the time Ingrid went to college, Mary had graduated and left China. Before high school, Mary used to tell Ingrid stories and play with her, but still, most days, they read different books, hung out with different friends, and played different games.

Before Mary went abroad, Ingrid had never seen her cook, not even so much as help their mother in the kitchen. Mary would accompany their mother to the market, but it was Ingrid, when she was old enough, who helped their mother with chopping and cleaning. Mary disliked being in the kitchen, and as soon as she put the grocery basket on the floor there, she would go to her room, leaving their mother to unpack the contents. What a miracle that Mary is now so into cooking! Ingrid thinks, while she herself has not the slightest interest in it.

In Ingrid's eyes, Mary has certainly changed since she left China: she is quieter, more withdrawn, and has developed such an enthusiasm for housework that no matter whether she is cooking, vacuuming, cleaning the windows, or tending the garden, she does it contentedly and joyfully, the way someone sinks into meditation, freeing herself from the bondage of earthbound souls.

Ingrid regards her sister's profile—slightly bent, head lowered—with both curiosity and sadness. What has changed her so much? Her marriage, her religion, her being a mother, or just the simple fact of growing older? If only she could be as peaceful as Mary. And if she could just understand what was on her mind. But Mary looks the most beautiful and gracious when she's in her own world, with an intense femininity, like their mother when she was young and still pretty.

The dinner is a feast. Apart from the soup and cold dishes, there are six main courses, including fried crabs with ginger and green onions. After dinner, they move to the family room, and Mary serves a chestnut-flavored birthday cake, Ingrid's favorite, that she has bought from a Hongkongese bakery. While eating the cake, Ingrid unwraps her gifts, which include a cashmere hat her mother crocheted.

After helping clean the kitchen, Ingrid walks to the backyard to smoke. Mary soon joins her, after starting a Chinese cartoon movie for their mother and Alex. In a short while, their mother comes to the back door. Wearing indoor slippers, she stays inside.

"It's so cold outside. What are you doing here?" She looks anxious.

"Ma, it's not that cold," Ingrid says. "Why don't you go and watch the movie with Dongdong? We won't stay out for long."

"Oh, Guo-Mei." Their mother turns to Mary: her lips move, but nothing comes out.

"Ma." Mary walks over to the door and puts her hands on their mother's shoulders. "There's nothing to worry about. Okay? Guo-Ying and I just wanted to chat a little." Their mother nods after a brief hesitation and returns to the family room, but a minute later, she appears at the door with two thick jackets.

"Guo-Mei," she addresses Mary, handing her the jackets. "It's your sister's birthday. Why don't we watch the movie together?" she pleads.

"We'll join you later," Ingrid says.

"Mary, what's going on?" Ingrid asks after their mother leaves. "Ma's acting weird."

Mary gives one jacket to Ingrid and puts on the other. "Ma was just afraid that we'd catch cold. You'd better put on your jacket now."

They sit on the bench facing the wisteria trellis.

"Do you mind?" Ingrid gestures with her chin at the half-smoked cigarette between her fingers.

"No, not at all. Go ahead," Mary says, almost too quickly, as if to prove that she is not as conservative as her sister thinks. She goes inside the house and brings out an ashtray. "Bob smokes sometimes."

Ingrid smiles, remembering Mary's vehement disapproval the

first time she saw her smoking. It was shortly after she came to the United States—in fact, she had smoked in high school and college but never in front of Mary. She draws a long drag and extinguishes the cigarette in the ashtray.

"I don't mind," Mary says.

"It's fine."

"I guess smoking relaxes you. Bob only smokes when he's stressed out at work."

"It does help."

"I read somewhere that more and more women have begun to smoke, especially in developing countries. Maybe it's a modern thing for women to do."

"Maybe. I like the feeling, though. It quiets me down."

"Oh, but—" Mary stops. "You know what I'm going to say anyway."

"No worries. I'm just a recreational smoker." Ingrid looks up. "You don't see such a dark sky in New York and San Francisco. There are too many lights in cities."

Mary raises her head too. "I wouldn't have noticed if you hadn't mentioned it. When you were little, you liked watching the sky and sometimes would sit outside for a long time after dinner. Once, you were holding a cookie in your hand while watching the sky, and when our hen took it away from you, you didn't even realize it. The neighbors said you'd become an astronaut someday. I got jealous and warned you, 'If you kept bending your neck backward, you'll grow up having a crooked neck.' "

"Did you say that? I don't remember." Ingrid laughs.

"Oh, yeah. When we were little, though I was much older than you, I always envied you. If the neighbors said that your smiles were cute, I'd say to myself, 'She smiles so much that she'll lose all her teeth by the time she's eighteen.' If the neighbors said that you sang beautifully, I'd say, 'Just let her sing until she ruins her voice and speaks like a male duck.' If the neighbors said that you grew fast and could reach five foot six someday, I'd say, 'When there's lightning, she'll be the first to get struck.' "

"No kidding! I didn't know that you were so mean! No wonder I have bad teeth and my throat is always itchy." Ingrid gives Mary a playful punch on the arm.

"I did a lot more. Several times, I spread dirt inside your rice bowl and coaxed you to eat it. 'The dirt is from a fairy lady. You'll be able to fly if you eat it,' I told you."

"That part I do remember. My goodness, I believed you! I was quite dumb, wasn't I? But I was also jealous of you. You were the top student in your class and were praised by teachers and even the headmaster all the time. Our parents asked me to learn from you. All my friends' parents knew about you. They didn't remember my name but knew me as Guo-Mei's little sister. They said that we two were so different. I was naughty and quite a troublemaker, while you were polite and well-behaved. We didn't even look alike. If we stood next to each other together, people wouldn't think that we're from the same parents."

"I guess not," Mary says after a delay.

"But I had my revenge," Ingrid says excitedly. "Once, after a teacher reprimanded me for not finishing my homework, using you as a model for me to learn from, I stole your textbooks, spread bread crumbs between the pages, and threw them outside a rat hole in the kitchen. Next morning, when you saw the destroyed books, you thought rats had dragged them out there. For a long while you cursed the rats and swore to skin them live."

"You did that? I should have guessed! You were so happy those days."

"Mary, I don't know if you remember or not, but you were a bully. You gave me your cast-off clothes and told our parents that I didn't need new clothes."

"That's not true! You just loved my clothes. Remember that sky blue sweater that our parents bought for me for my fourteenth or fifteenth birthday? I only wore it once before you stole it and wore it. You were quite tall for your age. You wore it every day, refusing to take it off, and even wore it to sleep."

"Of course I remember that sweater. There was a yellow bee on the chest. The first time you wore it, I was madly jealous. Our parents said that they'd buy one for me too, when it was my birthday, but I only wanted yours."

"You loved my toys as well. It wasn't like I had many. Just a few. You got obsessed with my rubber swan. Whenever you played with mud, you wiped your hands on the swan. Though I washed it each time you did that, it quickly turned from a white swan into a black swan. At last I had to give it to you. But the day you got it you weren't interested in it anymore and stuffed it under your bed."

They recall more childhood stories and laugh over them. Ingrid feels an intense happiness. It has been a long time since they talked like this, since she saw her sister so relaxed. Though Ingrid wishes that they would continue their conversation in this cheerful mood, Mary begins to ask about her life after their falling-out.

"What happened to Steven?" she asks hesitantly.

"We broke up right before I moved to New York."

"Why?"

"We weren't serious to begin with. We just thought we'd have fun for a while. I have to say I dated him partially to provoke you—I knew you wouldn't approve. But you weren't the only one who disliked us being together. His parents also didn't want him to be with a non-Indian. So, he dated me to irritate his parents. Ironic, isn't it? You didn't like his race and skin color, neither did his parents like mine. They belonged to a high caste in India, with aristocratic ancestors. His parents wanted him to marry a girl they had picked for him in India, someone from their caste. What's our family background? Our father came from an illiterate pauper family, and our mother's family was a combination of petit bourgeois and business owner. Well, if

I had been Steven's parents, I wouldn't have liked this relationship, either," Ingrid says sarcastically. She doesn't mention that she later became serious with Steven, yet he succumbed to his family's pressure and agreed to marry the girl they had chosen for him.

Even in the darkness Ingrid can detect Mary's embarrassment, so she adds quickly, "Let's forget about it."

"I'm sure you've dated after Steven?"

"Yes, there were a few guys."

"And . . ."

"None worked out."

"Really?"

"It's fine with me. You know, it's better for things not to work out than to be stuck with the wrong person."

"I'm sorry that none of these relationships worked out. I've told you before that it's important to be with someone who is responsible."

"Mary." Ingrid tries to repress her irritation. "You don't need be sorry for me. Could you just let me handle my own relationships? Please?"

"Well, if you say so." Mary smiles awkwardly.

"You don't get it. It's not that I don't want to talk about them with you. It's just that we have different views about certain things."

"But we're a family. We can talk about them."

"We can, but—" Ingrid doesn't want to continue discussing this subject, nor does she want to hurt her sister's feelings. "I'll tell you when I'm ready, okay?"

No longer relaxed, Ingrid looks up at the sky again while Mary fixes her eyes on the far end of the fence.

"Ingrid, how do you like your new company?" Mary asks, breaking the silence between them. "Do you get paid well? Do they have a good benefits package? You've yet to tell me the company's name."

Ingrid pities Mary's practicality, though, on consideration, she knows that her sister worries about her finances and is probably thinking about giving her money.

"There is no company. I lied so Ma wouldn't worry about me. But I have money. I saved when I was in New York."

"I knew it!" Mary stares into Ingrid's face. "Why don't you get a job in the South Bay? You'll be closer to Ma and me. I can pass your résumé to my friends in the big high-tech companies, like IBM, Intel, and Cisco. Though the economy isn't doing well, it's always easy for an accountant to get a job. And you're quite experienced."

"I didn't do accounting in New York."

"What did you do?"

"I did a lot of things. But in the past two years, I was a tour guide and did freelance translation and interpretation. I still get work from translation agencies, and I've built my own client list. The money is good. And I don't need to sit in the office nine to five."

Despite what Ingrid has said, Mary must have imagined that her sister lived a miserable life in New York. "I'm sorry. If I had known that, I'd have traveled there to bring you back."

Ingrid laughs. "Oh, come on, Mary, don't be ridiculous. I had a great time in New York."

Still not convinced, Mary says, "You shouldn't have sent me those checks."

"I owed you. You borrow money, you pay back. It can't be more straightforward than that. But you didn't cash them anyway. I put the money aside in a separate account. If you don't want it, it'll go toward Alex's college fund."

"You don't have to do that. Bob and I can surely pay for Alex's college. I'm your older sister, not a stranger, or a bank." Mary's body quivers slightly, and her voice sounds angry as well as hurt. "You should have told me when you didn't have money in New York."

A strange impulse comes over Ingrid: to embrace Mary and tell her that she appreciates what she has done for her. But Mary has to learn how to respect her choices: she is thirty-two, not a little kid, for God's sake. "Mary, I apologize if I hurt you, but I feel better returning the money. Besides, it was my choice to go to New York, to not do accounting. I had many opportunities to find an office job, and more than once I thought about doing so. Whenever I had to worry about my rent, I told myself that I was going back to accounting. I even tried to convince myself that sitting at a computer dealing with numbers and money wasn't as bad as I imagined. After all, I did that for more than two years after graduation, didn't I? Sitting in a big-windowed Bank of America office, wearing suits, doing balance sheets and income statements all day long, my brain filled with terms like *return on investment, equity, cash flow, abatement, estimated tax, revenue,* and all that stuff. I hated the job! The first thing I did when I got home in the evening was change into casual clothes. I told you that, but you wouldn't listen and kept telling me that I'd like the job better after I'd gained more experience."

While she is speaking, Ingrid blames herself once again for not standing up to her sister's manipulation earlier: she could have changed to a different major, or a different school, and she could have tried to find a different job, yet she did nothing until she went to New York. She gave herself too many excuses in those six years. Or was her idleness a way to punish herself for what happened in 1989?

Mary slides her hands from her thighs to her knees slowly, as if this movement will help her think. Then she sits forward, placing her hands between her thighs. For a while she remains silent. At last she looks at Ingrid. "You know why I chose accounting for you. I just didn't want you to have difficulty finding a job. Every company and every organization needs accountants. If it has to lay off people, it lays off marketing, sales, or other functions first. Even if a company is down to its last few employees, it has to keep at least one accountant to do the bookkeeping. And accountants get paid well. It's fine that you majored in history in China. I could care less. It's in China, your own country; you know people, the language, the culture. You can survive. But in the U.S., you had to start from zero. When you can't carry on a simple conversation in English and don't have money, I just don't believe that you have the luxury to talk about your interests and passions. What's the chance of getting a job with a history major? Have you seen many new immigrants studying history, or other arts and humanities programs? When we decided to leave China, wasn't it our principal goal to lead a better life?"

"No." Ingrid shakes her head. "We came here so we would have more choices."

"Choices? Your current, unstable life is based on your choices?"

"At least it's what I prefer now."

Mary sneers. "You remind me of some characters in Russian novels I read in college, who are called 'extra people' by the critics. I'm sure you've read those books too. These people long for spiritual freedom, living for their ideals and looking down on a worldly life. But you know what? They get disappointed soon—the society is real, not something they can control. You can hide in a cave, but you still have to eat, drink, and sleep. Now, you're young and can do whatever you want. But how about when you get old? You want to live on welfare and Medicare?"

Ingrid leaps from the bench. Something is burning in her chest. "Mary, I don't need your lecture, not as much as you might think. Yes, I'm your younger sister, but I'm over thirty. Wouldn't it be fair for me to run my own life? I won't mention all our previous conflicts, but you have to understand that I wouldn't exchange my life with yours even if I had your house, your fantastic office job, and your annual income."

Ingrid feels the chill in the air. She sits down and pulls up her jacket collar.

"We came here with nothing, having no connections and no heritage to speak of." Mary speaks slowly, not looking at her sister. "Our parents were lucky to survive the Mao era. When Ba died, I paid for his funeral because Ma didn't have money. Now, Ma's retirement income barely covers her daily expenses. If she had major surgery or if her factory changed its medical insurance and no longer covered her, what would happen? You know what the hospitals are like in China. They stop your treatment the moment your deposit runs out. And how about the bribes to the doctors and nurses? That's money too, right? Go ahead and laugh at me for being paranoid and practical, but I worry about Ma and I think I have good reason to worry." Mary pauses to breathe heavily. "I didn't want to have such a talk with you. I didn't mean to blame you or make you feel guilty. But it's just that you have to give some thought to Ma and your children. Do you know how difficult it was for Ma to raise us? How sad she would be if we didn't do well? The Chinese say 'Cookies won't fall from the sky' and the Americans say 'There is no free lunch.' It's the same everywhere."

Ingrid is irritated. She hates Mary for bringing their mother into the conversation to remind her of her duty as a daughter and a potential parent, yet she cannot deny that there is truth in what her sister has said. Inside, Ingrid has always sensed an undercurrent of uncertainty and trepidation, which makes her wonder what her next step is, where her future lies. She dreams of becoming a writer but has done little to prove herself. Allowing herself to drift, as she has found out, is easier than making a decision. During this drifting she has become a kite with a broken string. Now, Mary is trying to grab the string, to drag her back to reality.

Meanwhile, Ingrid sees Mary's sacrifice, her succumbing to family responsibilities and other obligations, not in a cowardly way, yet still pitiable in Ingrid's opinion. She remembers what Mary said to her right before she left China: "Just wait and see, I'll become one of the best chemists in the world." She had looked determined, her face glowing with youth, beauty, and intelligence. Now, a serene, gentle look has replaced this resolution.

"I only have one sister," Mary says. "And we only have our mother left."

At this moment, their mother appears. She opens the door and looks around until she finds Mary and Ingrid in the darkness. She doesn't speak right away, as if guessing what her daughters have been talking about.

"Ma," Ingrid and Mary call out at the same time, both putting on jovial voices.

"Ma," Mary adds, "we were talking about work."

"Guo-Mei just gave me some good advice," Ingrid says, not sure why.

Pleased, their mother says, "It's so cold outside. You don't want to get sick. I've made some soup with bird's nest and rock sugar. Drink some now. The soup tastes best when it's hot."

TWELVE

January

MARY DRIVES INTO HER company's four-story garage and parks on the ground level, where there are a dozen cars already. It's the first time she has come to the office this early: it's barely six a.m. She looks out the window at the dark sky, surprised that people are here earlier. They must live far and, to avoid traffic, have to hit the road before daybreak so that they can leave the office by three p.m., before the rush hour. Though the economy has slowed and jobs are fewer than the year before, traffic is still horrendous. Several of Mary's co-workers live in San Francisco and commute daily, driving more than one hour each way. They sometimes take Caltrain, but it usually takes much longer considering the waiting time and the time needed to get from the station to work.

Not only does the traffic remain heavy, but the housing market holds strong. Over the past year, Mary has been dreading a correction in the real-estate market, but so far she hasn't seen it. Maybe Julia was right, Mary thinks, as she gets out of her silver Toyota Camry, that California is a place everyone wants to come—for jobs, for the sun, and for the scenery.

She didn't have to start her day so early, but Claudia Dawn had sent her an e-mail late yesterday afternoon asking her to complete a PowerPoint presentation by ten a.m. and present it to a marketing team today. "These are the challenges that grow you in your career," Claudia likes to say to her employees about such short-notice projects. In Mary's opinion, Claudia just wants to show that she is the boss. She could have ignored the e-mail, pretending that she hadn't seen it until she arrived at work this morning, but it wouldn't be smart to confront Claudia, nicknamed "Stroppy Cow" by one of her co-workers—not now, with annual performance review time approaching. Who knows if this nasty woman would use this incident to say something unpleasant in her evaluation? Every year that Mary has worked for the company, she has been rated a top performer. She has had opportunities to be promoted to managerial positions, but she doesn't like to manage people, preferring to be an independent contributor.

She started the PowerPoint slides last night, but then Mingyi came over to discuss a new Bible study group at the church, which they had been asked to co-lead. Afterward they chatted. Mingyi has started to work four days a week, so that she will have more time for the church and for volunteering. Though Mary used to volunteer with Mingyi now and then, she hasn't been able to find time since her mother arrived.

The building where Mary works is quiet. The hallway carpet has dust, stains, paper scraps, and food droppings on it in many places. The janitors must have neglected their duty last night. She walks into her cubicle, places her handbag in an overhead file cabinet, and turns on her computer. Suddenly she realizes that she hasn't watered her plants for more than a week, a rare oversight. Luckily, the plants are still alive, though their leaves have begun to turn yellow. She hasn't been quite herself since she met Han Dong, she knows.

After she waters the plants, she begins to work, but she cannot focus. The recollections of Han Dong and her embracing and kissing, of him putting her on the hotel bed and taking off her clothes, return to her repeatedly. And the mysterious smile on his face while he stared at her half-naked body. Guilt, shame, and self-hatred well up inside her. She stops typing and buries her head in her folded arms on the desk, her temples pulsing with a dull pain.

For the past three weeks, Ingrid's arrival had cheered her up so much that she had almost forgotten her encounter with Han Dong in Berkeley—even if she did think of him, she managed to see him as a ghost from the past. Ghosts weren't real, and they'd go away, she consoled herself. After all, she didn't have sex with him and she wasn't even naked in front of him. American women wear bikinis on the beaches, she reasoned, while she'd had on not only her bra but also her long pants—she'd been much better covered than bikini wearers. No, it shouldn't be considered even a fling.

These self-deceiving arguments had helped her enjoy her family reunion, but now, she is overwhelmed with anxiety and fear.

After they met, Han Dong had sent her a stream of e-mails and called her cell phone frequently, but she had remained unresponsive. He will return to China in a month. As soon as he gets on the plane, he will forget her or remember her only as a reserved and unattractive woman, she knows. He might even mention her later as an object of scorn to new lovers, who will be much prettier, younger, and more liberal than she. "My heaven, she was something! So eighties. She should have been displayed in a museum." She imagines the amused expressions on his lovers' faces.

He hadn't gotten her, that was why he didn't give up, she believes. Men were like that. They always felt the need to make a conquest, however unimportant the time, place, and person might be to them.

She resolves to go back to her peaceful world, to be a good wife, mother, and churchgoer, to consider her single indiscretion as the kind of brief, unpleasant incident that is inevitable in one's life. She's not perfect, no one is perfect. She has sinned, but who hasn't? Somehow, she remembers that when she was little she stole a piece of candy from a store. If she had had the money, she would have paid for it, but she had only enough to buy a notebook, and she had to have the notebook for her class that day. As the store owner, a grandpa, went to the back room to get one—he didn't have it in the front—she opened a glass tin on the counter, took out a big White Rabbit, and slipped it into her pocket. It was easy: no one was around. She almost regretted that she hadn't taken more. A moment later the store owner returned with her notebook. She paid and walked out into the sunshine, whistling like an innocent lark.

It was the first time she had ever done something like this. But her happiness didn't last long. Approaching the school, as she was going to eat the candy, she suddenly thought of what her teachers had said about thieves: they were shameful parasites, people who should be thrown into jail. She was frightened. But the candy in her hand smelled so good! She couldn't help but lick it several times, sensing the sweetness on her tongue. Then she rewrapped it in its cellophane and ran back to the store as fast as she could, so she wouldn't have time to change her mind. No one was in the store but the owner. She asked to exchange the notebook for a different color. While the grandpa went to the back room, she opened the candy tin and replaced the big White Rabbit she had licked. She always remembers that day because she'd felt very proud of herself.

This time she knows that she cannot put the candy back as if nothing happened.

Her thoughts are tangled. She even wants to call Han Dong: she'd just tell him to stop contacting her, she thinks. But in fact, she longs to hear his voice, to hear him whisper her name. She lifts the phone and begins to dial but stops after pressing three numbers. If she did call him, what would happen next? She tries to imagine the outcome. Very likely she would drive to Berkeley to see him again, and then . . .

She stands and paces. She dreamed of Han Dong last night. They made love on a huge bed that allowed them to roll around freely. They changed positions often, and she was just as aggressive as he was. He licked all over her body, including her breasts and vagina. He sucked her hardened nipples. She moaned and laughed, just as she imagined a real slut would. She was happy, and momentarily she even thought that it wasn't bad to be a whore. Suddenly, in her dream, Han Dong disappeared and so did the bed. She found herself walking alone in a thick fog that had come out of nowhere, in a white nightgown as big as a tent. She looked around, seeing that the sky, moon, sun, stars, and oceans were all mingled together as in a mirage. Where was she? she wondered. Then she felt that her gown was melting. She looked down and realized to her horror that she had turned into a shapeless shadow. She must have shouted in her fright, which must have awakened Bob—he gave her a little shove on the shoulder, murmuring something before falling asleep again. His shove woke her up, and for the rest of the night she lay on her bed, her head aching, staring at the crucifix on the wall facing her bed.

Her computer monitor now changes to the screen saver: a family portrait in front of the entrance to Disneyland taken two years ago. Alex is sitting on Bob's shoulders, lifting a Mickey Mouse in his left hand and a Donald Duck in his right. Mary is holding Bob's arm, her head against his shoulder, smiling sweetly. She extends her hand to touch Alex and Bob, there on the screen, wishing that she could time-travel back to that moment, when she had no secret to hide, no shame to fill her heart, no sin to regret.

Besides Han Dong, her mother's confession about Ingrid's conception has shaken her: she can't believe her parents had hid such a big secret for so long. It disturbs her that she once disdained her father, who had saved the family. Since that evening, she and her mother have never mentioned their conversation, and though her mother had avoided her the first few days after they talked, as if she felt ashamed for telling Mary the truth, she soon warmed up to the new bond with her older daughter. As Mary talks with her mother, rather than the usual, strained politeness in her manner, she now has affection in her voice and attitude, and she has begun to go walking with her mother after dinner, holding her arm.

Many times, Mary has visualized how her mother lingered on strange streets, carrying a little baby in a basket. And Ingrid's innocent face. Just now, she recalls her mother's dreamlike voice; she can see her and her half sister, can hear her mother's heavy steps and her sister's giggling, can feel how her mother must have felt when she put down the basket outside a stranger's house.

Mary goes to the kitchenette to fix herself a cup of coffee. She usually drinks tea, but she feels like something stronger now. The coffee helps. She walks back to her cubicle and resumes work on her presentation.

After seven thirty, her colleagues start to arrive, saying hi to Mary as they pass her cubicle.

"Mary, did the janitor empty your garbage bin?" William Walker asks over the wall from his cubicle, which is right next to hers.

"I guess not, but I didn't have much in it," she replies.

Katherine Berry, the girl across from William, cries, "Didn't you see the e-mail from HR yesterday? Those Mexicans wanted a raise and started to strike the day before yesterday."

William chuckles. "We can't live without those Mexicans. Come and smell my cubicle, it's like a rat died in here. I shouldn't have dumped my leftovers into the bin yesterday. I don't think I can work unless I can find something to close my nostrils."

David Smith, another colleague, walks out of his cubicle opposite Mary's, a coffee mug in hand. "What's wrong with these Mexicans? They have no education and speak no English. They're lucky to have a job. If they don't like living in the U.S, why don't they go back to Mexico? No one forces them to stay."

Mary frowns at David's remark. Since the day he started working here she has disliked him. He's short and stout, has a fat nose, and tries his best to flatter the management team. Last week, he heard that a vice president in their department was helping his granddaughter sell Girl Scout cookies. He bought twenty boxes immediately and then bragged to Mary and his other colleagues about how he had talked with the vice president in his spacious office for more than ten minutes. His generosity with the cookies was ironic, considering that he would always refuse to pitch in for a colleague's birthday or baby shower gift, and when he went out with the team for lunch, he would calculate his share of the bill down to the cents.

No one on the statisticians' team likes him except Claudia Dawn. Recently, she promoted him to a managerial position, despite his inexperience: he graduated from an MBA program in New York last year and had never managed people before. The first day Claudia came to the team, he began to flatter her. He visited her cubicle often to update her on his projects and would say things like "You look fabulous today," "You're full of insights and vision," and "I can't agree with you more."

Since his promotion, he has tried even harder to please Claudia. During meetings, if he has to say something, he speaks with his eyes on her. If she nods, he raises his voice; if she frowns, he pauses and coughs or even excuses himself to go to the restroom. Claudia thinks highly of him, bringing him to meetings, trainings, and presentations, and even on business trips. They are often seen walking on campus together, on their way to meetings or lunch, Claudia tall and skinny, David short and tubby, holding his laptop, like Claudia's distorted shadow. Claudia often praises him in front of her other employees.

David knows what brands of clothes Claudia likes, what restaurants she frequents, what sports she plays; his opinions, hobbies, and even personal styles have become more and more similar to hers. She is a baseball fan, so he is too—he reads about baseball every day and can discuss her favorite players' performances expertly, as if they were his next-door neighbors. She walks fast, her arms swinging vigorously, her strides long, so he walks fast too, his body bouncing like a ball on his short legs. She wears Ralph Lauren shirts almost exclusively, so that brand has become his favorite. Just last week, he went to the Gilroy outlet mall and bought half a dozen RL shirts. Once she commented that Indians smelled of curry and Mexicans only knew how to produce babies. Since then, he has begun to make fun of Indians and Mexicans.

Sometimes Mary feels that she cannot tolerate David for another minute, but aren't people like him common in the workplace? And they always climb the ladder faster than their colleagues.

Whenever Mary's friends in China e-mailed her, complaining about nepotism and corruption at work, she told them that it wasn't much better in the United States, where adept use of connections and nepotism were often seen. If America could be said to be slightly better than China, she said, it was because there was no such thing here as the personal dossier, which records an individual's history from high school to the day he or she dies and is managed by a bureau called the Personal Dossier Management Bureau. Who didn't have a personal dossier in China? Without it, it was impossible to get a job in the government, at a school, or in a big company. And, in China, you couldn't access that file, which was transferred from job to job. If the dossier said that you weren't suitable for an important position, it was highly unlikely you would be hired.

But, of course, personal dossiers exist in the United States too, though the name is different, Mary thinks as her colleagues chat about the janitors. Isn't the performance review she receives from her company year after year a kind of personal file? If Claudia wrote negative comments about her in her review, those remarks could jeopardize her career—at least they would make it harder for her to switch to a different department. The good thing is that she can read her performance assessment and is even asked to sign it after reviewing it. But even if she didn't agree with Claudia's comments, it wouldn't make any difference. The Human Resources Department always listens to the managers. That's just an inescapable fact.

David pokes his head into Mary's cubicle, interrupting her thoughts. "Mary, how are those PowerPoint slides coming? The slides that Claudia asked you to put together for marketing."

"Almost done." She doesn't turn around to look at him. Despite her low opinion of him, she usually treats David politely. But today she is irritated: her slides are none of his business!

"That's good to know." David clears his throat, then raises his voice. "Could you e-mail them to me as soon as you're done?"

Mary senses the silence in the other cubicles: obviously their colleagues are listening to her conversation with David.

"Is that necessary?" She uses her toes on the chair legs to rotate her chair away from her computer, to face David.

David smiles, his tone softening. "You know, Mary, Claudia called me last night, saying that you and I should go through the slides together before I present them to the marketing department."

"I think I should present them myself. You don't know much about this project."

"Oh . . . well . . . Claudia said today's meeting is very important and all the participants are managers."

"I know them well and have presented to them many times," Mary replies. She can barely hide her irritation.

"Claudia wants me to do this presentation. If the marketing folks have questions, I could call on you to answer them, all right? Claudia will be in soon. If you have a problem, you can talk with her directly." He glances at his watch. "You know what? I'm having a meeting with some engineers in a few minutes. I'd better run. I'll let you go back to work. Let's catch up later."

After David leaves, Katherine, newly arrived from the United Kingdom, walks into Mary's cubicle on tiptoe and pats her shoulder, beckoning to her to follow. She takes Mary to a conference room, and after closing the door, she says, "Mary, don't be pissed off by this kind of rubbish. Last week Claudia asked David to do my presentation to the sales department. They didn't even let me attend the meeting. I heard later from a sales guy that David said he had done the slides himself. What a bloody liar! You've been with the company for a long time, and they're at least polite to you. But I've only been here two weeks and am applying for a green card through the company. They know they can order me around and give me bullshit."

Katherine paces the room. "You know why Claudia didn't want me to do the presentation? William told me that she said she couldn't understand my British accent. 'It's better to let someone who can speak proper English to do presentations,' she said. Brilliant! Doesn't Tony Blair speak English millions of times more proper and refined than that of the president-to-be, George Bush? In the U.K., you can stop any little kid on the street and bet he speaks better English than ninety percent of Americans. Today, you know, what David did to you—"

"I know. It's not just my accent. Claudia may also think that I smell too much of soy sauce and MSG."

"If I didn't need this job right now, I'd have given bloody hell to Claudia and David." Katherine waves her fist in the air. "By the way, do you know David's grandparents are from Mexico? William told me. He knows a guy who used to be David's parents' neighbor."

"Really? He told everyone that his grandparents were from Spain. He didn't have to lie about that."

"Well, he was probably afraid Claudia wouldn't like him being a Mexican."

They walk back to their cubicles. They can hear Claudia's loud voice on the phone: her office is only down the hallway. Mary gulps her coffee as if to suppress her disgust toward Claudia. For a moment, she considers deleting the slides from her hard drive and telling Claudia that it's impossible to put together a presentation with so little time. But didn't she already tell David that she was almost done? Of course she can blame the computer, explaining that it crashed suddenly and wiped out all the data before she could save it. But that doesn't sound convincing, and what a pathetic excuse! Would she have to apologize to Claudia for her mistake with feigned grief on her face? No, she wouldn't do that. Maybe she should tell Claudia outright that she's being unreasonable to give her such short notice for a big presentation. If she gets angry, they can go to Human Resources. Mary likes her last idea but knows that she won't carry it out—unless she's ready to leave the company, it's not worthwhile to make such a fuss.

Claudia has brought her thoroughbred Doberman pinscher to the office and is demonstrating to Mary's colleagues, including William and Katherine, how well-trained he is. David is in her office too.

"Sweetie, sit down!" Claudia's voice.

"Sweetie, turn right!"

"Sweetie, roll over!"

"Sweetie, shake hands with David!"

Each of Claudia's orders to the dog is greeted by applause and laughter—surely, that dog named Sweetie has fulfilled his mistress's orders perfectly. David, instead of being in his vaunted meeting with the engineers, is cheering for the dog; he couldn't have been more excited if he were watching the Super Bowl or the finals for the soccer World Cup.

Mary completes the last PowerPoint slide and e-mails it to David. She also e-mails Claudia separately to say that she is taking the rest of the day off because of family matters. She turns off her computer and exits the building via the stairs, where Claudia and her colleagues cannot see her.

Outside the parking garage, a crowd of janitors, more than thirty of them, are shouting slogans for a higher hourly wage in English and Spanish, holding flags and cardboard and printed signs; their slogans and signs tell Mary that they're not protesting against her company in particular but responding to the nationwide strike organized by the Service Employees International Union. They are asking for one dollar an hour more in their pay. She recognizes a few janitors who clean her building daily, such as the young girl in a red sweater and long floral skirt. Her name is Olga—she told Mary in one of the English classes that Mary had volunteered to give her. Standing in the front of the crowd, Olga holds up a yellow cardboard sign printed in red: *"Sí se puede!"* Compared with the other janitors, who are older and more determined, their heads high, chests sticking out, bellowing slogans rhythmically under a leader's instruction, Olga looks less sure, less bold, but the expression on her face says that she knows why she is here.

She is only nineteen, Mary remembers now. In one of their classes, Olga had said that she grew up near Mexico City and had been living in the United States for three years with her older brother, a self-employed porter, and four other Mexicans, in a two-bedroom apartment in Milpitas. The apartment had only one bathroom. Before she took a shower, she had to clean the tub. "Men are dirty and messy," she said, smiling innocently, showing her crooked but cute teeth. In the mornings she sometimes couldn't wait for her turn to use the bathroom and had to run to the Jack in the Box nearby. The bathroom there was much cleaner, she told Mary. She carried a picture of the Virgin of Guadalupe wherever she went, saying that it was a gift from her mother. She told Mary many things, including how her brother had injured himself while moving kitchen appliances for a couple who had found him outside Home Depot, as well as how she had hid inside a truck transporting tomatoes to enter San Diego from Tijuana.

At least Olga has the courage to face the world, to ask for fairness, Mary thinks, feeling more hopeless about herself giving in to David and Claudia. She runs to her car and starts the engine.

Mary arrives at her church. She parks next to Mingyi's green Beetle, remembering that today is the day to serve lunch to homeless people, a monthly event Mingyi organizes. She walks into the church through the side door that leads to the kitchen. The hallway is narrow and dark, shaded by several enormous oak trees outside. On both walls are excerpts from the Bible, events schedules, announcements, and other church-related brochures. Hearing the cheerful talking from the kitchen, she quickens her steps.

"Look who's here!" Mingyi sees her first. Wearing a blue print apron, Mingyi is washing vegetables at the sink. Since it's very warm in the kitchen, she wears only a short-sleeved blouse, and she has put up her short hair with a black barrette behind each ear. She looks young and energetic.

Apart from Mingyi, six brothers and sisters are there. Everyone greets Mary with great enthusiasm.

The pregnant woman cutting carrots is Wang Fang, who was baptized last week. She came to the United States two years ago, to be with her husband, who was doing his postdoctoral degree at Stanford's engineering school—he is now an assistant professor there. Though she's six months pregnant, she doesn't look like it. She's tall and thin, and her loose clothes hide her belly. She speaks Mandarin with a thick Beijing accent, her tongue rolling often to make the throaty sound of *er*, something Mary cannot do.

JG, a Singaporean, is cleaning the counter. He owns an import-export business and travels often to Southeast Asia and China. When he first visited the church, he claimed to be an atheist and liked to debate with Pastor Zhang and other church people. He was full of questions, from a word's origin in the Bible to comparisons between different religions and how God exercises control of the world.

Speaking Mandarin, Cantonese, Taiwanese, Shanghainese, English, French, Thai, and Malay, he was ready to attack anyone who believed in God. One of his questions to Pastor Zhang was how God knew in which language he was thinking and praying. JG was so well known for his tough questions that Mary and many brothers and sisters tried to avoid him. Only Pastor Zhang would talk with him for hours, not minding his hostility. Three years ago, to everyone's surprise, JG asked to be baptized and has since been passionate about advocating Christianity.

Of the other four, two are from mainland China, one is from Taiwan, and the last is from Hong Kong. Mary feels that only in the church can mainland people, Hongkongese, and Taiwanese abandon their political conflicts and live in harmony.

Mary helps Mingyi wash the vegetables.

"I thought you wouldn't be able to come. Don't you have a big presentation today?" Mingyi asks.

"It turned out that I had little work," Mary says.

"Mary, I heard that! May I join your company?" JG teases. "I've been thinking about selling my business for a long while. It's much easier to work for someone else. I'm just waiting for God's blessing."

"Hasn't God given you a lot of blessings already? Your business is getting bigger and bigger every day." Wang Fang laughs, stopping her vegetable chopping momentarily. "Mary, I'm glad you are here. Earlier, JG asked me to cook Guilin fried noodles. How can I, a northerner, know how to cook a southern dish? It's like asking a chicken to fly."

"Now you can relax," Mingyi says. "Our guests are lucky, and we are lucky too, to be able to eat Mary's famous fried noodles."

Qiu You, the Taiwanese, chimes in. "Last time a few people ate nothing but the fried noodles Mary cooked. One man, I'd say he was at least fifty, ate five plates. I worried that he wouldn't be able to stand after the lunch."

While all doing their assigned work, they begin to tell jokes. Ar

Chan, the Cantonese, mentions something he experienced as a criminal lawyer in a small city in Hebei Province in the early nineties. He says that he was hired to defend a convict who had been sentenced to life for murder. As he was speaking on his client's behalf, the judge stood suddenly, pounded the table, and ordered him evicted from the courtroom. Ar Chan mimics the judge, his hand trembling, his voice fuming with anger: "The Party and the country sent you to college and granted you a diploma. How could you side with a murderer? Where's your education? Where is your conscience? You've wasted the country's money. Get out of my court!" Everyone laughs at the story.

Before Mary starts to cook, Mingyi asks her if she wants to pick her mother up from home. "She is alone. Maybe she won't mind coming to the church."

"I've tried many times, but she doesn't want to come. She says churches are for Westerners." Mary smiles helplessly. "But she has begun to do morning exercises with some old people in the park. Sometimes she even plays mah-jongg or goes grocery shopping with them. I didn't realize that she knew how to play mah-jongg. She said that she learned it from my grandma. It was more than half a century ago and she still remembers it."

After eleven a.m. homeless people begin to show up. Some have come to the church before and walk directly to the yard outside the kitchen, sitting on the stone benches chatting or minding their own business. Mary and two other people take out water, juice, milk, and plastic knives and forks. After the food is served on three wooden tables placed end to end, a line is formed. Though most of the homeless wear shabby clothes, they look clean—they have probably shaved or washed before coming to the church—and are polite, staying in line. A few talk with the church people, thanking them for the food.

A bearded man in his fifties comes to shake hands with Mary. He hangs about near the Safeway in Mary's neighborhood, often pushing a rusty shopping cart that he found somewhere, in which he has stored all his possessions: a cotton blanket, an unlidded stainless-steel pot, empty Coke bottles, and used bike tires and other nondescript objects. He wears a tattered jacket year round, a pair of muddy hiking boots, and a red hat embroidered with "Peace" in the front. Mary had given him a few jackets and several pairs of shoes, but the next time she saw him he was still wearing the same old jacket and shoes. He never asks for change. As he pushes his cart around, he raises his head high, sniffing constantly, as if seeking something in the air. He once told Mary when she brought him clothes that he was looking for birds through his nose. "There ain't no birds around in this world. Cars and people killed them all," he said. When he isn't pushing his cart around, he likes to lie down in a hidden place, usually under a tree, smoking and playing with a wildflower.

"God bless you. God bless America. God bless China," he says after shaking hands with Mary. Then he bends, taking off his hat and placing it elegantly over his chest, saluting like a gentleman from the old times.

"Thanks. God bless you too," Mary says, happy to see him, then adds, "John, you look very good today." Though she has participated in her church's soup kitchen many times before, she somehow feels closer to John and the other homeless today.

A few steps away from Mary, Mingyi is chatting with a woman who has a face as wrinkled as a walnut and lacks two upper front teeth. The woman rolls up her pants to show Mingyi the cut on her right calf, telling her that a young man hit her with a brick when she was sleeping on a street in Mountain View last night. Mingyi squats to check her wound, and asks her if it hurts. No, the woman says, hissing through her teeth, she's been sleeping on the street for more than ten years and doesn't know what pain is like. Then she says that she hates to have such an ugly cut on her leg because she likes to wear skirts in summer.

A homeless man nearby says to Mingyi, "Don't listen to her. She's crazy. She did it herself. She just wants attention."

Mingyi walks into the kitchen and comes out with a basin, a small towel, and a first-aid kit. She asks the woman to sit and cleans the mud off her cut with the towel. After drying the cut with a cotton pad, she applies antibiotic ointment. Meanwhile, the woman hums and shakes her head, eyes half closed. Twice she utters a bright laugh, a little bit like the call of a magpie.

"Betty, come back here next Monday and I'll check you again," Mingyi says, pulling down the woman's pant leg and tying her shoelace.

Betty nods obediently like a little girl, then goes back to the line to get more food.

The leftovers are boxed for takeaway. As usual, Mary's fried noodles are all gone.

After the homeless people leave, Mary and Mingyi volunteer to clean the yard and the kitchen, telling the other church people to go home.

As Mingyi scrubs the pots and pans, she begins to sing a hymn whose beautiful melody quickly attracts Mary to join her. Both are good at housework, so the kitchen and the backyard look tidy in no time. Mingyi cuts a stem of bird of paradise from the yard and puts it in a vase on the kitchen table.

Mary boils a kettle and takes out a set of dark brown clay teaware, including a pot, a tray, and six matching tiny cups. She also fetches a package of tea from a drawer next to the fridge. After washing the pot and two cups with hot water, she puts them on the tray.

"I brought them in last week," Mary says, moving the tray from the countertop to the table. They both sit.

"Wow, we're drinking Gong Fu tea! Mary, you're more and more capable," Mingyi says, watching Mary drop tea leaves into the pot and, after a while, pour tea into the two cups as if she were watering flowers.

"Don't flatter me. It's my first time making Gong Fu tea. I know only a little about it. A friend of mine bought this set and the tea for me a few months ago, and I'd never had a chance to use them. You know, Bob doesn't drink tea and I'm too busy to think of drinking tea at home unless you, Yaya, and Julia come over. This tea is said to be very good oolong. I thought I'd just bring it to the church and share it with people who know how to appreciate tea. Gong Fu tea is meant to be drunk when you have time. But look at me! Where do I find the leisure to sit down to drink tea?" Mary lifts the cup to her lips and blows on it lightly to cool it. She downs it in one gulp. "Hmm, it's good."

Mingyi does the same thing, and after emptying her cup, she pours more for them both. "You're right about us being so busy here. It seems our countrymen in China know how to enjoy life better. Restaurants, teahouses, and bars are everywhere, packed from Monday to Sunday. Some restaurants open until four a.m. People seem to have a lot of time to hang out."

"Eating is always a big thing in China, isn't it?" Mary offers. "My friends there keep telling me that Americans don't know how to enjoy life. 'What do Americans eat?' they ask me. 'Burgers? Steaks? Italian pastas and pizzas?' Then they launch into long lists of dishes in China: eight major cuisines and local foods in each province and city. When my mother saw me eating salads, she said, 'Why do you eat raw vegetables? They can't be tasty. In China, they're for rabbits and pigs.' "

Mingyi laughs. "Your mother was quite right. I thought the same thing when I first lived in the U.S. Now we eat salads and pizzas, just like Americans." Mingyi drinks more tea. "Whenever I go back to China, I'm amazed at the changes and feel that my five senses are not enough to take in all the attractions and distractions. People who know that we've been living overseas say we haven't gotten used to the changes in China, but people who don't know we live abroad probably think we're peasants who are confused in the city. At my age, I'm probably more nostalgic than you. I sometimes wonder if young people care about China's history and culture at all, or if they'd rather be surrounded by McDonald's, KFC, Starbucks, and Nintendo games."

"I worry about Alex," Mary says. "What will become of him? Though he's learning Mandarin, he doesn't care about China. Once I told him about the Four Great Inventions. He looked uninterested, asking me why China didn't invent cars, submarines, or space shuttles."

"He's only six. He has a lot of time ahead of him." Mingyi pats Mary's back consolingly. "Let's talk about something cheerful. We sound like two hollow-cheeked, silver-haired old ladies with walking sticks, crying over lost glory." She licks her lips and smiles. "Hmm, you know what I'm craving right now? A piece of homemade sesame candy. Crispy and fragrant, perfect with the tea."

"My mother used to make them for the new year. Both my sister and I would help stir the sugar paste and then cut it into small squares. That was probably one of the happiest times for me in the entire year." Mary props her chin on her hands, eyes distant, thinking.

"Just the other day, Yaya talked about her hometown stinking tofu. This woman surely knows how to make your mouth water." Mingyi imitates Yaya's voice: "That smell, so strong that it seeps into your nostrils and brain and blood, turns into the most memorable aroma. Your stomach begins to ache from the craving, and before you know it, you are standing in front of the stinking tofu vendor's big vat."

Mary frowns to show her disapproval. "That Yaya! I was cheated by her once. Last year I was in Changsha briefly on business, and I begged a friend to sneak out of work to take me to eat stinking tofu. She said, 'Are you sure?' I said, 'Absolutely.' So she took me to a well-known vendor. Honestly, I smelled the tofu half a mile away, and instantly, I wanted to throw up. The smell was worse than from decayed meat on a scorching summer day. But I wasn't going to give up after such a long journey, so I bought a piece. I had to hold my breath before taking a small bite. I managed to swallow it, but threw away the rest."

"Aha, good you told me this, at least I'll be better prepared if I want to try it someday. I don't think Yaya is really so much into stinking tofu, though. She must be homesick. I always long for my hometown Tianjin's *ma hua*. It's so crunchy and tasty. I'm not kidding you. I spent my whole childhood dreaming of *ma hua,* my mouth watering even in my dreams. My biggest ambition used to be marrying a *ma hua* vendor. Whenever I go back home, the first thing I do is visit the best *ma hua* vendor in town and get a box. But as soon as I put a *ma hua* in my mouth, I'm disappointed with the taste: it's just not what I have been imagining day in and day out. Ironically, I buy it every time I visit Tianjin."

"I'm just like you. Sometimes I crave the soft, sticky rice cake and spicy river snails I liked so much when I was little. Even now, mentioning them makes my mouth moist. I buy them every time I return to my hometown, but they never taste the same as I remember. Maybe it is because my family was too poor when I grew up and we'd just be happy if we could have enough rice on the table. When you're hungry, everything tastes good. It's an illusion, more from your brain than from your mouth or your stomach. When I was a child, I spent a lot of time looking for food, and I ate weird stuff, like cicadas. They tasted like paradise. Now I can eat whatever I want, but nothing tastes like the stuff I ate when I was little."

The two friends toast to their health, their families, their faith, and their friendship, lifting their teacups and smiling.

"Do you know that my belief in God has something to do with food?" says Mingyi, beaming thoughtfully.

Mary shakes her head, awaiting the story.

"It was a long time ago," Mingyi starts, looking out the window as if struggling to recall everything here and now for Mary. "One day I was very hungry, so I went with a few kids in my neighborhood to a village nearby to steal yams. Those few yam fields, after the harvest, must have been scavenged many times by hungry people like us. After we searched for more than an hour, kneeling to dig the soil with our hands, almost fainting with hunger and exhaustion, we each had got only a few finger-size baby yams. But that was enough to cheer us up. Have you eaten raw yams?"

"Yes, of course. Sometimes I couldn't wait and just rubbed the yams against my clothes to get rid of the soil and crunched them like that. To this day I recall clearly the sweetness under the yams' dirty skins."

Mingyi nods. "We ate like that too."

"Did you find more food later?"

"We continued searching, hoping for more surprises, but the watchman found us. He ran toward the field with a stick in his hand. We ran away. I was seven or eight years old, the youngest and also the shortest in the group, so of course I fell behind the other kids. The watchman got closer and closer, and I thought I heard the wind from his stick and smelled the blood from its spanking on my buttocks. Then, in my hurry, I tripped over something. I fell, my chest hitting a solid object. Maybe a hungry person always has the sharpest nose. I knew right away it was a yam, a yam bigger than my four fists put together. The moment I realized it, I decided that I would just lie there, covering the yam, letting him spank me with his stick. Compared with eating such a big yam, getting spanked wasn't a big deal. But I was too excited and too dizzy with hunger to think clearly, so instead of following my plan, I jumped to my feet, holding the yam in front of my chest and exposing it to the watchman, who was now standing right behind me. He was not big, at most fourteen or fifteen, terribly skinny, his face looking like an upside-down triangle, his eyes deep-set, his arms no thicker than his stick. His ghostly white face suddenly turned red, as if lit by some mysterious light. He swallowed hard, staring at the yam."

"He took the yam, didn't he?" Mary cannot hide her disappointment. If she'd been the young Mingyi, she'd have taken a big bite of the yam before surrendering it.

"He reached for the yam, but I moved back a step; he advanced, I backed more. He moved his eyes from the yam to my face, startled, as if he had just realized my existence. We stared at each other like two tree stumps.

"I don't know how long we stood like that—five seconds, ten seconds, maybe longer—though it felt like forever. I saw the light in his eyes fade. Suddenly he turned and left, dragging the stick behind him as if he didn't even have the strength to lift it. He walked fast, almost running, looking straight ahead. I think he knew that if he turned he'd change his mind and take the yam from my hands. It would have been so easy for him. I didn't dare move until he disappeared into the darkness, my legs feeling like they could melt any second. It took me a while to walk to a place hidden by trees and bushes; I even took my time to wash the yam in a ditch before I sat against a tree to enjoy my precious food."

There is a long silence until Mary asks, "Did you meet him again later?"

"No, I wish I did. I should have gone back to the village to find him, to thank him. But like any little kid, I quickly forgot this incident, and it was not until much later, when I was almost an adult, that the evening came back to me. That watchman who had let me go must have seen on my face, an orphan's face, more hunger, more despair, and maybe even more death than he had seen in his own face. He backed off, giving me hope. I don't know if he's still alive or if he even remembers the girl holding a yam like it was her heart. Of course, he wouldn't know that what he did had saved this girl's life again and again in her later days.

"Whenever I was surrounded by darkness I thought of the yam, of the fading light in the watchman's eyes; then I knew I had to live, and I had the courage to live. Unlike many people from mainland China, who struggle for years before they abandon their doubts and follow God, I believed in God before I had the chance to read the Bible. My journey couldn't have been more natural." Mingyi moves her eyes back to Mary's face and gives her a faint smile. "Oh, the tea is cold. Let me fix another kettle. I don't want to waste such good tea."

Mingyi carries the kettle to the stove and lights the burner. Mary wants to go to her but instead remains in her chair, captivated by Mingyi's tale. She knew Mingyi's parents died a long time ago but didn't know that she had been orphaned so young. She thinks about herself living in the countryside, away from her parents. She was like an orphan too, during those two years, and she knew what it was to be hungry. She ate new grass roots in the spring; she picked wild fruit and mushrooms without considering whether they might be poisonous; she ate cicadas, grasshoppers, and other insects after baking them on the fire. Her need for food, her certainty that she could find more and better food if she kept looking, had given her hope for the future.

Mingyi returns with a plate of carrots and cherry tomatoes. "I'm hungry. I don't know if it's talking about the past or talking about food that makes me hungry. Want some?"

Mary lifts a tomato to her mouth and, after a long pause, says, "Mingyi, have you ever thought about getting married?"

"Hmm, no. I'm turning fifty in two years. It's not easy to find someone I can get along well with."

"But you look young." Mary hurries her words. "There are quite a few divorced men in the church, and most of them are very nice. I'd say you could easily find a match among them. You should at least try."

The kettle is boiling. Mingyi brings it back to the table and pours tea for them both. "My heart already belongs to someone. I haven't told you about it before because I liked to keep it to myself. I used to have a fiancé who studied architecture. He spent his childhood in southern France but later came to China with his Chinese-born scientist parents. We loved each other deeply and got engaged when I was barely twenty. But he was soon condemned for his research on protecting ancient buildings. He was sentenced to twelve years and sent to a labor farm in Qinghai. I went everywhere to fight for justice for him, but with my family background, I didn't stand a chance."

Mary remembers that Mingyi once mentioned that her parents had died in the fifties, just like her own grandparents. Though she doesn't know how they died, she has assumed that they were the victims of the Anti-Rightist campaign.

Mingyi continues. "Six months later I was sent to a labor farm as well, in the farthest northeastern area. He was in the west, I was in the east. We were separated by thousands of miles. The first two years, we could still get each other's letters. I read his letters so many times that I remember them by heart. He hid love poems in his writing, like puzzles, so the jailer wouldn't confiscate his letters. Many nights I'd lose sleep decoding those poems. Then for six months I didn't get a single letter from him.

"One night I decided that if I didn't get a letter from him in another month, I'd escape and go to Qinghai to find him. Of course, my idea was crazy. Anyone with any sense knew that escaping meant death. A week before my planned escape, he wrote to me, saying that he had been sent to build roads in a remote town and hadn't been able to write. Afterward, he wrote once a month, a poem in each letter. Beautiful poems."

Sensing where the story is going, Mary looks at her friend sadly. Why did Mingyi have to undergo so many misfortunes, to encounter so many hardships? she asks in her heart. Why didn't all-knowing, all-powerful God help her? It was easy for Him.

"Two years later, I was told that I would be released from jail soon. So I wrote him and told him that I'd travel to Qinghai to see him. The next letter I received was from a stranger, a previous cell mate of his. He told me that my fiancé had died more than two years earlier. He was severely injured while building a railroad and died a few days later. Before he died, he wrote me letters day and night. Afraid that I would commit suicide if I knew about his death, he asked his cell mate to send me those letters regularly."

Mingyi pauses, intertwines her hands behind her head, and looks at the ceiling, releasing a long sigh. But she soon recovers her composure. "Many nights I recite the poems he wrote me and feel that I'm having a conversation with him. You probably think I'm silly, so obsessed with a dead person. But to me he's still alive, living in my blood and with every breath I take. I'm with him every second, and I'm happy. God has given me my biggest joy by letting me love him so much."

They sit silently, looking away from each other—not because they want to avoid awkwardness but because each needs to be in her own thoughts. Silence sometimes is the best way to communicate, Mary believes. It's like the silence she experienced when she and her mother talked in front of the fireplace, when her mother told her how Ingrid came into the world. She had hugged her mother then, silently—a gesture of consolation and also of understanding.

Today, even a hug is unnecessary; Mingyi looks content and grateful, and there's something sacred in her smile. For the first time, Mary seems to see inside Mingyi.

"Did you ever ask God why all these things happened to you?" Mary asks.

"Oh, yes, many times."

"But still . . ."

"I didn't question Him again after I was baptized. He told me everything through the Bible. Without Him, I wouldn't have had the courage to live." Mingyi smiles again.

More silence.

An ambulance blasts its siren, shattering the stillness that has reached all the way into their souls as they sit together joined by reminiscence. A blessed stillness, Mary thinks.

"Thank you for listening," Mingyi says, taking the teaware and the kettle to the counter. She looks at her watch. "I've got to go. I have an appointment with someone in a senior center. Could you wash these for me, please?"

Mary nods hard. "Yes, of course. I still have time before picking up Alex from school."

Mary waves Mingyi away with a smile and watches her walk to the parking lot and get into her car, then sees her Beetle merge into El Camino Real, where the traffic is already heavy.

THIRTEEN

March

FENGLAN AND A GROUP of elderly Chinese people are practicing Chen-style *tai ji* at the park near where her daughter lives, occupying a shaded area under an umbrella-shaped oak tree. Starting a month ago, she has come here at seven every morning to exercise with this group. The air is fresh and soothing, vibrant with the melodious singing of birds. The grass quivers with dew that glitters in the soft March sunlight. Along the winding, paved path, a young Caucasian couple is jogging, wearing caps and sports gear of the same color and style. A bearded Middle Eastern man with a black turban is striding behind them. He is talking loudly and fast on his cell phone, laughing periodically. Near the pond flanked with beech trees, a black woman is training her puppy; he is more interested in the rawhide chewing bone in her hand than in chasing the dirty tennis ball his mistress just threw for him.

All this looks new and strange to Fenglan, just as when she first arrived, three months ago. She has to pinch herself, to feel the pain, to believe that she is thousands of miles from China in a country called the United States, which both of her daughters now call home. In her eyes, Caucasians, blacks, Indians, Arabs, fat people with legs thicker than her waist, heavily powdered old women, quiet parks, big lawns, undisturbed pigeons, even the blue sky, all belong to the United States, a country that has no relevance for her except that her daughters live here. She feels uncomfortable here, a trespasser; even now, listening to music played by Chinese instruments and practicing a Chinese exercise, she is conscious of the foreign environment around her.

She joined this exercise group because of her older daughter's urging—Guo-Mei had thought that it would help her get used to living in America. These people have lived here for many years and are all U.S. citizens, and though they speak only enough English to get by in their daily lives, they possess credit cards and driver's licenses, they know which Chinese restaurants are good and cheap, and they know how to withdraw money from ATMs.

It didn't take long for Fenglan to become acquainted with the group members, especially Mr. Jing and Mrs. You. Mr. Jing leads the *tai ji* practice. He's a Cantonese and came to America forty years ago. He used to own several shoe-repair shops but gave them to his three children when he retired. Mrs. You is from Fujian Province; her sole income is the rent from a duplex in Mountain View, purchased in the early nineties, when real-estate prices were low. She has a daughter in Los Angeles, a doctor, who rarely visits her. Mrs. You lives in a five-bedroom house owned by a Hongkongese family, and she cooks and cleans for them in exchange for room and board.

Apart from doing her morning exercises and playing mah-jongg with them now and then, Fenglan doesn't participate in their other activities. Mr. Jing and Mr. Wu just returned from a two-day trip to Las Vegas, which they visit at least once a month to play the slot machines and enjoy the cheap buffets. They like to talk about gambling, but it doesn't seem to her that they have won much.

She has difficulty understanding Mr. Jing's and Mrs. You's heavily accented Mandarin; she has to listen carefully. Where she lives in China, few tourists visit and most of the people she knows are local, so she is not good with accents. She complained about their Mandarin to her older daughter, hinting that she'd rather do her morning exercises by herself, but her daughter said, "Ma, why do you care which province they are from? You're Chinese and they're Chinese too."

The group takes a break before the next practice, called *mulan fist*, which Mr. Jing learned at a local *wu shu* studio and then taught everyone else.

Mrs. You asks Mr. Jing if he has made a will. Mr. Jing nods, then says that he may have to revise it because his oldest son—the one who puts in more time at the shoe-repair business than his other two children— thought it unfair and asked for a higher percentage of the inheritance.

"It's hard to be fair." Mr. Jing shakes his head. "I hope they won't argue after I die. I don't want my hard-won money to go to lawyers."

"It's easier for me. I have only one daughter. But she's already told me that she doesn't want my money," Mrs. You says. "Of course, I also can't expect her to look after me when I can no longer work."

"If you hadn't threatened to disown her, she wouldn't have acted like that," Mr. Jing says.

"But why did she marry a white guy? The guy looked so much older than her, with hair all over his arms and legs. She wasn't ugly, or fat, or too short, and she went to medical school. She could have found an Asian guy who is also a doctor. All her friends married Asians."

"We're old. We don't know what young people think. Why don't you just apologize to her? At least you'd get your daughter back."

"She hasn't called me even once in the past four years, not even during Spring Festival. What did I do in my previous life to deserve such a heartless daughter?" Mrs. You blots her eyes with the back of her hand before continuing. "Her father died early, and I worked as a nanny to send her to college. I didn't remarry—I had my chances, you know—because I was worried that she wouldn't get along well with a stepfather. She should have thought about what I had done for her. If she had called me, I'd have felt better and maybe I'd have accepted her husband."

Mr. Jing must have heard Mrs. You's story many times. He only murmurs, "You know, they are young. We're old. Young people are like that."

Mrs. You turns to Fenglan, who sits on the bench next to theirs.

"Mrs. Wang, don't you have two daughters?"

"I do. They both live here," she says softly. Seeing Mrs. You's sad face, her heart aches. Mrs. You's accent suddenly doesn't sound awkward to her; now they are just two mothers talking. If her own daughters hadn't contacted her for four years, she'd have been heartbroken as well.

"Are they married?" Mrs. You comes to her bench and sits with her. Mrs. You is a small woman with thick calluses on her hands and timid eyes.

"My older daughter is, but not my younger."

"Is her husband Chinese?"

"Well, I don't know," Fenglan says hesitantly. "His great-grandparents came from China. But he doesn't speak Mandarin or any other Chinese dialects."

"He is Chinese," Mrs. You assures her. "Just like my daughter. She was born here. She can speak some Mandarin but can't read or write it. Mrs. Wang, you're lucky that your daughter married a Chinese. Now their children are Chinese too, and have a Chinese last name." She rubs her eye before continuing. "I can't even pronounce my grandson's last name. It's very long. One of my daughter's friends once sent me a picture of my grandson. He didn't look Chinese, but he was cute, big blue eyes, and thick eyelashes. His hair was curly. It must be very soft." Her face brightens but soon dims. "It's no use talking about him. My daughter doesn't even let me see him. If I'd had a son instead of a daughter, maybe I wouldn't have cared that much whom he married. Now no one is going to carry on my husband's family name and roots. I don't dare go back to my hometown. People will look down on me."

"Maybe you should listen to Mr. Jing and apologize to your daughter," Fenglan suggests, though she sympathizes with Mrs. You and thinks her daughter is wrong.

"You think so? If your daughter married a white guy, would you be okay with that?" Mrs. You stares at her.

"I don't know," she replies honestly. After thinking a little more, she adds, "I live in China. I'm just visiting here. I can't tell my daughters what to do and what not to do. Like my second daughter, she's thirty-two and she doesn't even have a boyfriend. What can I do about her? Nothing. She's made up her own mind."

"You're right," Mrs. You says slowly. "My grandson's birthday is next Friday. I'm thinking about sending him a gift. He probably doesn't even know he has a grandma."

Mr. Jing starts his *mulan fist* music on the portable stereo. Mrs. You rises from the bench and joins the practice. Fenglan feels tired, so she tells Mr. Jing and the rest of the group that she will skip this round.

She goes to the water fountain to drink and then returns to the bench. She recalls her conversation with her older daughter two months ago, regretting again that she told her the truth when she had sworn to her husband that she'd never say a word about Guo-Ying's birth.

Will her older daughter treat her half-blood sister differently now? she wonders. Though her two daughters seem to be on good terms in her presence, chatting and smiling, she senses uneasiness in their suddenly downcast eyes or stiff smiles. Also, she has found out from her grandson that Guo-Ying didn't visit Guo-Mei for a long time. What has gone wrong between them? Fenglan has no idea, nor does she know how to ask. True, they're her daughters, but she hasn't lived with them for years and has rarely seen them, not to mention the fact that her daughters live in a country so different from China. She feels that she no longer understands them. Are they her Guo-Mei and Guo-Ying, or are they actually Mary and Ingrid? She is confused and even appalled, as if by changing names they had changed their identities and their pasts, and thus had somehow denied her and their father.

Another idea flashes through her mind. Will Guo-Mei tell her sister about her birth? Fenglan doesn't believe that she will, but she still worries.

If Guo-Ying knew the truth, she would certainly hate her mother and her father, Fenglan believes. Why hadn't she been able to keep the secret, as her husband had? She reprimands herself, the beautiful yet quiet park in front of her suddenly becoming unbearable.

Mr. Jing waves to her, saying they're starting another round of the practice, but she tells him that she needs more rest.

Walking toward her is an old couple with a stroller. They're in their late sixties, dressed stylishly. The wife wears a black and red striped silk scarf over a wide-collared suede jacket, the bottoms of her black pants covering most of her high-heeled shoes. The husband sports a wool cap and a brown sweater inside his unbuttoned, long black overcoat. His shoes are shined. Fenglan has seen them in the park before, heard them speaking Mandarin, but they've never greeted one another. Having lived in this neighborhood for this long, she has noticed that Asians typically don't greet strangers, while Caucasians usually do.

They sit on a bench near her and play with their grandchild, calling the baby "little darling," "sweet cookie," and other affectionate names. The baby soon falls asleep. They begin to talk about their son and daughter-in-law. Fenglan does not like to eavesdrop, but she cannot help. She looks away so as not to give the impression that she is listening: she does not want to embarrass them, or herself.

"They have no idea how tough it is for old people like us to take care of a little baby," the wife starts. "I held him for only half an hour yesterday. Today my shoulders and back hurt." She pounds her shoulder with her fist.

"He's almost fifteen kilos. Not a little thing," the husband says. "I can't even hold him for long. And now he's learning to walk."

"I thought I could finish reading a few books while we're here, but so far I've read only ten pages."

"I haven't even started to write the introduction I promised for Professor Liu's book. Last time when we talked on the phone, I lied to him and said I was halfway through. I think we should tell our son and daughter-in-law that we have neither the energy nor the time to babysit."

"But they are so busy at work. If we left—"

"You always say that! If they decided to have a baby, they must take care of him themselves. We aren't their nannies. You must make that clear to them. Didn't we raise three children all by ourselves? And we both had jobs too."

"But times are different now. Also, we're retired and don't have an excuse not to babysit our only grandson. Just look at our friends. Aren't half of them overseas, taking care of their grandchildren? Our daughter-in-law said to me just the other day that she was planning on having another child next year and would fly us over again on a six-month visa."

The man grows impatient. "You're too soft-hearted! Yes, we are retired, but there are so many things we can do. I can write a memoir, you can teach at an adult school or learn something new at a senior university. We can also travel. The Silk Road, Hainan, Guizhou, Neimeng—there are so many places in China we haven't been to. What are we doing here, spending our time with a baby who can't speak, cooking lunch and dinner for our son and daughter-in-law every day? If we could drive or speak good English, we might find more things to do. But the only foreign language we know is Russian.

It doesn't help us get around here." The man raises his voice. "More-over, our Chinese money is worth nothing here. If we want to buy anything, we must ask our son for money. Just think about our life in Beijing. So many friends, so many familiar restaurants, theaters, and teahouses. Bus stops and subway stations are within walking distance from our house. Here, you rarely see a bus."

Seemingly convinced, the wife nods, then says, "Are you going to tell them that we're returning to China next week?"

"Of course, yes. If you don't want to tell them, I will."

"I just don't want them to be mad at us for not looking after our grandson. You know yourself. You can be a little impatient at times."

"I'll just say that my stomach doesn't feel well and I need to go back to China for a checkup. Is that excuse good enough? I'll say that you need to get a checkup as well, for high blood pressure, or they might ask you to stay. Nowadays, children are too dependent."

"But I'll miss them and our grandson."

"I will too. But they can come to see us in China."

"That's true," the wife says, looking at the baby.

The husband puts his arm on the wife's shoulder. "I'll do the talking. Okay? You're too soft."

They stand and continue walking with the stroller.

Fenglan determines that it's also time for her to return to China. She will ask her older daughter to call United Airlines as soon as she gets home. She needs a medical checkup too. She's been feeling dizzy and nauseated for no particular reason, and now and then she has cold sweats and a racing heart. The heart medicine she has brought with her from China is almost gone. Though her older daughter has bought her a medical insurance plan, she knows the deductible would be high if she chose to see a doctor here. She's been hiding her dis-comforts from her two daughters, afraid that they'd insist on taking her to the hospital. Both Mr. Jing and Mrs. You have told her that American doctors always suggest surgery so they'll get paid more. It is better that she go to her hometown hospital, where she can use her own insurance and where she's grown acquainted with some of the doctors over the years. None of her discomforts is new, she reasons, and she just needs to keep taking her medicine.

One thing that pleases her is that her older daughter and her husband seem to be getting along better. She doesn't know what happened, but they have begun to talk more and do more things together, like cooking, grocery shopping, or fixing the house. Though Bob still often works overtime, when he is home, instead of going straight to his computer, he helps her daughter with housework or plays with Dongdong. A few nights, they left Dongdong with her and went out for a walk. When they came back, she could tell from the expressions on their faces that they'd had a good conversation. Last Friday night, the whole family, including Guo-Ying, went to a theater in San Jose to watch an acrobatic troupe from Beijing. Sitting between Dongdong and her older daughter, Fenglan noticed that Bob and Guo-Mei held hands for a while. After she leaves, she is now convinced that her older daughter's small family will go back to normal and the couple will be closer.

Mr. Jing, Mrs. You, and the others have finished the second round of *mulan fist* and are debating where to play mah-jongg. Fenglan tells them that she'll skip mah-jongg and go home.

"Are you going to the anti-Japanese seminar in San Francisco next Sunday? It's open to the public. It's organized by the Alliance for Preserving the Truth of the Sino-Japanese War," Mr. Jing says.

"A seminar?" she asks with surprise; she has never attended a seminar in her life.

The others explain to her about the seminar, to be held not far from the Japanese consulate in San Francisco, discussing Japan's atrocities in China and other Asian countries during World War II. "Did you read *The Rape of Nanking*?" one adds. "It's by an Asian-American writer. I have a Chinese copy. I can lend it to you."

Fenglan waves her hand. "I don't read books. Reading newspapers is hard enough for my eyes." Her parents were Nanking massacre survivors, and they had told her and her sister about it. Of course, they spared them the details so she and her sister wouldn't get scared. Later, through movies, newspapers, TV, and radio, she had learned more about the war, not just the war but also the Chinese government's protests against Japan's prime minister frequenting the Shinto shrine to pay his respects to the war criminals. Right before she visited the United States, she saw a group of Japanese tourists in the park near her apartment. They spoke softly to each other and smiled constantly at the passing Chinese. "Japanese devils!" she heard some Chinese cursing. But she couldn't see any devil in these tourists: they looked so polite and friendly—more so than any of the Chinese in the park.

Fenglan glances at Mrs. You, who is sitting on a bench, and remembers she once told her that during the Japanese occupation of her hometown, her mother had been forced into prostitution and her two uncles had been enslaved to build an airport and later tortured to death. She has forgotten exactly on which occasion Mrs. You told her that, maybe while they were talking about their parents' deaths. Fenglan didn't hide anything from Mrs. You: Mrs. You was her age, she was in China back then, she knew.

Mrs. You stands. Fenglan imagines that she will say something about her family, but Mrs. You sits again.

"Mrs. You," Mr. Jing says with irritable patience. "Are you going to speak out or not at the seminar?"

"Let me think about it." Mrs. You's voice wavers.

Mr. Jing turns to speak with the rest of the group, saying they should volunteer to distribute the flyers, posting them in all the Chinese supermarkets, like 99 Ranch Market, Marina Food, and Hai Yang. The atmosphere is boisterous, heated by condemnations of Hideki Tojo, the Japanese army, and criticism of the Chinese authorities, who in the view of Mr. Jing and two others, have been too soft in their confrontation with Japan, a compromise to win Japanese investment. Mrs. You sits quietly; she is obviously listening but makes no comment.

It's beyond Fenglan's comprehension that these people, who like to talk about gambling in Las Vegas, real-estate investments, and their children, would discuss a seminar so passionately. It's as though the women she used to work with in her factory had suddenly switched topics of conversation from baby diapers to world politics. She's an ordinary person. What do world politics have to do with her? she thinks. Even if Japan apologized, could that change the fact that Mrs. You's mother, her uncles, and other victims had suffered? How could one settle each of the many injustices of life? As her eyes meet Mrs. You's, Fenglan knows that's what she's thinking too.

After a while, Fenglan hears Mrs. You's voice. "I'll talk about my mother's and uncles' stories at the seminar." She turns to Fenglan as if looking for support. "Are you going?"

She shakes her head and says that she doesn't want to go; she realizes that they are different from her. They're like Americans, eager to express themselves, to have their voices heard, while she prefers silence.

She excuses herself. From the paved path, she can still hear Mr. Jing's loud talk about the seminar agenda.

At the other side of the park, Fenglan notices three people sitting on the grass with their legs crossed under them. Two look like Chinese, and the other is a white man. She stops to look at them curiously, but as soon as she realizes that they are performing *Falun Gong* she passes them hurriedly. She has seen *Falun Gong* supporters protesting outside the Chinese embassy in San Francisco, holding big banners and posters filled with pictures of how some practitioners in China had been tortured.

Two years ago, she followed the example of a neighbor and practiced *Falun Gong*, thinking that it was just a type of *qi gong*. But three months later it was pronounced illegal by the government and was prohibited across the country. So she stopped; if the government said it was illegal, it must be wrong, she reasoned. She was surprised when the leader in charge of ideology in her factory came to her apartment and told her that *Falun Gong* was an antigovernment and antiparty political organization and warned her not to practice anymore. Who had told the leader that she had practiced *Falun Gong*, she wondered, as the leader informed her that the practitioners had rallied in Beijing without permission from the government. She was scared and baffled, knowing nothing about the rally in Beijing and the claimed antigovernment element in the practice of *Falun Gong*. In fact, she had always practiced alone and had no contact with any practitioners other than her neighbor, a seventy-five-year-old woman. She promised the leader that she had stopped the practice and wouldn't do it again.

After experiencing so much political tumult in her life, Fenglan fears politics; on the other hand, she feels that life is complicated. Who would dream that doing a form of physical exercise could be political? Since then, she has practiced only *tai ji*, which, she believes, with its long history and popularity, is not political.

She continues to walk. Rather than going home, she turns onto a small road. She is perspiring, so she takes off the green fleece jacket her second daughter has bought her, which she wears often for her morning exercises.

Passing a white church with a huge cross on its roof, she sees a crowd of formally attired people enter, men in suits or tuxedos, women in dresses and high-heeled shoes. Apparently they are there for a wedding. She watches from a distance; she has never seen a church wedding before. After the groom goes inside, it is the turn of the bride, who is with an old man—the bride's father, she assumes, based on their similar looks. They walk toward the church, where the wedding music begins to play. The bride looks nervous in her beaded and flowing wedding gown, stopping to take a long breath. Her father whispers something to her, and she smiles. They enter the church, the bride putting her hand on her father's arm; right before they go inside, the bride plants a quick kiss on her father's cheek.

Fenglan is moved, recalling a moment thirty years ago: a line of nuns in black habits were standing outside a destroyed church, their heads weighed down by heavy wooden boards hanging from their necks, "I am a poisonous weed" written in black ink on the boards. Behind them were young Red Guards who shouted revolutionary slogans, lifting their fists again and again, while she, along with many other people nearby, were ordered to spit on the nuns and slap them. Convinced that Christianity was spiritual opium, Fenglan felt that these nuns deserved to be condemned and punished. Though she didn't want to spit on them and slap them, she followed the orders. A year later she was condemned as "a poisonous weed" herself, had to wear a heavy board just like those hanging from the nuns' necks, and was spat upon and slapped by strangers who stared at her with hatred and contempt in their eyes. As she listened to the roars of accusations against her, she asked herself, Why did these strangers detest her? Then she remembered that when she was spitting on the nuns and slapping them, she had had the same hatred and disdain in her eyes.

Her older daughter has asked her to go to the church with her a score of times, but Fenglan has always refused. The church is too clean, too quiet, too empty. She imagines that as soon as she steps over the threshold, she will be reminded of what she did to the nuns thirty years ago, then be judged and sentenced.

But why should she feel responsible for the cruelty she inflicted so long ago? Hadn't she been a victim herself?

She remembers that her older daughter once said to her that all human beings have sinned. No, she shakes her head. She hasn't sinned. She has never done anything deliberately to hurt others.

She likes the temples back home, which are colorful and always packed with people—you don't have to be a believer to go there. Incense burns in the burners; vendors sell red candles and paper money; monks chant. And there are so many gods, to each of whom she can pray about different things. No one judges her there.

The wedding music stops. She keeps walking. Except for the fallen leaves along the curbs, the road is clean, with no garbage in sight. On either side of the road, next to the sidewalk, evenly spaced evergreen trees extend like two walls, and their branches rustle in the breeze. Everything looks cheerful and bright, as if there were no such thing as darkness in the world.

Fenglan remembers her childhood as bright and cheerful when her parents and sister were still alive. Her father liked to hold her on his lap and tell her stories; her mother was always soft-spoken and gentle, a good cook and housekeeper; and her sister, naughty and smart, often played house with her and took her to see puppet shows and street performers. In the evenings, after dinner, her father would tell her and her sister a story from *The Classics of Mountains and Seas* or *Strange Tales of Liao Zhai,* an ancient collection of stories about foxes and ghosts. He sat them both on his lap, and while he was telling his stories, her mother would set out snacks or sweet soups she had made on the small table in front of them, to consume after her father had finished. Fenglan's favorite story was about Nuwa.

"Nuwa is Emperor Yan's youngest daughter. One day, Nuwa went to swim in the East Sea and was drowned by huge waves," her father had said dramatically, moving his hand in the air to show the motion of the waves. "After she died, she turned into a little bird with red feet and a white beak." He now flapped his arms, like a bird flying. "She missed her father so much that she cursed the ocean that had taken her life. But the ocean ignored her, rising and ebbing as if nothing had happened. Every day, from dawn to dusk, she circled above the ocean, making the sad sounds of *jing . . . wei, jing . . . wei,* and picked up stones and tree branches from the mountain nearby and threw them into the ocean, wanting to fill it."

"You can't fill an ocean. It's too big," Fenglan had responded to her father, her eyes wide.

"But it doesn't matter, does it? The most important thing is that Nuwa lived her life bravely," her father had answered, stroking her head.

"Ma, is that right?" She had turned to her mother, who was dividing red-bean soup into four small bowls.

"Your father was right," her mother had answered, straightening her back. "In the future, no matter how difficult life is, you and your sister must live bravely like Nuwa."

At that time, Japan had already established a puppet government in northeastern China, and had bloodily occupied Nanjing, where her parents used to live. They had traveled to Hangzhou, Wuhan, Jiujiang, then finally settled in Nanyi, where Fenglan and her sister had been born. Though they had lived in a small rented house in a run-down neighborhood, her mother had kept the house clean and organized, with her father's books neatly shelved or stacked, their favorite paintings and calligraphy on the walls.

Half a century has passed, and now Fenglan is a white-haired old woman, and her parents and her sister are dead. If they knew about her life in the afterlife, she wonders, if they knew that, even though she is alive she has suffered and is merely an ordinary retiree who has achieved nothing in her life, would they feel proud of her? She stops at an intersection, looking around, as if hoping someone will answer her questions. But all she sees are silent roads, silent houses, and silent trees. Heaving a deep sigh, she unwittingly holds her arms in front of her, as though she were pushing away a huge rock from inside her chest.

Without realizing it, she arrives at Dongdong's kindergarten. It's a one-story building with a red roof and blue outside walls. Flowers grow along the walls. Under the awnings are colorful wind chimes made of glass disks shaped like animals. When the wind blows, the animals run in circles, jingling merrily.

In front of the building is a playground with swings, seesaws, monkey bars, slides, climbing structures, and a sandbox. Fenglan has seen kids playing there many times when she comes to pick up Dongdong. But the playground is empty today—the kids are inside.

Standing outside, she debates what she should do—go home or wait for recess. In China, she has often seen old people waiting outside a kindergarten's high fence. Some stand on tiptoe, looking over the fence or through the gaps between the bars, hoping to spot their grandson or granddaughter in the classroom. They usually have brought fruit, snacks, or toys with them, waiting for the break to give them to their grandchildren. Whenever a staff member sees these old people, he or she yells at them, telling them not to disturb the class. They smile apologetically, pretending that they are going to leave. But as soon as the staff member disappears, they turn around and stay.

Dongdong's kindergarten has neither a fence nor rude staff members who will ask her to go away. Nor old people with food and toys waiting for their grandchildren. Fenglan suddenly misses her grandson terribly. She paces on the sidewalk before mustering enough courage to walk to a half-open window and peek inside.

There are more than twenty children in the classroom. The teacher, a round-faced Indian girl, is helping a boy draw a house. Fenglan spots Dongdong in the middle of the room. Lying on his stomach, legs swinging back and forth, he is drawing an animal on a piece of paper with crayons. The animal is a combination of a horse, a dragon, and a bird, with colorful wings, a thick tail, and a long body. After he's done, he stands and holds it up in front of him. He smiles proudly and shows it to a white girl with a ponytail. They both wave their arms up and down, as if flying. After a while, Dongdong says something to her, and they sit on the floor facing each other.

"You slap my hand once, I slap your hand once, now let's tell the story about a kid playing with mud." Fenglan hears Dongdong's childish voice in Mandarin. She feels her heart skip a beat.

The little girl must be familiar with the game. She chants with Dongdong and slaps his hand once. Though she cannot speak Mandarin and is merely humming along, she looks serious, staring at Dongdong's mouth, trying to figure out how he pronounces those foreign sounds.

"You slap my hand twice, I slap your hand twice, now let's tell the story about two eagles looking for wizards," Dongdong continues. Fenglan finds herself chanting silently with him. "You slap my hand thrice, I slap your hand thrice, now we have a story of three monkeys crossing the mountains . . ."

As she leaves the kindergarten, she feels relieved, knowing why she is still alive, full of hope. In her imagination, she is standing in her apartment in China right now, surrounded by her parents, her sister, her husband, her two daughters and their families. For the first time, her dim apartment is filled with chatter, laughter, and kids' cheerful singing.

"Qiang." She calls out her husband's name silently, smiling. "Look! Four generations are finally together."

FOURTEEN

March

AT A CAFÉ NEAR San Francisco's Union Square, Ingrid sips an espresso. She looks out the window, watching people burdened with shopping bags. Stores are still giving steep discounts, hoping to dispose of unsold spring stock and prepare for the new summer lines. It is a sunny but chilly Saturday afternoon, following a week of rain; the streets are crammed with tourists holding maps, cameras at the ready. They hesitate at intersections, looking around, sometimes turning to their maps before deciding where to go. San Francisco is a visitors' town.

Inside the café, three teenage girls, each with multiple shopping bags, at least one printed with "Macy's," at her feet, occupy a window table. A girl with shiny purple eye shadow takes a halter-topped, silver satin evening dress from a bag to show her friends, saying that it cost $150 after a 60 percent discount. "But it's a BCBG!" A girl with a wide copper-studded, red belt remarks and shrugs. The other girl agrees, assuring the owner of the dress that her money was well spent, especially because she is in college now and needs something a little "classy." "And you got the money from your parents anyway," the girl adds. The girl with the red belt now extracts a jewelry box from her purse and displays a glistening silver bracelet.

"Gosh! So beautiful!" the other two girls exclaim simultaneously, startling a middle-aged woman next to them who was reading a Harry Potter book and also has a Macy's shopping bag at her feet. At first she gives the girls a stern look for interrupting her reading, then she beams a forgiving smile when hearing the bracelet's proud owner announce that it's a gift from her mother, celebrating her first year at college.

The sight of the girls reminds Ingrid of her gift from her father when she went to college in China: a notebook with a cover picture of Zhang Haidi, a highly accomplished disabled young woman promoted by the Party as the model for youth since the early eighties. Under her picture were inscriptions from a Party leader: "Learn from Zhang Haidi. Be a Communist with revolutionary ideals, sound morals, good education, and strong discipline!" Ingrid had used the notebook as a diary but burned it after her college boyfriend died. She glances at the three cheerful American girls, thinking how different her life was at their age.

Ingrid is waiting for Matthew Stein, an editor from a San Francisco-based small press. Last week, Matthew e-mailed her, saying that he had received her contact information from Bing'er, whom he had encountered in Toronto not long ago. "She sent me your travel blog, and I enjoyed reading it. I heard you live in San Francisco right now. Why don't we meet?" he'd said. Not having heard of the press, Ingrid first thought it might be one of those vanity publishing houses, but after research she discovered that it had been in business for more than thirty years and had published quite a few critically claimed books. So she replied and made an appointment with him.

Ingrid had started the travel blog the day after she moved to San Francisco, on a whim. Since then she has made a dozen postings, each about a city she has visited. They're supposed to be a writing exercise, and she isn't serious with them, though she tries to write her best. Bing'er loves them and has been begging her to write more. When Ingrid received Matthew's e-mail, she thought it was odd that her travel blog interested him.

Along with the blog, she began a novel, about which she hasn't talked with anyone, not with Bing'er, not with Angelina, not even with Molly Holiday. Three weeks ago, she enrolled in a private writing workshop in Palo Alto, an effort to discipline herself to write. The teacher, Susan Frazier, a former Stanford Stegner fellow, is a sixtyish woman with a wide range of publications, including novels, short stories, poems, and essays. Ingrid wouldn't go so far as to say that she loves her writing, but there are certain things about the teacher she admires, especially her warmth toward her students and her sincerity about writing, not as an occupation but as her indulgence, something essential in her life. There are ten students in the class, with whom Ingrid's begun to be friends more or less—at the least, they are all quite committed to the workshop. Last week, Ingrid submitted a short story for critique but not her novel excerpt; she wasn't ready for that yet.

Now, sitting in the café, hearing all the light talk about shopping and bargains (the café is getting crowded), she ruminates on her characters, a family of three separated by wars and other turbulence. She has modeled the wife on her aunt; though her aunt died long before she was born, the first moment she saw her pictures, Ingrid was drawn to her—her beauty, her liveliness as a child, her melancholy and defiance as an adolescent and a young adult.

As for the father, she has borrowed from a middle school classmate's father, a silent janitor with ashen hair and a prominent mole at the right corner of his mouth, who swept the campus every morning, meticulous about his work. Her classmate was ashamed of his father, and the only thing he had said to her about his father was that he was a lunatic. She had thought the father illiterate and dull until one day she saw him against a wall behind bushes, his broom beside him, when she was on her way to fetch hot water in the canteen. He was sobbing, a thick book open in the middle on his knees. She walked over, half out of kindness, half out of curiosity. "Uncle Luo," she called out to him. Startled, he closed the book. She saw the cover: *Doctor Zhivago*. Her sister had read it the summer before, so she knew it was by a Russian writer, a Nobel Prize winner. Later, she made fun of this incident to a few of her friends, unaware of her cruelty until much later, when she went to college and read the book herself.

Before she started her novel, her plan was ambitious, to cover nearly a century, from the end of the Qing Dynasty to the present. Her major in history in China had helped her lay out the historical terrain. Research was challenging but not too difficult; she had gotten a stack of books from the San Francisco Public Library and some university libraries.

She was well into the third chapter. Until a week ago: since then she hasn't been able to write one more word. She is at a loss about how to continue. And she's begun to have a strange feeling that part of the book demands to be written in Chinese. For certain scenes and characters to sound authentic, she believes that they will have to be in her mother tongue. Furthermore, she is afraid that her having lived outside China for a decade has made her thinking and her writing too Western, has made her subconsciously absorb Western stereotypes about China and Chinese people. Moreover, she needs more Chinese books for reference, books she has to buy in China because they are unavailable in the United States.

Now, I have two second languages, and no first language to claim, Ingrid thinks, laughing at herself. She finishes her espresso and walks to the counter to order a double latte. She'd like to forget her writing for a while. She walks back to her table and picks up the newspaper her neighbor left behind: only the real-estate pages.

She reads them anyway, knowing that she will never be able to afford to buy in San Francisco. She takes a look at her watch: fifteen minutes past the scheduled meeting time. But she is not in a hurry, so she doesn't mind. Then she takes out two books from her purse and flips through them. A translation agency gave them to her just this morning to translate from English to Chinese, both with decent advances.

One is by an author whose investment books are always *New York Times* best-sellers. Under the large-print title *You Can Become a Millionaire Too!* is the author's triumphantly smiling face, her eyes glittering like those of a leopard. The other book, also a best-seller, is about how to enrich one's sex life, with explicit descriptions of love-making positions, sex tools, and fantasies, including group sex, outdoor sex, anal sex, bondage, and other curious activities. "Imagine the unimaginable!" the author invites on the cover.

Are these the books Chinese people like to read nowadays? she wonders and meanwhile makes fun of herself: she'll be an expert in sex and investment after translating them. She signed the contract because she needed the money, but she knows she is lucky to have the work—she cannot complain about the payment. However, how long she can make a living doing translations remains unknown. She faces competition from China, where translation agencies have grown rapidly in the past few years and charge much less than their American counterparts. She read in a Chinese newspaper that more and more English books are translated into Chinese by college students, who get the assignments from their professors, commissioned by a translation agency or a publisher; sometimes, translation agencies give the work to students directly. Each student gets a chapter and a dictionary, and at the end the translations are compiled and edited—at this speed, a book of 250 pages can be translated in weeks or even days. Ingrid's agency once showed her a novel translated thus from English to Chinese. The translation was awful— poor word choices, grammatical errors, no difference in sentence structure between English and Chinese. If she hadn't read the novel in English and known how beautiful it was, she would have thought it unworthy based on the Chinese translation. She feels fortunate to have read many well-translated books when she grew up, such as Tagore's poetry by Bing Xin, Hemingway's novels by Feng Daiyi, Byron's poetry by Cha Liangzheng, and several French writers by Fu Lei. Those translators were either writers themselves or scholars who were experts on the writers they translated. Ironically, Ingrid is aware, some of these writers had chosen to do translation in Mao's era because they feared persecution for writing something Mao disliked.

Ingrid has been considering going to China with her mother at the end of June—granted a visa extension, her mother won't return to China until then, one and a half months longer than planned—and living there for a while, to keep her mother company and extend her savings. It has been more than a month since her birthday, when Mary criticized her for being reckless with her life and not caring for their mother. Mary apologized the next day.

"There's no need to. You were telling the truth anyway," Ingrid said to Mary.

"You're my sister. I only have one sister. I only wish you well," Mary said affectionately, even a little too seriously. Though Ingrid always knew that Mary cared about her, she feels her sister has been a bit too much lately: she calls often, sometimes daily, when there is nothing specific to talk about. Ingrid wants to tell her to stop calling her so frequently but doesn't have the heart.

"I wish we had another sister," Ingrid once joked to Mary. "So she could share your calls with me."

"Well, I think she'd just get the same amount of calls," Mary responded and smiled good-humoredly.

"I'd better escape somewhere for a while. Somewhere with no cell-phone towers," Ingrid joked.

"Why don't you visit China?" Mary suddenly said. "It's very different from before. Even if it hadn't changed, you should go back. After all, it's where you came from, where you spent your first twenty years."

Mary was right, Ingrid admits. The thought of visiting China makes her restless, bringing back her suppressed memories, but she knows that it is the right thing to do, for her mother, for her writing, and most important, for her to make peace with herself—she cannot live in self-exile forever. She needs time to think about what to do next, and she feels that being in China might inspire her.

After her years at San Jose State, she began to travel. At first, they were domestic trips, mostly driving since she had little money. She slept in youth hostels or camped. Sometimes she went with friends, other times alone. After graduation, when she had a full-time job, she traveled internationally whenever she had time off. But it was not until she quit her day job and became a freelance translator and tour guide that she began to travel widely: some business trips but most for leisure. Traveling had given her excitement and inspiration, but six months ago she began to feel lost and anxious, like tumbleweed blowing in the wind, without purpose or direction. Sometimes, the moment her plane landed at another country's airport, she agonized about being a tourist, a temporary resident, a shallow foreigner in the locals' eyes.

For instance, four months ago, she spent two days in Florence after interpreting at a furniture trade show in Milan. She had been to Florence before and had always liked the city. She visited the Duomo one morning. Such a formidable piece of architecture in the center of a boisterous downtown! The grandness and antiquity filled her with awe. Climbing the stairs inside, she realized that she knew little about it beyond what was said in those beautifully printed pamphlets and travel books. She was no different from those despicable tourists who rush to each point of interest and, after taking photos of themselves against popular backgrounds, leave contentedly for the next destination on their itinerary. Every minute she spent in the Duomo she felt more ignorant about it.

Then, one week ago, another business trip took her to Tokyo—in her opinion, a place too futuristic to be real. Again, it wasn't her first time there. Though she used to be fascinated by its congested concrete jungle and tremendous energy, this time she felt only its foreignness, a feeling strengthened by what she saw as she lunched on pasta at a restaurant in Shibuya. The waitresses were all young girls in white aprons with fancy hairstyles and cute jewelry, who bowed often and whispered amiably as they spoke to the customers.

A woman in a ridiculously big red hat had walked in and sat in a corner, four or five tables from Ingrid. She ordered a glass of Asahi, nothing else. Then she extracted seven or eight makeup boxes of various sizes from her handbag—also ridiculously big. She opened all the boxes and began to put on makeup, without removing her hat. She applied layer after layer, slowly and meticulously. During this beautification, a line had formed outside the restaurant, and the waitresses had quickened their steps to serve the customers, sweating visibly; a traffic accident had occurred, and an ambulance had arrived with lights flashing and sirens blasting. But nothing seemed to matter to the woman other than her makeup. She examined herself intently in a silver costume mirror, adding new dabs of eye shadow or applying more mascara. Ingrid couldn't guess her age: the lighting was dim and the shade from the brim of her hat concealed half her face. She could have been in her twenties, thirties, forties, or even older. Ingrid was too fascinated to leave and ordered a dessert that she did not even want.

Two hours elapsed before the woman completed her makeup, then, after putting some money on the table, she left suddenly, her Asahi untouched, her head bowed low. It seemed to Ingrid that only in Tokyo could one encounter a woman who would have done something like that. The loneliness she saw in that woman spoke of her own loneliness in a strange city. It was at that moment, when the woman with the perfectly made-up face disappeared from view, that Ingrid decided she would go back to China with her mother and live there for a while.

As she ponders, a finger taps on her table. She looks up and sees a man wearing a green-and-white checkered shirt under a denim jacket a bit too tight for his broad shoulders. He face is red and he is breathing heavily, presumably from running. Only slightly taller than she, he has disproportionately long arms and an extremely wide forehead. With a round face, big brown eyes, and a dark complexion, he would have looked childlike if not for his black-rimmed glasses. His stomach has begun to bulge, though not too noticeably. He must have had a haircut recently—his soft, straight hair looks tidy, the part significantly to the left.

The mix of a cowboy and Truman Capote. A thought flashes in Ingrid's mind.

"Hi, Ingrid. I'm Matthew Stein. Call me Matthew." He offers a hand.

Ingrid rises and takes his hand. She wonders how Matthew recognized her amid the crowd, which includes quite a few Asian women, then remembers that there are a few pictures of her on her blog. Matthew says that he will order a drink and be back.

As he takes his wallet from his jeans pocket at the counter, the coins slip out and fall on the floor. He squats to gather the coins and thanks the people in line for helping him. On his way back with his Thai iced tea, he bumps into an empty chair and almost trips. He apologizes profoundly to the young couple at the table.

Ingrid is amused but slightly disappointed—Matthew does not resemble in the slightest what she has imagined an editor should look like: composed, witty, with skeptical eyes. She guesses his age at between twenty-nine and thirty-five.

They introduce themselves—the usual stuff two strangers typically exchange when first meeting. Matthew says he grew up in Glendive, Montana, and his parents are farmers, raising horses and Texas longhorns.

Ingrid asks him how he met Bing'er.

"She worked in the restaurant I happened to dine in. I was in Toronto for business," Matthew says. "It was cold that night, and I was the only customer. I asked her to recommend a dish, Szechuan flavor, a little spicy but not too greasy. She said, 'Ants on the Tree.' I laughed and said I didn't know Chinese eat ants. She looked dead serious. 'We do. It's time consuming to make this dish. Better to have big and juicy ants or the dish would be too dry.' "

Ingrid laughs. "You believed her?"

"She was a good actor. Chinese eat snakes, rats, chicken feet anyway, why not ants? I decided to try it. I asked her where to buy ants, those big and juicy ones. She said there was an ant-raising factory near Chinatown. The workers there fed the ants a little wine in the winter to keep them warm and make their meat more tender. She then asked me if I added wine to my pasta sauce sometimes. It all made sense to me. It was not until the dish was served that she confessed that, despite the real name, it is just minced pork mixed with thin bean noodles. She was a funny girl."

"I hope you liked the dish."

"I *loved* it! I just ate it again yesterday at a restaurant on Clement Street. So anyway, we started to talk, and after she learned I am an editor, she told me about you. She adores you."

"She did?" Ingrid chuckles. "Did she tell you about her traveling plan?"

"Not just that, she even showed me her '88 Jeep Cherokee. Other than a bowl-size dent on the rear bumper, it looked pretty okay. I asked her if she was sure about her bold adventure. She said she was from Hubei."

"Yeah, people from Hubei are called *jiu tou niao,* nine-headed birds. They're famous for being smart and fearless."

"That's something, spending a month driving in a strange country alone. Since I was five, I have been dreaming of something like this, but it's still a dream to this day. Oh, well, I guess I have time. Steinbeck did it when he was almost sixty. Have you read his *Travels with Charley?* An excellent book." As Matthew continues to speak, the earlier shyness on his face turns into a relaxed expression, as if talking has helped calm him. He then summarizes his background: unqualified math teacher, mediocre keyboard player, terrible actor, unsuccessful small-business owner, inexperienced editor, and baffled writer.

"At least you've tried them all," Ingrid says.

Matthew glances at the two books at Ingrid's elbow. Noticing his bewilderment, she explains that they are translation projects she has just received, not something she buys or reads for pleasure.

"It pays my rent," she tells him and holds up the investment book. "And this one"—she takes up the other, about sex—"pays for my food, clothes, car insurance, and all the other stuff."

Matthew nods sympathetically. "When I quit teaching, I did various odd jobs. I painted houses, and for a few summers I played cartoon characters for an amusement park. That was a terrible job, wearing hairy clothes on a hot day. By the end of the show I thought I'd die from heat and dehydration. But it's a piece of cake compared with the job one of my friends has. He works at a cemetery, carrying bodies and digging graves. The pay is pretty good. Random House just bought his suspense novel, which I have read already. The protagonist works at a cemetery, and most scenes take place between midnight and four o'clock in the morning, inside the cemetery. I had goose bumps reading it. My friend called me a few days ago, saying he was quitting his job to write full-time and asking me if I wanted to work at his cemetery, to get some fun experience."

"Then you might write a suspense novel too. Or a thriller."

"Yeah, maybe. But I don't mind working at a small press right now. I get a chance to talk with literary agents. Before taking the job, I sent many pitch letters to them but never heard anything back. I thought they were gods, really. Now I call them for coffee or lunch. Maybe one of them will represent me someday, who knows? Having connections doesn't hurt. Also, I get books for free. Of course, I have to read a lot of junky manuscripts. But unless I complete a novel, my boss won't be interested in me as a writer. He pays me to edit other people's writing, not to write my own books."

"We Chinese say that reading ten thousand books is like traveling ten thousand miles. You must have accumulated pretty good mileage. Not enough to cross the U.S., but enough to cover the distance between San Francisco and Los Angeles."

"Aha, that's a wise saying," Matthew responds, then asks Ingrid if she has thought about writing a novel.

Instead of telling him the truth, she says, "I'm thinking about starting one." She just doesn't think she can say she's working on a novel if she isn't sure about the ending.

"I have no problem starting. My problem is finishing," he says. "Oh, I've forgotten why I'm here. My boss asked me to find books with multicultural themes, especially memoirs. Are you interested?"

Ingrid leans back. "I can't write a memoir. Last year, I met an agent in New York, and she asked me to write a memoir about the Cultural Revolution, saying those kinds of books were hot. I told her I was only seven when it ended. Also, aren't there many overseas Chinese writing memoirs about that period already? They are the people who went through it, being Red Guards or Intellectual Youth, exiled to labor farms or put in jail."

"You're right. But memoirs do sell better than novels." He pauses. "I don't know what made me want to write fiction; it just feels good to invent characters and see how they develop, you know. After spending years on a book, you have to find an agent, then the agent needs to find a publisher. You can bet it's much easier to find a husband or a wife. But my press is quite good, and we publish literary novels that don't make money or make little money. My boss loves money, but he loves good books more. Of course we must make a profit or we can't stay in business. If we went under, I'd have to update my résumé, changing 'inexperienced editor' to 'homeless editor.' "

"Think about your friend's offer of working at a cemetery," Ingrid says jokingly.

"You never know. I might take the job. Also, being a janitor or a night watchman may not be bad, either. Raymond Carver used to work as a janitor and a deliveryman. I believe he painted houses too."

"Good for you. It looks like you have something lined up."

"We'll see. One thing I can tell you is that I don't fancy a life of eating dry bread and drinking beer. I've had enough of those days." He glances at his stomach. "I don't lose weight easily. Even if I only drank water every day, I doubt I'd shrink much. I'm the opposite of you Asians. No matter how much you eat, you don't gain weight. Just look at the old people in Chinatown. It seems to me that they eat many meals a day, but they're skinny. I bet that if they stood on eggs, the eggs wouldn't break. But it's not bad to be a little fat in San Francisco, you know. If there were an earthquake and I got stuck in my room, my fat might save my life."

Ingrid laughs at his self-deprecation; she has realized that Matthew isn't the kind of authoritative editor she had agonized about but a wannabe writer just like herself.

"You Chinese writers exist in the shadow of the Cultural Revolution, while we Jewish writers live in the nightmare of the Holocaust," Matthew remarks. "In fact, both my grandparents managed to escape the Holocaust, and none of my relatives died unnaturally. Still, somehow I get the feeling from my writer friends that I'd better write a book about the Holocaust if I'm serious about writing; they even get jealous of me because they have no holocausts to write about."

"When so many people write about the same theme, they could ruin the theme or make it seem less important, don't you think? Mass production, it sounds like to me," Ingrid says. "Reminds me of IKEA furniture."

Matthew agrees, then begins to talk about writers he likes, mainly contemporary ones, including those his age. Though Ingrid has heard of most of them, she is not familiar with their work. In the end she has to interrupt him and tells him that the writers she typically reads are from the eighteenth or nineteenth century or the first half of the twentieth. She explains that her reading habits reflect the fact that she was slow reading English the first few years she was in the United States, so she tried to read the classics first. "The list is long, so I'm still working through them," she says. She also explains that, influenced by her Mexican roommate in New York, she has been reading several Latino writers.

"Do you read only the masters? Or writers who are dead?" Matthew asks. "One of my friends is like that. He calls it 'digging out treasures from the dead.' He says those masters are his spiritual friends. One day, we had barely sat down at a restaurant when he told me that Nabokov was on his way to his apartment to discuss one of his characters with him. Then he just took off, leaving me there. To learn from the masters, he copied their writing for an hour in longhand every day. He said it was important not to write with a computer or you wouldn't be able to enter the masters' brains. I once read a short story he wrote. The plot, structure, and tone totally copied Chekhov's 'The Lady with the Dog.' My friend wrote about a married farmer in Napa meeting an illiterate prostitute during his vacation in San Diego. That kind of feigned melancholy almost killed me. After reading his story, I had to eat lobster for dinner to make up for my suffering."

"Ha-ha, you were quite mean. Does your friend still write?"

"He still copies the masters' books in longhand now and then, waiting for inspiration."

"Do you read the classics?"

"I used to, when I was in college. But they require patience, don't they? A lot of them are slow and boring. Fifty or one hundred years ago, people had time to read big books like *War and Peace, Jean-Christophe,* or *Crime and Punishment.* Nowadays we have distractions from TV, radio, the Internet, movies, piles of newspapers and magazines, not to mention a full-time job and a messy apartment waiting to be cleaned—not by a maid, that's for sure. You've probably heard that some of the classics' publishers are doing compact editions, meaning abridged editions, of some classics."

"That's too bad. That's like fast food to me."

"I don't like the practice, either, but I understand why they do it. At least the readers get a chance to read something intelligent. I can tell you've read a lot of classics from your blog. I liked how you inserted certain scenes or dialogues from a classic novel into your description of a tourist attraction. You know what? Forget about memoirs. I think you should do a travel book. Travel books sell big-time. And after you have money, you can write as you please. Like Anaïs Nin and Henry Miller, who once wrote porn stories for a dollar a page for an old man in Oklahoma to supplement their income so they could write what they wanted. As for me, since I don't want to have anything to do with the Holocaust, at least not now, all I can write about is coming of age, friendship, divorce, homicide, adultery, or family conflicts. Just last night, I was wondering how to make a hard-core Roman Catholic widow with three little kids in Montana fall in love with an ambitious young atheist politician."

"What's the time period?"

"The early nineties? Or maybe earlier."

"Hmm, that widow must have been bored with her unromantic and undramatic life."

"Do you think that a young politician could fall in love with the widow?"

"Why not? In his social circle, all the women are politicians, attorneys, businesswomen, or others who are just as ambitious as he is. That widow's unconditional motherly love and care and her submissiveness are just what he needs when he comes home from a tiring day. But their relationship won't last. The young man will soon seek a new mistress who can help him rise in the world and challenge his manhood."

"What do you say about making the politician a married man and a father? That would make the plot more intricate."

"It's better if he's single. A young, ambitious bachelor, intelligent, passionate, a good lover. If he had a family, he'd worry about the media and wouldn't dare get involved with the widow. Just look at our previous president to see how powerful and omnipotent the media are nowadays. In my opinion . . ." Ingrid pauses deliberately.

"Go on!" Matthew looks engrossed, almost impatient.

"How about making the widow a traditional, religious, high-class woman whose husband is a boring business guru? To make the husband donate to his campaign, the young politician approaches the wife and seduces her, only to realize later that he has fallen in love with her. But, for his future, he must choose another woman with more social status. He meets such a woman: stunningly beautiful yet too naïve and girlish for his taste. But it doesn't matter; all he cares about is his career."

"Wow, it's getting more and more interesting. How will you end the story?"

"Let me think . . ." Seeing Matthew take the bait, Ingrid can barely contain her laughter. She picks up her lukewarm latte and sips it with a thoughtful expression. "Hmm, it's a moot question."

Matthew grasps his iced-tea cup with one hand and lifts it to his lips, his eyes fixed on Ingrid, but instead of drinking he puts the cup down: he too is thinking about the fate of this forbidden love.

"I've got an idea!" Ingrid wipes her mouth with her napkin. "He's afraid that the widow will publicize their affair and ruin his political career, so he decides to kill her. Of course he isn't so stupid as to hire a mafia hit man or professional assassin to do it—these people always come back to threaten you later, you know. Also, he's arrogant and proud: if he starts something, no matter whether it went well or poorly, he faces the consequences and finishes it himself. His campaign for governor will be officially launched in two weeks, and he has to kill her before that. His decision is timely because the widow is planning to expose their affair to the media. In her despair and depression, she has confessed to her priest about her adultery, and her priest has urged her to publicize her affair, to humiliate the candidate. In fiction, priests always like meddling in others' business. Isn't that so? If you haven't read E. L. Voynich's *The Gadfly*, you should check it out. That book used to be extremely popular in China and Russia, read by millions of people. There is a famous priest in the book. Anyway, the widow hasn't wanted to damage her young lover, nor has she been paid either by the media or the politician's rivals. She loves the man dearly and only wishes him well, however heartbroken she is by his betrayal."

"I like the idea to have a priest in the book. I can write plenty about them. One of my uncles is a priest."

Ingrid continues. "One evening, this young man—he's not that young anymore, but still very good-looking—invites the widow to meet him at a secret place on a mountain where they used to make love, saying he's been missing her. When they meet, he shoots her. In his haste, he doesn't kill her, though he thinks he did. When he gets home, he's tortured by guilt; after all, he still loves her. He doesn't dare read the newspapers or watch TV, afraid that he'll see her body. He locks himself up in his country house, responding to neither his new mistress nor his aides. In the end, nearly losing his mind, he turns himself in. A bit like Rodion Raskolnikov in *Crime and Punishment*. Only then does he realize that she is still alive, bedridden in a hospital, and she hasn't said a word to the police about him. He's overjoyed, realizing that his true love is the widow. I know little about American law. It's up to you what kind of sentence he'll serve. I think he'll commit suicide over his career failure and his guilt toward the widow. As for the widow, I'll let you decide her fate."

Matthew nods, sighs, smiles, all the while looking at Ingrid with a sense of wonder. Ingrid cannot hold in her amusement any longer; she buries her head in her arms to muffle her laughter. Matthew's smile turns into a puzzled frown.

"The story I just told you," she confesses at last, "is just a variation of Stendhal's *Le Rouge et le Noir*—*The Red and the Black*. The politician is the recalcitrant Julien Sorel, the widow is Madame de Rênal. Didn't you say that classic novels are boring and out of date?"

Matthew blushes. He clenches his right hand into a fist and waves it at Ingrid, pretending to be angry, but then he laughs. "Okay, you won this time. It looks like I have to kiss my Montana widow good-bye for a while until I figure out what to do with her."

Matthew looks at his watch and says he must go to another café, not far away, to meet several volunteers from the International Action Center office. He is one of the organizers for a pro-gay rally in April.

"Since Bush began to campaign for the presidency, I've been volunteering with several activist groups," Matthew says. "I'd thought he wouldn't have stood a chance to get elected. If not for his old man, he wouldn't even have been a governor. My friends and I had planned a big celebration. But . . . anyway, we got very drunk when the returns came in. If we hadn't, we'd have gone out and vandalized cars and stores. In the past few months I've helped organize a dozen demonstrations and conferences, supporting equal marriage rights and immigrants' rights, and protesting against the Bush administration. Did you notice that Bush Street here was renamed Puppet Street on Inauguration Eve? I didn't do it. I wish I had." He looks happy about this prank. "Oh, I forgot to ask you. Are you an American citizen? You didn't vote for Bush, did you?"

Seeing Ingrid shake her head, he is relieved, assuming she was replying to his second question. "Call me up if you want to volunteer. There are a lot of things we can affect. The world won't get better if we just sit around letting politicians abuse our trust."

His big eyes are filled with enthusiasm—Ingrid sees herself, her younger self, in his face. Since coming to the United States, she hasn't participated in any political events—she just cannot bring herself to be passionate about American politics, about which she knows little to begin with. Moreover, she has deliberately stayed away from parades, rallies, or other big gatherings, which somehow always lead to an unpleasant memory. In San Francisco, New York, or other places, whenever she came across such an event, she walked away, going to a mall or a restaurant where people seemed utterly ignorant of what was happening on the street. Is the past so present in her mind that she's forever caught in this bind? she asks herself. To hide her unease she says, with a faint smile, "I didn't know you are so into politics."

"It's not politics. It's just exercising our rights as citizens. It's in the First Amendment. By the way, there is an anti-Bush rally outside the Civic Center right now. I'll be there after the meeting. If you have time, stop by." Matthew rises and finishes his iced tea in a few gulps, not noticing that it has dripped on the front of his jacket. "Also, when you're ready to write your novel, let me know."

Though Matthew keeps telling Ingrid that he's running late for his meeting, he doesn't get going. Finally, he says good-bye, only to return a moment later, asking her for her phone number.

After he leaves, Ingrid sits at the café a little longer, then walks out and goes into a gallery at the intersection of Grant and Sutter, where expensive paintings and lithographs by Miró, Chagall, Dalí, and Picasso are displayed artfully in a high-ceilinged and well-lighted space. She admires Miró, an artist who in her opinion never abandoned innocence and conscience. How peaceful it is to be in a gallery! She thinks of the husband character in her novel, an ink-and-brush painter who locks himself up in his studio to paint whenever he hears bad news from the teahouse he frequents—that's his way to deny the real world, struck by endless wars and injustices. One day his studio is bombed, and when he wakes up alone in the hospital, he no longer remembers who he is. The only thing he does remember is that he is married and his wife is pregnant. Then he is forced into service by a local warlord and sent to a battle far from home.

What's next for him? Ingrid thinks. What should she write in the fourth chapter and those that follow? Of course, he will look for his wife, but how can she advance the plot? And she doesn't know how to end it, either, a terrible mistake according to Susan, her workshop teacher. Writing a novel, Susan once said in class, is like climbing a mountain—your goal is the peak and you know where you're heading all the way—while writing a poem is like picking wildflowers in an open prairie—you stop wherever you feel like. Though Ingrid doesn't believe in rules in creative writing, she has to agree with Susan on this one. Without knowing the direction of her novel, she cannot seem to develop the characters and the plot. Or maybe it's just her; she cannot write like Henry Miller or Jack Kerouac.

She wouldn't mind hopping from one gallery to another—there are many in this neighborhood—but she decides to roam on Market Street toward the Civic Center. All along the way are scattered demonstrators carrying signs and banners, saying things like "Bush is a thief," "He is not my president," "Where's democracy?" and "Gore had half a million more votes. Gore won the election!" As she approaches the Civic Center, she sees that thousands of people have gathered in the plaza. An effigy of George Bush, at least fifteen feet tall, is visible from far away. At each intersection are uniformed and fully equipped policemen, including some on horseback; despite their formidable batons and riot gear, they look friendly and even greet passersby. They can be harsh to protesters should there be conflict, arresting them and charging them with disorderly conduct or other crimes, Ingrid knows, but there won't be machine guns and tanks.

As she stands across from the Civic Center, she hears a loud, cheerful voice behind her. "Hi, I knew you'd come."

She turns: it's Matthew, pink-cheeked and short-breathed, his jacket askew and open. "I cut the meeting short. I went back to the café to look for you. You know what, I think I'll write about the Montana widow anyway. But there won't be any young, good-looking politician. Just a manipulative philistine priest."

Before she can say anything, Matthew takes her by the arm and drags her across the street, into the crowd.

Not until Ingrid arrives home does she realize that she wants to see Matthew again. She's both surprised and amused. Matthew has nothing in common with the men she used to see; he's like a big boy, passionate yet reckless. And he cannot be called handsome. Or knowledgeable or artsy—at least he hasn't demonstrated that side of him. Though she doesn't know his exact age, it's very likely that he is younger than she, perhaps barely thirty. She thinks of his dropping his change all over the floor in the café, tripping over a chair, his impatience in urging her to tell the modified story from Stendhal, his clumsy way of asking for her phone number, and later his dragging her across the street. Even just a few months ago, she wouldn't have imagined herself being with someone like him. Glendive? Where is Glendive? She looks it up on the Internet and learns that it's a tiny town, with fewer than five thousand people. She wasn't completely wrong about his association with cowboys—there are rodeo competitions around that area every summer, not to mention that he grew up with horses and cows. Despite all these things, she felt relaxed and comfortable with him, a feeling she hasn't experienced for a long time with men. Then she recalls his support of gay groups and wonders whether he is straight or gay.

It's an April morning. Ingrid is driving her Volkswagen on Highway 680, with Bing'er in the front passenger seat and her mother in the back. They're heading to Lake Tahoe: Ingrid has reserved a cabin in South Lake Tahoe for two nights. It'll be a four-hour drive. Two weeks ago, her mother had expressed an interest in visiting casinos—not to gamble but to satisfy her curiosity. "All the people in my morning exercise group say that I must see them and play the slot machine," she said to her two daughters. "They say that'll bring me and our whole family good luck."

"Ma, casinos aren't temples, and slot machines aren't gods." Ingrid told her and laughed. But then she thought it was not a bad idea to take her mother to Lake Tahoe to see some shows and do a little sightseeing. Coincidently, Bing'er was visiting, so Ingrid decided that she'd take both of them; Bing'er could ski. Mary and Bob wouldn't be able to make the trip because of a five-day retreat in Sonoma County organized by Mary's church. There would be activities such as hiking, wine tasting, and horseback riding, as well as preaching and seminars about marriage, finances, child rearing, and other matters. Mary had invited their mother to go with them, but she didn't want to.

At the end of March, her mother had told both Ingrid and Mary that she had decided not to emigrate to the United States. "I like living in China, and you can come to visit me. When Dongdong is recovered from asthma, he can come see me too," she had said with resolve. Mary had cried that night, in front of Ingrid, after their mother went to bed.

This morning, Mary and Bob left early for Sonoma County, taking Alex with them. Ingrid could tell they'd both slept poorly; she heard them talking around one a.m., when she was getting ready for bed after reading Zweig's *Letter from an Unknown Woman*. In the morning though, they looked normal; they even kissed on the lips swiftly before getting into the car. Ingrid hadn't seen them kissing for a while.

Outside, the bougainvilleas clinging to the sound walls along the freeway are blooming, purple, crimson, or yellow. Now and then, slim, tall cypress trees, which help block the traffic sounds further, can be seen above the wall. There aren't many cars on the road, so Ingrid sets the cruise control to seventy.

Bing'er is telling Ingrid's mother about her aborted cross-country trip while munching on a tea egg Fenglan made this morning as breakfast. Back in March, toward the end of the second week of her road trip, Bing'er's Jeep broke down in Colorado, not far from Rocky Mountain National Park. With more than 150,000 miles on the car already, it was not worthwhile to fix it, a mechanic told her. So she disposed of it and flew back to Canada.

Bing'er says that when she was in Texas, an old couple let her stay with them for two nights. They asked her if Chinese still wore Mao-style jackets and worried about her family being persecuted because she lived overseas.

"Didn't they know that was the old times?" Fenglan says.

"I don't think so. They probably haven't watched TV or listened to the radio for years."

"Don't they read newspapers?"

"The newspapers they read probably don't say much about China. But I really shouldn't make fun of them. I made a ridiculous mistake myself in Mississippi. I thought there were still a lot of Ku Klux Klan members around, wearing white caps and hoods over their faces and long white robes. I always remember a movie called *Mississippi Burning*."

"Who are these people?" Fenglan asks.

"Bad people, white supremacists."

Obviously impressed by Bing'er's solo adventure, Ingrid's mother keeps asking questions.

Ingrid wants to join their conversation but cannot help thinking about her interview for a contracting research position with KQED last week. The San Francisco-based public broadcasting station is planning a documentary series called *China in the New Millennium*. Should she be hired, there would be a chance for her to travel with the camera crew to China, helping with interpreting, interviewing, and researching. Matthew Stein had heard of this opportunity from a friend and immediately informed Ingrid. Though the pay is not generous—the work is only two days a week—Ingrid hopes she can get the job. Of course, she would have to continue doing translation and interpretation to supplement her income.

It's turned out that Matthew is straight, though he has more gay and lesbian friends and neighbors than anyone Ingrid has known. He lives in the Castro March. The day after the anti-Bush rally in January, he called and they dined at a Mexican restaurant in her neighborhood, eating tacos and drinking tequila. Since then, they have been seeing each other a few times a week. He's a good chef and likes camping. So far, they've camped out three times, in Big Sur, Lassen Volcanic National Park, and Death Valley. Instead of a short stay in San Francisco for the sake of her mother, Ingrid now feels she'd like to live here longer: maybe KQED will hire her, maybe she and Matthew will get along well, who knows? Anyway, she called Angelina and her other friends in New York about her interview, and they wished her good luck and asked her to promise to visit them soon. As for the Italian student who's subletting from Ingrid, she thrilled that she doesn't have to move.

"Guo-Ying, don't drive too fast," her mother suddenly says.

"It's only seventy." Ingrid glances at the speedometer. "We're in the slow lane. Look! The other cars are going much faster."

"I drove eighty-five on some roads when I was in Texas," Bing'er says with pride.

"That's probably why your Jeep broke down," Ingrid teases.

"I thought it could at least reach Arizona, if not California. Well, I'll have to do it again sometime. A friend is selling her car, a Honda hatchback, one hundred thousand miles on it. What do you think? You can put a lot of stuff into the trunk."

"Are you becoming a nomad?" Ingrid smiles. "That sounds a lot of miles to me."

"But she's only asking eight hundred Canadian dollars. You know, Japanese cars run forever."

"Well, maybe it's a bargain."

Ingrid's cell phone rings. She puts on the headset. It's Mary. "We just arrived," she says. "The driving was smooth. Only a little over an hour. How's Ma doing?"

Ingrid unplugs the headset and passes the phone to her mother. Her mother speaks with Mary first, then Dongdong, then Mary again. Mary then asks to speak with Ingrid, reminding her of safety.

"Ma, I think Guo-Mei is going through a midlife crisis," Ingrid says to her mother in the rearview mirror with a naughty wink after shutting off her phone.

Before Ingrid hits Highway 80 to Sacramento, her mother has fallen asleep in the backseat; she has taken carsickness medicine, which makes her drowsy. Ingrid exits the freeway and stops at a gas station to put a blanket over her mother before continuing to drive.

"You're very nice to your mother," Bing'er says.

"When I was your age, I only wanted to be as far from my parents as possible. And the last thing I wanted was to go home." Ingrid thinks of what Mary once said to her about her not wanting to go home: she had a different reason from her sister's, but the result was the same.

"That sounds like me. I don't want to go home at all."

"The day will come when you'll want to."

"Maybe when I am down and out." Bing'er extends her head outside the window, shaking it in the wind like a happy dog, her hair flying.

The radio, tuned to the National Public Radio station, is broadcasting the news about Slobodan Milosevic, former president of the Federal Republic of Yugoslavia, who was arrested in his Belgrade apartment by Special Forces recently.

"His name was in the news all the time when I was growing up," Bing'er says, looking puzzled. "My classmates and I nicknamed him Old Mi. I always thought he was a hero. How can he be charged with war crimes?"

"You don't get the full story from the media. Not in China, nor in the U.S."

"Which means that people will *never* know the truth." Bing'er laughs. "Anyway, Old Mi is history now. My memory of him as Dear Old Mi is also history now." She rummages in the backpack between her feet. "Politicians come and go, but artists don't. Let's play Bob Dylan. I have his CD here." She finds the CD and inserts it into the player. The singer's unique voice rises: a little hoarse, a little nasal, a little melancholy.

"I recently began to watch sitcoms," Bing'er says. "It seems a good way to learn English, especially slangs. You don't get those from news."

Ingrid agrees, then says she watched a lot of sitcoms herself the first few years she was here. And she tried to memorize the whole *Oxford American Dictionary.* "I think I managed one hundred pages before giving up."

"Wow, that would kill me fast," Bing'er marvels. "Speaking of sitcoms, there are shows about Caucasians, about black people, but nothing about Asians."

"TV producers don't think Asians are funny, I guess."

Bing'er grunts her disapproval but doesn't say more. Then she changes the subject. "I don't think I want to see Tom anymore." She looks out the window. "Remember the boy I told you about a while back?"

"The American boy you met through language exchange? What happened? I thought you liked him?" Ingrid glances at Bing'er before looking back at the road. The traffic is getting a little busy. She presses the brake gently.

"Well, I've been thinking. He is doing his master's in linguistics at the University of Toronto. I haven't even been to college."

"You're a nine-headed bird. When did you start to worry so much? It doesn't matter, does it? As long as you like each other. Also, you can always go to college in Canada. It's not as difficult there as it is in China."

"But the thing is . . . the thing is that I lied to him. I told him I had earned a bachelor's degree in art." Bing'er's voice is dismal. "From the Central Art Academy in Beijing. I don't know why I lied, somehow those words just slipped out of my mouth. I guess I did like him a little."

"Cheer up! How can he check? You're a good painter. That's more important than having a degree. Look at me! I have a degree in accounting, but I wish I didn't."

"He surely can find out," Bing'er mumbles. "Sooner or later. Then he'd call me a liar."

"Then just tell him the truth and apologize."

"There's more, though." Bing'er pauses. "Don't laugh at me for being oversensitive if I tell you."

Ingrid nods.

"One week ago I met his parents and spent a night in their house in Buffalo. They were kind to me. His father is some kind of boss at a computer company, his mother a housewife. After dinner, Tom went to the basement to do laundry—he had brought some of his dirty clothes from school. Since I'd spilled orange juice on my jacket and jeans during the dinner, he took them and threw them in the washer too. A few minutes later, his mother went to the basement and stopped the machine. It wasn't until later that night that I realized she had washed my clothes in a separate load, and I overheard her saying to Tom's father that she thought the clothes made in China were of poor quality and she didn't want Tom's clothes to get stained if the colors bled."

"Did his father say anything?"

"Well, he just said a lot of things were made in China now and he wouldn't worry about that."

"Did you tell Tom that?"

"No, and I don't plan to. What can he say about it? He loves his mother to death. Since that night, I haven't seen him. I just told him I was busy and I was going to visit you. He has a paper due, so he's overwhelmed right now. Anyway, better not to think about it. So, did you have a boyfriend when you were at college in China?"

"I did."

"Why did you break up?"

"We didn't."

"Then what happened? Where is he?"

"I guess somehow we just couldn't be together."

"Sounds like a mystery novel." Bing'er drums her fingers on the dashboard. "Well, I like Matthew."

They are silent for a while, listening to Bob Dylan:

I'm drifting in and out of dreamless sleep
Throwing all my memories in a ditch so deep

Bing'er yawns and says she is sleepy—she woke up early this morning. If Ingrid doesn't mind, Bing'er says, she'd like to take a nap. Bing'er puts on her thick jacket and soon falls asleep, her head against the window, her body shaking slightly because of the uneven road. Despite the sad nature of her earlier story, she has a carefree, hopeful expression on her face, like a baby in a cradle. Several times, Ingrid glances at her admiringly.

Ingrid drives through Sacramento on Interstate 80 and soon reaches Highway 50. She likes driving—it makes her feel free. The first day she got a car, during her second year at San Jose State, she took it out for a spin. It was a blue '85 Ford two-door sedan, the paint on either side faded in so many places that the gray primer underneath showed through. She drove off the campus, up Interstate 80, all the way to Napa, in the wine country. As she drove by a winery, a full moon appeared from behind the clouds, illuminating the silhouettes of the distant mountains and the bushes nearby and spreading a silvery sheen on the road. She stopped the car and walked into the bushes nearby feeling the chilly air like a purifying energy, cleansing her blood and soul. If there were ever a moment in which she believed that God existed, it was then. The sky, the moon, the mountains, and the quietness of the night seemed to be delivering a message from God about the truth of a life—to her, it was a new life in a new country.

With equal clearness, she remembers another moment when she embraced such a freedom, such an intimacy. It was in China, her sophomore year. She traveled with her boyfriend to Qinghai Province, to his hometown. His uncle, a truck driver, drove them around. For a long time, their truck cruised on the desertlike land, no people or houses in sight. They saw many deer and wild goats, as well as coyotes. These animals must not have learned to be afraid of humans.

They watched them curiously, and it was not until they were very close that the animals trotted away; some even galloped along as if keeping them company. The sky was so blue that it seemed to have absorbed all the oceans in the world. One day they arrived at Qinghai Lake. The huge prairie around it extended all the way to the horizon. She and her boyfriend ran, jumped, sang, danced, rolled on the grass, hollered at the lake like animals.

Ingrid's grip on the steering wheel tightens. She inhales deeply and straightens her back. To her amazement, it begins to snow. Though she knows it's not uncommon for snow to fall in the Lake Tahoe area in April and has brought tire chains with her, she still cannot believe her eyes as she sees small white dots sailing toward her and landing on the windshield, melting as quickly as they hit. She turns on the windshield wipers. Soon the small dots become feathers, thick and threatening, pattering on the windows like raindrops. She's barely passed Echo Summit on Highway 50 when she sees the "Chains required" sign. Cars have formed a line, going no more than fifteen miles an hour. She knows the checkpoint is ahead. She pulls off the roadway to the right, turns off the engine, and begins to install the chains—she has done it before. She overhears people talking about an unexpected storm hitting the area. "But it will clear soon," an old man in a North Face down jacket assures a woman in a red parka, who looks anxious as she stands next to her car just ahead.

When Ingrid returns to the wheel, her mother is still sleeping. Ingrid reaches over to move her mother's head slightly and wedges a pillow between her head and the window; she also rearranges the blanket. She starts the engine, which wakes up Bing'er.

As soon as Bing'er realizes that it's snowing, she cries out merrily. "It snowed a lot when I was a kid. Every winter I so looked forward to the first snow that I couldn't focus on school. If the forecast said there'd be snow in the evening, I'd press my nose to the window, waiting for the first flake to appear in the sky. I could never stay up long enough for the snow, and when I woke it was daytime and the world was already white, reflecting on the ceiling of my room. How I hated my parents for not waking me up earlier! I made snowmen and snow angels, marked new snow with my footprints and fingerprints, played hide-and-seek with other kids. Those days, nothing was more painful than going to school. I learned how to fake stomachache; I was so good at it that I could even produce a cold sweat on my forehead. After my parents went to work, I sneaked out. I never got tired of playing in the snow. Nowadays it rarely snows in my hometown, and even if it does it melts fast, turning into slush. It must be because of global warming."

Ingrid tells Bing'er she likes snow too; she also faked sickness to play in the snow, and was spanked often by her father for playing hooky. Before she left China, she says, it snowed every winter in her hometown, especially around the Spring Festival, but since she hasn't been back for so long, she doesn't know if it still snows much or even at all.

"Well, you'd better visit me in the winter then," Bing'er says cheerfully. "There's tons of snow in Toronto. Heavier than any snow I've experienced in China."

Seeing Ingrid become preoccupied, Bing'er asks, "Are you thinking about your interview with KQED?"

Ingrid shakes her head. "No, I'm just imagining what my hometown is like on a snowy day."

Bing'er takes out a pencil and pad from her backpack and begins to draw the snow, the trees, the slow-moving cars. She is soon absorbed in her world.

Snow comes from all directions. If she were outside, Ingrid imagines, she wouldn't be able to open her eyes. She wants to be outside, to let the flakes fall on her palms and see them melting, as she liked to do as a kid. She rolls down her window and extends her hand. Afraid that the cold wind might awaken her mother, she quickly closes the window.

They have more than ten miles to go. At the speed they are traveling, it could take quite a while. But if the old man in the down jacket was right about the storm clearing soon, Ingrid thinks, they might arrive before sunset. She doesn't mind driving in snow, as long as she can see the road ahead.

FIFTEEN

May

MARY STANDS AT THE kitchen sink peeling a cucumber, looking out the window, a hollow feeling inside her. She doesn't awaken from her trance until the overpeeled cucumber snaps in half. She dumps the fallen half into the garbage disposal and presses the switch. Hearing the loud grinding, she pictures the crushed cucumber, feeling that her life is not much better than its.

Her mother died suddenly last Saturday. In the morning she went to the park as usual. Barely twenty minutes had passed before she returned, telling Mary that she was a little tired and needed a nap. "Where is Dongdong?" she asked. Mary told her that Dongdong had gone to a swimming class with Bob. Her mother nodded pensively and yawned. Mary thought that her mother hadn't slept well the night before, so she made up the bed for her. Her mother lay down and asked her to stay a while. "Wake me up when Dongdong is home," she said.

Mary agreed, then sat beside her mother, leaning back against the wall. They chatted, mostly about inconsequential things, and soon her mother fell asleep.

Mary didn't leave but slipped into a reverie. She had been overwhelmed at work, taking on extra projects after a staff reduction, and hadn't slept properly for days. Before dozing, she heard vaguely the raindrops beating on the windows and roof, even remote thunder; but rather than awakening her, they lulled her to sleep. An hour later, she opened her eyes, refreshed. She felt her mother's forehead to see if she had a fever. Only then did she realize that her mother had stopped breathing. She looked peaceful and calm, her wrinkles smoothed, as though she were sleeping soundly.

Her death had probably resulted from a stroke or heart failure, the doctor said. He gave more details, but his explanation sounded cold and distant to Mary, as if he were speaking the language of aliens.

During the past half a year, she had gotten used to her mother being around. In the afternoon, before she even turned in to the driveway, her mother heard her car and would come to open the garage door for her. It was nice to be greeted by family after a long day's work; Mary liked it. When she stepped into the house, the light was burning and a cup of hot green tea was on the coffee table. Her mother would also hand her a warm face towel. If Mary had to work from home in the evening, her mother made porridge or a snack for her, and they'd chat while eating. Since her mother arrived, Mary had kept the heat on during the daytime, but her mother always turned it off after she and Bob left for work and didn't turn it on until half an hour before they came home. Mary knew that her mother wanted to save money for them. She understood that her mother's generation had lived in poverty for years and become accustomed to being thrifty: they didn't know how to enjoy themselves even when the situation allowed.

One day in March, her mother had insisted that Mary book her return airline ticket. She said she needed a medical checkup. Mary said that she would take her mother to see her and Bob's family doctor. But her mother didn't want to go. Okay, Mary said, she would book the return ticket the next day. The next day, Mary's company announced a layoff plan; four people on her team had to go, though the list was not yet finalized. Mary must have looked gloomy that evening, because her mother guessed what had happened. She told Mary not to worry, saying Bob and Mary should focus on work and she'd help with the housework and look after Alex. She also said that she wouldn't leave until Mary's job stabilized: she even asked Mary to file an application with the embassy to extend her visa. Then, only two months later, she was gone.

Mary glances down the quiet hallway that leads to the guest room, mourning silently.

"Mary," Bob interrupts her thought, entering the kitchen with handfuls of Safeway bags. "I bought chicken, beef, brown onions, asparagus, and button mushrooms. I hope I didn't miss anything. I also bought cereal, yogurt, juice, and bananas for breakfast."

"Thanks for doing it." Mary takes a few bags from her husband and helps him load the groceries into the refrigerator.

"Is Alex still sleeping?" Bob asks.

"I guess so. Let me wake him up."

"I'll do it."

"Did he say he wanted to go to Marine World?"

Bob nods and closes the refrigerator. "I'm thinking about taking him there today."

"Hopefully it'll make him less sad."

"When will Ingrid be back?"

"Maybe in an hour. The travel agency is in Palo Alto."

Mary coughs and cups her mouth with both hands.

"You still have some cold," Bob says as he pulls a tissue from a box on the countertop and hands it to her.

She wipes her mouth and hands. "It's almost gone." Then with a smile, she says, "I thought I'd never get sick."

"Mary." Bob places both his hands on her shoulders. "I could try to take some time off from work and go with you for your mother's funeral, you know. We can ask Mingyi or Julia to take care of Alex for a few days."

"It's too much trouble, with visas, Alex, and everything else. And I know it's difficult for you to leave work right now. Besides, we already had a ceremony here."

"But I want to make sure you're okay."

"I'll be fine. Ingrid will help me out there. And I worry about Alex. It's better you're here with him. We can all go to China next year to see her, our whole family and Ingrid. My mother would like that." Disturbed by mentioning her mother, Mary breaks away from Bob's hands and walks to the sink, looking out the window. "Mingyi, Yaya, and Julia will be here soon," she says, as a way to change the subject.

"Are you sure you want to cook for so many people today?"

"They are old friends. It's nice to see them before I go to China." She gazes at a small basket of flowers against the bay window, arranged by her mother before she died. The petals of the yellow miniroses and golden daisies have fallen off, but the leaves are still quite green. Mary's tears drip into the sink. She feels Bob behind her, his arms around her, pressing her against his chest. She turns around and buries her head in his shoulder, her hands clasping him tight. She sobs, her eyes and nose running freely, her body shivering, just like eleven years ago, when she was biking in the December evening rain, empty-stomached, hopeless, toward her dorm, or like that Friday night in January when she lay next to Bob on the bed, looking into his eyes, and told him how she wished they loved each other like they had: that Friday night, they finally talked, and they talked for the whole night, each apologizing for neglecting the other.

Bob tightens his embrace and rubs her back soothingly.

"Mom, Dad." Amid her sobs, Mary hears Alex calling in his room. She straightens her back and cleans her face hurriedly.

"You stay here. I'll go," Bob says gently while taking off his jacket, which has been soaked by her tears. He hugs her once more.

Forty-five minutes later, Bob and Alex head for Six Flags Marine World in Vallejo, an hour's drive away.

"Sister, I'm back." Half an hour after they leave, Ingrid returns. She hands Mary her plane ticket. In their grief and preoccupation, neither realizes that it is the first time since Ingrid moved to New York that she has called Mary "Sister."

Mary takes the ticket, studying the details. "Are we seated next to each other?"

"No. The plane is full. There were only three seats left when I called. We can try to switch seats with someone." Since their mother passed away, Ingrid has been staying with Mary, helping with the arrangements: looking for a crematorium and a beautician, calling relatives about the funeral to be held in their father's hometown, picking an urn for the ashes, booking the plane tickets. She started her part-time job at KQED one month ago, but she doesn't need to go to the office unless there is a meeting.

"Where are Bob and Alex?" Ingrid asks, smelling the white lilies in a vase on the countertop. There are fresh flowers in every room, sent mostly by Mary's church friends.

"Bob took him to Six Flags Marine World; they won't be back until late afternoon. We thought it'd make him feel better. Since Ma passed away, Alex has been crying every day, asking to go to the hospital to see her. I said *wai po* is now living in paradise. He didn't believe me, saying that *wai po* didn't go to church so she wouldn't be living in paradise. I said *wai po* was a very nice person, that of course she would live in paradise, and that someday we'd visit her there. He burst into tears and said he knew *wai po* had died and would no longer tell him stories and make him a rat with her handkerchief." Mary's eyes turn red.

"Kids his age are forgetful. Soon Alex won't be so sad," Ingrid consoles her sister, though she can barely hold back her own tears. To compose herself, she squats and extracts an apron from a lower drawer. She slips the neck strap over her head and ties the apron around her waist. "Is there anything I can help with?"

"It's fine to eat a bit late. Mingyi, Yaya, and Julia won't mind."

"When will Mingyi begin her seminary studies in Pennsylvania?"

"In another two months. She's already quit her job and devoted herself to volunteering and church affairs. Next Monday she'll go to China with a few sisters and brothers to start a documentary film about Christianity's development there. They'll travel to more than twenty provinces and interview more than more hundred people. There won't be much time between her trip and her school. I hope I can still see her now and then after she goes to the seminary." Mary mopes. "Oh, let's not talk about it right now." She walks to the fridge and takes out a piece of beef. Ingrid finds another apron and puts it on her sister. Mary smiles appreciatively and begins to chop the beef on a cutting board. She asks Ingrid to pick some basil leaves and chives from the backyard.

The day before her mother passed away Mingyi had told Mary that she had decided to study at a seminary in Pennsylvania, and afterward serve as a missionary in the Congo for five years.

"Why do you want to be a missionary?" Mary had asked.

"I think it's the right thing to do," Mingyi had said calmly. "I've been waiting for this day over the past twenty-plus years, waiting for God to summon me. It's only through serving God wholeheartedly that I feel my life has a meaning."

If these words had come from Pastor Zhang or other sisters and brothers, Mary wouldn't have been so shocked, but this was her best friend. Though Mingyi had told Mary before that she was considering doing missionary work outside the United States, Mary didn't think she really meant it—especially not in Africa. She just couldn't imagine that a friend with whom she had been so close would choose to do something like this. She had secretly hoped that a nice man in their church would change Mingyi's mind about not getting married. After all, Mingyi was so kind, gentle, wise, and beautiful, the sort of woman who attracted men easily; such a woman deserved a good family.

Now, standing in the kitchen, Mary feels despair. Though she had thought she and Mingyi were similar, she has come to see they are actually very different in their thoughts and attitudes, Mary's feet always on the ground concerning secular things like house payments, bills, food, work, and children's schooling, while Mingyi lives at another level, focusing on a simple life and spiritual devotion.

The distance between them, Mary has now recognized, is vast, unbridgeable.

After Mingyi completes her seminary degree and returns from the Congo, will they still be able to share sorrow and joy as they did before? Will they still be able to enjoy cooking together and chatting? Mary isn't sure. She tries to think positively, to cheer herself up by respecting Mingyi's new endeavor, but meanwhile, she cannot avoid the thought that their friendship is destined to fade with time, with them living far apart, with their different priorities. In her mind's eye she has already begun to see Mingyi's face acquiring an amiable yet distant smile. If she hadn't been so distressed and exhausted by her mother's sudden death, Mary would have tried her best to dissuade Mingyi from going to the seminary, though she knew that Mingyi had made up her mind. Now she doesn't have the energy.

After chopping the beef into thin strips, she uses a new cutting board to slice a brown onion. Usually she would place the board on the sink and cut the onion under cold running water so that she wouldn't cry, but today she forgot. Soon, her tears flow, and as she rubs her eyes, absentmindedly, more tears emerge. She stops chopping the onion and closes her eyes, waiting for the stinging to go away; she begins to sob, her shoulders shaking.

Hearing Ingrid closing the backyard door, Mary hurries to the hallway bathroom, splashing cold water on her eyes and patting them with the tips of her fingers to reduce the swelling. She flushes the toilet and pauses for an appropriate moment, then comes out.

Ingrid must have been crying in the backyard too. Her eyes look red. When she sees Mary, she looks away.

"It took me a while to get enough," Ingrid says hastily, attempting an excuse for being away so long. Then she tries to smash a garlic clove with the side of a Chinese knife on a cutting board—she has seen Mary do this to peel the skin. Unused to housework, Ingrid holds the knife as if it were a brick. She uses too much force, and a piece of garlic flies out and hits the end of her nose. Both Mary and Ingrid laugh at this small incident. The grim atmosphere that has hung around the house suddenly lightens.

"Did Ma bring this knife from China? It's so heavy. Americans don't use this kind of knife," Ingrid says.

"I asked Ma to buy it for me. It works much better than American knives when you chop bones or slice meat. It's good for vegetables too. I don't like the knives here. They're only good for cutting bread or fruit. Ma even brought me an iron caldron because I once complained to her that I could find only thin, flat-bottomed pans in the U.S. and it was hard to stir-fry with them. She remembered what I had said. Imagine how heavy her suitcase was! Now, with the iron caldron, I can cook much more efficiently. Bob said that he'd have the vent hood replaced with a more powerful one so I can do more stir-fry."

"Bob is very considerate. I've never heard him complain about eating too much Chinese food at home."

"He knows that cooking is my biggest hobby. I'm lucky he likes my cooking. Though he's allergic to pollen and dust, he is fine with oil and the fumes from stir-fry. When he was little, he told me, his grandma cooked only Chinese food," Mary says. "I don't know why, but I haven't been able to make myself like Western food. No matter how delicious and sophisticated French or Italian cuisines appear, they don't stimulate my appetite. However, a bowl of fish fillet porridge or a plate of sweet-and-sour chicken does. Before Bob and I got married he ate mostly Western food, but now he is more used to Chinese food." Mary's face lights up as she talks about Bob.

"That's true. He's eaten more Chinese cuisines and dishes than I have," Ingrid says and pauses. Then she says, "You and Bob seem to get along well. These days, Bob has helped a lot, taking care of Alex, doing housework, and even cooking. He cooks very good pasta."

"He usually didn't do housework, which I don't mind. But you're right. He's been very helpful."

Mary takes more food from the fridge, and while Ingrid washes the spinach and *baichai*, Mary does the chopping.

"Ma liked to help me in the kitchen," Mary says, slowing down her chopping to wait for Ingrid to hand her more vegetables. "Every day, when I got home, she had already cleaned and chopped the vegetables and meat. All I needed to do was cook them. She rarely cooked because she was afraid that Bob and Alex wouldn't like her cooking. But for each meal she'd fix two or three small plates of cold dishes. Alex loved them."

"They were very good. I loved them too, especially the spicy cucumber strips."

Mary nods and says she also likes that dish. Again, she glances at the empty hallway to the guest room.

Ingrid follows her sister's eyes. Both of them stare at the hallway for a moment.

"I don't know if you knew, but for years I didn't get along well with Ma." Mary looks down at the half-chopped vegetables on her cutting board as she says this.

Ingrid doesn't reply but stares at her sister, holding a small bunch of spinach leaves over the washing basin.

"I went to college when you were only twelve," says Mary, "so you probably don't remember things so well."

"You came home only once a year when you were in college. And you rarely wrote. When I complained about you, Ma and Ba always said that you were busy studying. 'Your sister is with the smartest students in the country. The competition is intense and she has to study hard,' they'd say."

"I didn't study that hard. I just didn't want to go home."

"Why?"

Mary doesn't reply right away. After chopping a *baichai*, she says, "At that age, we only think about ourselves. Nothing matters more than our own pride, our own feelings."

"True. I treated Ba poorly when I was at college. Later, I regretted it, but I never told him."

Mary turns to look at Ingrid. "Was I too selfish? If I hadn't asked Ma to stay, maybe she wouldn't have left us so quickly."

Ingrid puts down the spinach leaves and holds Mary's shoulders and looks into her eyes. "Don't blame yourself. Didn't the doctor say that Ma had a weak heart? Even if she hadn't traveled to the U.S. she might have experienced the same problem, and wouldn't it have been worse if she had been alone when she died? I think when Ma left us, she was happy that she had lived with you and Alex for so long."

"Yes, she was smiling." Mary's voice breaks and she cannot continue.

"I think you were right," says Ingrid, knowing that she must try to console Mary somehow. "Telling Alex that Ma is in the paradise, waiting for us."

Mary knows that Ingrid has said this to make her feel better. "Let's cook. Our guests will be arriving soon."

Ingrid withdraws her hands from Mary's shoulders and continues to wash the vegetables. "If anything, I was to blame. I didn't even go back to China to see her once in all these years. I always thought I could do it later. Well, there isn't always a later."

Seeing Ingrid's pensive face, Mary feels that it's her turn to cheer her sister up. "Ingrid, today's vegetables are very fresh! The meat looks good too. I can't wait to have lunch. I didn't eat any breakfast."

"Neither did I. I forgot it completely." Understanding Mary's intention, Ingrid tries to lighten her mood. "When I was in New York, whenever a friend recommended a Chinese restaurant to me, I'd say that I didn't think the chefs there were as good as my sister. My sister, I'd tell them, could cook just about any Chinese dish they'd ever heard of. Sweet, sour, salty, spicy, bitter, whichever flavor. You were famous among my friends, and they kept asking when you were coming to visit. I'm not kidding—I could see their mouths water when they asked. I want to learn how to cook from you this time. Maybe someday we'll open a Chinese restaurant in New York together."

"Now, I don't dare go to New York. If your friends found out that you were just bragging, they wouldn't let you off easily." Mary glances at her watch. "Mingyi, Yaya, and Julia will be here soon. The lion's head meatballs are done. The pork-rib soup is almost done. Why don't you help make the sauce for the chicken? I don't think I can cook well today, but I'll try. The good thing is that all the guests are my friends and they won't be picky. The lunch is more for a get-together."

Ten minutes later the doorbell buzzes, and Mary opens the door for Mingyi, Yaya, and Julia.

Everyone helps. Food is soon served. Mingyi has brought a bottle of rice wine, and everyone drinks a little before starting to eat.

Mingyi asks Mary about the funeral arrangements in China.

"Ingrid just got the plane tickets," Mary replies. "Our flight is to-morrow evening. Bob will take us to the airport. After we land, we're taking the long-distance bus to our uncle's village. Our father's grave is there. My mother's ashes will be buried in the same grave. When my father died, the villagers were very poor, so his funeral was quite simple. Now my uncle says that we must have a big funeral for our mother. You know what it's like in the countryside—funerals cost more than weddings. My uncle said that we must invite every vil-lager to the banquet, and on top of that, he proposed to hire a band to play the funeral music and a dozen monks to chant blessings. And of course, we must buy paper houses, paper furniture, and paper money to burn at the grave."

Ingrid chimes in. "We told my uncle that hiring monks would be fine, since our mother sometimes visited temples, but not a band—it is too noisy. But he said that the band was essential if we wanted to draw a crowd. Believe it or not, after the funeral music, he would ask the band to play pop music so people would come to listen. He believes that the more people who attend the funeral, the more honor will be given to our mother. He also suggested hiring a dancing troupe. How ridiculous!"

"I agree with you," Yaya says. "I don't like that kind of funeral, either. I still recall very well my grandpa's funeral, held in his village in Hunan Province. The banquet went on for three days. My uncles and aunts even hired a professional model team to draw the crowd. The grave site was built like a pavilion, and the carving on the marble base itself took two masons a week to complete. My father didn't want to do all this, but he didn't have a choice. It was the local custom to have a big funeral, and he was the youngest child. He had to listen to his brothers."

Mary says, "We don't have a choice, either. You'd think that since both Ingrid and I have been living overseas for so long and have had a good education, our uncle would have listened to us. That's simply not true. When it comes to things like this, we have to listen to the older generation. I negotiated with him on the phone, and he finally agreed not to ask the band to play pop music. We just sent him the money he asked for. Now I understand why having a funeral can bankrupt a family in China."

"In my opinion, the banquet, the extravagant tomb, and the monks are all feudal country customs," Ingrid remarks.

"You're too Americanized. It's China," Julia says. "Chinese people like big occasions—noise, excitement, and food. Funerals, weddings, a baby's one hundredth day celebration, which doesn't need a banquet? Old customs or not, they're what Chinese people cherish."

"It's much easier living in the U.S.," Ingrid says.

"That's so true. Far fewer hassles," Yaya says.

Julia shakes her head, disapproving. "Don't forget that we're foreigners here. Even if we wanted to invite a lot of people to our events, where are the people for us to invite? Most of our families and relatives are in China, and they need a visa to visit us. Not to mention how expensive a plane ticket is for them. When Wang Wei and I got married here, we didn't have a wedding. Of course, we had no money then, but it was also because we knew very few people. If you asked me to choose, I'd rather go into debt to have a proper wedding than not have one at all. That's a once-in-a-lifetime thing, you know."

Her words make the other women think.

"Let's eat!" Mary says with a smile to break the silence. "At least we have one another here now."

They begin to eat, praising every dish, and though they manage to have some light discussions and even a few laughs, they are generally reserved and serious; they don't seem to have much appetite, either. After they put down their chopsticks, most of the plates still have a lot left on them.

Mary wants her friends to enjoy the meal: she wants it to be a thank-you for their help and a farewell to Mingyi. She lifts her chopsticks, picks a meatball, and pops it in her mouth. After chewing and swallowing it, she says, "That was so delicious! Now, you all must have one. Mingyi, you've been very quiet. Still thinking about your volunteer work? You don't like meat, so how about finishing this plate of mixed vegetables? Julia, you know you're too thin. You must eat more. Ingrid, you're my sister. You needn't be so polite. Yaya, I've never seen you eat so little. Don't be shy. We all know that you ate half a sheep for lunch in Inner Mongolia."

Yaya laughs. "That was years ago." She picks a meatball and eats it. The rest of the women start to eat too, finally.

Mary feels better. She turns to Mingyi and asks her about her trip to China.

"The more I prepared for it, the more I felt anxious," Mingyi says. "I pray every day, asking God to give me wisdom, strength, and willpower. I'm actually only an assistant, and my main job is to record interviews, but even so I feel pressure. In the past few weeks, I've interviewed more than fifty people over the phone, and some of them cried so much that they couldn't speak. I wonder what it'll be like when I meet them in person. I don't know if I'll be strong enough to listen to them."

Since Mingyi quit her day job, she seems to Mary younger and healthier, her face showing a new, pink glow. Her soft, gentle voice now sounds more charming, as if it contains wisdom from God. Maybe she made the right choice, going to a seminary and becoming a missionary, Mary thinks, looking at her friend affectionately. With Mingyi's personality and devotion, she will win people's friendship and trust in the Congo very soon; she will lead a busy life, a happy and eventful one. As for herself, she will just have to accept her flaws, weaknesses, and imperfections Mary decides.

After dinner, Ingrid leaves: she has to go to San Francisco to pack. Mary and her friends move to the family room to have tea.

Mary notices that Yaya is winking at Julia, so she asks, "Yaya, what's going on?"

"Hmmm, I . . ." Yaya stammers and turns to Julia. "You start first."

"No, you start first." Julia looks hesitant.

"Mingyi, you must know what they're hiding from me." Mary turns to Mingyi.

"Yaya and Julia, I think you should just tell Mary. You can't hide it from her forever anyway. Why don't you start, Yaya?" Mingyi says.

"Oh well, you know, it's like this," Yaya says, frowning at Mingyi to show her unhappiness at being asked to go first. "Daming has been in China running his business for a year now. Before,

I thought that I'd stay here and travel between the two countries. Now I feel more and more worried about him. If I call him and can't reach him, I worry that he might be with another woman. If he tells me that he must cancel his planned trip to see me, I sleep poorly for days. It's not that I don't trust him, but my parents call so often to warn me about the dangers of a long-distance relationship. They say that young girls nowadays go after rich men aggressively, not caring whether these men are married or not. I say that Daming not only doesn't have money but also owes the bank a loan. My mother says what the girls focus on is potential, and Daming is like a promising public stock to them. I can't believe that a conservative Communist like my mother actually knows something about stocks!"

"So you're moving back to China?" Holding her teacup, Mary feigns a smile.

"I talked with my boss last week. He said that our company is setting up an office in Beijing and asked me if I were interested in being a manager there. I'd get the expatriate deal for the first two years, with my United States salary and a housing subsidy. Afterwards I could either stay or come back to the United States. I couldn't have dreamed of a better deal."

"Grab it, Yaya. It's too good an opportunity to pass up. Congratulations. Daming must be thrilled," Mary says.

"Yes, he's very excited. He'll fly back in a week to help with the moving. We haven't gone through all the details yet, but I think we'll rent our house here."

Mary turns to Julia. "You aren't moving back to China, are you?"

"I won't follow Yaya." Julia smiles, then says after a pause, "But we're moving to Phoenix. In Arizona, you know."

"Did Wang Wei find a job there?" Mary asks.

"That's right. You know he's been looking for a job since he was laid off. It's difficult; few local companies are hiring these days. I can't make much money, either. Though the real-estate market is still okay, there are too many agents in this area, and competition is fierce. A few days ago, Wang Wei received an oral offer from IBM, but the job was in Phoenix. We talked about it and decided to move there. We can get a four- or even five-bedroom house for less than one third of the price it would be here. Schools there are better too. So Wang Wei took the offer. He'll start the new job in a week. He'll go there first. We're selling the house. Of course, George and Sophia didn't want to leave their friends, but after we explained our financial situation, they agreed."

Mary puts her teacup on the table and clasps her hands on her lap. She feels a cold wind blowing. Noticing that her friends are looking at her with concern, she controls her emotions. "Wow, more good news. Julia, you used to say that California's sunshine is priceless. Well, I guess Arizona's sunshine is very nice too. The good thing is that we're not that far apart. The flight is only two hours from San Francisco to Phoenix." She turns to Yaya. "Yaya, ask your boss to let you travel to the U.S. at least once a quarter. When you're here, you stay with me."

"That's for sure. Maybe Daming's company won't do well and he will want to come back to the U.S. You never know," Yaya says. "Maybe I'll be back in two months."

"I've not seen a woman like you who doesn't wish her husband a success." Mary pours tea for Yaya. "I'm sure you'll like living in Beijing. It's a nice city."

"As for Mingyi"—Mary now pours tea for her third friend—"I can call you every week, right? So, it's not that bad."

"We should set up teleconferences at least once a month. We all have computers," Yaya says enthusiastically.

"I like the idea. Wang Wei can be our technical support," Julia says.

For a while, everyone discusses this high-tech possibility with much laughter and suggests more ways to keep in touch, though each knows that their overly optimistic conversation is just a way to hide their sadness about their upcoming separation.

"Is something burning?" Yaya suddenly asks, sniffing.

"Oh, my goodness." Mary leaps from her chair and runs to the kitchen. "I forgot the dessert!" She turns off the oven and opens the door. Smoke pours out.

Mingyi, Yaya, and Julia all follow Mary to the kitchen.

Mary puts on an oven mitt, takes out a tray, and drops it on a pot holder on the countertop. "Well, the taro cookies are burned. I'm sorry. When we had dim sum in Milpitas a month ago, you all said you loved the taro cookies there. After I came back, I tried to make them. I failed twice, but I thought it'd be okay this time. I can't believe I forgot them. I've never burned my food before."

Mingyi takes a pair of chopsticks and flips over a few cookies that are blackened on the top. "Maybe they're only burned outside." She picks up a cookie with a napkin, blows on it to cool it, peels the charred skin, and bites off a morsel. Mary stares at her and asks eagerly, "How is it? Still okay?"

Mingyi doesn't reply right away but closes her eyes and chews slowly. After she swallows it, she smiles. "Mary, it's ten times better than those we ate at the restaurant."

Yaya grabs one and bites it before it's cooled. She purrs her approval.

"Don't try to make me feel better." Mary takes a cookie. So does Julia.

After peeling the skin, Mary nibbles at the cookie, feeling the fine taro paste, sweet and soft, melting on her tongue, leaving its fragrance and a desire for more. "Yeah, it's not bad. Not bad at all." She can barely hide her joy.

"I need the recipe!" Julia says after eating her cookie. "I'll make them as soon as I get home, so my husband and children know that

I can make good dessert. Just the other day I spent a whole evening baking an apple pie, but George and Sophia didn't even touch it. I tried hard to persuade Wang Wei to take a bite. You know what he said afterwards? He said, 'Please, no next time.' "

Within a few minutes, Yaya finishes five cookies. "The skin is good too. Very crispy. If you don't want yours, give it to me. I like the skin. Mary, I'm telling you, it's the tastiest cookie I've had in a long time."

"Even tastier than stinking tofu?" Mary teases, extremely pleased by her friends' praises.

Yaya smiles. "Nope. I'm sorry, but nothing can beat stinking tofu."

They go back to the living room and eat more cookies. They chat, catching up with what's new about themselves and their families in the past week.

After swallowing her tenth or eleventh cookie, Mary gulps some tea and delivers a loud and satisfying belch. She covers her mouth with her hand and is about to apologize to her friends when she hears Yaya's belch, even louder. She bursts out laughing, and so do her friends.

The phone rings. Mary picks it up. It's Bob, on his cell phone from Marine World, asking Mary if she is okay and telling her that they are watching killer whales perform. "Alex has stopped crying. He likes big animals," Bob says, then adds, "I miss you."

"I miss you too," she says, not feeling shy saying so in front of her friends.

After putting down the phone, Mary eats more cookies. The living room is filled with the warm aroma of the taro cookies and the green tea they're drinking, a smell that seems to be visible, like some kind of soothing color painted on the ceiling, the walls, the window trim and sills, all the furniture. Against the light-colored sofa, chairs and the creamy carpet, the mahogany coffee table, four cups of tea holding, stands out like a piece of art. Facing Mary are silk-framed

Chinese paintings of the four seasons, hanging from the top of the wall almost touching the floor.

Mary is warm and relaxed. She looks around at her friends with a feeling of contentment, of joy. Julia and Mingyi are teasing Yaya, saying that she has finally admitted she isn't as modern about her relationship as she had claimed. Mary suddenly has a strange feeling that her mother hasn't passed away at all but is making hometown-style snacks in the kitchen, just as Mary remembers her doing for the new year when she and her sister were little, back in China, so long ago and so far away.

"Guo-Mei and Guo-Ying, come and taste what I've made for you!" her mother would say, holding out a plate of sesame balls.

"Coming!" The two girls would run toward their mother cheerfully, hand in hand.

After dinner, Mary and Bob sit on the sofa in the living room. Alex has gone to bed, exhausted from a few days' crying and his day at the amusement park.

"Did he have a good time?" Mary asks, feeling comfortable with her head against Bob's shoulder. It's so quiet now, just her and her husband. Knowing her friends are leaving her one by one, Mary is overcome by a longing to be closer to Bob, feeling blessed because she still has him.

"He didn't smile, but he seemed to like the rides." Bob strokes the small of her back gently.

"Are you okay taking care of him by yourself while I'm away?"

"Of course, yes, and I'll work from home for a week. Mary, are you sure you don't want me to go to China with you? I can just get a ticket tomorrow." Bob pauses. "I know I said it before many times, but really, I'm sorry that I've been spending so little time at home."

"It's not easy for you. It's not like you can slack off at work." She turns to face her husband and runs her fingers through his hair, which has grown a little too long; there's also a few days' growth of beard on his chin. "You haven't slept much these days," she says.

"Well, you haven't, either," he replies.

"Now, you just got another promotion. It's probably more work ahead."

"I talked with Shirat yesterday, and he said he's quitting. He's found a job in Bangalore, as an entry-level manager in a bank. He's moving his whole family back to India. He said it's not worth it to sacrifice his marriage and family life. I've been thinking too. I like the job, you know, but—"

"Just take your time. Whatever decision you make, I'll support you. Just don't feel you have to stay with this job until the company goes IPO. We don't need a big house, and if it's necessary, we can even sell our current house and rent. We rented before and it wasn't bad. And we have enough savings to last a while, don't we? We're probably better off than most Americans. If you wanted, you could even quit for a while and have some rest. I have a good salary too. Even if I lost my job, that's still not the end of the world. We can always find jobs somewhere, you know, with our educations and work experiences. Julia's husband just found a job in Phoenix, and they are moving there. We could move too, to somewhere cheaper so we won't have such a mortgage burden. I know it's a cliché, but money doesn't buy happiness." She rushes through her speech as if to assure Bob that he has nothing to worry about: meanwhile, she is pleasantly surprised how fluent her English was this time.

"Thanks for saying that." He cups her face in his hands, his thumbs brushing across her skin, staring at her with softness in his eyes, the kind of softness she had thought long lost in their marriage.

"Do you love me?" she blurts out in a half daze, not sure why she asked.

"Of course I do. I cannot image not having you in my life." Bob bends to kiss her on the forehead, the cheeks, the nose, the area behind her ear, then her lips. "Do you love me?" he whispers.

She nods hard, then tears come. Oh, you foolish woman, she chastises herself. Why are you crying? But more tears arrive. Bob dries those tears with more kisses. His warm breath and soft lips send chills down her spine. She stops sobbing and opens her mouth to meet his tongue. She closes her eyes dreamily, reveling in the feel of his strong arms, his familiar body scent, their tongues intertwined in a deep French kiss. A stir of desire arises within her, strong, irresistible, and she feels, to her embarrassment, her panties' dampness against her. No, not right now, she says to herself, not today, yet she pushes her body against Bob's greedily, wanting to touch him, and to be touched. As they take a break from kissing, they stare at each other with a sense of appreciation, of newly found love. Bob picks her up and carries her through the kitchen toward their bedroom, like he did on their wedding night.

"Oh, Bob, but Alex . . ."

"He's sleeping," Bob says with a mischievous smile.

The phone is ringing; then the answering machine starts: it's Ingrid.

Mary turns her head to look at the phone.

"Want to talk with her first?" Bob asks.

"No," she says, with a slight hesitation. "No, I'll call her later." This time, she's firm. Strangely, for the first time in her life, she feels she's happier than Ingrid: yes, her sister has made love with many men in her life, but she, Mary, is the one who is going to have wonderful sex with her husband.

Circling her arms around Bob's neck, Mary regrets that she hasn't combed her hair properly, hasn't put on something nicer than her jeans and a plain blouse. She doesn't even remember what kind of underwear she put on this morning. Probably those white cotton ones that she had gotten from JCPenney's recent sale, for $9.99 a set, bra and panties. It was Julia's fault; she can never say no to sales and has to find someone to go shopping with her. Mary feels a gentle resentment toward her friend. And she must look ugly, with swollen eyes and tear marks on her face. She won't allow Bob to turn on the ceiling light in the bedroom, she decides. And the shaded lamp on the nightstand will have to be on low. Then she thinks of her mother. Oh, well, her mother will forgive her. She didn't plan it. She raises her head and places her lips by Bob's ear. "Let's close Alex's door."

SIXTEEN

June

INGRID OPENS THE DOOR and turns on the light with Mary behind her: they have just returned from their mother's funeral in the countryside. Their parents' apartment, unoccupied for six months, is dusty, stifling, smelling of mildew. After putting away their suitcases, they open every window to air out the place, then begin to clean.

"I can still hear *suo na* and gongs in my ears. The music was awfully loud," Ingrid says, using a broom to sweep away the cobwebs in the corners. She hadn't wanted to talk about the funeral, but the subject has somehow remained on the tip of her tongue. The funeral was so surreal, it seems to her that only through talking about it again and again with her sister can she make sense of the fact that her mother has indeed left them forever. "If you hadn't stopped Uncle, he'd have hosted a three-day banquet. But even the one-day banquet was a lot of work. After everyone left, I filled five fifty-*jin* rice bags with empty liquor bottles and cigarette boxes." Ingrid recalls several drunkards singing and making a fuss.

"Luckily Yaya warned us about what a country funeral is like." Mary washes a piece of cloth in a basin—she is cleaning the windows.

"It looked less like a funeral, more like a chaotic stage performance."

"It was a sort of show, in a way."

Yes, it was a show, Ingrid thinks. When she and her sister were burning the paper sacrifices, she heard a young woman with a naked-buttocked little boy next to her commenting on the ritual. The woman said it was such a waste and how nice it would be if the money could have been used to buy a piglet, or a fruit tree, or send a kid to school. Ingrid had felt bad: it was not the money that upset her but her and her sister's caving in to her uncle, to the old customs. Why couldn't they mourn their mother's death in their own way?

Mary continues. "But what could we do about it? Uncle wouldn't have listened to us anyway, neither would the villagers. Uncle said to me, 'After the funeral you just go back to the U.S., but I have to live here. If the funeral wasn't good, I'd become the laughingstock. How could I continue living here with that kind of shame?' "

"We could have insisted. Don't you think? Uncle just wanted to set an example for his children, so they'd have a funeral like this for him when he dies."

"Don't be so hard on Uncle, and don't think we can change him. He has rarely traveled outside his village. If you were him, you'd probably have thought the same way. 'Face is bigger than the sky.' It's all about maintaining face."

"I don't think Ma would have liked such a funeral."

"We don't know. Maybe she would. Ma once told me that she always burned paper money for Ba on his birthdays and the holidays. People of her age like to observe the old customs." Mary speaks slowly and calmly, wiping the window.

Ingrid glances at Mary, thinking that her sister is more accommodating than she is, though she doesn't necessarily share Mary's views. Or is she so Americanized, as Julia claimed, that she no longer understands the old rituals in China? Has she somehow abandoned her roots?

Without Windex, or a squeegee, or stain and spot remover, cleaning the windows is painstaking, but Mary doesn't seem to mind. To remove tough stains, she uses her fingertips and fingernails. "Whenever I came home," she says, "the windows were always very clean. I hope Ma had hired a helper to do the job. I don't know why I never asked her." Her voice conveys barely concealed grief, suggesting that she is convinced their mother actually did all the cleaning herself.

Throughout the funeral, Mary had worked with their uncle on the arrangements. While their uncle treated Ingrid like a girl, an outsider, ignoring what she said, he listened to Mary's suggestions. Without Mary, Ingrid has come to realize, the funeral would have become a farce—their uncle had even considered hiring professional mourners, not an uncommon practice in the village. Of course, Mary was the older daughter, but something in her—perhaps her calmness or her understanding expression—made their uncle and the other villagers take her more seriously than they did Ingrid.

After the funeral, they stayed a few more days. Every evening after dinner they walked for half an hour to visit their parents' grave, located in the middle of a hill, surrounded by wild azalea, with several thick-branched pine trees nearby. Their uncle had told them that their father had hired a feng shui master to pick this location during one of his trips to the village. This surprised Mary and Ingrid; they wouldn't have guessed that their Communist father, who had criticized feudal traditions so vehemently when he was alive, would have done something like this. But the grave site is indeed a nice place, especially in the evening, when the daytime noises have abated, replaced by insects chirping and tree leaves rustling in the breeze.

They sat down together on a rock near the grave, overlooking the square fields and several adobe houses. In the dark, in the silence, they talked about their father, their mother, their memories of them, both good and bad. They had never been so frank with each other. Despite their reservations about their mother's funeral, they felt relieved that their parents were buried together in their father's hometown, remembering what their father liked to say when he was alive: that fallen leaves return to their roots.

Ingrid now sits on the floor to take a break. She scans the room. "After all these years, the furniture remains the same, even its arrangement. The TV is the same brand, in the same spot. Ba's wicker chair is where it used to be. It's like déjà vu, like stepping into an old dream. I can almost see Ba opening the door and going out for a walk in his warden's uniform after dinner and Ma doing dishes in the kitchen, her head bowed."

"Wasn't Ba very thin? His lozenge-shaped face and bony hands. When I was leaving China, he traveled to Beijing to send me off at the airport. After handing me the luggage, he said in a flat tone, 'Take care of yourself and don't worry about us.' Then he said good-bye and left, not looking back once. He didn't like to show his emotions, you know, being a typical Chinese father. I used to think him cold and strict." Mary looks absorbed in her narration. "I knew little about Ba at that time. Now, I think that he didn't leave the airport after saying good-bye to me but waited in the lobby to see the plane take off through the window. He probably even cried in the men's room if no one else was there."

"That was like Ba. I sometimes wished that he'd hugged us and praised us like an American father does. I'm sure he was very proud of us, especially you—you were always a top student—but he never told us anything."

"We weren't very nice to Ba. Maybe he thought we despised him."

Ingrid is silent, remembering again how she treated her father outside her dorm room in Beijing. Then she says, "I just thought of something. Do you know that Ba had several big scars on his right leg? One ran from the knee almost to the ankle. That was why he wore long pants year round. No matter how hot it was, he never wore shorts or rolled up his pants."

"How did you find out?"

"I saw them when Ba was washing his feet in the sink. I was in high school then. As soon as he saw me, he rolled down his pants legs. Those scars were deep and ugly. I asked him how he'd gotten them, and he said that he fell from a tree when he was a teenager. I believed him at the time; I just didn't think much about it, I suppose. Oh, Mary, did Ma tell you a lot of things from the past?"

"No," Mary replies hastily. "The past is the past. What's the point of keeping on thinking about it?"

Ingrid ignores her sister's comment. "Have you seen the photo of Aunt and Ma taken in 1947? Aunt looks extremely cute. She has a high forehead, her short hair permed into small curls. She is smiling mischievously. Ma looks nice too. She wears a fur-collared coat, her head high, like a proud princess. Our grandparents must have been quite well off before the Liberation, or at least they had money for a while. There's also a photo of Ma and Ba, taken one month after my birth. Though they're wearing decent clothes—the type of clothes everyone wore at that time, you know—they look like skeletons. Especially Ma. Her cheeks are hollow, and her lips are ashen. When Ma was in the U.S., I asked her if she had a problem giving birth to me. She said the labor was easy and she looked sallow in the picture because of lack of nutrition. Mary, do you remember the time when Ma was pregnant with me?"

Mary avoids Ingrid's inquiring eyes. She squats to rinse the cloth in the basin again. "I was only five or six. How could I remember? I think Ma was telling you the truth, that she didn't get enough nutrition." Mary looks up at Ingrid and says cheerfully, "But look at you! You weren't affected. You're pretty tall for a Chinese woman."

Ingrid catches Mary's momentary hesitance, so she asks again, "Ma really didn't tell you anything?"

"No. Nothing at all." Mary smiles. "Don't sound so skeptical. If Ma had told me anything, you bet that I wouldn't have hidden it from you. We're sisters."

Mary takes the basin to the kitchen. A moment later, she hollers. "I'm cleaning the stove now. Don't come in. There are cockroaches here. Those big ones. You probably haven't seen one for years."

Ingrid walks in anyway. "Don't forget when we were little you were the one who was afraid of cockroaches. When you found one in your room, you sent me to kill it."

"That's true." Mary chuckles. "Okay, you can clean the cabinet."

Ingrid is going to ask more questions about the time their mother was pregnant with her, but Mary says first, "Who is the guy who called you yesterday? Matthew something?"

"Matthew Stein. Just a friend."

"Only a friend?"

"Yes." Ingrid gives Mary a discouraging look.

"Okay. I got it," Mary says in a half-serious, half-joking way. "In our next lives, let's switch; you'll be the older sister and I'll be the younger one. Then you'll know how I feel."

Ingrid laughs. She takes a wet towel Mary hands to her and begins to clean the cabinet. "I only got one call, while you got many. Mingyi, Yaya, Julia, your church friends. Your phone kept ringing. Bob called you at least five times, right? He and Alex must have been missing you a lot."

"Rather than missing me, they're probably missing their chef, janitor, and gardener," Mary jokes. "Believe it or not, Bob cooks every day. Now he doesn't have time to play computer games or watch sports on TV. Alex said that his dad is a good cook and he played with him and told him stories every night."

"How is Bob?"

"He's doing all right. Though many small companies are going bankrupt, his just got funding from a venture capitalist, and it can last at least another year. They're actually hiring. His ex-boss at Santa Clara University contacted him a few days ago and said that he'd love to take him back. Bob is considering it right now. He was just promoted to director. He has to work much harder at a start-up and the job isn't secure, but it's more challenging and he gets paid more. In Silicon Valley, having a mortgage is a big financial burden." Mary lowers her voice. "It was I who asked him to join a start-up, but now I want him to go back to the university, to get some rest. If the housing market crashed, we could always move to a smaller house or sell our house and rent."

"How about your own job?"

"I don't think about it. If I were laid off, I'd probably get a pretty good severance package, and I could also apply for unemployment benefits." Simulating a cheerful voice, Mary adds, "Capitalist countries aren't always bad."

"But if you don't like your job, why don't you change?"

"What's the difference between this job and that job? I'm not like you. You still have a dream. Fourteen or fifteen years ago, I dreamed of becoming someone like Madame Curie, but now my focus is my family."

"Sister, I hope you don't mind me asking. But do you get along well with Bob? I mean . . . really."

Mary puts the oven racks in the sink and runs water to wash off the dust and soot. "Love is like a plant. You must take care of it, remember to water and fertilize it regularly. I used to complain about him spending little time with the family. The truth is that I didn't spend time with him, either, to listen to him, to understand him better. I just ignored him, pretending everything was all right. There is one thing I didn't tell you before. I went to see Han Dong. Remember him? My first boyfriend. You even told me that he was very handsome. He was in Berkeley for business training."

Ingrid nods and stares straight into Mary's eyes.

"You look like you don't believe me. In your mind, your sister must have been an old-fashioned, boring, and dull woman."

That's what Ingrid thinks, but she denies it so as not to hurt Mary's feelings. The effort makes her blush. "No, not at all. I just didn't know Han Dong was in Berkeley. Did you tell Bob? Did he forgive you?"

Mary shakes her head. "You thought I slept with Han Dong? No, I didn't. But maybe I'm just fooling myself. What we did wasn't much different from having sex. Sharing intimacy starts in the mind. The body follows. We came close, very close. My thoughts were a betrayal. I can't deny it, even if it wasn't—how should I say it?—consummated. I didn't dare tell Bob. I didn't even tell Mingyi, afraid that she'd think I was a bad woman, an unqualified Christian."

"Mingyi isn't like that. She'd help you."

"Yeah, I know, but still . . . You know what? She seemed to have sensed my problem. She asked me a few times if I was all right and if Bob was all right. Well, I just didn't know how to start. I guess I was afraid of losing her as a friend. And I haven't decided if I should confess to Pastor Zhang or not after I go back to the U.S. Nothing is worse for a Christian than not to confess her sins and ask God for forgiveness. God knows what I have done, and it's up to Him if He will punish me or forgive me. I don't know." Mary walks over to the window and rests her hands on the sill. She breathes deeply. "Bob and I have been working on our marriage. I do love him. Maybe that's why it's so difficult to face him and Alex."

Ingrid walks over and stands beside her sister. "You're a good mother, a good wife, and a good sister. Everyone makes mistakes. I don't believe God is as perfect as you Christians claim. If He was so perfect, why did he create human beings who are so imperfect? He could have made Adam and Eve perfect all the way through, couldn't He?"

"You don't know about God and His love."

"I surely don't, and I'm glad you don't try to convert me."

"Maybe I should."

"Aha, not in a million years. I don't trust your God. Just look, the Crusades, the Reconquista, and many, many other religious wars. If there is a God, He seems quite volatile and egoistical to me. I'd rather be a rotten sinner."

"Ingrid, you . . ." Mary pauses, shaking her head, smiling, as if saying, "I'm not trying to convince you, someday you'll talk with God yourself." Then her smile subsides as she remembers something. She hesitates before speaking. "I've never told you this, but Bob has stopped going to church."

"Did he tell you why?"

"We talked in Sonoma, during the retreat. He said he sometimes had a hard time understanding God's ways, and he didn't find churches or pastors particularly inspiring. He asked me to give him some time to think."

"Isn't it better for him to live his faith in the real world?"

"I'm not sure about that, but I'm praying for him, hoping one day he'll return to God." After a brief silence, she goes on. "People are vulnerable by themselves."

"I think people are stronger than you think."

At this moment, a piano begins to play on the floor right above them: Schubert's Serenade. The music goes fast but unsteadily, as if the player can't wait to finish it. Then a woman's harsh voice interrupts. "I've told you one hundred times to play it slowly. You don't listen! Where are your ears? Just yesterday the teacher said that you had to play this song slowly, with emotion, while imaging beautiful forests, wide rivers, fragrant flowers, and a blue sky where birds are flying. Why can't you do that? How often must I ask?"

"I've never seen beautiful forests and a blue sky except in movies." a little girl cries out.

"Stop arguing! If you don't play well today, there won't be ice cream for you after dinner. Your ba and I have saved hard to pay for your piano classes."

The piano plays again. Though the music is much slower, it is flat and unemotional.

"Good! Just like this. Slow, slow, slow . . . one . . . two . . . three . . ." The mother sounds excited now. "Play for your ba when he gets back. Then you'll have ice cream."

Both Ingrid and Mary laugh, covering their mouths. They walk back to the sink. Mary gestures up to the ceiling. "Poor kid! She reminds me of Alex. Now I see that I'm no better than this mother. Oh, I forgot to tell you, Bob said that the clivias are blooming. Also, there's some news about Niuniu, the cat. You've seen her in our backyard. Bob said that it was raining heavily one evening so he opened the garage side door to let her in, as we always do when it rains. She paced back and forth outside under the awning, meowing, but didn't dare come in. Bob stood in the garage, calling her name and luring her with food. It was like that for ten minutes. Just as Bob was about to give up and close the door, the cat dashed into the garage. The funny part was when Bob pointed at the door and urged her to go out, the cat meowed loudly as if protesting, as if she understood that he was just playing a game with her. The same night Bob bought a litter box and a cat bed for her. Next morning he went to the garage and saw the cat sleeping comfortably in the bed. She had also used the litter box. Now, she goes out during the daytime and sleeps in the garage at night. When I get home, we'll take her to the vet and adopt her officially."

"Why don't you go back to the U.S. earlier?" Ingrid suggests. "I can stay one more week. There's no need for both of us to be here. I can handle the rest."

"You sure?"

"Sister, trust me this one time, okay? You have a family there. I don't."

"How about your job with KQED? That's a good job. You don't want to lose it."

"I already talked with the team. The real work won't start for another month. So everything is fine."

Mary smiles and nods, her eyes fixing on Ingrid with a strange mix of affection and concern—only briefly—then she looks away and begins to wash the oven racks vigorously. She blushes as if she had betrayed a deep secret, but she seems happy.

Ingrid smiles—she too feels a strong kinship at this moment. "Let's finish the cleaning and then we'll have a nice meal," she says.

Three days later, after sending Mary to the airport for the two p.m. flight to Shanghai, where Mary will catch her connection to San Francisco, Ingrid returns to her parents' apartment and climbs into bed to take a nap. Since she arrived in China a week ago, she hasn't had any good rest. Unaccustomed to sleeping on wooden planks padded only with a thin cotton blanket—her parents didn't have a mattress—her back hurt the first few nights. Now she is so exhausted that as soon as her head hits the pillow she passes out.

She doesn't wake until five a.m. Not being able to fall back to sleep, she sits in her father's wicker chair and browses a few old magazines she found in the living room. She is restless, waiting for daybreak. Whenever she hears a sound from the street, she gets up to see what it is. It occurs to her that she is like a first-time tourist who cannot wait to explore a new city; in her case, it's the city of her birth, where she spent her childhood and adolescent years but hasn't visited for almost ten years. When Mary was here, they were both consumed by practical matters, mainly concerning their mother: Whom else should they notify about her death? What paperwork must be completed for the local police and her mother's factory? Should they keep or sell the apartment? (Their decision was to keep it for one year and then discuss the matter again.) They also had several long conversations about each other's views on relationships and religious beliefs. Whereas before they had both been quick to ridicule the other's opinions, this time they listened carefully, avoiding arbitrary judgments.

Now, alone, Ingrid can put practical matters aside temporarily and experience the city. At five thirty, she sees several street sweepers in straw hats pass by, riding a rickshaw filled with bamboo-handled brooms, shovels, plastic buckets, and other cleaning tools. The sight of them fills her with happiness, for they remind her of her childhood.

Then come the early-shift buses. With green lights all the way, they drive so fast that when they have to stop at the station near the apartment to pick up one or two passengers, their tires skid.

She also hears the family upstairs getting up, their shoes making slight yet audible sounds on the wood floor. She knows that they are the couple running the tiny dim sum and noodle restaurant on the ground floor—she and Mary ate there once. In a short while, the couple's quick steps resonate on the external stairs, then the iron chain lock of the restaurant is opened. Ingrid imagines that they start to work immediately and with their usual efficiency—one chops the meat and vegetables and mixes them to make the stuffing for *baozi* or *hundun* or other dim sum items, while the other makes various wrappings with corn flour on a big table.

From somewhere comes a man's voice: "Junjun, you'd better go to bed! You fell asleep at your desk again." This must be a concerned father, Ingrid speculates, and Junjun must be his only son, who is about to take the college entrance test. Years ago, when she was preparing for the test, Ingrid remembers, her father used to get up after midnight and check on her, making sure she hadn't fallen asleep at her desk. He wanted her to be diligent but was afraid that she would catch a cold if she fell asleep without a blanket to keep her warm.

Ingrid takes a shower and then goes downstairs to the dim sum and noodle restaurant for breakfast. While eating, she hears the garbage collector's chanting.

"Do you have old newspapers and magazines to sell? Do you have iron and steel products to sell? Do you have old fridges or TVs or washing machines to sell?" The garbage collector hollers repeatedly in the Nanyi dialect, his voice drawling. This man has been collecting garbage in this neighborhood since the early eighties. In Ingrid's memory, rain or sun, holidays or normal days, he rode a rusty rickshaw from one street to another, advertising his business with his characteristic chanting. Before Ingrid went to the United States, his chanting hadn't included electric appliances—they weren't common at that time. No one knew where he lived, and people called him Young Wan. Whoever had something to sell would open his or her window and shout, "Hi, Young Wan! I have something to sell." And the garbage collector would stop his rickshaw and look up to see where his client was. "Sure, I'm coming!" he would say happily and proceed to complete the transaction.

Ingrid looks out the window and watches the garbage collector, who is parking his rickshaw under a tree waiting for business: she remembers that swarthy face, though it's now wrinkled. She wonders if people still call him Young Wan or if they've changed to the more proper Old Wan since he's now in his forties. She tells the restaurant owner that she will be back shortly to finish her food. She rushes back to her parents' apartment, and after gathering old newspapers and magazines, she pokes her head out the window and hollers in the Nanyi dialect, "I have something to sell."

"Coming!" Young Wan or Old Wan looks up and replies. Then he adds, smiling, "I've not seen your mother for a while. She always sold me newspapers on Mondays."

Seeing the man's cheerful face, Ingrid decides not to tell him about her mother's death—he'll figure it out sooner or later, or one of her mother's neighbors will share the news with him.

After completing the trade, Ingrid finds herself in a lighter mood, as if this simple act has proved that she was a local.

There is more chanting on the street. Different accents, different rhythms, different volumes, different offers of items for sale.

"Tea eggs! Big tea eggs. Sixty cents each. Two for one yuan."

"Tofu soup! Sweet or salty!"

"Gas canisters!"

"Efficient pesticides! Kill your rats, cockroaches, flies mosquitoes, and other insects."

Ingrid is familiar with all this chanting—she grew up listening to these messages. She cannot help but wonder if time has reversed or if she's just dreaming.

After breakfast she strolls to Progression Park nearby, which is new to her.

The park is crowded. People, mostly the elderly, are engaging in various activities: practicing *tai ji* or *qi gong,* dancing folk or social dances, playing chess or poker or just watching others play, doing sports like jumping rope, kicking a Hacky Sack, or playing badminton. Bird owners hang their cages on the tree branches, listening to the birds chirping in the morning light. Some people jog on the gravel pathway along the river, rolling their heads, shoulders, and arms without stopping, and a few shout at the top of their lungs now and then as some type of *qi gong*. In certain parts of the park are narrow paths specifically designed for foot massage, where colorful small pebbles are aligned nicely, their smooth edges protruding above the surface. Following a few elderly people, Ingrid takes off her shoes and walks on the stones barefoot, feeling the pebbles with her soles, getting the sense of a massage.

Ingrid continues to roam, listening to people chatting. She hears two old men talk about the Long March, which they participated in when they were in their late teens; they miss the camaraderie they experienced then and keep saying how cold people are to one another nowadays. Near a huge flowerpot, a man in a white short-sleeved shirt is using a giant brush to write calligraphy with water on the concrete. Ingrid recognizes the sentences from one of Chairman Mao's poems: "The rivers and the mountains are so gorgeous that they impress numerous heroes."

The orange sun is glaring. Though it's only early June, it feels as though real summer has arrived. Cicadas stridulate loudly and monotonously in the trees, and the concrete under foot seems hot enough to melt shoe soles. It's dry too. When cars whiz by, they stir up the dust, visible in the sunlight like little shiny metal particles. Ingrid cannot recall a June this dry, this warm.

She is now in the Ten Mile Street neighborhood, one of the city's oldest, where her mother and her sister used to go grocery shopping. Women in flowery pajamas and oversize flip-flops walk to the food stands to buy breakfast, their hair uncombed, their faces unwashed. After giving the vendor a handful of coins or a few crumpled bills, they rush home with a plastic bag of warm *mantou*, meat-stuffed *baozi*, or fried Chinese noodles—they hurry because they must wake their husbands and children. Amid the newly built apartment buildings is a spread of dilapidated bungalows scheduled to be torn down soon, to be replaced by an entertainment center with a shopping mall, a movie theater, and restaurants—a big sign on the roadside says so. From those dark, dingy houses, a humpbacked old woman emerges magically, holding a wooden night stool, limping toward the public bathroom. Before she reaches the bathroom, she coughs and spits. Small stores are now open for business, and the owners turn on their radios, listening to the morning news from the central broadcasting station; it will be the Official Word, true or not.

By seven a.m., every street is turning into a river of bicycles, cars, motorcycles, and pedestrians. Bikes swerve like small fish between cars that keep honking to warn bicyclists and pedestrians against getting too close. Among the fearless bicyclists are young women in expensive-looking dresses or tight suit skirts and high-heeled shoes. They pedal fast, seemingly unaffected by their formal attire. To avoid getting tanned, they wear wide-brimmed straw hats decorated with fake flowers and gloves covering the exposed areas on their arms. As for the older women, most wear foldable fabric hats, plain but functional, sold at small shops for three yuan each in a wide selection of colors. Some male bicyclists are afraid of sunlight too—they hold the handlebars with one hand, an umbrella with the other.

It's time for young parents to send their children to school. The children, each an only child in his or her family, sit on the backseats of their parents' bikes. They are nicely dressed, some with red scarves, and their cheeks are pink and healthy. Some are half asleep. Eyes closed, they hold their parents' waists with both hands, their heads against their parents' backs, their legs dangling on both sides of the seat.

Standing at a busy intersection, Ingrid watches the city of her birth awakened by noises, then breathes in the mixture of car exhaust, dust, and industrial emissions. At this moment the United States seems far away; she even doubts that she has lived there for eleven years. On the other hand, she questions her existence in this city, which she is now an observer, a tourist. She lost contact with her school friends long ago; the buildings where she studied have been either torn down or renovated with new names. Where is the Happiness Alley she used to bike through to get to high school? Where is the bookstand with the red door and crooked windows she liked to visit and borrow foreign novels from? Where is Granny Zhou, who liked to sit on a plastic chair outside her tiny stationery store on hot summer days, fanning herself with a yellow oil-skin fan? Ingrid wonders as she walks from one street to another, looking for the remains of her past. Though she has seen the changes all around China in the past decade on TV and in other media, only now does she realize how much the cityscape has been transformed, how it has become almost alien to her.

But has it really changed? she asks herself, seeing two middle-aged women bickering at the end of an alley, something she came across almost daily when she lived here. One woman stands on her balcony, the other sits on a stool downstairs. The woman on the balcony leans against the banister, knitting a sweater unhurriedly, while the downstairs woman plucks a dead rooster in a wooden basin filled with water. They curse, throwing words at each other such as *bitch, whore, moron,* each saying that the other woman's husband has a mistress somewhere. Then they curse each other's husbands, parents, children, and ancestors.

A crowd has gathered to watch them. No one interferes; Ingrid knows that the onlookers actually enjoy the spectacle and urge them on—whenever there is a car accident or a street fight, people gather like this, as if their pleasure lies in seeing others' misfortunes. Encouraged by the onlookers, the woman on the balcony finally drops the sweater she has been knitting and storms down to the street, while her rival leaps from her stool, hurling the half-naked rooster into the basin. Just when the fight is about to start, a policeman arrives. The cause of the incident, as Ingrid has overheard from people's discussion, was that one woman's cat ate the other woman's fish, put out on the porch to dry. The fish was less than a quarter pound, its value less than one yuan.

These bored onlookers! Ingrid remembers an article by Lu Xun, a twentieth-century writer she admires, criticizing the apathy of the Chinese people. The city may have changed, but the people haven't, she says to herself.

A bearded white man is striding toward her on the sidewalk, a backpack on his back. He's short and slim, and his face is dusty. A few beggars, all kids, are following him, extending their dirty hands toward him.

"Mei you le, gei guang le," the white man stops and says to the beggars in heavily accented Mandarin, pulling both his pants pockets inside out. "Look! No money." He now speaks English. The beggars giggle and mimic his English but still follow him, hands extended. The people who had been watching the two women now turn their eyes to the man—foreigners are rarely seen in this city—and begin to comment on his physique and speculate about what he's doing here. The foreigner takes a map from his shirt pocket and studies it. Then

he looks around, as if wanting to ask for directions. Discouraged by people's stares, he looks back at his map.

Ingrid walks up to him and asks in English if she can help. Learning that he's looking for a Taoist temple, she asks a woman in the crowd for the directions and then translates them for the foreigner. The temple is nearby—she used to know how to get there, but with all the new streets and houses and road constructions, she no longer knows. Afterward she and the foreigner chat briefly, and he tells her that he's from South Africa and is taking a year off to tour China and several other Asian countries.

They bid each other good-bye, and the foreigner leaves. Now the beggars ask Ingrid for money. Ingrid gives them some and they disperse. A young man with a brown suitcase approaches Ingrid. "Can you ask that foreigner if he has American dollars?" he says to her. "I'll give him a good exchange rate. You can take a cut."

Ingrid ignores him and keeps walking.

The man shoots her a contemptuous stare before turning away. "Who do you think you are? You think you're somebody just because you can speak English? You're still a black-haired, yellow-skinned Chinese!" he blurts out.

Rather than feeling angry, Ingrid finds herself smiling. Isn't that the truth? She says to herself.

She walks into an Internet café to check her e-mail—she hasn't done so since arriving in China. Other than the e-mails about the progress of her translation projects, she has received quite a few personal e-mails. Molly said that a university press had accepted her poetry chapbook with a five-hundred-dollar advance. "Well, it won't make me rich but at least I'm a published writer," she wrote. To celebrate her hard-won breakthrough into print, Molly treated all her friends in a Chinese restaurant.

Angelina asked Ingrid when she was coming back to New York. "There's this Mexican dude named Hugo Martinez, a mustachioed theater critic, and he's been asking me to move to Puerto Vallarta with him to run a bed-and-breakfast," she said. After describing how charming Hugo was and how exciting it was to make love to him, she wrote, "Who knows what God has planned for us? Life is like blind wine tasting: you've got to taste the wine to know if it's any good."

Bing'er wrote from Vancouver, where she had enrolled, part-time, in an art school. To pay her tuition, she started to work at a Vietnamese restaurant. "Believe it or not, they made me the chef yesterday. And my first order was fusion-style Ants on the Tree!" She couldn't travel for a while because of her class, she complained at the end. She didn't mention Tom.

There were several e-mails from Matthew, and the latest one told that his boss had read the first three chapters of her novel and was interested. "He may offer a $3,000 advance!!!" He was overjoyed. As for his own writing, he was "so inundated with organizing demonstrations and human rights activities" that he simply didn't have time for it. He asked Ingrid what she thought about him pursuing a career in public service.

As Ingrid replies to the e-mails, she hears three people beside her chatting.

"Do you think a lot of college students died in 1989?" a young man's voice asks.

"I don't know. But the government said a lot of soldiers died. Don't you remember the photos of ten 'Soldier Heroes' who died putting down the riot? I remember one of them was burned to death," says a girl.

"It wasn't a riot." Another young man chimes in.

"I was only fourteen at that time. I don't remember much about it. And I was studying hard for finals. My parents didn't even allow me to watch TV," the first man says. "Ling, how about you?"

"Well, I was twelve," says the girl after a pause. "But I watched on TV, and it seemed that many people fainted or got ill during the hunger strike in Tiananmen Square and were sent to the hospital. Some refused to leave. Many students wore white headbands saying 'democracy' or 'freedom' or 'anticorruption' in red ink or maybe their own blood. I also remember seeing tanks driving down the streets in Beijing."

"Wow, you remember a lot." The voice reveals admiration.

"Don't you envy those people who participated in the protest? I do. They have done something amazing in their lives, you know." The second young man's voice is quite loud.

"Let's not talk about it here," the girl whispers, hushing her friend with a gesture. "It's a sensitive topic."

Ingrid glances at them out of the corner of her eye. The girl is looking around furtively, and her paranoia is catching. Ingrid feels her anxiety.

It suddenly occurs to her that today is June 4. Twelve years ago, on this very date, she witnessed the massacre in Beijing; she, a twenty-year-old, saw her boyfriend, another twenty-year-old, killed by a bullet. "Run! Run for your life!" Sitting in the Internet café, she seems to hear a male voice pounding in her ears. She recalls Tiananmen Square covered with tents, flags, and banners; students' and activists' speeches about freedom and human rights; the people who were carried to the hospital on stretchers during a hunger strike. A torrent of emotion grasps her, paralyzes her.

She sits silently for a while, and after she feels better she leaves. As she looks around, everything is peaceful, even cheerful. Endless streams of pedestrians, bikes, and cars. Huge billboards on top of commercial high-rises. Multilaned streets flanked with foreign-brand boutiques and fast-food restaurants. Passing her, a group of teenagers, with misspelled English words printed on the backs of their T-shirts—such as "Kis me! Make lov to me!" and "Feel fuk good!"—are chatting and laughing. It's yet another day, without the smallest trace of memory, without the slightest grief.

Here is her birth country, eager to forget and to march forward without any burdens from the past, thinks Ingrid.

*   *   *

At noon, she returns to her parents' apartment after writing in a café for a while. There, she jotted down the final chapter of her novel in one straight shot, mixing English and Chinese. Half a century after the couple separated, both assuming the other long dead during the wars, and having remarried and borne children with their new spouses, they meet at a common friend's house. The man is now a widower, a retired bank clerk, but the woman's husband is still alive, and they have three children, including the one fathered by the man, the painter. Shocked, they avoid each other, and when the man finally gathers enough courage to speak with the woman, he sees her pleading eyes and realizes that all he can do is say good-bye, to the woman, to her husband, and to their three children.

Now, as Ingrid enters the apartment complex gate, she begins to consider the ending she just wrote primitive, tentative. She debates with herself. The couple has to talk, and they must tell the truth to their common child; if she was him, she'd want to be told. Then she counters that the truth doesn't do anyone any good. Isn't it better to keep it buried so everyone can move on?

Move on, that's the essence of life, she thinks as she starts up the stairs. Then she hopes that she can at least continue the novel, which, excluding the ending, has only the first three chapters written.

At this moment she hears a female voice behind her. "Are you Wang Fenglan's daughter? And your aunt is Wang Fengzhu?"

Ingrid turns and sees a woman in her late fifties or early sixties standing a few steps away. The woman is thin, of medium height, looking elegant with her short-sleeved green silk top, black knee-length suit skirt, and black leather handbag on her left arm.

"You know my mother and aunt?" Ingrid asks, surprised.

The woman removes her sunglasses. "Finally, I found the right place. I'm your mother's old neighbor. We lived in the same court-yard compound for several years, both before and after the 1949 Liberation. Your mother used to call me Big Sister Zheng, and your aunt was a few months older than I and called me Little Sister Zheng. You can just call me Aunt Zheng." She sizes Ingrid up. "You look very much like your aunt, especially your eyes; they seem to be able to talk. The moment you entered the gate, I suspected you were Wang Fenglan's daughter, but I didn't want to appear rude, so I followed you until I was sure. I haven't seen your mother and aunt for more than forty years. How are they doing?"

Ingrid is speechless. Can it be possible that the neighbor her mother had as a little girl is standing in front of her?

"Is your mother home? Where does your aunt live?" Aunt Zheng can barely contain her excitement.

"They both passed away. Aunt died in the early sixties, and my mother died last month in the U.S., while she was visiting my sister and me," Ingrid whispers.

Aunt Zheng's smile freezes. She raises her right hand slowly and presses her temple with her fingertips as if she had a headache. After a silence, she says, "Oh, no. I am so sorry. Please forgive me. I didn't expect that news."

Ingrid invites Aunt Zheng to her parents' apartment. She boils water and makes tea for her according to Chinese custom. Then she tells Aunt Zheng how her mother and aunt died and also how her father died.

"They left too soon." Aunt Zheng keeps shaking her head, and a few times wipes tears from her eyes. "How I wanted to catch up with your mother and aunt, and talk about our childhoods in the courtyard compound! When we lived there, there were five families. Though the Civil War had broken out, we lived a relatively peaceful life behind the brick walls. After work, men discussed what was going on with the Communist Party or the Nationalist Party, predicting how soon the war would end. Women didn't talk about politics. Our mothers would wash rice or vegetables out in the yard, listening to their husbands talk . . ."

Ingrid listens attentively, her mouth agape, like that of a kid. She imagines her myopic grandfather delivering a political speech in the courtyard, his hands inserted into the wide sleeves of his blue *chang-pao* over his chest, his feet apart, one slightly ahead of the other, and as he talked of something exciting, he gestured like an orchestra conductor.

She also imagines her grandma making peanut candy, sesame candy, and sticky rice cakes during a Spring Festival. She had a small stone mill to grind beans, rice, corn, and other ingredients. Whenever she used the mill, the kids in the compound would all gather around, listening to fairy tales, and of course, when the food was prepared, each would get a taste. She was particularly fond of Aunt Zheng, treating her like her own daughter.

"When the Five-Antis Campaign started in 1952," Aunt Zheng continues, "my father was arrested on charges of bribery, tax evasion, and exploiting workers. He was running a small furniture company at the time. After this incident, most of our neighbors and friends shunned us; some even provided fake evidence to the government, saying my father had hidden a lot of gold and jewelry in our 'country mansion,' which didn't even exist! Your grandparents were the only ones who remained our friends; they actually told people that my father was wronged and would be released soon. Though my father denied all the charges and insisted that he was innocent, he was sent to a labor farm in a different province, and we lost the factory. Without income, my mother decided to take me and my two younger brothers to live with a relative in Henan Province, so she didn't have to borrow money from your grandparents, who had sold all their valuables to support us."

"So, the charges against your father were made when there was no evidence at all?"

"Evidence didn't mean much at that time." Aunt Zheng smiles bitterly.

"It must have been hard for my mother and aunt to see you leave."

"Indeed. With our departure approaching, they cried every day and begged me to stay. I cried with them too, but there was nothing I could do to change my mother's decision. After we arrived in Henan Province, our relative changed his mind and didn't want us to stay, so we kept traveling north to try another relative in Changchun. She took us in. As soon as we were settled, my mother wrote your grandparents, but they never wrote back. It was not until a year later that we were told they had both died. We began to write to the people we knew back home about your mother and your aunt, but to no avail. Afterward, there was one political movement after another, and we had to give up looking for them."

"Do you know how they died?"

"Didn't your mother tell you?"

"She was vague about it. She said they died of sickness."

"Sickness? Hmm, I don't know." Aunt Zheng shakes her head slowly. "All I heard was that your grandfather was accused of some kind of crime. Didn't your parents later get any documents from the government saying that he had been wrongly accused? My father was rehabilitated in the early eighties and received a small monetary reparation."

"Even if there were such documents, they never mentioned them to me and my sister."

"You might be able to find something about your grandfather in the municipal library archives. Don't expect too much, though."

"I'll go to the library tomorrow," Ingrid says, imagining roomfuls of dusty files.

"I'll go with you. I know someone there."

Aunt Zheng holds up her tea mug, then puts it down without drinking. "In the past ten-odd years, I traveled to Nanyi at least once a year to look for them, but there was no news. Five years ago I managed to get a teaching position at the University of Finance and Economics here and began to spend more time searching for them. I don't know how many times I visited the government's human resources bureau. Several times I thought I'd found your mother, only to realize that it was a false alarm. After I retired I joined the senior university to learn calligraphy—by that time I'd almost lost hope of finding your mother and aunt."

"Too bad. You were in the same city."

"Sometimes the world is small, sometimes it is big. My luck finally came. This morning, I went to a folk art exhibition organized by the university and spotted a paper cutting—a strolling hen followed by three chicks. The artist was Wang Fenglan. I can't tell you how excited I was; I almost fainted. You might find my reaction strange—Wang Fenglan is a common name, and in all the years I was looking for your mother I came across at least fifty people with the same name. But you know, the paper cutting was based on one of your grandmother's ink-and-brush paintings. I saw her paint it and was told that she was the hen and your mother, your aunt, and I the three chicks. I immediately went to the administrative office and found your mother's address. I pressed the buzzer, but no one answered the door, so I waited. Then I saw you . . ." She sighs. "But I was too late."

Aunt Zheng begins to sob. Embarrassed to cry in front of a young person, she turns her back to Ingrid, using a tissue Ingrid has handed her to wipe her eyes and cheeks. Ingrid remains silent in her chair, fighting back her own tears.

Aunt Zheng stops crying. She turns and smiles at Ingrid. "I should feel happy. At least I saw you. Tell me, how was your mother's life? What was your father like? I want to know everything about them."

Ingrid starts to tell her, alternating between her childhood and adult memories. As she talks, she is surprised how she is moved by small, trivial things about her parents and the insignificant events that took place within the family. Aunt Zheng interrupts her frequently, requesting more details. "Tell me more. I want to know," she says sincerely, as if hearing about her childhood friend will erase the separation from her.

During a break, Ingrid asks about Aunt Zheng's family.

"My father is still alive," Aunt Zheng says, no longer sad. "He's very healthy. Just two weeks ago, he went to Anhui Province to climb Huangshan Mountain. My mother is also very healthy, and she practices *tai ji* fist for two hours every day. They live with my husband and me. We have one son and one daughter, and both teach in college. You must come to see us tomorrow. I can't tell you how happy they'll be to see you. My father has kept a photo of him and your grandfather. He cherishes it so much that he doesn't allow us to touch it." Aunt Zheng laughs.

They keep talking till dusk, till they can hear neighbors' kitchen exhaust fans and smell stir frying. They eat at a restaurant nearby, and afterward Ingrid asks Aunt Zheng to take her to the courtyard where her mother and aunt lived when they were little; she cannot wait.

The taxi stops in front of a nightclub. Aunt Zheng and Ingrid step out and stand on the street. "Here it is," Aunt Zheng says, pointing at the club, which has a gilded double door and a neon sign of a long-haired white man playing the saxophone like a drunkard. At one side of the door stands a scrawny girl in a red Qing Dynasty dress with blue and green edging and an elaborately decorated hairdress, who curtsies to every client who goes in and out. On both sides of the carpeted stairs and in the space outside the door are dozens of flower baskets; on the ribbons hanging from the handles are written auspicious phrases such as "Business flourishes," "Treasures all year long," and "Plentiful money." Apparently the club has been opened recently. Across the street is a commercial building with underground parking.

"Was the courtyard here?" Ingrid asks with skepticism.

"That's right. It took me a while to find it. Well, it's the most expensive nightclub in the city," Aunt Zheng says. "It opened last week. It looks neither Chinese nor Western." She shakes her head with a helpless smile. "Before, it was a Japanese restaurant. And before that, it was a real-estate office. Things happen fast here. All the alleys, houses, stores, and trees I remembered are long gone, and the only things left are the traces of the three wells."

"Three wells?"

"Yes." Aunt Zheng walks toward a sycamore tree. Ingrid follows her. The receptionist in the Qing Dynasty costume looks at them curiously.

"Here is one." Aunt Zheng stops at the tree, pointing at the space in front of it, between two parked cars.

Ingrid looks down and sees a slightly protruding ring on the road. "You mean this?" She bends to look closely.

"Yes. It's a well's opening. Two others are over there. I'll take you to see them. The construction workers filled in the wells with dirt and ran the paving machines to build the street, but over time the dirt and asphalt compressed." Aunt Zheng begins to walk with measured steps. "It's fifteen steps from this one to the second. I was little then, so my steps were small. Then it's twenty more steps to the third one. Your mother, aunt, and I called our courtyard Three Wells and called ourselves Three Wells' Three Pirates."

Walking behind Aunt Zheng, Ingrid counts her steps. After they check out the remaining traces of the last well, Aunt Zheng, squatting, begins to draw a map, tracing the outlines of the past onto the street. "Your grandparents lived right about here . . . my family lived here . . . here would be the garden . . . the walnut tree . . . the date tree . . ."

Ingrid squats next to Aunt Zheng and gazes at her invisible drawing, trying to visualize the courtyard's layout.

When both feel sore from squatting, they raise their heads simultaneously to look at the front of the nightclub. Aunt Zheng is silent, her eyes glittering, as if she could pierce the brassy façade, recover history, and see the brick houses, the walnut tree, the date tree, and the arched door to the garden.

Earlier today, Ingrid recalls, she had sighed over Chinese people's forgetfulness. Now she's been brought back to an earlier time, a past laden with puzzles, secrets, and unspeakable subtleties.

Why should I know about all this? she wonders.

She has no answer, though she isn't looking for one. But she knows in her heart that her existence is connected with the past, that she is a witness to history whether she likes it or not.

At this very instant, the ancient bell from a Tang Dynasty temple nearby rings. The sounds are deep and soulful, resonating in the sky.

ACKNOWLEDGMENTS

I'm grateful to my agents Jennifer Joel and Toby Eady. From the very beginning, they have believed in my work and have provided all the support a writer could wish for. I feel fortunate to have Johanna Castillo as my editor, whose talent, intelligence, and enthusiasm have made this book possible, and our delightful conversations span much more than writing. My gratitude also goes to Jamie Coleman, Laetitia Rutherford, Sam Humphreys, and John Joss for their generous editorial advice, and to Susan Brown, my copy editor, for her meticulous reading.

Thanks to Judith Curr for her trust, and her staff, especially Amy Tannenbaum, for being so helpful and efficient.

And, finally, my gratitude goes to my husband, Mattias Cedergren, whose love, patience, and support have helped me go through all the ups and downs during the writing of this book.